THE
OTHER
NINETEENTH
CENTURY

TOR BOOKS BY AVRAM DAVIDSON

The Avram Davidson Treasury
The Other Nineteenth Century

Edited by

GRANIA DAVIS
AND HENRY WESSELLS

TOR®

A TOM DOHERTY ASSOCIATES BOOK
NEW YORK

THE OTHER NINETEENTH CENTURY

A STORY COLLECTION BY

Avram Davidson

*Containing Startling Revelations of the
Lives of Literary Persons; also, Truthful
Accounts of Living Fossils, Montavarde's
Camera, The Irradiodiffusion Machine,
and El Vilvoy de las Islas; with Heinous
Crimes, Noble Ladies in Adversity,
Brilliant Detections, Imperial Eunuchs,
Political Machinations, etc., etc.*

THE OTHER NINETEENTH CENTURY: A Story Collection by Avram Davidson

Edited by Teresa Nielsen Hayden

A Tor Book
Published by Tom Doherty Associates, LLC
175 Fifth Avenue
New York, NY 10010

www.tor.com

ISBN 0-312-84874-9

First Edition: December 2001

Printed in the United States of America

0 9 8 7 6 5 4 3 2 1

ACKNOWLEDGMENTS

"The Account of Mr. Ira Davidson" first appeared in *The Magazine of Fantasy & Science Fiction*, May 1976.

"Buchanan's Head" first appeared in *The Magazine of Fantasy & Science Fiction*, February 1983.

"Business Must Be Picking Up" first appeared in *Ellery Queen's Mystery Magazine*, May 1978.

"The Deed of the Deft-Footed Dragon" first appeared in *Night Cry*, Fall 1986.

"Dr. Bhumbo Singh" first appeared in *The Magazine of Fantasy and Science Fiction,* October 1982.

"Dragon Skin Drum" first appeared in *Kenyon Review*, Vol. XXXIII, No. 1, Winter 1961.

"El Vilvoy de las Islas" first appeared in *Isaac Asimov's Science Fiction Magazine*, August 1988.

"The Engine of Samoset Erastus Hale, and One Other, Unknown" first appeared in *Amazing Science Fiction Stories*, July 1987.

"Great Is Diana" first appeared in *The Magazine of Fantasy & Science Fiction*, August 1958.

"The Lineaments of Gratified Desire" first appeared (as "Price of a Charm") in *Ellery Queen's Mystery Magazine*, December 1963.

"The Man Who Saw the Elephant" first appeared (as "What More Is There to See?") in *Yankee Magazine*, October 1971.

"Mickelrede" (with Michael Swanwick) first appeared in *Moon Dogs* by Michael Swanwick (NESFA Press, 2000).

"The Montavarde Camera" first appeared in *The Magazine of Fantasy & Science Fiction*, May 1959.

"O Brave Old World!" first appeared in *Beyond Time*, ed. Sandra Ley (Pocket Books, 1976).

"The Odd Old Bird" first appeared in *Weird Tales*, no. 293.

"One Morning with Samuel, Dorothy, and William" first appeared in *Isaac Asimov's Science Fiction Magazine*, December 1988.

"Pebble in Time" (with Cynthia Goldstone) first appeared in *The Magazine of Fantasy & Science Fiction*, August 1970.

"The Peninsula" first appeared in *Amazing Science Fiction Stories*, November 1985.

"The Singular Incident of the Dog on the Beach" first appeared in *Alfred Hitchcock's Mystery Magazine*, December 1986.

"Summon the Watch!" first appeared in *Ellery Queen's Mystery Magazine*, October 1971.

"Traveller from an Antique Land" first appeared in *Ellery Queen's Mystery Magazine*, September 1961.

"Twenty-Three" first appeared in *Asimov's Science Fiction*, July 1995.

"What Strange Stars and Skies" first appeared in *The Magazine of Fantasy & Science Fiction*, December 1963.

To Owlswick, without whom . . .
And to our readers, families, and friends

CONTENTS

THE
OTHER
NINETEENTH
CENTURY

O BRAVE
OLD WORLD!

All morning long the bells had been ringing, those bells which had
been for a while silenced so that the sound of them might instantly
signal if enemy troops were to land. But, by common consent and
by clerical permission, they now sounded something else entirely.
The reddish-gray-haired man looked up from the sheet of parchment, of which he must by now, it seemed, know every letter, so
often had he scanned it. Immersed though he was in his text and
his thoughts, still he lifted his head at length and spoke.

"It sounds as though every church in the city is ringing its bells,"
he murmured.

The friend and countryman who had so long and so often stood
by his side, figuratively and literally, said, "Yes, and even in the
suburbs . . . the Liberties, as they call them here."

The reddish-gray-haired man made a soft, musing noise, turned
again to the document, then half-raised his head once more. "One
might call them liberty bells, then," he said. Another thought
brought his head all the way up. "What was it," he asked, "that text
from Scripture—you recall, don't you?—on the bell in Philadelphia?"

His friend and countryman considered, nodded. " 'Proclaim liberty throughout the land—' "

"Aye, liberty. The Jews had a word for it. And 'unto all the inhabitants thereof,' aye. . . ." He nodded, sighed. "Philadelphia," he said.

"Williamsburg."

"Richmond."

"The Chickahominy."

"The Rapahannock."

At the door, a burly, tousle-headed fellow, cheeks stubby and shirt (none too fresh) open at his shaggy breast, looked in, listened. His face showed a mixture of impatience and compassion. Often had he listened to these and other refugees recounting, as a litany, the names of their towns and provinces. (One could not always tell them apart.) Sometimes the names of the New World (perhaps Brave, perhaps just Bold) merely echoed the names of the Old. (O servant exalted above the master!) Sometimes they seemed a concatenation of barbarous sybilants and gutterals from the aboriginal tongues. Ah, well. To duty.

"Are you quite ready for us, then?" he asked the two. They turned.

"Ah, Charles. I should think—"

"Ah, Charles. Just one more moment. A last look. You understand."

"Of course. Of course. No wish to rush you." He coughed; he raised his eyebrows. The reddish-gray-haired man went back to his text. The friend moved quietly and, gently and tactfully (he was not always quiet, or gentle, or tactful) eased the newcomer away.

"He won't be much longer at it, I promise. I know."

"Yes, yes. You've known him a long time."

"Since his hair was quite red."

Arm in arm they moved out into the corridor. There, all was controlled turmoil. Country squires and yeoman farmers with mud on their boots spoke confidentially to craftsmen smelling of machine oil and the forge. Bishops, white sleeved, listened with modified majesty to inferior clergy, all in black save for the white bands at the neck. And a member of the old peerage, head covered with a wig of archaic cut, nodded to the comments of an old man wrapped in a ragged—and still, technically, illegal—tartan. It was at least as likely that this last anachronism had crossed, recently and hastily, from long exile in France, than that he had descended from Scotland. The Estates, as the Scottish parliament was called since the revisions of the Act of Union, had done little more with the use of their regained powers than to pass innumerable acts of outlawry and attainder upon each other. But this, too, would soon enough pass away.

Very, very soon, in fact.

On seeing the two approach, one gentleman, evidently in a condition of total confusion as well as in court dress (court dress, sword and all), buttonholed the burly fellow with an agitated air.

"Where will it end, Charles?" he asked. "Where will it all end?"

"All's well that ends well," was the half-muttered reply, then added, after a moment's recollection, "Doctor."

As though needing no more than this acknowledgment of his profession, the doctor at once said, "As to where it all began, why, say I, it all began with the fatal tennis ball. Or, if I may be permitted to say it—" here he glanced around, defiantly "—the insufficiently fatal tennis ball."

"Water under the bridge," Charles muttered, tugged a watch out, glanced, then muttered again, "Water under the bridge. . . . London Bridge. . . ."

But the medical man's phrase was overheard, was appreciated, was at once repeated and passed from mouth to mouth. *"The insufficiently fatal tennis ball. . . ."*

And the bells rang out and the bells rang on. St. Paul's, St. Martin's, St. Clemens, Bow, St. Mary-le-Bone. . . .

"The insufficiently fatal tennis ball. . . ."

The Stuarts, as even the handful of still-unreconstructed Jacobites would needs admit, the Stuarts had their faults. But they had not hated their heirs. That is, the Jameses and the Charleses had not hated one another. Anne, to be sure, now, Anne—Anne had certainly shown no fondness for, first, Sophia, Dowager Electress of Hanover, and for Sophia's son, George. But they were only Anne's distant cousins, and were far off in what someone later was to term "a despicable Electorate." Poor Anne! Last of the Stuarts actually to occupy the throne, thirteen (thirteen!) pregnancies, and no heir to outlive her, she might have been (and was) excused for not wishing the sight or presence of her so-distant kin.

But it was left for the kin themselves to exemplify the phrase of Elizabeth, her sentiment that "she could not bear to hear the mention of a Successor." And yet, even so, Elizabeth, too, had had some reason. Had she not? "The Queen of Scots hath a bonny Babe, and I am but a barren stock." Thus Elizabeth. But what reason had the sovereigns of the House of Hanover for hating, and for so hating, their own heirs? Heirs who were of their own bodies lawfully begotten—and lawfully present. Had not George I, at a court levee, publicly cursed his son, the future George II, forbidding him thenceforth to attend cabinet meetings, cabinet meetings from which, there no longer being any interpreter whom German George felt he could trust, the king thenceforth absented himself from. (And a good thing, too, said many.)

Even this, however, had faded beside the subsequent hatred of George II for his own heir, Frederick, Prince of Wales. The English, not used to the sort of thing which was evidently traditional in Hanover, the English had murmured, "Poor Fred. . . ." Poor Fred, indeed. The king could not, after all, immure the Prince of Wales in a palace prison, however much he called him "scoundrel." Nor could he cut his son off from revenues which either had been voted as "supply" by Act of Parliament, or accrued by ancient English law and custom, via the duchies of Cornwall and Lancaster. However much he thought and called him "fool."

Frederick, Prince of Wales, was, however, subject to all the coldness, the scorn, hatred, spleen and exclusion of which his father, George II, was capable. He was left to molder in his own petty counter-court, attended only by those politicians who were not merely out of favor but entertained no hopes of ever being again in favor while George lived. The prince was left to admire the poems of Pope. And he was left to play tennis.

It was the blow upon or near the breastbone, the blow from a hard-struck tennis ball, which gave the princely physician a concern. "I fear me," the meddlesome apothecary had murmured, "I fear me that this blow might be the occasion of an imposthume. And that, should Your Royal Highness suffer at some future date from a severe cold . . . an inflammation on the lungs. . . ."

"Is nothing to be done?" inquired the prince, somewhat languid from opium and ipecac. "Am I so soon to leave nine orphans? [There had been, after all, one other thing in which the king was powerless to constrain him.] Should we send for the chaplain?" But the physician-in-ordinary was not ready to send for the chaplain.

"I should propose to bleed Your Royal Highness once again," he said. The Prince of Wales, however, was not ready to be bled once again. "Then I should propose to purge Your Royal Highness once again." But the prince absolutely refused to be purged once again.

The physician-in-ordinary threw up his hands. "In that case," he said. And stopped. "In that case. . . . In that case, I must recommend . . . in fact. . . . In that case," he said, firmly, "I indeed must insist upon Your Royal Highness taking a long and immediate change of air."

As was to be expected, the king managed to contain his grief.

"A change of air? Vhere?" he demanded.

"The Isle of Wight has been suggested, Your Majesty."

"Der Isle of *Vhat?*" A map was brought and the Isle of Wight pointed out to the king, who was pleased to give a grunt, interpreted as a Gracious Assent.

However and however.

"His Royal Highness does not, it seems, desire to go to the Isle of Wight."

The king had been playing backgammon with his mistress and already felt bored with this interfering subject.

"*Teufelsdreck!* Dhen vhere he vants to go?" It was intimated that the prince had expressed a preference for either Hanover or France as the scene of his recuperation. The king gave a shout of rage and kicked the backgammon board across the room. Hanover? Never! Hanover. . . . In Hanover. . . . In Hanover the air was sweeter, the water purer, the food better, the populace more loyal ("—than in England" being understood). Hanover was reserved for the king him- self to go to for changes of air. And as for *France*—

"He vould intrigue vhit der French king! He vould efen intrigue vhit der pretender!" It was pointed out to him that the pretender now lived in Italy, and rather meanly, on a papal pension. But the king would hear no arguments. Once let Frederick set foot upon the Continent, why, what would prevent his going even to Italy? *"Der force of graffity, maybe?"* he screamed, with immense sarcasm.

"Nein! Nein! He can go to der Isle of Vight—or he can go to Hell— und—und—if he doesn't vant to go to Hell, den he can go to America!"

At this, the royal mistress was unwise enough to allow a snort of laughter to escape her lips. The entire court waited breathlessly for the lightnings. But the king, having had his attention called to the fact of his having made a joke, abruptly decided to enjoy it. His hard-bitten little red face grew redder still, and the court, breathing inward sighs of relief, joined in the now royally permissible laughter.

And on this merry gale, the prince's vessel was wafted out to sea.

First aboard the *Anna Maria* was the royal and proprietarial gover- nor. His cocked hat showing above the railing as he climbed the ladder, he was demanding, "Have ye got me snuff with ye? Have ye got me madeira? Have ye brought me mail, me newsletters?" With a heave and a ho he clambered on deck, looked all around. "Have ye got any pretty wenches that have come to seek their fortunes in the new-found world? Have ye—" And here his face, which had just that moment focused on a slender and somewhat pale passenger, underwent an absolutely fascinating transformation.

"Your Royal Highness!" he bawled, and did not so much fall upon his knees as on his face.

It was in this manner that Frederick, Prince of Wales, came to America.

The king, it was reported, had near had an apoplexy when he heard the news. But he had, after all, he *had* given his permission. After a fashion, no doubt, but given it he had. And in the hearing of all the court. There was, then, nothing he could do about it.

From *The Court Circular and Gazette:*

> *His Royal Highness the Prince of Wales, Her Royal Highness the Princess of Wales, and their Children [here followed a list], have, by Reason of His Majesty's Most Gracious Solicitude, engaged upon a visit to the American Plantations, in order that His Royal Highness may recruit his Health.*

No member of the royal family had ever before set foot upon the soil of the American plantations ("the colonies," as it was now becoming fashionable to call them). And, suddenly, in one stroke, here were eleven of them! They moved into the home of the royal and proprietarial governor, the r. and p.g. moved into the house of the lieutenant-governor and the lieutenant-governor moved into an inn. The governor's home was, for the Americas, palatial. But it was, after all, crowded with all of them there. It was *damned* crowded!

"Let's build a little house," the prince suggested. "Eh, my dearest? Shall we build a little house along the river? Is that not a capital suggestion?" The princess thought that it *was* a capital suggestion. All her life, after all, she had lived in houses built for others. The notion that she might now have a voice in designing one for her own use fell upon her ears like harpsichord music played by an orchestra of angels. The house was to be on the Delaware River, and not on the Thames? Bless you, it might have been on the Styx for all she cared! And in the meanwhile . . . in the meanwhile . . . for it *was* crowded in the governor's house . . . well, what about a visitation of the *other* colonies?

And so it was arranged. The youngermost ones of the royal infants remained in Pennsylvania with their nurses; the eldest of the royal infants accompanied their royal parents. New Jersey and New York had heard with curiosity what they now beheld with enthusiasm. Connecticut had been cool, but the coolness was now warmed. Massachusetts, New Hampshire and Rhode Island and Providence plantations had, in fact, been skeptical about the whole thing: who knew but that it was some sort of a flummery tale concocted down there in Pennsylvany? What would a prince be doing in America, anyway? It was all obviously, or half-obviously, a sort of granny's tale. Prince? There was no—

And then, thunderation! *Here he was!*

And would you just look-see what he was *do*ing!

Previous examples of British officialdom had merely sniffed at the coarse foodstuffs of the frontier, hastily ordered their cooks to prepare some French kickshaws ("Or at least a decent dish of mutton!"). Not Fred. The capacity of Frederick for the New England dinner, boiled or otherwise, was prodigious.

"*Look* at him a-tuckin' inta the baked beans!"

"Didn't do a injustice to the hasty puddin', either!"

"*How* many bowls o' chowder and *how* many quohogs'd the prince eat down't the clambake?"

Up came the First Selectman of the Township of East Neantic, which was, so to speak, catering the affair; sweating and smiling slightly (in East Neantic they smile slightly where others would beam), he called his order for "more o'th' ha'nch o'venison fr His R'yal Highness!"

And, not very long later: "More roast beef fr the Prince o' Wales!"

In England, venison came from the King's Deer, and the king was not inclined to share. In England, one had not known that bears could be roasted; in England, one had, in fact, never even *seen* a bear!

The New Englanders looked at each other, looked at their prince—who gave them back a hearty grin, somewhat greasy about the chops—looked at each other again.

"Likes our vittles, do he? He *do!*"

"Guess we ain't sech barbarious critters after all!" they said to each other.

And they said: "Well, sir, I snum!"

"I snum!"

Even at this date one may wonder: *why* had Fred such an appetite, such a zest for things? Well, for one thing, the provinces of the New World were . . . well, they were *new!* The hand of man had not yet had time to tame them as in Europe, trim them into shape like yew hedges, turn their sparkling rivers into tame canals or drainage ditches. And, in that pure air, under that clear sky, the despised son of what a later New England writer was to call a "snuffy old drone from the German hive" seemed to enter a new youth—almost without ever having, under the cold gaze and hot scorn, almost without ever having had a previous one.

Here, no one called him "fool!"

Here, no one called him "scoundrel!"

And, perhaps best of all, here, no one called him "poor Fred!"

After a while, the weather commencing to turn cold; prince and princess turned south, were reunited with the royal infants in Philadelphia, examined the progress on what people were already beginning to call the Prince's Palace. . . . The Prince's Palace was not really quite ready yet. . . . Not quite ready yet, eh? Hm, well, there were colonies to the south of Pennsylvania, were there not? There certainly were! And, having heard of their sovereign's son's reception by the colonies to the north, they were restlessly waiting to show him what they could do in Delaware . . . Maryland . . . Virginia . . . North and South Carolina . . . and even in far-off Georgia, hard upon the borders of the Spanish dons.

It was all very pleasant. It was all *most* pleasant. And so, as he was bound to do, sooner or later, the king heard about it.

It is His Majesty's pleasure that the Prince should now return.

The prince did not return.

Those listless days of playing cards before a smoky fireplace under a lowering London sky, listening to the slow babble of a second-hand and second-rate set of courtiers were over. The Prince's Palace was finished now, but the prince had no intention of turning it into a copy of what he had left behind him. It was brought to his attention that what the colonies, menaced by French and Spanish and Indians, what the colonies needed was a well-regulated militia. Very well, then; he began to regulate—that is, to organize and reorganize and drill one. And, at the first occasion—another outbreak on the frontier—he led it into battle. There was no nonsense of bright, gaudy uniforms (such as his father so loved), preceded by loud-sounding brass and drums. In their native buckskin and hickory-dyed homespun, slinking through the wilderness as stealthily as Indians, the colonial troops met the enemy. And he was theirs.

More shouts of rage in far-off London. Once again the backgammon board was kicked across the room.

It is His Majesty's command that the Prince shall now return forthwith.

In tones practicedly smooth and outwardly respectful, the prince replied that his health did not, alas, permit him to return . . . just yet. And, in fact, he—but let the story follow, turn by turn.

The king was of course not without resources. And one of them was to commandeer the resources of the Prince of Wales. These were collected as soon as ever they fell due, and at once closed up in the Privy Purse. The king did not, to be sure, confiscate them. He merely neglected to forward them to the prince.

"Let der vild backvoodsmen pay Fred's bread *und* board," he said. Or was said to have said. And, so, might as well have said.

The Assembly of Pennsylvania voted the prince a subvention of a thousand pounds, Pennsylvania. The Assembly of Maryland voted a similar sum. The Virginia House of Burgesses voted him fifteen hundred. The race was on. From colony after colony the money rolled in. It rolled in—until word arrived that *His Majesty has refused the Royal Assent to the subvention.* By now the colonial temper was hotting up. What was to be done?

"The king be a-tryin' tew take our prince away from us, be he? A-tryin' to starve him out, be he? Well . . . *he bain't a-goin' tew!*"

The Selectmen and Town Meeting of East Neantic voted the

prince the best three lots in the township available, and promptly voted to rent them back at the best rent possible; they then voted to send the money forthwith; as a further act, they also voted the prince's household "twenty pecks of cornmeal, two barrels prime salt pork, a barrel of oysters, a barrel of clams, a hogshead of hominy and one of samp. . . ." The list rolled on.

"The king, he bain't able tew veto the Township of East Neantic, no, sir, not even he!"

It caught on. It caught right on. Within two months the prince's storehouses not only bulged with victualry, peltry and wampum, but he had become the largest landowner in any single colony one might care to name. There was lots of land.

Could not the prince be said to have "fled the Realm" and hence to have abdicated, as was said of James II? The cabinet dubiously said that it rather thought not. The Privy Council respectfully said, not. And even the law lords, with many a regretful harrumph, said, absolutely . . . absolutely not. Well, then, what could the king *do?* Once again the king was politely made to know that he could do—nothing.

Of course, he could die. And, of course, he did.

What happened next was compared to the Flight of the Wild Geese, the Flight of the Earls, when the leaders of the Irish almost *en masse* took to their heels and, not waiting for the completion of yet another English reconquest, took refuge on the Continent. Of course, it was not the same. It was, well, it was because no one really knew how one stood in regard to the new king. ("Frederick, by the Grace of God"; how odd it sounded! There had never been a King Frederick before. Well, there had once never been any King George before, either.) And, for that matter, no one knew how the king himself stood in regard to . . . well, anything!

The Atlantic was white with sails. London Pool was left bare of any vessel capable of crossing the ocean, and Bristol, the same. Every man with a place to lose or hope of a place to gain was posting o'er the white-waved seas. Was London the capital, still? Well . . . Parliament sat in London. But only if the king summoned it to sit. The king was, after all, still very much the Fountain of Honor . . . and of power. And each cabinet minister, each member of the Privy Council, each powerful marquis and viscount and earl, each of them had the thought that if *he* were the first to bring the new king the news, if the new king, panting for the crown, were to accompany *him* back to England. . . .

For bringing back an earlier exiled Prince of Wales, General Monk had been created Duke of Albermarle.

Historians dispute who actually was the first to bring Fred the news. There was, after all, quite a crowd of them. They found him— and a hard journey of it they had had, too, in finding him—they found him sitting on a split-rail fence the other side of the Alleghenies, wearing a coonskin cap ("Sitting on a *what?* The other side of *where?* Wearing a *which?*") and buckskin breeches stained with grease and blood. They babbled out their news. Their great news. And waited for the new king to cry for his horse.

"I shan't budge," said the new king. And he spat a stream of something which they soon learned was tobacco juice.

"I ain't a-gonna go," the king said.

He rid himself of his chaw and called—not for his horse—for a dipper of rye whiskey. "To rense out my mouth."

Nothing was ever the same afterwards.

Parliament was summoned to sit, and Parliament sat. A royal and Ducal uncle opened it in the capacity of "Captain of the Realm." *But the Privy Council was held in Philadelphia!* True, only a Parliament could, only a House of Commons, in fact, could vote the king "supply." But, secure in his colonial rents and revenues, the king did not need their supply. "Ship money"? Bless you, he had all the ships, and all the money, as ever he could need, right where he was! London? The king called London "a cesspool full of snobs." He said that if London did not like it, London could kiss his royal arse.

He did suggest that Parliament should make provision for American members. Parliament was dazed but it did not feel itself to be as dazed as that. Parliament's term eventually expired. The king simply did not summon another one.

What he *did* summon, by and by, was a sort of American parliament, called a Continental Congress, with the new privy council acting as a sort of House of Lords (a prominent member of which was the First Selectman of East Neantic). The prime minister was a colonial, a native of the American Boston, who had moved to Philadelphia in his youth. His name was Benjamin Franklin. The detested Navigation Acts, so hostile to colonial manufacture and shipping, were in effect nullified. Before long, American shipping—so much closer, after all, to wood and sailcloth and resin and pitch, and just as close to iron—had begun to supplant British preeminence in the trade upon the seas.

Who does not remember the great invasion of England planned by one Bonaparte? Who has not thrilled to the story of the sailing of the American armada, which, under the command of John Paul Jones, swept the French from the seas in a twinkling? Who, then, could object to the fact that American troops now spat their tobacco juices in the streets of London?

Franklin retired and was replaced by a Virginia planter by the name of Washington. "I detest your Party, sir," was his common word; "your Faction, sir, I abhor." But he grew old. (And, for that matter, so did the king.) And presently Washington stepped down, and was replaced, of course, by another colonial. The king grew very old. But the king, though he did not die, less and less attended to the business of state, leaving it more and more in the hands of his first minister. And this one was one who did by no means despise party or faction. Intrigue was middle name to him. The Americans had had little or no experience in such matters. The power slipped bit by bit from the hands of the old congressmen before they even noticed it. And the prime minister, securing the lord presidency of the privy council as well, began that which some said he had aimed at all along: a dictatorship after the old Roman model.

The old king no longer roamed the wilderness frontier delighting in the hunt and in the rough but genial banter of the backwoods-

men. He stayed in the by now truly palatial Prince's House—the
name had stuck and would never be changed—drinking rum cock-
tail and watching what were known as minstrel shows. One by one,
the old champions of liberty slipped away, slipped across the seas,
took refuge in an England which their forefathers, in the name of
that same liberty, had long ago left behind them.

The old king lived on and on and on.

Though the prudence of retaining the American troops in England
seemed clear to many (mostly in America), the costliness of doing
so was also clear. The troops could hardly go and shoot game enough
to feed themselves. England grunted at the first of the new tax acts.
Stamped paper was to go up, was it? Well . . . they did not like it,
but, after all, it was the same both sides of the sea. One by one the
Acts of Congress descended. Congress, as such, could not act for
England. But the Privy Council could; it could act anywhere in the
realm. An Order in Council. Another Order in Council. And another.

England, it was being said, now groaned beneath an American
tyranny.

And still there was not enough money. The American troops
needed new clothes. The troops were protecting England, weren't
they? Well, then let the English pay for it.

To be sure, some of this expense had to be shared by American
taxpayers, too. One had to step delicately here. The prime minister-
president cautiously considered. What source of revenue was there
which would least vex the colonies? It did not take him long to find
it. After all, in all the Americas, how many folks really drank tea?

That had been the back-breaking straw. The British were long suffering, slow to wrath. They were loyal. They endured the absence
of their king. They had submitted to the loss of their Parliament.
They had accepted the presence of what were more or less foreign
troops. They had muddled through the dismal diminution of trade.
But—

Raise the tax on their tea?

On TEA?

The bells tolled in the churches, but not to summon the faithful to prayer. Fishwives and bishops, coal porters and Whig gentry, Thames watermen and bishops, cheesemongers and prentice boys, the beggars and the whores and the learned Proctors of the Doctors Commons, all rose up as one:

There was an East India vessel of the Honorable Company then in the Pool of London, laden with the newly taxed hyson, oolong and pekoe. A mob, calling itself the Sons of Liberty (said actually to be composed of the younger sons of the younger sons of peers), stormed the vessel and threw the tea chests into the harbor (whence the well-sealed containers were promptly and clandestinely pulled out, to be sold, *sub rosa* and *sub* counter, and sans tax, by members of the Worshipful Company of Grocers). And, as though to express their opinions as to the source of the oppressive tax, the mob had dressed themselves as Indians!

Could contempt and defiance go further?

For almost the first time in English history, a Parliament met without being summoned by the hand of a sovereign. The precedent, the so-called Convention Parliament—which had outlawed James II and confirmed the Crown to William and Mary—the precedent was uncertain. But when a precedent is wanted by a people close to rebellion, any precedent will do. They did not meet in the old Houses of Parliament, long empty—though empty in a sense only, for the House of Commons had served for some years as a choirboys' school for Westminster Abbey, and the Commons itself was now used as a quartermasters warehouse for the American soldiers. They met in the Guildhall, under the great statues of Gog and Magog. First they repealed the old Act of Union. Then, under a slightly different style, they reenacted it. Then they passed resolutions. This delay was almost fatal.

The American troops, marching down Leadenhall Street in their brave new red-white-and-blue uniforms (symbols of oppression), and

with their newly equipped bands playing—rashly, oh so rashly—
"Yankee Doodle," were met by a withering crossfire from the newly
re-formed Trained Bands, hiding in the thickly clustering houses.
And, abandoning their intended attack on the Guildhall, they were
obliged to fall back, retreating across the Thames in the direction of
Southwark.

And so, now, all day, behind the barricades, the refugee American with the reddish gray hair had toiled over the document. And
now at last he looked up, and he nodded.

They marched into the great hall. They read the document aloud
as the Liberty Bells rang out, proclaiming liberty throughout the
land, unto all the inhabitants thereof. And when the words were
reached, "RESOLVED, *That these United Kingdoms are, and of right,
ought to be,* FREE AND INDEPENDENT"—ah, then, what a
shout went up!

"Charles James Fox should be first to sign," the American said.

Charles James Fox scratched his bristly chin and shaggy chest.
Shook his unkempt head. "No, sir," he declared. "You have written
it, the honor of signing it first belongs to you. Let that scoundrelly
American prime minister-president, let the tyrant who has driven
you all from your homeland, let him see your name there for himself."

The American nodded. With a wry smile, he said to his friend,
"Well, Pat, I now commit treason . . . eh?"

His friend's comment was, "If this be treason, let us make the
most of it."

The other, with a sound assent, picked up the proffered pen and,
in a great round hand, wrote: *"Thomas Jefferson."*

"There," he said in grim contentment. "Now Aaron Burr can
read it without his spectacles. . . ."

AFTERWORD TO "O BRAVE OLD WORLD!"

Avram Davidson's fantasies of the nineteenth century are explorations of neglected incidents or alternative explanations of well-known events. "O Brave Old World!" is a classic example of alternate history, now known in academic circles as "counterfactual history." What if, Davidson asks, Frederick of Hanover didn't die young in 1751, and the British monarchy evolved along quite different lines? What if the seat of government were moved to North America?

Many of those who write alternate history betray monarchist leanings. The portrait of the down-to-earth King Fred is quite sympathetic, but Davidson takes his politics several twists further: as England bears the brunt of an occupying army sent to combat Bonaparte in Europe, London becomes the seat of a revolution in which Thomas Jefferson raises the voice of liberty. Note also the cameo role of "that scoundrelly American prime minister-president," Aaron Burr.

—Henry Wessells

GREAT IS DIANA

"Whenever the sexes separate, at a party like this, I mean, after dinner," Jim Lucas said, "I keep feeling we ought to have walnuts and port and say *'Gempmun, the Queen!'* like in the old English novels."

"Naa, you don't want any *port.*" Don Slezak, who was the host, said, opening the little bar. "What you want—"

Fred Bishop, who had taken a cigar out of his pocket, put it back. "Speaking of the old English," he began. But Don didn't want to speak of the old English.

"I want you to try this," he said. "It's something I invented myself. Doesn't even have a name yet." He produced a bottle and a jug and ice and glasses. Jim looked interested; Fred, resigned. "It's really a very simple little drink," Don observed, pouring. "You take white rum— any good white rum—and cider. But it's got to be *real* cider. None of this pasteurized apple juice that they allow them to sell nowadays as cider. So much of this . . . so much of that. Drink up."

They drank. "Not bad at all. In fact," Fred smacked his lips, "very good. Strange, how fashions in drink change. Rum was it until gin came in; then whisky. Now, in the seventeen hundreds . . ."

Don got up and noisily prepared three more rum-and-ciders. "Ah," he said, quaffing, "it goes down like mother's milk, doesn't it." Jim put his glass down empty with a clatter. Don promptly made more.

"Mother's milk," Jim said. He was reflective. "Talk about fashions in *drink* . . . dextrose, maltose, corn syrup, and what the hell else they put into the babies nowadays. How come the women aren't born flat-chested, explain me *that,* Mr. Bishop?"

Fred smiled blandly. "Proves there's nothing *to* this evolution nonsense, doesn't it. Particularly after that sordid Piltdown business . . ."

Don Slezak poured himself another. "Got to go a little bit easy on the cider," he said. "Rum, you can get rum anywhere, but real cider . . . That's a *revolting* idea!" he exclaimed, struck by a delayed thought. "Flat-chested. Ugh."

Jim said, defensively, that it would serve the women right. "Dextrose, maltose, corn syrup. No wonder the kids nowadays are going to Hell in a hotrod. They're rotten with chemicals before they can even *walk!*"

"The poor kids." Don choked down a sob. Jim waved his glass.

"Another thing. Besides that, Nature *meant* women to nurse their babies. Nature meant them to have *twins.* 'Sobvious. Or else they'd just have *one.* In the middle. Like a cyclops or something. And how many women do *you* know or do *I* know, who have twins? Precious damn few, let *me* tell you. . . . Oh, Margaret Sanger has a lot to answer for," he said, darkly.

Don smirked. "Spotted the flaw in *that* argument right away. According to *you,* cows should have quadruplets." He began to laugh, then to cough. Jim's face fell. Fred Bishop at once put his cigar back again.

"Curious you should bring that up. The late Alexander Graham Bell passed the latter years of his life developing a breed of sheep which would produce quadruplets. In order for the ewes to be able to nourish these multiple births they had to possess four functioning teats instead of the usual two."

Don squirmed. "I wish you'd pronounce that word as it's spelled," he said. "It sounds so *vul*gar when you rhyme it with *'pits.' "*

Jim crunched a piece of ice, nodded his head slowly. Then he spat
out the pieces. "Just occurred to me: Doesn't something like that
sometimes occur in women? *'Polymam-'* something? Once knew a
woman who was a custom brassiere-maker, and she claimed that—"

Fred waved his arm. "All in good time," he said. "In the seventeen hundreds—"

A dreamy look had come into Don's eyes. "Suppose a fellow was
one of these whatdayacallits? a breast-fetishist." He got the latter
word out with some difficulty. "Why, he'd go *crazy*—"

"Why don't you mix up another round, Don?" Fred suggested,
craftily. "Jim could help you. And I will tell you about the interesting
career of Mr. Henry Taylor, who was, in a way, an example of what
Aldous Huxley calls the glorious eccentrics who enliven every age by
their presence."

Mr. Henry Taylor [Fred continued] was an Englishman, which
is a thing glorious enough in itself. He was not, even by our foolish
modern standards, too much of an eccentric; which is an argument
in favor of free will over heredity. His grandfather, Mr. Fulke Taylor,
in unsolicited response to the controversies between the Houses of
Hanover and Stuart, had managed to plague both—and the Houses
of Parliament as well—with genealogical pamphlets he had written
in favor of the claims (which existed only in his own mind) of a
distant, distaff branch of the Tudors. He also willed a sum of money
to be used in translating the works of Dryden into the Cornish
language. The task was duly carried out by a prolific and penniless
clergyman named Pendragon, or Pendennis, or Pen-something; it
did much to prevent the extinction of the latter's family, but had,
alas, no such effect upon the Cornish language.

Trevelyan Taylor, Henry's father, was much taken up—you will
recall this was in the seventeen hundreds—with what he called *"These
new and wonderful Discoveries"*: meaning the efforts of Robert Bak-
ewell and the brothers Bates in the recently developed science of selective breeding. *"Previously,"* wrote Trevelyan Taylor, *"Animal Husbandry
was left entirely to the animals themselves. We shall alter that."*

Others might inbreed, crossbreed, linebreed, and outbreed in the interest of larger udders or leaner bacon; old Trevelyan spent thirty devoted years in the exclusive purpose of developing a strain of white sheep with black tails. There has seldom been a longer experiment in the realm of pure science, but after the old man's death the whole flock (known locally as Taylor's Tails) was sold to an unimaginative and pre-Mendelian drover named Huggins, thus becoming history. And mutton.

The flock, if it produced no profit, at least paid for itself, and its owner had spent little on other things. Henry Taylor, who had enjoyed a comfortable allowance, now found himself with an even more comfortable income. He turned ancestral home and estate over to his younger brother, Laurence (later, first Baron Osterwold), and set forth on his travels. London saw him no more— *"London, where I have passed so much of my youth,"* as he wrote in a letter to his brother, *"in profligate Courses as a Rake and a Deist."* These two terms are, of course, not necessarily synonymous.

Henry Taylor crossed over to the continent with his carriage, his horses, his valet, clothes, commode, dressing case, and toilet articles. No one had yet begun to vulcanize or galvanize or do whatever it is to rubber which is done, but he had a portable, collapsible sailcloth bath—all quite in the Grand Tradition of the English Milord. Throughout all the years that he continued his letters—throughout, at least, all of the European and part of the Asiatic term of his travels—he insisted that his tour was for educational purposes.

"I devote myself," he wrote, *"to the study of those Institutions of which I count myself best qualified to judge. I leave to others the Governance and Politick of Nations, and their Laws and Moral Philosophies. My Inquiries—empirick, all—are directed towards their Food, their Drink, their Tobacco, and their Women. Especially their Women! Glorious Creatures, all, of whatsoever Nation. I love them all and I love every Part of them, Tresses, Eyes, Cheeks, Lips, Necks, Napes, Arms, Bosoms . . .*

"Why do Women cloack their lovely Bosoms, Brother?" he demands to know. *"Why conceal their Primest Parts? So much better to reveal them pridefully, as do the Females in the Isles of Spice. . . . I desire you'll*

send [he adds] *by next vessel to stop at Leghorn, 6 lbs. fine Rappee Snuff and 4 cases Holland Gin.*"

Taylor passed leisurely through France, the Low Countries, various German States, Denmark, Poland, Austria, Venice, Lombardy, Modena, Tuscany, the Papal Dominions, the Kingdom of Naples and the two Sicilies, and—crossing the Adriatic—entered the Turkish hegemonies in Europe by way of Albania . . . the tobacco was much better than in Italy, but he complained against the eternal sherbets of the Turks, who were, he said, in the manner of not offering strong waters to their guests, "*no better than the Methodies or other dehydrated Sectarians.*" He was not overpleased with the Greek practice of putting resin in their wine, and noted that "*they eat much Mutton and little Beef and drink a poor sort of Spirits called Rockee.*" He liked their curdled milk, however, and—of course—their women.

"*The Men here wear Skirts,*" Henry Taylor says, "*and the Women wear Pantalones. . . . I have made diligent Inquiry and learned that this unnatural Reversal doth not obtain in* all *Matters domestick, however.*" He cites details to support this last statement.

There is a picture of him done at this time by an itinerant Italian painter of miniatures. It shows a well-made man in his thirties, dressed in the English styles of the year of Taylor's departure, with a line of whisker curling down his jaw; clean-shaven chin and upper-lip, and a rather full mouth. He began to learn Turkish and the Romaic, or vernacular Greek, to sit cross-legged and to suck at a hookah, to like the tiny cups of black and syrupy coffee, and—eventually—to dispense with an interpreter. He spoke face to face with the pasha of each district he passed. He rather liked the Turks.

"*There is among them none of this Hypocritical Nonsense, as with us, of having One Wife, to whom we are eternally yoked unless we care to display our Horns and our Money to the House of Lords.*" He reports a conversation he had with "*a Black Eunuch in Adrianople. I asked him quite Boldly if he were not sensible of his Great Loss, and he pointed to an Ass which was grazing nearby and said with a Laugh—*" But I really cannot repeat what he said.

Taylor said he *"admired his Wit, but was not happy at the aptness of his Analogy."*

From the Balkans he went on to Asia Minor, where he made a closer acquaintance of the famous Circassian women—the raising and the sale of whom was seemingly the chief business of their native hills. He pauses in his flow of metaphors to ask a question. *"If I compare the Breasts of the Turkish Women to full Moons, with what shall I compare those glorious Features possessed by the Circassians? I would liken them to the warm Sun, were the Sun Twins."*

"Polymastia!" Jim exclaimed. He smiled happily. Fred blinked, Don said, "Huh?"

"Not *'polymam-'* something, but polymastia: 'Having many breasts.' Just now remembered. Came across it once, in a dictionary."

"Just like that, huh?" Don asked. "Were you considering becoming a latter-day A. G. Bell with the human race instead of sheep?"

"Go on, Fred," Jim said, hastily. "I didn't mean to interrupt."

Taylor's next letter [Fred continued, after a very slight pause] was dated more than a year later, from Jerusalem. He had conceived a desire to visit the more remote regions of Western Asia Minor, eventually heading for the coast, whence he hoped to visit certain of the Grecian islands. As large areas were impassable to his carriage, he was obliged to hire mules. He gives a description, as usual, of the nature of the country and people, but without his usual lively humor. Suddenly, without any connecting phrases, the letter plunges into an incident which had occurred that day in Jerusalem.

"I visited a synagogue of the Polish Jews here, having some business of minor Importance with one of their Melamedins, or Ushers. It is a small room, below Street-level, furnished as well as their Poverty permits of. There was an Inscription of some sort at the Lectern, but they had been burning Candles by it for so long that it was obscured by Soot and Smoke.

"Only the single word Hamatho *was visible, and I confess to you, Dear Brother, that when I saw this word, which means, His Wrath, a*

Shudder seized me, and I groaned aloud. Alas! How much have I done to merit His Wrath. . . ."

And then, without further explanation, he reverts to his ramble in Asia Minor. His party had come over the Duzbel Pass to a miserable Turkish village east of Mt. Koressos, *"a wretched marshy neighborhood where I was loth to stop, fearing the Ague. But some of the Mules required to be shod, and we were preceded at the forge by some Turkishes officers, Yezz Bashy or Bimm Bashi, or like preposterous Rank and Title. So there was no help for it. It promised to take Hours, and I went a-walking."* Henry Taylor soon left the village behind and found himself in wild country. He had no fears for his safety, or of being lost, he explained, because he had pistols and a small horn always about him. By and by he entered a sort of small valley down which a stream rushed, and there, drinking at a pool, he saw a woman.

"She was dark, with black Eyes and Hair, buxom and exceedingly comely. I thought of the Line in the Canticle: I am black but beautiful. Alas! That I did not call to mind those other lines, also of Solomon, about the Strange Woman. And yet it was, I suppose, just as well for 'Out of the Strong came forth Sweet.' "

On seeing her, he freely confesses, he had no hopes other than for an amorous adventure, and was encouraged by her lack of shyness. He spoke to her in Turkish, but she shook her head. She understood Greek, however, though her accent was strange to him, and she said that her name was Diana. She offered him a drink from her cup, he accepted, and they fell into conversation. *"Although she gave no Details about her Home, and I pressed her for none. I understood that she was without present Family and was in what we should call Reduced Circumstances. For she spoke of Times past, when she had many Maid Servants and much Wealth, and the tears stood in her Eyes. I took her hand and she offered no objections."*

The next lines are written in ink of a different color, as if he had put off writing until another time. Then, *"In short, Brother, I pursued the Way usual to me in those Days, and although she gave me her Lips, I was not content to stop, but was emboldened to thrust my Hand into her Bodice . . . and thus perceived in very short order that she was not*

*a Human Female but an Unnatural Monstrosity. I firmly believe, and
was encouraged in Belief by a worthy Divine of the Eastern Church to
whom I revealed the Matter, that this Creature who called herself* Diana
*had no Natural Existence, but was a Daemon, called forth, I first
thought, by the Devil himself.* . . .

"*I am now convinced that she was a very Type of Lust, sent to test
or prove me. That is, to horrify me in that same Sin in which I had so
long wallowed, and to turn those Features, in which I had intended to
take illicit Delight, into a Terror and Revulsion. I ran, I am not
ashamed to own it, until I fell bleeding and exhausted at the Forge, and
was taken by a Fever of which I am long recovering* . . ."

According to the standards of his time there was only one thing
for him to do under the circumstances, and he did it. He got religion. There had lately been established in Jerusalem an office of the
British and Overseas Society for the Circulation of Uncorrupted An-
glican Versions of the Scriptures; Henry Taylor became a colporteur,
or agent, of this Society, and was sent among the native Christians
of Mesopotamia, Kurdistan, and Persia.

He never knew, because he died before it became known, that
the Turkish village where he had his shocking experience was near
the site of the ancient city of Ephesus. Its famous Temple of Diana
was one of the Seven Wonders of the World and was served by
hundreds of priestesses and visited by pilgrims in throngs. But that
was before the Apostle Paul came that way and "*Many of those which
used curious arts brought their books together and burned them before
all men.*" But not every one in Ephesus was so quickly convinced.

A certain "*Demetrius, a silversmith, which made silver shrines for
Diana . . . called together the workmen of like occupation, and said . . .
that not alone in Ephesus, but almost throughout all Asia, this Paul
hath persuaded and turned away much people, saying that they be no
gods, which are made with hands: So that not only this our craft is in
danger . . . but also that the temple of the great goddess Diana should
be despised, and her magnificence be destroyed, whom all Asia and the
world worshippeth. And when they heard these sayings, they were full*

*of wrath, and cried out saying, Great is Diana of the Ephesians. And
the whole city was filled with confusion. . . . "*

"I am also filled with confusion," Don said. "First we hear about
this Limey, Taylor: he tries to grab a feel and gets the screaming
meemies. All of a sudden—a Bible class."

Jim clicked his tongue. "That *word*—it's slipped my mind again
Poly—? Ploy—?"

"Patience," Fred pleaded. "Why aren't you more patient?"

The confusion in Ephesus [Fred said] was finally ended by a city
official who *"appeased"* the mob by asking, *"What man is there that
knoweth not now that the City of the Ephesians is a worshipper of the
great goddess Diana, and of the image which fell down from Jupiter?
. . . Ye ought to be quiet, and to do nothing rashly."*

Long after Henry Taylor's time, the archeologists uncovered the
temple site. Among the many images they found was one which may
perhaps be that same one *"which fell down from Jupiter."* It is carven
from black meteoric stone, and was obviously intended for reverence
in fertility rituals, for the goddess is naked to the waist, and has, not
two breasts, but a multitude, a profusion of them, clustering over
the front of the upper torso . . .

"Well, you're not going to make too much out of this story, are
you?" Jim asked. "Obviously this condition was hereditary in that
district, and your pal, H. Taylor, just happened to meet up with a
woman who had it, as well as the name Diana."

"It is certainly a curious coincidence, if nothing more," said Fred.

Don wanted to know what finally became of Henry Taylor. "He
convert any of the natives?"

"No. They converted him. He became a priest."

"You mean, *he gave up women?*"

"Oh, no: Celibacy is not incumbent upon priests of the Eastern
Church. He married."

"But not one of those babes from the Greater Ephesus area, I'll
bet," Don said.

Jim observed, musingly, "It's too bad old Alexander Graham Bell didn't know about this. He needn't have bothered with sheep. Of course, it *takes* longer with people—"

Fred pointed out that Dr. Bell had been an old man at the time.

"He could have set up a foundation. I would have been *glad* to carry on the great work. It wouldn't frighten *me,* like it did Taylor. . . . Say, you wouldn't know, approximately, how *many* this Diana had—?"

"It must sure have taken a lot out of Taylor, all right," Don said. "I bet he was never much good at anything afterwards."

Fred took one last swallow of his last drink. The jug and bottle, he observed, were empty. "Oh, I don't know about that," he said. "In the last letter he wrote to his brother before the latter's death, he says: *'My dear Wife has observed my sixty-fifth Birthday by presenting me with my Fifth Son and ninth Child . . . I preach Sunday next on the Verse, "His Leaf Also Shall not Wither" (Psalms).'* "

AFTERWORD TO "GREAT IS DIANA"

This story is part of Davidson's long sequence of writings exploring the notion of the survival of mythical beings. Further examples include "The Case of the Mother-in-Law of Pearl," "Something Rich and Strange," and the essays on mermaids, unicorns, and werewolves in *Adventures in Unhistory.* There are also echoes of the club story as practiced by Buchan in *The Runagates Club* or Dunsany in the Jorkens stories. Its quasi-epistolary form—letters from an expatriate Englishman to his brother—evokes that most literary of outcasts, the remittance man, whose activities past and present bar him from his native soil. The story's resolution stems from Davidson's abiding interest in the many obscure sects of Eastern Christianity, so that there are strands linking "Great Is Diana" to the magisterial essay "Postscript on Prester John," also in *Adventures in Unhistory.*

—*Henry Wessells*

ONE MORNING WITH SAMUEL, DOROTHY, AND WILLIAM

Samuel came down with red eyes, seeking coffee and a biscuit. William was not there. Dorothy was, looking pale, and twining her hands together. "Dorothy," he said, "coffee, please, and a biscuit." She looked very pale, uttered a stifled exclamation, and twisted her hands together. After a moment he said again, "If you please, Dorothy, I desire you will direct the servant to bring me coffee and a biscuit."

"Oh God! Samuel!" she cried. "How can you sit there talking of coffee and a biscuit—" "Because it is far too early in the day to talk of butcher's meat," he said. She uttered a stifled shriek and tugged at the opposite ends of her cambric handkerchief. "—and butcher's meat, when—" "No no, far too early for that," he muttered; "coffee and a biscuit."

"—when it must be evident to you by my appearance that I am laboring under the greatest conceivable strain to which a passionate and virtuous woman can possibly be subject, particularly when her sentiments are of a loyal and patriotical nature?"

"Java, preferably," he said. "But mocha will do tolerably enough. I've no great objection to mocha. Dorothy, for pity's sake take pity on me and ring for the servant to bring me a cup of—"

Dorothy uttered a stifled scream. "Oh God, Samuel, do you wish to drive me mad?" she exclaimed. She gave the bell-pull a tug, and staggered.

"Less of that French brandy, Miss W., is my advice to you," he said.

"It is not the minute quantity of French brandy, which I take purely upon the advice of my medical man, who pronounces it a sovereign alexipharmacal against the vapours, it is that Mr. Fitzgeorge has again offered to place me in an establishment which—"

In came Jenny the servantgirl, dropping a courtesy. Samuel leered at her behind a copy of the *Unitarian Intelligencer*.

"Jenniver, a cup of coffee—java if we have it—and a biscuit, for Mr. Samuel."

"Yesmum," said the girl. "Almond, caraway seed, currant, sugar, or plain?"

"Provoking girl!" exclaimed Dorothy; "leave the room at once and bring a cup of coffee, do you hear, and a biscuit of any description. Go! They all want to kill me," she said, in a low, strained voice. William came in, looking pale and spiritual.

"I don't want to kill you, Doll," said Samuel. "You've got the vapours again. Tell me all about your fat friend, do."

Dorothy pressed her hand to her bosom. "I have often desired you not to refer to Mr. Fitzgeorge by that oleaginous descriptive," she said. "You know that he assures me he holds a very high though confidential position in His Majesty's Government. William! Why are your knees green again?"

William sighed, staggered suddenly, sat down suddenly, looked dreamily at his knees.

" 'Tis grass! Of all substances exceedingly difficult to a *degree* to remove from the knees of linen unmentionables, William, grass is the—"

"It was the loveliest daffodil, dearest Dorothy," William said.

Samuel sniggered. "Was *that* her name?" he enquired. "No wonder you look so weak."

William gazed at him, ethereally. "I do. I do? Ah, you see, you observe it also, Samuel. There is something about flowers which— Ah, Jenniver, bless you, gel, I needed that coffee and that biscuit." His fingers touched her, lightly. She jumped and gave a small scream, "La Mr. Wulliam sir!"

Samuel watched with open mouth and working throat as William, his eyes raised politely, drank the coffee. Samuel turned to Jenniver, but she, with a flounce and a simper, had already left the room, after pausing at the door to smile at William, who gave a gentle and benevolent ogle.

Dorothy said, "I have informed Mr. Fitzgeorge that although I have not been unmindful of his regard, whilst his dear Papa is unable to give consent to his son's offering marriage, all other considerations, such as a carriage, a cottage, a curricle—

"Samuel! Samuel, where are you going, Samuel, with that horrid look upon your face? Samuel, Samuel, not that dreadful substance in the vile vial again?"

But Samuel was already halfway up the stairs. Behind him he heard William say, "Dearest Dorothy, it is merely med'cine, Samuel's nerves are not strong . . . Eh? What is that? My knees? Ah, 'twas the loveliest flower, so soft, so swee—" And then the bed-sitting-room door closed.

Samuel half-groaned, half-sighed his relief, opened the huge Bible on his table to the Apocrypha, and, bending his head, from in between The Book of Tobit and The Song of the Three Children, took out a small bottle containing a ruby tincture of which he promptly filled a wineglassful, and tossed it down with a glottal sound of gratification. Then he seated himself and reached very slowly for some sheets of blank papers and the bottle of ink. He stayed thus for quite some time whilst an expression of serenity and of knowing slowly spread across his face, totally replacing the look of confusion and vexation which had been there before. And, so, at last, with an air of dreamy beatitude, he trimmed a fresh point to the quill and dipped it and wrote and wrote and he wrote and—

"I see that it is quite useless for me to endeavor to act the part of a true friend, Samuel," the voice of Dorothy rang in his ears. He wrote on. He wrote on. "Nay, Samuel, have the modicum of common gentility which would oblige you to give ear even to the address of a servant, and set aside your pen for one mere moment, Samuel: There is a person to see you."

Presently he became aware that she had left and that a strange face was looking at him. Slowly his hand faltered. He tried to go on with his writing, but the face grew larger and redder and sterner and then began speaking to him and although he urged it to go away, go away it would not. "The Doge of Venice?" he asked, hissingly. "The Great Cham? The Old Man of the Mountains?" *Sssss.* "The Negusss of—"

"None of them coves," the red face said. "Samivel 'Uggins, h'of 'Is Majesty's Hexcise Sarvice, sir. Sarvint, sir. Hin regards now, to that 'ere little flagon or as yer might call it h'a flask sir, h'of hopium, sir, now, no doubt you 'as the recee*p*t to show h'as 'ow the proper hexcise tax as been paid h'on it?"

Numbly, dumbly, Samuel shook his head.

The gager nodded. "Just has I thort. One a them gents has thinks yer habove the Lore, does yer? Well, we knows 'ow to 'andle the likes of you, come along now and no strugglin', see, hor it's the mace—" Then his expression changed as he saw Samuel's eyes rolling about like those of some cornered beast; instead of brutal, became sly. "Hunless, h'of course, now, you 'appens to want to settle hout of court; say, two guineas, to cover hexcise tax, fines, costs, h'and—"

A furious voice shouted, "What's this? What's *this?*" It was Dorothy's fat friend again. Mr. Huggins' red face went white and he fell to his knees. "Ho Gord, hit's the Prince!" he cried.

Mr. Fitzgeorge's fat fist, covered in greasy hand-lotion and bright with jeweled rings, came down upon the head of the terrified gager with a thump. "Get out of this, never come back, don't breathe a word, or it's Botany Bay!" Thump, thump, thump, he thumped the revenuer out the door; turned and gave Samuel a look and a wink and placed his index finger alongside his nose, and was gone.

In came William. In came Dorothy. "Was it about the French brandy?" asked Dorothy.

William said, "Ah, you've been writing again, Samuel. Oh, good. Excellent. Let me see." Samuel's eyes were very red. His throat and mouth dreadfully dry. He opened his lips and he croaked his want. "Not bad," said William indulgently.

Dorothy said, "What, Samuel? *Coffee? Again?* No wonder your eyes are red!"

William said, "Not bad. *For he hath fed on honeydew, and drunk the milk of paradise.* Rather a nice image, and not at all bad for a closing line."

Samuel's head jerked up. "Closing line? Nonsense? What do you mean? There are at least thirty more verses!" Sheet after sheet of paper he scattered and scanned; but all were blank. "I had them all in my head," he muttered, stunned. "In my mind . . ." But his head ached, and his mind was as blank as the paper.

Dorothy said, "You must endeavor to lead a more regular life, Samuel, and avoid low associates. What did that vulgar person from the Porlock Excise Station want with you?"

Samuel uttered a wail. He *had* to regain his lost images. He snatched for the vial of laudanum. But there was only a bottle-shaped dent in the pages of the Apocrypha to show where it had been. "My poem!" he screamed. "My beautiful poem! Gone! Everything gone! I'll never get it back, never! That bloody nark! He's busted my stash!"

Dorothy shrieked, pressed her hands to her ears. But William, tolerant, indulgent, merely looked at him benignly. "Sometimes you use very curious expressions, Samuel," he said.

AFTERWORD TO "ONE MORNING WITH SAMUEL, DOROTHY, AND WILLIAM"

The composition of Coleridge's poem "Kubla Khan," reduced to a fragment through the inopportune arrival of "a person on business from Porlock," is one of the central episodes of the Romantic period

in English literature. Davidson here offers a compact, briskly or-
chestrated explanation that accords with Coleridge's opium use. Davidson wrote this story late in his career and adopted narrative
structures quite different from those he used fifteen or twenty years
earlier. The black humor of "Traveller from an Antique Land" yields
to a lighter tone in this piece full of incidents and asides; there are
memorable sketches of the differing characters of William Words-
worth and his sister Dorothy. "Kubla Khan" was written in late 1797
or early 1798, but not published until 1816, "at the request of a
poet of great and deserved celebrity," namely, Lord Byron.

—Henry Wessells

TRAVELLER FROM AN ANTIQUE LAND

"I met a traveller from an antique land
Who said: Two vast and trunkless legs of stone
Stand in the desert. Near them, on the sand,
Half sunk, a shattered visage lies, whose frown,
And wrinkled lip, and sneer of cold command,
Tell that its sculptor well those passions read
Which yet survive, stamped on these lifeless things,
The hand that mocked them and the heart that fed;
And on the pedestal these words appear:
'My name is Ozymandias, king of kings:
Look on my works, ye Mighty, and despair!'
Nothing beside remains. Round the decay
Of that colossal wreck, boundless and bare
The lone and level sands stretch far away."
                                    —Shelley, *Ozymandias.*

It was in April 1822, on the third day after his friend had sailed off into a lead-grey, oil-smooth sea only a few hours before the storm broke, that Tregareth, fearing the worst, made his way to Lord Gryphon's villa, to consult with him. Was not Gryphon the nominal head of the English *literati* hereabouts?

The time was past noon, Gryphon had already had his cup of strong, green tea, and was lunching on the invariable biscuit and soda-water as he lay abed. He looked up when the tall figure entered, long black hair in disarray, striking his fist into palm.

"Surely there is *some* news, Tregareth," Gryphon said. "Are they safe? Have they been . . . *found?*"

Tregareth shook his head. "I have no news, my lord," he said, trying to mask his agitation with formality. "Every vessel putting into Leghorn has been questioned, but there has been no sign of the *Sea Sprite*, of Shadwell or Wilson or the ship's boy. I thought that you might have had a letter, or at least a note, from their wives at the Villa Grandi, saying that they had arrived."

"I have had nothing!" Gryphon cried.

"Fulke Grant has heard no word, either. He blames himself, poor fellow—'It was to welcome me and get me settled that they sailed to Leghorn,' he says."

"Oh, God, Tregareth!" Gryphon moaned, covering his fat, pale face with a trembling hand. "They have been drowned! They have surely been drowned!"

Tregareth, looking away from him, turning his gaze out of the window to the hot sandy plain, said sturdily, "It does not follow, my lord. Not at all. I conceive of at least two other possibilities— no, three. First, they may have been carried away off course—to Elba, perhaps, or even to Corsica or Sardinia. Second, assuming the vessel *did* come to harm, which Heaven forbid—though she *was* cranky and frisky—there were so many other craft at sea that evening—" Tregareth spoke more and more rapidly, his broad chest rising and falling as his agitation increased. "Surely it is not unreasonable that they have been taken aboard one of them and are even now disembarking in some port. And, third, I fear we must also consider the possibility that a piratical felluca may have ridden them down—pretending accident, don't you know, my lord—and that presently we shall receive some elegantly worded message which in our blunter English speech spells 'ransom' "

Gryphon had begun slowly to nod; now his face had cleared

somewhat. He reached for his silver flask, poured brandy into the tiny silver cup. "What must we do?" he asked. "You have been a sailor—in fact, if we are to believe your own account of it—wilder than any tale *I* dared to write!—you have been a pirate, too. Command me, Tregareth! Eh?" He drained the cup, looking at the Cornishman with raised brows.

Ignoring, in his concern, the implication, the other man said, "I thank you, my lord. I propose, then—in your name, with your consent—to obtain the governor's permission to have the coast guards scan the beaches. Perhaps some flotsam or wreckage will give hint of—" He did not finish the sentence. Gryphon shuddered. "And also, I will have couriers sent out on the road to Nice, enquiring of news, if any, of their having reached another port. In the event of their having been captured by brigands, we must await that intelligence."

Gryphon muttered something about—in that event—the British Minister—

Tregareth's grey eyes grew fierce and angry. "Let Shadwell's *wife*, my lord, let poor Amelia appeal to the minister and to diplomacy. Let *me*, but hear of where they are constrained—give me a file of dragoons—or if not, just a brace of pistols and a stiletto—I have stormed the corsair's lair before!"

"Yes, yes!" Gryphon cried. He rose from bed, thrust feet into slippers, and, with his queer, lame, gliding, walk, came across the room. "And I shall go with you! This is no coward's heart which beats here—" He laid his hand on his left breast.

"I know it, my lord," the other said, touched.

And, telling him that he must make haste, Gryphon thrust a silken purse into Tregareth's hands, bade him godspeed, and gloomily prepared to dress.

The two ladies met the Cornishman with flushed cheeks—cheeks from which the color soon fled as he confessed that he brought them no news. Jane Wilson essayed a brave smile on her trembling lips, but Amelia Shadwell shrieked, pressed her palms to her head, and repeated Gryphon's very words.

"Oh, God, Tregareth! They have been drowned!"

But Mrs. Wilson would not have it so. She knelt by the side of her hostess's cot in the "hall" of the Villa Grandi—a whitewashed room on the upper story, not much larger than the four small whitewashed rooms which served for bedchambers—and taking the distressed woman by the hand, began to comfort her. Wilson was an excellent sailor, she said. No harm could come to Shadwell while Wilson was aboard. The storm had lasted less than half an hour—surely not enough to injure such a stoutly built vessel as the *Sea Sprite*. Tregareth added his assurances to Jane's, with an air of confidence he did not feel.

By and by the cries gave way to moans. Amelia pressed a handkerchief to her lovely eyes and turned away her head. Tregareth would have lingered, but Jane drew him gently away. They descended the stairs together. The sea foamed and lapped almost at their feet.

For a moment they were silent, looking out over the beautiful Gulf of Spezia to the terrace. To one side was the tiny fishing village of Sant' Ursula; to the other side, a degree nearer, the equally tiny town of Lorenzi.

At length Jane spoke. "Poor, poor, dearest Amelia!" she said. "She has been far from well. It is not only her body which is weak, you know, Tregareth. She has been sick in spirit, sick at heart. It is the loss of her dear children. To bid farewell to two such sweet babes in so brief a time—no, no, Tregareth, man knows nought of what woman feels. It is too much." And so she spoke, mantling her own concern for the missing. Even when her husband's name, it was only in connection with Amelia's illness.

"Did you know, Tregareth, that scarcely more than a week ago, when she was in truth barely able to turn on her couch, that we missed her one night? Wilson found her down below, her slippers sodden and her hem drenched, and she seemed like one who walks in a dream. I have not dared to part from her for even a moment since. We had better go back—but no word of this."

Amelia smiled at them as they returned, a sad and worn little smile. "I am ready to hear what you have to tell me, now, with more composure," she said.

And so Tregareth recounted to her what he thought she might safely hear. How Shadwell and Wilson came sailing the trim little *Sea Sprite* over the wine-dark sea to greet the poet Fulke Grant and his family. How Grant and Shadwell had fallen into one another's arms for joy. How they had settled the new arrivals in satisfactory quarters. And how, finally, it was decided that the *Sea Sprite* and the *Liberator*—Lord Gryphon's vessel—would return together, with Tregareth captaining the latter, while Gryphon stayed behind.

"Oh, why did you not do so, Tregareth?" cried Amelia Shadwell. "With a skilled sea-captain such as you to convey them—"

It was the fault of the harbormaster, Tregareth explained. At the last minute he had refused clearance to the *Liberator* on some petty point or other. And so Shadwell and Wilson, by now impatient to see their wives once more, had sailed off alone, with only Antonio, the ship's boy, for crew. Not for worlds would he have told her of his fears. Of Wilson's being—for all his wife's pride—but a gentleman-sailor. Of how awkwardly Shadwell handled the craft. Of what others had said—

"Crank as an eggshell, and too much sail for those two sticks of masts," remarked the master of a Yankee ship, spitting tobacco. "She looks like a bundle of chips going to the fire."

And the *Liberator*'s first mate, a Genoa-man: "They should have sailed at this hour of the morning, not the afternoon. They're standing in too close to shore—catch too much breeze. That gaff topsail is foolish in a boat with no deck and no real sailors aboard."

There had been only a slight wind. But in the southwest were dirty rags of clouds. "Smoke on the sea," said the mate, shaking his head. "A warning . . ." as the fog closed around the trim little *Sprite*. The air was sultry, hot and heavy and close. Tregareth had gone below to his cabin and fallen into a doze. He dreamed of Shadwell, his dark-fair hair only touched with grey, ruffled by the breeze, the light of genius in his eye, the look of exaltation on his face—a boy's face still, for all he was approaching thirty—a boy's fair skin and light freckles, and a boy's look of eagerness. The world had never gone stale for Archie Shadwell . . .

Tregareth had thought, as he often did, of his own good fortune in being the friend of Shadwell and of Mrs. Shadwell; and somehow he found himself envying Wilson, who not only had a beautiful wife of his own—Tregareth's wife was dead—but the company of the beautiful Amelia Shadwell . . . and then he had fallen asleep.

And then had come the gust of wind—the *temporale*, the Italians called it—and the squall broke. It thundered and lightninged and he rushed on deck to help make all trim. In twenty minutes the storm's fury was spent, but Jane Wilson was wrong in thinking that was too brief a time for deadly damage. Twenty seconds could do for so light a boat as the *Sea Sprite*.

Thus three days had passed—three days of ceaseless enquiry. From Gryphon, Tregareth had gone directly to the governor, mentioned the name of *il milord Gryphon*, doucely slid the purse across the desk.

"A courier? As far as Nice? Of course! And the coast guards to patrol the beaches all about? Certainly!" The purse vanished. Orders were given, messengers scurried. Tregareth had left in a flurry of assurances, and come straight to the Villa Grandi.

He had intended to leave as quickly, to pursue his own search, to flag (and flog, too, if need be!) the coast guards into vigilance—for who knew if any of Gryphon's gold would trickle down to them? But Amelia would not hear of it.

"Tregareth, do not leave us!" she begged. And he, looking at her sweet face, could not refuse to tarry a little while. Jane summoned a servant to make fire for tea. Jane herself was busy pretending the matter was no more than that of, say, a diligence whose lead-mule had delayed the schedule by casting a shoe; she bustled about with needles and thread. But Amelia would not play this game.

"Oh, Jane, in Heaven's name, be still," she pleaded.

"I am looking for the beeswax, to help thread my needles," Jane explained, hunting and peering. "I promised dear Shadwell to finish that embroidered shirt for him. Where can it be? Is that not strange? A great lump of unbleached beeswax—"

Amelia began to weep. "Shall he ever wear a shirt again? And this creature wants to kill me with her talk and her scurrying—"

But the next moment Tregareth himself was kneeling and holding her hand and vowing that Shadwell would live to wear out a thousand shirts, ten thousand. She smiled, allowed her tiny white hand to become engulfed in his great brown one. But she gave a little cry of pain.

"Why, what is this, Amelia?" he asked, astonished, opening her fingers, and looking at the scarce-healed marks there.

"I was sawing wood, kindling, for the fire," she said in a small voice; Jane and Tregareth exclaimed against such foolishness. There were servants. Amelia pouted. "They care nothing for me," she said. "Look at that slut, there—do you suppose she cares about me?"

The servantgirl, perhaps sensing she was being mentioned, turned at that moment. She smiled. Not at all an ill-looking wench, Tregareth observed, almost abstractedly—though of course one could not even consider such coarse charms in the presence of lovely Amelia. The girl smiled, "The *signore* will soon return," she said.

Amelia spat at her, cursed, called her *puta*, struggled to rise.

"Madame!" cried Tregareth, shocked.

"She meant but to reassure you, dearest Amelia," said Jane, as the girl scuttled away, frightened.

"She did not mean to! She meant to scorn me! Does she think I am blind? Does everyone think I am blind? Do *you*, Jane?" But the hysteria passed almost as soon as it had come.

"Tregareth, forgive me," she said. "I am not well. Such sickly fancies cloud my mind . . . Oh, I know that Shadwell must be living! So great a genius cannot die so young! No age ever had such a poet. Does not Gryphon himself agree? Was he not proud to have the little ship named after his own poem? Oh! I little thought, the day he carved his initials in her mainmast, that she would give us so much grief . . . I have had such presentiments of evil—such a sense of oppression that I have not felt for years, not since poor Henrietta . . ."

Tregareth felt the little hairs rise on his neck. Never before had he heard the name of Shadwell's first wife mentioned in this house. It seemed—he scarcely knew why—it seemed dreadful to hear it now on Amelia's lips, on Amelia's smiling lips.

"Do you believe she drowned herself?" she asked. He could only stammer. "There are those who say—" Amelia paused.

"No one says—" began Jane.

But the sick woman smiled and shook her head. "Everyone knows of Shadwell and me, how we eloped while he was still a married man," she said dreamily. "Everyone knows that only Henrietta's death set us both free to marry. Everyone knows of Shadwell and Clara Claybourne," she continued. "First she bore Gryphon's illegitimate child, then she bore Shadwell's—everyone knows . . ." Her accusing eyes met those of Jane, who stood by, her face showing her pain. "But only you and I, Jane, know . . ." And she seemed to fall into a reverie. Then she chuckled.

So pleased were they to have this sign of her mind passing to anything which had power to please her, whatever it might be, that they beamed. "Do you remember, Jane, your first night here? Were you listening? How Wilson said. 'To think that my wife and I are privileged to be guests under a roof which shelters two such rare geniuses! Archie, the author of that exquisite poem, *Deucalion,* and Amelia, the author of the great novel, *Koenigsmark*—' Do you remember, Jane, what Shadwell said?"

"I did not hear, dear Amelia. What did he say?"

"He said, '*Koenigsmark!* Ha-ha!' "

For days Tregareth rode the shores, scanning the waves, the scent of the salt sea never out of his nostrils. Some few bits of flotsam from the *Sea Sprite* had come ashore, but this was not proof positive. However, he no longer had doubts. He drove himself, unrelenting, in his quest. Not only grief for his friend spurred him on now, but guilt as well.

"You have travelled so far, Tregareth," Amelia had said to him; "you are, yourself, that *'traveller from an antique land'* who brought back word of Ozymandias. In the East, of which you are so much enamored, and of which you have made me so much enamored—do they have love there, as we know it? Or—only lust?"

Tregareth had considered, throwing back his head. After a moment he said, "In the East they have that which is stronger than either love or lust. In the East they have *passion*."

She considered this. She nodded. "Yes," she had said. "For love may fade, and lust must ever repel. *Passion*. Do not think that our English blood is too thin and cold for passion, Tregareth."

Now he asked himself, again and again, spurring through the sand, was it covetousness to desire a man's wife for your own—if the man were dead? Would not Shadwell himself have laughed at such squeamishness? Would not Gryphon?

He almost did not see the coast guard until the man called out to him. When he did see, and reined his horse, he still did not imagine. Then the man gestured, and Tregareth looked.

And there on the margin of the sea he saw him.

"There is no doubt of it being Shadwell, I suppose?" Gryphon asked.

Tregareth shook his head. "None. Shadwell's clothes and Shadwell's hair, in one pocket Shadwell's copy of *Hesiod*, and in another, his copy of Blake."

Gryphon shuddered. He looked at a letter which he held in his hand. "From Amelia," he said. He began to read.

" 'You have heard me tell that my grandmother, a Scotswoman, was reputed to have been fey, and to have visualized the Prince's defeat at Culloden before it happened. I, too, at times, have had presentiments of future misfortunes. I had them at the time of poor Henrietta's death. But never so strong as during this Springtime did I feel the burden. The landscape and seascape I saw seemed not of this earth. My mind wandered so, as if enchanted, and oftimes I was not sure—and still am not sure—if the things I saw and did were real—or were the products of an ensorcelled mind, musing on ancient wrongs: and all the time, the waves murmuring, *Doom, Doom, Doom* . . ."

They were silent. "What shall be done with the body?" Gryphon asked. "The nearest Protestant cemetery is in Rome."

Tregareth said, "Shadwell a Protestant? If ever there lived a man who was a pagan in whole heart, body, and soul—Besides, in this weather, it is out of the question to convey the corpse to Rome."

Distressed, almost petulant, Gryphon flung out his fat hands. "But what shall we *do?*" he cried.

"He was a pagan," said Tregareth, "and shall have a pagan funeral. The Greeks knew how. And I have seen it done in India."

Gryphon began to quiver. He reached for the silver flask.

The widow received the tragic news with an agony of tears. Presently she recovered somewhat, and said, "I knew it would be so. I have had no other thought. Now he is young forever. Now," her voice trembled and fell, *"mine* forever."

They parted with a gentle embrace, she accepting Tregareth's counsel not to attend the immediate funeral. Later, he said, when a second interment would be held at Rome, if she felt stronger . . .

Tregareth's emotions, as he rode back, were mixed. In great measure his activity on Shadwell's behalf had absorbed the grief he would otherwise now be experiencing at Shadwell's death. Moreover, thoughts he had earlier suppressed rose now and had their will. Had there not been, in Shadwell's friendship for him, some measure of condescension? Had Shadwell not indicated from time to time— though less openly than Gryphon—a lack of complete belief in the stories Tregareth told of his youth in Nelson's Navy and his adventurous career as the consort of buccaneers in India?

But—sharpest of all—Shadwell was dead! And he, Tregareth, was alive! It was dreadful about the former, but it was impossible not to feel gratitude and joy in the latter. As he rode between the forest and the sea, Tregareth felt the keenness of delight in the fact that he lived and could experience all the rich pleasures of the living world.

The body had come ashore near a place called Via Vecchio. A

small crowd had gathered, but the dragoons scarcely needed to hold them back. The people looked on, half fascinated, half horrified at the strange scene, and kept crossing themselves.

Tregareth was in full, undisputed charge.

"I might have spared myself the trouble of bringing wood," he said. "See—not only is the forest there full of fallen timber, but here are all these broken spars and planks cast up on the shore."

He gave directions in loud and resonant tones. The workmen dared not resist, though they looked as if they would have mightily liked to. A pyre was soon built up, and the body lifted onto it. Tregareth heaped on more wood. One piece he glanced at, put it under his arm.

Gryphon was pale and ill at ease, but gentle little Fulke Grant did not even trust himself to stand, and remained sitting in the carriage.

"I think all is ready," Tregareth said. He cleared his throat. Hats came off in the crowd.

"Surely Shadwell's shade is watching us," he said, "as we prepare to bid farewell to his clay. Behold the verdant islands floating on the azure sea he loved so much, and which he took to his final embrace! Behold the ruined castles of the antiquity whose praises he sang in incomparable numbers, 'for the numbers came'! Behold the snowy bosoms of the ever-lofty mountain peaks! All these, Shadwell loved. Shadwell! *Vale!*"

He poured over the body a quantity of wine and oil, then took the waiting torch and thrust it under the pyre. The wood was tinder-dry and flared up directly. *"Vale,* Shadwell!" Tregareth cried again. He cast into the fire the copy of Blake which had been in the drowned poet's pocket. He tossed on a handful of salt, and the yellow flames glistened and quivered as they licked it up.

"Behold!" he exclaimed, "How peacefully the once-raging sea is now embracing the land as if in humility, as if to crave pardon! O Shadwell, thou—"

But here Gryphon interrupted him. "Tregareth, cease this mockery of our pride and vainglory," he said in a stifled, low, voice.

Tregareth, his long black hair floating on the wind in magnificent disorder, looked at him with some surprise. Then he looked over to Fulke Grant. But little Grant, still in the carriage, now had the silver flask in his hand. The only sound he made was a hiccup.

Tregareth shrugged. He tossed in a handful of frankincense. The flame mounted higher. The heat grew more intense.

"I cannot endure to remain much longer in Italy," Gryphon said. "Every valley, every brook, will cry aloud his name to me . . . We must go off together somewhere, Tregareth, you and I. For now I have no one left. America, Greece—somewhere far off." He sobbed aloud, then turned and walked away. The fire crackled and hissed.

Tregareth stood all alone by the pyre. Slowly he took from under his arm the piece of driftwood. It seemed a portion of a ship's mast. On it were carved the initials *G. G.* He clearly called to mind that happy day, only a short while back, when Gerald, Lord Gryphon, had carved the letters. The top of the piece was all rent raggedly. But on the lower part the breach was only partly so. The rest of it—

He could envision the scene. The sudden trumpets of the storm, the terribly sudden blast of wind, the foremast crashing down before the frightful pressure of the wind-caught sails, mast and sail falling as dead weight upon the gunwales, and the ship careening and filling and then going over, going down, as the sea rushed in and the lightning served only to make the blackness deeper . . .

Tregareth ran his fingers over the smoother surface of the wood. Someone, plainly, had sawn half through the mast and then hidden the cut with unbleached beeswax of the same color.

He lifted his fingers, bent his head. Despite the wash of the sea and the scouring of the sand, Tregareth could still note the scent of the wax. He thought, for just a moment, that he could even detect the scent of the soft bosom in which the wax must have rested to soften it—but this was only fancy, he knew. It need not, however, remain only fancy.

Love, he reflected, can fade; and lust must ever repel—but passion is stronger than either.

He came as close to the pyre as he could, threw in the shattered section of the mast, and watched it burn fiercely.

Then he turned and went to join the others.

Postscript to "Traveller from an Antique Land":
A Letter from Avram Davidson to Robert Mills, 03 October 1960

> October 3/60
> 410 West 110th St.
> NYC 25

Dear Bob,

Thank you for sending along Fred Dannay's very interesting comments on TRAVELLER FROM AN ANTIQUE LAND. I think I see exactly what he means. Some of the changes he suggests have been already made, others, I shall make. For instance:

Historical Names	Fictional Names
Trelawney	Tregareth
boat "Don Juan"	boat "Sea Sprite"
boat "Bolivar"	boat "Liberator"
Mary	Amelia
Harriet	Henrietta
Claire Clairmont	Clara Claybourne
"Epipsychidion" (poem)	"Deucalion"
"Frankenstein" (novel)	"Koenigsmark"
Villa, Casa Magni	Villa Grandi
Via Reggio	Via Vecchio
Williams	Wilson
copy of Keats*	copy of Blake
Leigh Hunt	Fulke Grant

| Lord Byron | Lord Gryphon |
| Shelley, Percy | Shadwell, Archie |

forget actual names of towns I call: Sant' Ursula and Lorenzi "if other vol.* was really Sophocles—so, change to Hesiod (The cities of Nice and Rome are, of course, both fictitious.)

The letter from Mary/Amelia is from an original. I should have liked to essay another in the same vein, but I eliminate as directed. Fred does not mention my having pointed out that much of the funeral oration is in Trelawney's (and, to a much lesser extent, Leigh Hunt's) own words. I guess he simply forgot, and, as I am sure he does not want it to stand so, I have paraphrased.

I am sure I do not know what he means about asking me not to play any tricks or try to fool him. "The ox knoweth his stall, and the ass his master's crib . . ."

On second thought, I *will* try to compose another Mary/Amelia letter. If not desired, it may be eliminated, so that this part of p. 12 would then read simply, "Gryphon shuddered. They were silent."

The date I supply as directed on p. 1 is the actual one; if this was not what was wanted it may safely be changed to—say—five years before or after. I trust these revisions will do the trick. I did not feel up to retyping the whole MS a third time.

Yours,

Avram Davidson

AFTERWORD TO "TRAVELLER FROM AN ANTIQUE LAND"

Davidson was not the first to treat the history of English literature as the setting for crime fiction (Lillian de la Torre's stories of Sam: Johnson, *detector*, are probably the earliest sustained series). The suggestion Davidson makes about the death of Shelley is novel. The letter from Davidson to his agent, Robert Mills, printed here, identifies the actors in this thinly veiled account of the death of Shelley at sea in 1822. Perhaps the most accurate portrait is that of the unsavory Trelawney ("Tregareth"), who is notorious as the designer of Shelley's sailboat and the man who found Byron a doctor in his final illness. Few men have had the distinction of causing the deaths of two poets of such stature: Trelawney dined out on his fame for the rest of his long life.

—Henry Wessells

THE MAN WHO
SAW THE
ELEPHANT

The story is short, and quickly told.

There was a man of the people called Quakers whose name was Ezra Simmons, and he and his wife had a farm in the hills behind Harpervill. Esther Simmons was a woman who never rested during the hours she was awake, and the hours of her slumbers were few. It is recalled that she did once go down to the main road and sit on the stone fence there to see John Q. Adams go by, the year he became President. It is also recalled that she took her spinning along to keep her hands busy. "Waste not, want not," was a common word with her, and another such was, "Whatsoever thy hands find to do, do it with thy might."

In short, she was one of those of whom the Scriptures speak, saying, "Who can find a virtuous woman? for her price is far above rubies. The heart of her husband doth safely trust in her. . . ." There was good reason for Ezra Simmons to trust in her, for had he trusted in himself the cattle often as not would have gone unfed, the sheep unshorn, and the meadow unmowed. It was not that Friend Simmons was a lazy man. The summer of Eighteen Hundred and Froze to Death, as some light-tongued folk called it (it would have been the year Sixteen, give or take a year or two), he toiled late and early on an engine he intended should make shoe-pegs. It never did make enough to fit his own shoes, and meanwhile his kine and his swine alike should have laid stark and cold, had not his good wife Esther tended to them. Snow and hail in July! Truly, a heavy judgment upon a nation overgiven to vanities; but that is neither here nor there.

Simmons Farm was neat and trim enough, and so was Ezra Simmons's grey coat, but his grey eyes looked beyond his farm. They looked beyond his native hills, and, as he confessed, beyond his native country as well.

"Suppose," he said once to his wife, "suppose a Friend had a concern. He might go and preach unto those lost in darkness, and even now groaning beneath the spiritual tyranny of the Muscovite Caesar or the Grand Bashaw of High Barbary."

"Suppose a Friend had a concern," Esther answered, tartly, "he might pick up his scythe and commence on the home acre."

Too, Ezra had a great interest in curious and foreign beasts, and this too, he voiced to his wife, from whom he concealed nothing.

"Does thee suppose, Esther," he would ask her, "that the Bengal tiger, for an instance, is striped merely as our Tabby, in grey and darker grey? Or is it indeed striped in yellow-gold and black, as Captain Piggott says?"

Esther, for her whole answer would hand him the milk-bucket—and point to the barn. In truth, she was not over fond of Captain Piggott, considering him and his tales an unsettling influence on Ezra. "How large would thee say the whale-fish is, Captain Piggott?" her husband asked him once, when he came a-visiting. "As large as this farmhouse?"

"As large as the meeting house!" the old mariner declared.

Ezra exclaimed in wonder, but Esther was unimpressed. "It is no affair of ours, John Piggott," she said, "if the whale-fish is as large as the meeting house or as large as two meeting houses. When was the last time thee was inside the meeting house, John Piggott?"

John Piggott coughed behind his hand, and shortly afterwards he took his leave.

It was, accordingly, with no great surprise—and, for that matter,

with no great attention—that Esther heard Ezra say to her one afternoon, after returning in the shay from Harpervill, "There was a
broadside given out in the town, Esther, telling of a travelling show
which will make a visitation to the county seat come next Second
Day."

Esther was at her churn, and the day was hot, and she spoke in
a sharp voice without much heeding her words.

"Must thee be forever a-gadding after vanities, Ezra Simmons?"

He stood a moment, silent and taken aback, then turned and
took up his axe. She heard him splitting firewood for a good long
while, and then, scarcely giving time for the echo to die away, he
was in the springhouse before her, as she paddled the roll of new-
made butter. "Does thee do well to rebuke me, Esther?" he asked.

She looked up, surprised, for she had clean forgotten the matter.
"In what way have I rebuked thee, Ezra?"

"Is it a vanity to look upon the great beast which the Lord hath
made? Can it be that He hath made it for nought? I doubt not that
the showman is one of the world's people, but can the great beast
be less a marvel for that?"

Esther dabbled her fingers in the shallow pool fed by the spring,
and touched them, absently, to her face. "I do not understand thee,"
she said. "What marvel and what great beast is it of which thee
speaks?"

"The elephant, Esther Simmons! The elephant!"

There was buttermilk to be put in crocks, and the crocks to be
put in the well; potatoes to be peeled and the peels fed to the hogs
and the potatoes to be put up for supper. There was a dried-apple
pie to be baked and linen to be spread in the sun against yellowing
and mildew. There was a labor of work, and scarce daylight to do
it in, and Esther said, "I have lived in this world five-and-forty years,
Friend Husband, and I have never seen the elephant, nor have I ever
been moved by the Spirit to see him yet."

Ezra stood before her, his head bowed, his broadbrim dusty from
the wood he had been splitting, his hands folded on the handle of
the axe. He stood there, thus, for quite some moments, and then,

in a low voice, he said, "I have lived in this world for nine-and-forty years, Friend Wife, I have lived in this world for a jubilee of years, thee can reckon. I have never seen the elephant either, but I tell thee, Friend Wife, that I feel moved by the Spirit to see him now, for I truly believe that else I do I shall never have chance to see him again."

There was hay in the meadow, ripe for the mowing, and shingle-trees in the yard needing to be split for the roof of the barn. A cartload of corn stood as it had stood for two days—unloaded. Esther did not hesitate.

"Thee feels moved by the Spirit to see this elephant?"

"They say it is the great beast Behemoth of the Scriptures."

"Thee feels moved by the Spirit to see this elephant?"

"I do."

"Thee has a concern to see this elephant?"

"I have."

"Then thee must see him," she said.

She rose before dawn on Second Day and baked fresh bread and put it in his wallet. She put in a roll of butter wrapped in green ferns, and sliced meat, and three apples and a jug of water and one of buttermilk. She paused to reflect if she had forgotten anything. It occurred to her that the world's people took money for preaching the Word of the Lord, and, this being the case, might also require to take money for showing the Lord's creatures. She took a brick out of the fireplace and, reaching in her hand, pulled out a sock. From the sock's scanty store she selected a Spanish milled dollar, and she put this in her husband's wallet, too.

He led out the horse and harnessed it. "Will thee not come with me, Esther Simmons?" he asked.

Again, she shook her head, and again she made the same reply.

"I have not been moved by the Spirit to see the elephant, nor am I moved to see him now."

The old shay rolled down the lane, and she turned her work. And, to his work, too.

Ezra drove down the white, dusty country roads. He rode past fields ripe with grain and past orchards heavy with fruit. People called out to him, but he did not pause to talk. He rode over rattling bridges and beside mudflats covered with eelgrass and salt hay, and turned inland again, through granite hills. He stopped at times to water the horse, and then he drove on again. The sun was on the decline when he arrived at the county seat, and he drew up and called out to a man afoot, "Friend, can thee tell me where the show-man is, who has the foreign beast to see?"

"Showman? There bain't no showman here."

Ezra lifted his hat slightly. The evening breeze cooled his head. "There was a broadside given out to Harpervill," he said, "which related that such a person was to be here, come Second Day."

"Showbill, ah. I recollect, now. Someone did arrive in a caravan, all painted in outlandish colors, yes. A foreign-looking man, as you say. But the Selectman wouldn't give him leave to stay, so he went on. Who knows what mischief he might be up to?"

Ezra set his hat down. "How old of a man would thee say he was, Friend?" he asked.

The townfellow scratched his head. "Hard to say. Might 'a' been thirty. Might 'a' been forty. Why?"

"Thirty or forty. The Lord has given him leave to tarry in this world for thirty or forty years, and thee would not give him leave to tarry in this town for so much as a day." He shook up the reins and drove on, leaving the townsman with mouth agape.

The sun set, the sweet smell of the earth rose into the night air. The moon came up, broad and yellow. "Thee sees how it is, Friend Horse," Ezra said, to the plodding animal. "It was not the Lord's will, it seems, that I should look upon the countenance of His great beast Behemoth, which men call the elephant. So be it. I have dwelt all my days within the circle of these hills, and if at times I have felt it to be a somewhat smaller circle than I could wish, still, I have never wished to go against His will."

The horse whinnied, and then it shied. Startled, but not so much as to forget the account of Balaam and the ass, Ezra Simmons peered into the silvery road ahead. He saw no angel there, he saw a wagon painted over with strange devices, drawn over to the side of the road. Horses tethered to a tree raised their heads and nickered. A curtain at the back of the caravan parted and a man appeared. In his hand was a lamp. Rings glittered in his ears.

"Is thee the person called a showman?" asked Ezra.

"I am that very one, Reuben."

"My name is not Reuben, Friend. It is Ezra. I have come to see your great beast."

The man gestured Ezra inside. There was a bright quilt on the wagon bed, and a woman sat on it, with a child at her breast. Her legs and arms were bare, and so, though she smiled at him he turned aside his head. The man led him to a door in a partition, and held out his hand. "There was no money at all in the last town," he said. "And no bread grows by the sides of the road."

"What money is the fee?"

The showman shrugged. "I take any money that will pass muster. York shillings, United States gold and silver, fips and thrips and picayunes. I take paper notes of all New England states, as well as New York and Pennsylvany. Virginny and Caroliny, I take at a discount, but as for the wildcat currency of Tennessee and Missouri, them I do not take at all."

Ezra felt in his wallet. "I have nought but one old piece of eight," he said.

"I take them, too. Come along."

It smelled musty in the large space beyond the partition. It smelled odd and wild, it smelled of strange places and strange things, and it smelled most of all of strange beasts. Shadows danced and something rustled in the soiled hay, something made an odd sound. The showman held out his lamp. "There he be," he said. "Have you ever seen the like before?"

"Nay, Friend," said Ezra. "I never have. And never will again. Hold the lamp steady." He looked into the eyes of the strange beast, and the strange beast looked into his own eyes. There was silence. "Thee has a canny look about thy face," Ezra observed. "I believe that thee would laugh, if thee but could. So. And this is the Behemoth of the Scriptures."

The showman took out a piece of pigtail tobacco and thrust it into his mouth. "Now, as to that, I cannot say. On that subject I am coy."

"The elephant, then."

The showman mumbled his chew. "Hmm," he said. "Hmm, hmm."

"This is the only foreign beast thee has? Thee has no other?"

After spitting a brown stream into the straw and wiping his mouth on the back of his hand, the showman shook his head. *"Had* another one. It died. Over a week ago. A great loss, believe me."

Ezra took another look at the beast, and the beast at him. Then, tentatively, he reached out his hand and touched it. The creature nuzzled at his hand, then sniffed his pockets. "Would thee eat an apple? I believe thee would." He watched it eat the apple. Then it turned away. "Thee is right," Ezra said. "It is time I was gone."

At the door, foot on the step, he turned around. "If thee has by chance a likeness of the beast . . . ?" he asked. "But I have no more money with me."

The showman waved his hand, rummaged in a box, produced a sheet of paper with a woodcut on it—the precise likeness of the beast. "No need to mention money. Take it. My compliments. You're the only gent I met today." He stooped, grunted, took out a demijohn, gurgled it. "Splice the mainbrace?"

"Nay, Friend. I thank thee. But I must be getting back to Esther Simmons." He peered at the paper, lips moving slowly. "What is the meaning of this strange word?" he asked.

The jug gurgled again. The showman lowered it a bit. "Oh, that. Why, commodore, that there is the animal's name in its native language."

Ezra's lips moved again. "The Hebrew is a sacred tongue. How full of awe its syllables be. *Kan-ga-roo.* There. I have it now." He took the showman's hand. "Friend, I thank thee," he said. "With all my heart. Thee little knows what thee has done for me. My soul is now at rest within me, like a weaned child."

Earrings glittering, wet mouth smiling, the man said, "Don't mention it. But, say. Like to take a look, scot-free, at the very hat Old Boney wore at St. Helen's Island? Or a parmacetty-tooth? Hey? Do."

Ezra shook his head. His eyes were grey, and very gentle. "What care I for such things, Friend? I have seen the elephant. What more is there for me to see?"

AFTERWORD TO "THE MAN WHO SAW THE ELEPHANT"

Friend, I hope you got a chuckle out of this story. I certainly did. I once lived near a community of Quakers (or Friends). They were gentle people who still drove horses and buggies when everyone around them was driving steel and chrome. Were they simple, or were they simply as satisfied as the man who saw the elephant?

Henry Wessells reminded me that "the man who saw the elephant" once meant someone who had been to San Francisco during the gold rush of 1849, so perhaps there is more in this simple story of "bait and switch" than first appears.

—Grania Davis

PEBBLE IN TIME

(with Cynthia Goldstone)

The City of San Francisco is certainly *my* city! I wouldn't live anywhere else than "The Port of Zion" for anything in the world. Perhaps my favorite worldly spot—next, of course, to Golden Gate Park—is the Embarcadero. Only two people have ever known how much thanks is due to one of them (now passed from Time into Eternity) that the sailors and seafarers have helped spread the Restored Gospel throughout the seven seas to the four corners of the earth. Of course its spread was inevitable, but I do think that if we Saints had stayed in, say, Missouri, our message would have been much slower in making its way around the world.

Not that I mean for a moment to indicate anything but the most wholehearted approval for the work done by our regularly appointed young missionaries, but of course nothing can equal the zeal and energy of sailors! And, walking down the Embarcadero and seeing the vigor with which they toss their Orange Julius drinks down their thirsty throats, I think how different the scene must be in (for example) that terribly overgrown and misnamed large city in Southern California, where seafarers may be seen abusing their systems by the use of alcohol, tobacco, tea, and coffee—all, of course, forbidden by *The Word of Wisdom* of the Prophet Joseph.

When I speak of the role played in this by one of the only two people who know the whole, true story, I am referring to my maternal grandfather. *I am the other.* And I suppose I'm a chip off the old block—or, perhaps, stated more exactly, a chip off the stalwart old Mormon family tree, so well set up (on paper, of course) by Grandpa Spence during the later years of his retirement. How he spent the earlier years, we will see very shortly. As is usual among L.D.S. people, I take a great interest in my ancestors, but most of all in Grandpa Spence. It may be because I inherited (if such things be hereditary) both his interest in genealogy and inventions, as well as that slight speech impediment which becomes troublesome only at moments of excitement. I have always said to myself, "Nephi Spence Nilsen, your grandfather rose above this, and so will you." It invariably helps. Grandpa was aware of all that and it constituted another bond between us. To sum it up: he and I both tended to stammer, both were interested in Mormon history and genealogy, both loved to consider mechanical devices.

It was a combination of these characteristics of Grandpa's which brought about a certain incident which I feel can now, safely, and *should* now, properly, be made known to one and all. And above and beyond that, my grandfather specifically (though in veiled language) asked me in his will to speak out on this matter at this particular time.

Grandpa was a peach. Perhaps it was the very enthusiasm of his devotion to the Latter Day Saints (though Grandma drew the line when he dutifully considered taking a second wife) which accounted for his unfailing good humor and zest even when he was quite old. Needless to say that he was a respected and responsible citizen, having for many years been Mechanical Supervisor for the various industries operated by the Latter Day Saints Church, and was valued for his circumspection as well as for his technical competence. Unfortunately (or fortunately: let History decide) his circumspection failed him at one crucial point in his life when—

But let me simply state the facts.

Grandpa had left England with a party of immigrants (all converts like himself) as an already full-grown young man of fifteen, crossed the plains to Great Salt Lake City, and within a short time was hired by President Brigham Young to copy letters in his clear and graceful longhand. His promotion in the Church was rapid, and after fifty years of remarkable service, he retired to his own three-story home on First North Street. Grandma had passed from Time into Eternity years before, and all the children had homes of their own; a neighbor lady acted as part-time housekeeper, leaving him free to follow his own inclinations in his own now fully free time.

The inspiration for the chief of these inclinations arose out of the only real regret that he had ever had. Much more out of his reverence for Mormon history than personal pride, he wished so much that he had not missed by only a year or so having been present on that great day when Brother Brigham led the weary pioneers to the bluff overlooking the great Utah valley and announced that they would stay and make the desert bloom like a rose. In his retirement, Grandpa Spence secretly determined to build a device which would transport him back to that decisive moment.

"I was born in the age of the covered wagon," he declared to himself, "and have lived to see the age of the flying machine. Eternity is one thing, but Time is another, and surely to a Saint nothing is impossible!" He was of course not certain of being able to *return,* he might even be scalped by an unconverted Lamanite, but to these considerations he gave but a shrug and a smile. His enormous dedication to the idea of fulfilling himself in this singular way enabled him to work like a steam engine (he *had* helped drive the Golden Spike at Promontory Point—Utah!—incidentally); he was a vigorous man with great inventive ability, and he was inspired. He completed the machine one bright May morning and got to Observation Bluff one hour and seventeen minutes before Brother Brigham and his advance party arrived.

Grandpa had not calculated on finding a smooth or barely downy chin instead of the full beard his hand automatically sought to stroke in satisfaction, but after a moment he realized what had happened: he had traveled back in time so successfully that he had become a stripling once again! Fortunately he had always been moderate in diet and his 20th-century clothes were only slightly loose. *Un*fortunately he no longer had the gravity and patience of his former years and soon became overanxious and restless. And as the pilgrim travelers approached, his excitement drew him away from the machine, which was well hidden by the bushes on the bluff above the new arrivals. He was recklessly determined to get as close as possible to the principals of this historic moment and to hear the historic words, *This is the place!* And in moving towards the travel-worn Saints, creeping along in the low bushes, he accidentally dislodged a stone, which tumbled down the slide, gaining momentum.

Forgetful of all else, he stood up to warn them out of the way, but in his excitement he found his speech impediment rendered him unable to release a sound . . .

The stone rolled and bounced and hit Brigham just above the worn and dusty boot on his right leg. The square, heavy face winced and swung around and saw the still-speechless stranger above on the bluff. All the weariness and travel of the long journey west, all the tragedy of the Mormon martyrdom, all the outrage of the persecuted was in Brigham's roar of pain and astonishment. "Look ye there!" he cried. "Who's that? Not a speck of dust on him! Throwing stones already! I thought this place was empty and I see that the Gentiles have got here before us!" And while poor young-again Spence struggled vainly to give utterance, regret, and denial, Brigham turned and swung his arm in a great, determined arc.

"This is not the place!" he cried. *"Onward!"*

Not for a moment did anyone dream of controverting the word of the President, Prophet, Revelator, and Seer. *Onward!* they echoed. And *onward* they went. And the conscience-stricken young stranger, where did *he* go? Well, where *could* he go? He went after them, *onward,* of course. Of course they couldn't make heads or tails of his stammering explanations, nor even of the ones he attempted to write. But they understood that he was sorry. That was enough. Mormons have suffered too much to be vindictive. And that night when the band camped, he was brought to the leader's wagon, where a small lamp burned.

"Young man," said Brigham, "they tell me that you have expressed a seemly contrition for having raised your hand against the Lord's Anointed; therefore I forgive you in the name of Israel's God. They also say you write a good, clear hand. Sit down. There's pen and ink and paper. *Dear Sister Simpson. It cannot have escaped your attention that I have observed with approbation your*

—no, make that—

the modesty of your demeanor, equally with your devotion to the doctrines and covenants of the Latter Day Saints, which is of far greater importance than the many charms with which a benign Nature has adorned your youthful person. My advanced years will always assure you of mature advice, and in my other seventeen—is it seventeen? or nineteen?—pshaw, boy!—a man can't keep all these figures in his head—*my other eighteen wives you will find a set of loving sisters. Since it is fitting that we be sealed for Time and Eternity, kindly commence packing now in order to depart with the next party of Saints heading for our original destination which as you know was tentatively the peninsula called San Francisco in Upper California. Yours & sic cetera, B. Young Pres., Church of J.C. of L.D.S.*—sand it well, son, for I hate a blotty document."

You've all read your history and must certainly have often felt thankful that Brother Brigham did not yield to the momentary impulse he admitted he had, and that he did not stop in Utah. Despite its impressive name, Great Salt Lake City is just a tiny town with a pleasant enough view, but even that can't compare with the one from my window alone. It's a pleasant thing to sit here in my apartment atop the hill on Saint Street, sipping a tall, cool lemonade, and admire the view. To the west is the great span of Brigham Young Bridge across the Golden Gate, with its great towers and seven lanes of cars; to the east is the Tabernacle, its otherworldly shape gracing the Marina Green, with the stately Temple nearby. I see a network of wide, dignified streets feathered with light green trees, giving the city the look of a great park. And, being truly a *Mormon* city, it is undisfigured by a single liquor saloon, tearoom, tobacconist, or coffee house.

And Grandpa? After his retirement, he sold his house on Joseph Smith Esplanade and moved to the fine apartment in the Saint-Ashbury District where I now live. Having decided to leave well enough alone the second time around, he devoted his *last* last years entirely to the study of Latter Day Saint genealogy. He felt right at home here, as do I, and why not? After all, the Saint-Ashbury can boast of more lemonade and Postum stands per square block than any place in the U.S.A. and one is always seeing and hearing those inspiring and exciting initials: L.D.S.! L.D.S.! L.D.S.!

AFTERWORD TO "PEBBLE IN TIME"

Cynthia Goldstone is a highly regarded San Francisco artist. Ray Bradbury once wrote her a letter of appreciation. Cynthia and her late husband, artist Lou Goldstone, exhibited their work at many science fiction conventions, and were a much-loved couple in the Bay Area science fiction community. Avram and the Goldstones were good friends in San Francisco during the lively 1960s and 1970s, before Avram relocated to Washington State. Cynthia has always been fond of her Mormon heritage. I can imagine the fun Cynthia and Avram had, writing this story—perhaps while passing around a pitcher of lemonade.

—Grania Davis

THE SINGULAR INCIDENT OF THE DOG ON THE BEACH

Sitting here in the sunshine and looking at my orange trees, I know there was no way I could have stayed in that awful English climate. But there I was, just gotten off the train in what they call Paddington Station, London, and my arm hurting something bad; however, I tried not to scratch it. A station official gave me pretty clear directions to a nearby doctor, so off I went and in I went. Took off my coat, rolled up my sleeve, lit my pipe as much to distract my mind as because I wanted a smoke, and waited. And waited.

And waited. No sign of the servant who had let me in, but by and by I heard men's voices, and called out. In came two men.

"I hope you haven't had a long wait," said one. Burly fellow. "My friend and I are just at the point of leaving. But Dr. Anstruther, round the corner, or Dr. Jackson, down the street, will be pleased to attend to you on my behalf."

"I had understood that your office hours were going on now, sir."

He gave a look at his companion—a tall, spare, limber man— and said, "Well, well, yes, but, ah, you see—well, Jones?"

"Well, what, sir? Let's just have a look. Hm." It was just a look he gave me. And then he said . . . and then he said this . . . all this: "Your arm has a bad case of creeping eruption which you no doubt picked up on the beach in Florida where the dog was. It must itch badly and no doubt has much bothered you all the way from Liverpool, and may even have bothered you while you were grafting the sweet oranges on to the bitter orange root stock."

Many years as a poker player had given me control of my face. Merely I asked, what made him say all that?

He smiled. "Your clothes, my dear sir, are American-cut. Your hip pocket sags, as though it had long carried the weight of a pistol or revolver; this is not the usual custom here in the United Kingdom, although, I believe, far from uncommon in the United States . . . though, I understand, far less common in the northern than in the southern states. The raised weal of the concentric circle on your arm is certainly that of creeping eruption, an infection often picked up on a tropical or subtropical beach, where the parasite is evidently carried by dogs. Your clothing, if you will pardon me, has a definite tang of pine wood, and it is not the season when our timber merchants receive their Baltic pine. And although your trousers have been brushed, hotel servants are often careless, and there are still some slight traces of the unmistakable mud of the Merseyside, where the timber-boats from Florida often put in. Is there not in your pipe tobacco the aromatic herb, deertongue, a product of the Florida forest? Do I not observe that a drop of the sap of the orange tree has fallen on your sleeve and dried? And had you been cutting down sweet orange trees because they had become infected with the disease to which they are, alas, prone, you would surely have taken off your coat so as to swing the axe more freely. And—"

And in another minute he would have reminded me that we certainly do graft sweet orange onto the bitter orange root stock which is so much more resistant. I said, "And my arm, sir? My poor afflicted arm? Is nothing to be done for it?"

They had the gaslight on, and barely noon; and they needed it on, too. This fellow—Jones?—gave a slight shrug. "Well, sir, surgery, even minor surgery, is out of my line. I would suppose that

my medical friend here would wish to numb the skin and subcu-
taneous tissue with applications of ice, and then use the lancet—
one, two, three—to excise the tiny parasite which has caused the
trouble; eh, doctor, what, sir?"

The doctor said, somewhat shortly, somewhat ruefully, that he
had no ice. "I never have ice. I should advise him to go see Creevey,
at St. Stowe's. Creevey is by way of being somewhat of a specialist
in tropical medicine and surgery, removal of the guinea worm, and
such. St. Stowe's is very well-furnished, very up-to-date, and has an
ice machine. Meanwhile let me put on a soothing ointment, and try
not to scratch—Eh? No charge, no. The servant will let you out,
my friend and I must be on our way, now; pray excuse haste."

His friend had already forgotten me. I heard him say, as they
went out, something which has stuck in my mind forever. But I did
go to St. Stowe's, by way of what they call a four-wheeler; the other
kind of cab, the hansom, has only two. Huge place, St. Stowe's! In
came a heavy-bodied, short-legged man: stamp-stamp-stamp: this
was Mr. Creevey, the surgeon. He scarcely listened to me.

"Dr. Who? Never mind, don't signify. Eh? 'Creeping eruption?'
I daresay; be glad it's not guinea worm! Eh? 'Ice,' what do you want
ice for, do you think this is a lolly-shop, this is a surgery; we don't
serve ices here! Dresser! Scrub down that arm! Dresser! A clean lancet! One-two-three: *there!* All over. Dresser! Patch him up! *'Day!'"*
Stamp-stamp-stamp; exit Mr. Creevey the surgeon.

The dresser said, "If you feel faint, sir, put your head between
your knees while I set this carbolized bandage on your arm. You are
lucky to have had one of the foremost up-and-coming men in this
hospital, sir. In London, sir. D'you like London, sir? *I* don't. Coming
from our dispensary at Gravesend this morning I saw that new ship,
the *Ballarat*, starting to get up steam; if I had a purse of gold I'd be
off like a shot and aboard her. Ah, sunshine!"

Wonder what the man's name was; the dresser, I mean. He put
the idea in my head, and an hour later my satchel and I were in the
steam launch, heading down river for the *Ballarat*.

Doothit had had no business sicking his dog on me or pulling that pistol when I bashed the critter. It was Doothit who'd shot the bank cashier, not me; I never wanted him shot. I only wanted my fair share of the gold, but things being the way they turned out, why, I took Doothit's share, too. It came in handy while waiting for my new-planted trees to bear. I took a new name here, to go with my new life; they are used to that sort of thing here, anyway. And I raise as good oranges in Queensland as ever I did in Florida.

It's not that I think too much about the past, but just that just now this little bitty old scar on my arm reminded me. That first doctor back in England—his name . . . what . . . what? No matter. I even kind of forget his face. Funny way to neglect a medical practice, running off from patients because a friend says, *such* an odd thing to say! "Quick, what, sir! The game's afoot!"

But I don't forget his friend's face, though. Sharp as a hatchet and just as keen. Yes! *Very* keen! And *very* smart! What a beautiful system of logical deductions he had, too. Look what he smelled out about me in a few seconds. Good thing I lit right out for Australia and never came back there, or he might soon have smelled it all out. Yes, he likely might right soon have smelled it all out. I know his methods.

Afterword to "The Singular Incident of the Dog on the Beach"

Nowhere do the names Watson or Holmes appear in this glorious pastiche, which carefully blends the precise recall of events with just five instances where the most celebrated names in detective literature are misheard. The perspicacity of that "one look," and the "beautiful system of logical deductions" that unfolds as a result, leaves the reader certain that it was Sherlock Holmes who provided the off the cuff diagnosis—and who spooked the narrator enough for him to take ship for Australia.

—*Henry Wessells*

THE ENGINE OF SAMOSET ERASTUS HALE, AND ONE OTHER, UNKNOWN

THE WITNESS
[H. Nickerson, accused]: Debts which I had first incurred in order to keep my family whilst I was at sea a-hunting parmacety whales. Which trade I wish to my Redeemer I had never left off, nor settled ashore into another.

THE CORONER
[Mr. Salathiel Adams]: Best leave off such vain wishings. Where be my notes. Now, in regard to an electrical or magnetical engine of sorts. You worked on it.

NICKERSON:
Yes. He called it a radiatoring engine or such.

CORONER ADAMS:
The deceased freeholder was the sole inventor?

NICKERSON:
He and one other. I don't know the other.

CORONER:
You merely performed mechanical work upon it as directed
by the Deceased?

NICKERSON:
Yes.

MR. SALTONSTALL, THE FIRST SELECTMAN:
Had it been told you by the Deceased that he believed the
said invention or engine might be of considerable use to this
Nation in the event of a pretended dissolution of our Federal
Union—

MR. QUINCY SLOCUMB, THE SECOND SELECTMAN:
Which must and will be preserved.

THE JURY AND SUNDRY OTHERS PRESENT:
Hear, hear! Huzzah! et cetera.

FIRST SELECTMAN:
A secession. Had you?

NICKERSON:
Yes. He said something about sending intelligence. Communications, an audible semaphory. Whatever that be. I didn't
much reckon what he meant. A trumpery music-box sort of
thing, I reckoned it. The Negro pumped it like a church organ. I sot the fire to hide my traces.

SECOND SELECTMAN:
Were you prompted by those in favor of dissolving the
Union?

NICKERSON:

No, no. I have never sot my hands to commit sedition nor treason.

CORONER

[Mr. Adams]: Then how come you to set your hands to commit a crime as most would say be almost as bad?

NICKERSON

(after some silence): Not having the fear of God before my eyes, I was seduced and instigated by the Devil.

> from *Records of the Township of Tusquokum,*
> *100th Folio, 2nd Series,* 1861 (2nd Quarter)

Samoset Erastus Hale stood at his window. The weather vane was still and so was the strip of muslin which served as gage for lesser and more trifling breezes. Hale made a very slight sound. In weaker men it might have been a grunt; in far weaker ones, an oath.

"Esau," he called. "Esau, Esau." Gradually his voice rose. Stopped.

"Why, what is the matter with you, Esau," a female voice asked below. "Don't you hear Professor Hale a-calling of you? Why bain't you already in his cabinet, or 'office' as some will say it? Esau? What? What? Why no, it is not neither the hour for midday meal, it lacks a full quarter-hour thereof, and you may be certain, Esau Freeman, that I will give you no midday meal if you do not get body, boots, and breeches up the back stair directly. Go now!"

Feet were heard, laggingly ascending. Esau stood at the stairhead by and by, with hands at sides and lower lip outthrust.

"Time passes," said Professor Hale. "Time passes. To work, Esau. Connect the wires to the lightning rod, as thee calls it. Good. Pump the engine, now. Pump the engine."

"Some people think that I am a mere beast of burden," Esau said. "I say, some people thinks I be a mere beast of burden. Am I not also a man and a brother? I asks, am I not also a man and a brother? I asks—"

Professor Hale's features did not shift. "Thee is not a mere beast of burden," he said. "Thee is also a man and a brother, Esau Freeman. And as a man and a brother, thee must work. Also. Does thee not see that there is no breath of air to turn the windmill? Does thee not see that I am twisted with age and infirmity? Does thee not know this, without seeing? Get thee to the pump, Esau Freeman."

"Directly."

Nothing in the back room where Professor Hale had his engine was in the least gaudy or worldly; everything was solidly wrought and of the best substance, though some of his natural history equipment was certainly most curious. Hale thrust out his stick and opened the double doors of the large polished maple-wood box which housed the mysterious engine; the engine itself, behind the doors, was concealed by a stretched-taut cloth on the face of which was embroidered, THERE IS NO SPEECH NOR LANGUAGE WHERE THEIR VOICE IS NOT HEARD. A creaking sound began, died away.

"I doesn't *like* this work," Esau said. "I ben't *used* to it. I doesn't *like* them huge cylinders as drips acid sometimes. I doesn't *like* them spook voices. I doesn't *like*—"

Hale's gnarled hands moved on his walking stick. "Thee will become used to it if thee does thy duty as befits a man, Friend Freeman. And as for *like*, why, what has *like* to do with life? Has thee not heard Professor Longfellow say with his own lips that life is real, life is earnest? I swear no oath, as thee well knows, but I assure thee, Esau, that if thee does not directly commence to pump I shall directly commence to prod thee with my walking stick, even as my own father did me, for my own good, when I dallied, which was not often. Pump."

In the cabinet, or office, the bitter reek of chemical substances mingled with the smell of furniture polish, the scent of slightly damp wood and slightly damp plaster, the smoke from the Franklin stove, and a whiff of cinnamon and clove from the downstairs kitchen of Emma Coolidge, who was baking the pie for tomorrow's breakfast.

Esau's mutters continued, but so did his pumping. By and by a crackling sound came from behind the taut embroidered cloth. Samoset Erastus Hale took out his pocket watch, looked at the grandfather clock in the corner. A small bell sounded, somewhere else.

"I wun't *do* it! I wun't *do* it! I be afeard of this irradiator magnet ingine."

Hale's time-carved face moved slightly from side to side. "Thee speaks as one of the foolish people, not as one to whom I have given my word that he shall have my second-best broadcloth coat this coming First Day if he continue to work well. Continue pumping. Thee is working well. I am proud of thee."

Suddenly a burst of melody, as though from a Swiss music box, was heard behind the cloth covering of the great maple-wood chest-front on its sturdy legs. Esau gave a squeak of fear, thrust his head out from the other side of the strange engine. His eyes stared imploringly. But Professor Hale was looking at his watch. All at once a pair of voices were heard singing. As though automatically, Esau's lips began to move. Slowly his head withdrew. His voice was now blended with those of the others, as they hailed Columbia, Happy Land.

A moment after the song ceased a voice began to speak. "The President had audience this morning with the retiring Minister of the Two Sicilies," it said. ("Popery," said Hale. "Tyranny.") "The President had audience this morning with Chief Red Fox of the Pashimauk Nation and with Captains Bobcat, Several Spots, and Medicine Wolf of the Up-River Tacsabac Nation. The President presented the Indian Allies with the customary silver medallions, and assured them—"

"Stuff," said Hale. "Graven images. Shining baubles. Gewgaws. What of their *souls*, Friend President? What of them, I say?"

"I says so, too, but another thing I doesn't like is that them voices is never respectable, they never gives you a civil answer no matter what you may ask, Friend Professor Hale, does—"

". . . first-chop hyson is down one cent," the voice declared. "First-chop first gunpowder stays stable at four and one-half cents.

At the haymarket, well-cured hay is down one quarter of one cent, with sufficient supplies coming in from the country districts. Sassafras continues strong, as does summer-strained whale oil at one dollar, with winter-strained oil asked for at one dollar and a quarter of a dollar but not available. Sea-island cottons including nankeen or slave-cotton—"

Samoset Erastus Hale's hands again shifted on his cane. " ' . . . no man might buy or sell, save he that had the mark, or the name of the beast, or the number of his name,' " he murmured.

Esau implored, "Oh, Friend Samoset Erastus, *please* don't talk mention of the number of the beast, for it—"

Implacably the other voice continued, "In Richmond, prime men field hands fetch $1100 as per report of the magnetic telegraph, while the same fetch $1300 in Montgomery. In New Orleans—"

Esau said nothing whatsoever, but Professor Hale said " 'My heart shall cry out for Moab; his fugitives shall flee unto Zoar.' "

By and by the voice stopped speaking. A throat was cleared. Then the voice, in a different tone, said, "That's all on the paper."

Another and an older, a much older and much weaker, voice said, "Then that is all for today."

"Then I'll have my dollar."

"I am getting it, Mr. Booth. Be patient."

"Patient? I think I am patient. I come here three times a week and sometimes there is a brief dramatic recitation and sometimes we accompany the music box in a song and whatever you have written I always read into the pipe, very patiently, but I'm blamed if I understand."

Was there a sigh from . . . somewhere? "The time will come, sir, when I trust you will understand. In the meanwhile, you are not being paid because you understand but because you have a strong, clear voice, as befits an actor. And here is the dollar. Thank you. I will see you on Monday."

"Monday."

A door was closed, but not in Professor Hale's back room. The very old voice said, and it was difficult to hear it against the background of crackling sound, "Professor Hale, if you are listening, kindly note the time and quality of the speaking."

Professor Hale was already noting it in a small, leather-bound book. After a moment or so the very old voice resumed speaking. Hale leaned close and cupped his ear. "In two weeks I hope to take the train of cars and meet you in Philadelphia, as planned. We have much to discuss. I am not feeling well these days, not at all, but I trust that a merciful Providence will spare us both to complete the work on the irradiodiffusion machine, as I am increasingly confident it may be of much service to our nation in the dark times ahead which I foresee. Though you may not agree."

Hale said (to whom? perhaps to Esau) that he did agree, indeed. But still hoped the machine would be used "Mainly for spreading the Gospel of the Peaceable Kingdom, as well as for mercantile intelligence, especially for such as dwell where there is no telegraph office."

The old voice spoke for about a half-minute more, but it was no longer possible to make out more than a word here and there through the continuous crackling sound. "Needs more work," Hale said. "Needs more work. Must speak to Mechanic Nickerson when he comes with my money." As he finished saying this, a sound came clearly over and through the crackle, as though a small signal-bell had been struck.

"Can I stop pumping now, Friend Sir?"

"Thee may stop now, Friend Esau." A sigh of more than mere relief came from behind the big box on legs, and Esau stepped forward. "Thee has done well, Friend Freeman, and may go to get thy midday meal, not forgetting that tonight is a school night." Samoset Erastus Hale had stipulated that his hired boy must continue in learning as a condition of employment; one third of the expense he bore himself, one third came from Esau's wage, and the Whipple school discounted one third more. Esau declared later that Hale had said nothing more on that occasion. More concerning this entire conversation, later.

(The entire conversation has been principally reconstructed, though with difficulty, from the evidence—some of it hearsay—subsequently provided by Schoolmaster Dwight Whipple and his two sons, as well as from Esau's own testimony, though, of course, Emma Coolidge was not silent.)

Esau declared later that Hale had said nothing more on that occasion. Hale, to be sure—Someone came and visited Hale that night and quarreled about a debt and when someone left Hale did not leave with him. No eye saw for a while what else was left behind as it crept here and there, silently and uncertainly at first, then leaping forward with a great roar. The papers, purposely scattered, went first, then the well-polished furniture and the philosophical equipment and then the walls and floors. No one saw vanish into flames the sampler-like embroidery with the citation from the Psalms which covered the front of the engine behind its paneled doors, and no one saw the melting of the copper wiring and the aerial rod perhaps (though who can say more than *perhaps* . . . ?) not intended entirely to deflect lightning; no one saw the liquefaction of the battery of large cylinders and their zinc plates, and no one saw the acid vaporize. Every tangible evidence of what the engine, the "sending intelligence," the "audible semaphory" and "trumpery music-box sort of thing," "irradiator magnet ingine" and "irradiodiffusion machine"—every tangible evidence of what the singular-sounding device might really have been—was gone in the immense conflagration which brought fire fighters from ten townships roundabout. Details are to be found in the document entitled *Office of the Coroner of the County of Mitchingham: Inquisition into the Death of Samoset Erastus Hale, a freeholder in said County.*

It was well for Esau Freeman that he had spent the entire evening at the Whipple school, as it was far from well for Hannibal Nickerson, Mechanic of Tusquokum Township, that he had (as was well-proven) called that same night upon Samoset E. Hale in the matter of the overdue note for one hundred and thirteen dollars. Nickerson wanted this extended. Hale declined. Nickerson showed a proper and edifying repentance before he was hanged, but the records do not show that he said, or was asked to say, much about the curious "magnetical irradiofusion machine" destroyed in the fire he admitted setting.

The question of the identity of the "one other" still remains "unknown." Both Professor Bell and Mr. Edison have recently [1883—Ed.], and entirely independently, made investigations, but have not been able to find whomever it may have been in Washington City and with whom S. E. Hale was concerned in the perhaps joint invention. Still, we must ask ourselves, Who *was* this person of mystery, allegedly there at that time? A fragment from the correspondence of General W. Scott refers to "Cranky old Smith and his talk of Message Injines to run without wires," but as the facts seem to be that there can be no such engine, the reports purporting to describe one man or one hundred men can after all be nothing but phantasies, however ascribed, and it is vain, were it possible, to seek for any "Smith" among multitudes. What we have collected and placed in apparent order here must be a fiction, tastefully tricked out to while away the dull night moments when the outside world cannot divert.

It is certainly true that some doubt has been cast upon parts of the testimony of both the hired man Esau Freeman and the housekeeper Emma Coolidge, these parts seeming (until not long ago) so very improbable, even phantastical; but it is unlikely that anything further will ever be learned. Emma Coolidge was drowned at sea six months later whilst returning from a visit to Nantucket. Esau Freeman (who it will be remembered was not subject to the draft) fell in an attack by Rebel sharpshooters upon United States Colored Troops in the course of a nameless skirmish somewhere in the Carolinas during the year 1865, in the month of April. May the dogwood and the crepe myrtle gently drop their fragrant flowers upon his grave.

Afterword to "The Engine of Samoset Erastus Hale, and One Other, Unknown"

This late Davidson gem, concerning a vanished technology considerably in advance of its time, works with characteristic misdirection and uncharacteristic concision. We might call the "irradiodiffusion machine"—created in early 1861 for the purpose of "spreading the Gospel of the Peaceable Kingdom, as well as for mercantile intelligence"—a radio. But the surviving witnesses to the fire in which inventor and invention perished have no such vocabulary to draw upon. Where R. A. Lafferty's television story "Selenium Ghosts of the Eighteen-Seventies" employs a baroque narrative of duplicity succeeding treachery, Davidson's story seems terse and straightforward— at first. Hale might be communicating across the aether, or perhaps he is simply muttering to himself.

In the story's final three paragraphs, Davidson cites the names Bell and Edison to send further ripples of historical suggestion that linger in memory. He undercuts the narrative we have just read, creating a sudden leap in time from 1861 to 1883, and pointing to flaws in the evidence and the death long ago of all parties directly connected with the curious events.

—Henry Wessells

BUCHANAN'S
HEAD

Grant lived in sin with a buxom shrew; Tumbleton was in effect director of a privately endowed museum. After Eustace Williams had somewhat slightly recovered from his second nervous attack, Doctor Douglas McFall told him straightforwardly that he must give up the cottage-studio. He told him this in the presence of Williams's friend Tumbleton and Grant, who had come down with McFall from town on the 9:15; and of his friend Harrison, who had already been staying with Williams in the country since having learned of the attack. The sick man's condition was of such a nature that he required and would (for a while, as yet to be determined) require constant medical attention; and McFall, regardless of the fees, could not constantly be coming down to attend him; other medical men in the neighborhood of Troy Barns there was none. The cottage-studio stood nearer to two miles from the station than not. Sometimes there was a dogcart waiting, or a trap; more often there was not. The weather was un-predictable: McFall could neither be expected to burden himself with mackintosh or oilskins nor risk exposure to pneumonia as an alter-native. Troy Barns was an out-of-the-way and brutish place, no neighbors for a full mile in any direction, and the sullen groom who acted as manservant could not be expected to prepare decent food if such were always available, which was not the case; upon neither the butcher's cart nor the baker's could one rely. McFall wound up this speech from, as it were, the throne, by saying he wondered Williams had not died of scurvy by now.

"Which he damned well would have," said Grant, in his usual growl, "if Harrison had not come down ahead of us."

Harrison said nothing, but touched his light gold beard, a gesture which often did him in place of speech. Williams gave evidence of desiring to say something, but he was still too feeble, and McFall racked on. "No chemist in case you run out of medicine, which you might, or you or that oaf Crutchett spill it, same thing it would come to: no. I want you where I can look at you and look you over as often as I think proper. You can't go on living on bacon and bad potatoes and stale bread and stewed tea, you'll be able to have fresh meat—chops, a joint, a nice fowl—and sprouts and greens, some decent wine, whatever I think best for your diet as we go along. If you have another of these moods in which you feel you cannot stay in the house, why, step to the curb and call a hansom or a four-wheeler—instead of rushing out into this barbarous wilderness and risk falling into an old quarry."

Williams moved forward in his chair, his lips began to move, he licked them, moved his right hand. But McFall gave him no chance. McFall said he didn't care how "romantic" the cottage-studio was for a painter or poet, he wanted Williams within short distance of a hospital, *if need be* (he emphasized those words), and in particular St. Olave's, where McFall stood high, though he did not say so; what he said was that Professor Schneiderhaus of Lepzig, a man knowing more about nervous diseases than any other man in Europe, including Charcot, was spending a year at St. Olave's. Even McFall had to pause for breath, at which Williams said something at last, but so weakly that he could scarcely be heard to speak at all.

Tumbleton it was who spoke and was heard, preening his left side-whisker, then his right: "After all, Williams," he said, "you can paint and write in London as well as anywhere. Lots of chaps do."

No: McFall, ignoring Tumbleton, pointed a thick finger at the sick man and said, in rolling tones, "I absolutely forbid you to touch brush to paint or pen to paper for at least six months. You are to undergo no exertion at all. For at least six months. For at least six months you are to do nothing requiring the expenditure of nervous energy more than to dress, climb into a smoking jacket, put your feet on the fender of the fireplace, and pick up a newspaper or a magazine. You are to take naps in the afternoon. One evening a week, if one of your friends—and you may thank your good stars that you have such good friends—if one or two or all three of these gentlemen here for that matter, wish to take you out for dinner at a quiet place, or to a music hall or a concert, why, very well, I allow that. But mind you: *no drama.*"

He stopped, indicated by a rise of his tufty brows that Williams would at last be allowed to speak. After a moment, Williams did so.

"What is the alternative?" he whispered.

"Death or the straight-waistcoat," said McFall, with quite terrible promptness.

Williams collapsed back into his chair.

"Well, there's no more to be said," said Grant. "We'll pack you *up*"—he thrust the poker into the smoky fire as though it had been a mortal enemy; but still it smoked—"and take you back to *town.* You'll live a quiet life, we'll all see to that, we'll all look after you, and I understand from Dr. McFall as we were coming down, that at the end of six months, when you will be much better, that there would be no objection raised if you'd wish to try the sea air; damn these coals, they aren't proper coals at all, they're half slate; in London you'll have decent coals, you'll be *warm!*"

"*Warmth,*" said McFall, "is of the utmost importance in illness of your sort. You *must* have a good fire." The lamp smoked, too, in its sooty globe, but Grant, having failed to do anything with it a moment earlier, did not try now. The wavering small light of the lamp, the dim sun through the grimy windows and dusty skylight, did little to show what might be on the unfinished canvas in the corner where an armor breastplate hung askew on a tailor's dummy and a mass of cobweb had settled on a plumed hat; or what might be written on any of the dusty sheets of paper on the desk in another corner, loosely confined by what looked like a dictionary—something clattered in the kitchen, something smashed, somebody swore. Briefly.

"There is a problem," Harrison said. His voice was rather high, but it was not effeminate. "I live with my father and my brother, my brother is somewhat simpleminded, a gentle soul and no trouble to *us,* we know his ways, but he is not a fit companion for an invalid. Tumbleton is a married man with a small child, and, I understand, another soon to be expected." Tumbleton did not precisely preen, but he did straighten himself a bit. And nod. "Eustace could hardly stay *there.*" Tumbleton suddenly looked grave and slightly shook his head. "Grant has his own arrangements." Grant lived in sin with a buxom shrew whom only Grant could manage, and then only within certain limits, and within those limits there could be no place for Williams. Grant said nothing; his face, smooth-shaven save for a moustache, did not move. Grant exported cheap bottled spirits to the Colonies under a variety of bright labels, all of which he himself had designed; now and then when the sale of one label flagged, Grant designed another: this had become the extent of Grant's work as an active artist.

The wind wuthered down the chimney, driving more smoke into the room; Dr. McFall reproved it by coughing and waving his hands. "Very well, very well; what is the problem? Shall I tell you what is the problem? The problem is that your friend Williams is a very ill man. I have done my best for him before. Has it helped, no it has not helped. This is his second breakdown. The tonic which I prescribed after the first, I see it untouched. The elixir, on the contrary, is all over the floor, and the bottle is still where it fell. The diet pudding? In the larder, untouched, save for what the rats have mucked about. The claret, on the other hand, which should have lasted another month, is gone, it is clean gone, there are not even any empty bottles, but there is a barrel of beer which I did not order, and a case of gin, which I absolutely forbade; *that* is the problem, *that,* and the minor matter that your friend Williams had the good fortune to be found lying by the road, well-nigh insensible, by perhaps the only police-constable to have passed this way since the Chartists marched on London; what is the time, I must not miss my train, I have a Harley Street office with patients waiting for me, I have a practice in the Borough with a rather young partner who wants being looked in on rather often, I have wards to walk to St. Olave's—problems? problems? Do not speak to *me* of problems, Mr. Harrison."

He glanced at his watch, raised his eyebrows, began next to put things back into his black case. Harrison touched his beard, but, nonetheless, said, "There is a problem of money. And where Eustace is to live. Not here, certainly, but—"

McFall would be butted no buts; his red face grew redder. Williams had money of his own, had he not? What? It had been somehow anticipated? There was a shortage in the last quarter's income and there were no accounts, no hopes of recovering any of the shortage? (Things were suddenly very quiet in the kitchen.) Well, he, McFall, had not said that Williams must take rooms in the Albany, neither did he advise him to live in a doss house in Stepney. There were other places, quite livable, places respectable and yet inexpensive. "Mr. Grant and Mr. Tumbleton and I have already discussed this." He snapped the crocodile-bag shut.

Tumbleton blinked, taken slightly by surprise, fluffed his whiskers. "Ah, yes, Williams, Harrison, we did. We did. Old Solomon, you know old Solomon, the painter's cousin? Picturesque old fellow, 'the artists' friend,' they call him, buys and sells used canvases, picture frames, easels, and such things, buys . . . rents out . . . sells . . . ah, theatrical costumery and painter's props and ah—"

Grant was suddenly as impatient as the physician. "Oh, damn it, man, don't give us an inventory of old Solomon's business affairs. He is in the *cheap* business, and he had a *cheap* house on lease in Upper Welchman Street and is willing to rent the first floor *cheap*, rent not on an annual but on a quarterly basis—so you needn't be hung up for a year's money when you'll likely not be needing the place for more than six months. Eustace Williams may store all his things in one of the rooms on the second floor, or in two of them, for that matter: so long as Solomon continues to have access to his own rubble and rubbish also stored up there on the same floor. It is just the thing for you, Williams, and there is no other thing for you, Williams, and thank God for you that you needn't depend for pennies, to say nothing of pounds, on the sale of a painting or a poem, Williams." Williams blinked very rapidly and for a very long moment after Grant said this last.

Things did not, really, go at all badly.

Crutchett vanished without trace, and with him the possibility of a detailed explanation of the perhaps not precisely alchemical mystery of how an amount of Williams's money had been transmuted into dross—or even how several dozens of claret had become, somehow, changed into at least one barrel of beer and a quantity of gin. But it was felt that this was a fair price to pay for a total absence of Crutchett. Old Solomon, it turned out, slightly to Grant's annoyed surprise, was surprised to think that the gentleman had thought the furniture of the apartments in Upper Welchman Street was not included in the rent: it was; it was old furniture, but it was good enough: so *there* was a saving, *there*. And, perhaps equally surprising, perhaps even more, only Grant could have said, and Grant did not say; Kitty—whom Grant referred to, when he referred to her at all, as "my slut"—Kitty undertook to see that the apartments were cleaned, and Kitty *did* see to it that the apartments were cleaned. It was Kitty who hired the cook-housekeeper, and Kitty who swooped down at irregular and unannounced intervals to see that the cooking was done and that the house was kept, and kept as well as anyone could expect. She came usually, and departed, usually, while Williams was being taken somewhere which made very little demand on his nervous energy; Harrison once asked, curiously, "Have you ever actually *seen* her?"

"No," said Williams, incuriously, "but I have heard her. Once." Perhaps Dr. McFall might not have approved. But no one told him. Dr. McFall, it is true, did not come to see Williams as often as Williams's friends had expected. Not quite as often. However, his directions were scrupulously carried out: Williams drank the claret, and he drank it *as prescribed*. And Williams was taken regularly to St. Olave's, where Professor Schneiderhaus asked him many questions and grunted a great deal and peered at the insides of his lower eyelids, and other things like that. Eustace had little to do, otherwise, except to thrust his feet into his slippers and place his slippered feet on the fender of the fireplace in which burned real coal, and to read the papers. The daily papers arrived twice a day; the reviews were lent by Tumbleton, who brought them himself, but did not pay for them himself, they being paid for by the Duke's Museum, of which Tumbleton was Vice-Director. The Hon. Director was the present Duke himself, who never set foot in the Museum except for the Annual Meeting, or when there was an exhibition of Landseer. Or Bonheur. The Duke was very fond of Bonheur. "There, Tumbleton, you *see?* A woman, a mere slip of a woman, and a *French* woman, at that: and just see what she does with horseflesh. Eh? Now, why cannot our English artists all paint that sort of thing? Eh? Tumbleton?"

The Duke, of course, never dreamed of looking at the list of periodicals to which the Museum subscribed, and, to the one single member of the Board who ever had, and who had asked why the Museum subscribed to literary publications "as well," Tumbleton solemnly replied, "Because, Sir Bascomb, it is part of the whole duty of man." Sir Bascomb never asked again. Williams, of course, never asked at all.

Though from time to time he would exclaim, almost with a note of despair in his voice, "Oh, God! Another exhibition of *that* fellow's wretched daubs!" or, "Dear Lord! *Another* edition of this man's wretched doggerel?" To which Tumbleton might reply, with a good-natured shrug, that this man or that fellow seemed to have the knack of pleasing the public taste. "The public *taste*. Oh, God. Dear Lord." Williams might actually strike his own head with his fist.

His friends were divided as to how to reply to such scenes. Harrison did once suggest that perhaps some of the reviews should be withheld, Tumbleton (unhappy) had pointed out that Williams would be sure to notice their absence. Harrison (unhappy) had perforce agreed. Tumbleton suggested that an edition of Williams's unpublished poems was just the thing to raise his wasted spirits. Harrison said that he was merely the junior partner in the firm and that his father, who was the senior, had more than once pointed out how meagerly the single publication of Williams's other poems (". . . although, mind you, certainly the best . . .") had sold. Harrison suggested that an exhibition of Williams's paintings was what was really needed. And Tumbleton sighed, stirred, said that, even *should* the Duke agree (and one feared he wouldn't), why—the excitement! No, no. Williams must on no account be allowed to become excited. And Grant had made a very coarse suggestion as to what *he* felt that Williams needed.

"To buck him up," said Grant, growling.

"Eustace is still fearfully ill, you know."

"Eustace can *try,* can't he? What I have admired about him is that he always did try, never mind what the critics said, damn the critics, he would *try!* Again. Reason why he went to that bloody place in the country: to try. No, I tell you that what he needs is—"

"But it is *exciting,* and the doctor—"

A shaft of light lit up Harrison's pale beard and hair, but Grant grimaced, said, "About as exciting as any other natural function, I'm sure the doctor would agree."

The doctor did not say if he would agree or not agree, when, not very long after, Grant ran him down in the private bar of a place near the Hospital. He grunted (perhaps a habit picked up from Schneiderhaus), asked, "Is he sleeping well these days?"

Grant rubbed his smooth cheeks and chin, fingered his sleek moustache, and said, No, he believed not. Fellow was complaining about that just the other day, said Grant. "Well," McFall declared, heavily, "he damned well should be sleeping well. Why hasn't he been sleeping well? Should be sleeping well. Lack of sleep must inevitably lead to death or the straight-waistcoat. Why hasn't he been taking a sleeping-draught?" Grant stared a moment. Then, with a degree of uncustomary tact, suggested that perhaps "the Professor" had neglected to prescribe him one. McFall grunted again.

"Shouldn't wonder. Foreign fellows don't know everything, look at Charcot and his hysterical cow-maids turning somersaults, *I* shall damned well, prescribe him one. By Zeus and by Apollo." He called for pen and he called for ink, wrote so firmly that the nib at one point dug into the paper. Called for brandy.

"More brandy, Doctor?"

"Yes, damn it, waiter, more brandy. Do you think that I drank the ink? I shall pay for it *instanter,* too, more than I can say for some of my patients, I have a Harley Street office to pay for, and the lease on a house in the Borough to pay for where I have an incompetent partner to pay for and I have a house and a wife and two unmarried daughters in Belgrave Square and an unmarried son to pay for and carriages and horses to pay for, and if you were obliged to walk the wards with me and observe the immense amount of human misery which can never be paid for—" McFall stopped abruptly, stared at Grant. Who stared back. McFall tried to hand Grant the pen, then handed him the prescription. "The chemist will put the directions on the bottle," he said. "I used to dispense when I first began practice but I don't now. Do not even think of sending your friend to try the sea air as yet. It would be death or the straight-waistcoat. Wait-*ter.*"

Williams felt much better. "Sleep, sleep, is nature's sweet restorer," he informed Harrison. "It is sleep which knits up the raveled sleeve of care."

"Eustace, you have no idea how happy I am to hear you say so."

Williams was happy to be saying so. "It makes all the difference. The difference between strolling in a rose garden and tossing on a bed of thorns."

"I say, you ought to write that down, you know."

"Ought I? Well, perhaps you are—No." He settled into his easy chair again, a faint smile on his face. "You forget that I am forbidden to touch pen to paper for a good while yet." He pronounced himself restless on this point before, but now seemed content, quite content.

Harrison remembered, apologized. "Though I thought you had been. Doing so, I mean."

"No, no. Devil a bit of it."

Harrison moved about on the heavy oaken settle. "Well, in that case, perhaps I—It is really too good a line to—Paper? Ink?"

"All the newpaper you want. Ink? Don't know if there's such a thing in the house." Harrison seemed faintly discomfited. Williams said that the lines would keep. "I shan't forget them. I have a good many more, you know, all up here," he tapped his brow. "They come to me in dreams, visions. Strolling through the rose garden, gently pushing away the crystal ball." And, in reply to his friend's inquiring look, he explained that, as he would lie abed, relishing the soon-to-be-expected slumber, sleep would (as it were) slowly approach in the form of a crystal ball, floating, floating slowly toward him. "And I, knowing that it will keep on coming no matter what may be, I take a sort of curious pleasure in pushing it away for a while. Once. Twice. Perhaps a third time. Then, finally, I allow it to snuggle close." He smiled. "Delicious."

"Excellent. Excellent."

But this excellence did not endure. By and by Harrison, coming into the sitting room one day, observed his friend to be walking back and forth, back and forth, restless, and, in fact, groaning. He started on seeing the visitor: "Eustace, what is wrong, my poor fellow?" "I cannot sleep. I cannot sleep, I lie awake, and then I have such sick and troubled fancies, and I get up and walk about, walk about, hoping to tire myself so that—"

Then it was Harrison who gave a start. Williams was indeed wearing the smoking jacket. But he was wearing it over his night-garment. "Surely, Eustace, you have not, I hope that you have not been pacing the floor since last night? Do not say, 'No, no.' Look: you are not yet dressed. Eustace."

Williams glanced at his attire, gaped, pressed his hands to his temples, groaned. "What can this mean?" asked Harrison. "And you gave me such a good account of the effects of the sleeping-draught—" Williams burst out laughing.

"The sleeping-draught! Of course! Edward! God bless you! Will you believe that I had forgotten to have it refilled! And that I had forgotten that I had forgotten!" The two friends laughed heartily at this. Then Williams said that he would dress at once and take care of the matter; but his friend raised a hand which protested this decision.

"Dress? By all means, dress. However, you are not to exert yourself: I shall go and have it refilled, this *is* it, here on the chimneypiece, is it not? Yes? Shan't be long." Then he clapped his hand to his own head. "Good Heavens, your forgetfulness is contagious! *Where* am I to refill it? Where is the chemist's?"

"Just round the corner to your left, second door down: *Jessup. Chemist*. At least I believe Grant said so."

Grant was quite correct. The chemist came out from his dispensing room, on his ruddy face a smile of inquiry which ebbed a bit as he looked at the bottle Harrison set on the counter, requesting that it be refilled. "Directly. . . ."

"Well, sir. Yes, sir. But do you think it altogether wise, sir?"

Harrison was surprised, and, in fact, rather put out, thinking of his afflicted friend waiting at home. "What do you mean, sir. 'Do I think it wise?' I have nothing to think about it, Doctor Douglass McFall has thought about it, *the* Doctor Douglass McFall; you are Mr. Jessup? Be so kind, Mr. Jessup, to let me have the mixture as before. Directly." Mr. Jessup was so kind, he came back directly, and he said no more except to say that that would be one and eightpence, sir.

Williams was already dressed, smiled cheerfully, took the bottle and replaced it on the chimneypiece, thanked Harrison very much; and then, some new thought occurring to him, said, "Edward, *would* you mind. This being the footman's day off"—the (mythical) footman was a favorite joke between them—"and Simmons being such a heavy, slow old thing, and I being so forgetful, and the steps so steep and dark, *would* you go down and ask her for the measuring glass? Then I needn't worry about its being here when I need it tonight."

The steps were indeed steep and dark, and Simmons, seated and staring into her own fire in her kitchen, was indeed a heavy, slow old thing. Eventually, however, she was able to focus her mind and to say that the measuring glass was on the night table next to Mr. Williams's bed; and from this declaration she would not budge; so Harrison went upstairs and repeated to his friend that Simmons had said . . . what she had said. "No, it isn't," Williams said promptly. "While you were gone I found it there, over there. Silly old slattern; never mind." Suddenly his face changed, he repeated the words, *"Never mind?"* in such an entirely different tone of voice that Harrison was astonished, and, thinking that it was the woman's mistake which was bothering, said that Williams was not to be peevish—

He could, the next moment, have bitten his tongue; instead, said, "Forgive me, Eustace, of course you are not being peevish," but it was too late. The man *was* being peevish, suddenly took up several of the publications from the low table where they lay, waved them furiously in Harrison's face. "Don't be *peevish?* Never *mind?*" His voice rose, his teeth actually grated; almost, he ripped the magazines apart to open them before his friend's greatly troubled eyes. "Poetry? Do you call this *poetry?*" His breath trembled, his voice as well. "And as for *this*—" He held up an open page from an illustrated: "Is this worthy to be called *painting?*—And as for the characters of these men, which are too vile to—"

"Eustace . . . Eustace. . . ."

But now Eustace actually did rip them apart, or rather, he began to do so, but Harrison, pleading Tumbleton's embarrassment at having to excuse this to the librarian at the Museum, gently dissuaded him from any further destruction.

He also insisted on staying for dinner; then on taking Williams to a music hall, the nearest, the Vicereine. The Vicereine was the nearest, but it was nowhere near the best. Williams showed no pleasure in seeing and hearing the tunes, muttered, slumped in his seat, nodded off for a bit from time to time, groaned, awoke. "I perhaps should not have brought you here, Eustace, this is wretched stuff, not even third rate. Would you like to go?"

No: Williams, in a dreary voice, said that it was better watching a superannuated *artiste* than watching Buchanan's head. But after the curtain dropped on Madame Adelaida, or whatever she was called, he rose abruptly and made his way through the mostly empty row, with Harrison, taken by surprise, half-scuttling after him. He found him waiting, found him glaring, heard him saying, between clenched teeth, *"And as for Rossetti—!"*

It was easy to humor him, here. "Well, true, Eustace, true; Rossetti is not the thing nowadays, no one looks at his pictures, no one reads his poetry, the man is quite *démodé.* I quite agree." Williams became placid as he heard these words, the slightest touch of his arms persuaded him to move. At the door, with the voice of some aged buffoon comedian echoing dimly from within, he stopped. Turned to face his companion.

"Rossetti also tossed upon the bed of thorns and yet he too found the key to the rose garden, you know." He said this very quietly.

"But still," Tumbleton observed, some while later (it proved not then possible for the three to meet at once). "But still. Whilst in some ways certainly he is better than, say, after his first and even his second, ah, nervous crisis, in other ways, ah—"

"—he is worse," Grant finished. Grant was never patient with word-fumblings. "Furthermore, it is my opinion that he may be taking too much of that sleeping-draught. Don't know how many times I've refilled it for—"

"You! *You* have refilled it for him many times!" Tumbleton's face was half astonished, half aghast. "Why, *I* have done so, I don't recall how often, but, ah, ah, *often,"* he concluded hastily, in the face of Grant's awful glare.

Then it was Harrison's turn to speak about that.

It was agreed that McFall must be spoken to, and at once; they divided their forces: Tumbleton went to Harley Street, Harrison to the Borough, Grant to St. Olave's. Grant stopped first at Williams's, found him alternately snoring and muttering, shaving kit laid out but not used; removed the medicine bottle, stopped at the establishment of *Jessup. Chemist,* looked in at the private bar of the place near the hospital; finally ran down McFall, who was washing his hands in a basin on a cart, in one of the wards. He thrust the bottle at the physician, asked, sans preface, "What is in this sleeping-draught you prescribed for Williams?"

McFall looked at him from red-rimmed eyes, then looked at the bottle, dried his hands, took the bottle, then sniffed it, then held the besmeared label close. "Ah, yes. 'In it'? Basically, chloral and water."

"Chloral? Chloral. Good God. Isn't that the stuff that Coleridge and De Quincey both went stark mad from using?"

"No. No, no. That was laudanum. Tincture of opium. I did not say laudanum. Neither did I prescribe it for your friend. This is chloral, chloral hydrate, a synthetic; different sort of thing entirely . . . though sometimes the effects of overuse: fantasy, hallucination, addiction . . . what is this you are thrusting into my face now?"

This, on a billhead elaborately engraved *Jessup,* et cetera, was a list of dates and of the quantities of chloral dispensed to Williams on those dates. Jessup was probably not required to have provided this list to a layman, but Jessup had perhaps his reasons for doing so; besides, Grant was a great bully. McFall scanned the list, slowly. It was then his turn to say, *"Good God!"* After a moment more he said, more quietly, "He should not have been allowed to have had that much. How is he?"

Grant told him how Williams was. "And in addition to all that, he has developed a hatred, which I can only describe as maniacal, of every artist being exhibited and every poet being published, and has been writing letters on the sneak to the reviews and magazines and newspapers accusing them, these people, I mean, of every imaginable vice. Harrison suspected something when he saw ink stain on Williams's fingers, oh, a good while ago. Admitted, that jealousy is a very natural human emotion, still—"

McFall gave a very deep sigh. "Yes. 'Still.' Go on."

Grant did go on. He went on to say that Williams had first denied it all, then insisted that it was all true and that he acted out of public duty, then he had shrieked and babbled and wept and said that all of it and much more had been revealed to him by what he called Buchanan's head.

"He called it—*what?*"

"Called it Buchanan's head. Said that first there was a sort of crystal ball in a rose garden, then gradually this had changed into a human head, says it spoke to him . . . speaks to him . . . tells him all these things, tells him that *x* is a fornicator and *y* is an adulterer and *z* is a pornographer, and so on and so on. Says he doesn't *know* how he knows it's *Buchanan's* head, just that he *knows,* nor does he know who 'Buchanan' is, and he must have the drug or he cannot sleep, which is horrible, and when he takes the drug, and he has taken more and more of it—What? 'Miracle that he is still alive?'—We must, I suppose, have you to thank for this miracle, Doctor Douglass McFall; yes, I am also 'sorry.' "

As for the appearance of the head, aside from there being no body attached to it, it was most remarkable for its expression of jealousy, malignancy, and hatred; also that it appeared to have been badly marred on one side; how, Williams could neither explain nor adequately describe. "What is to be done?" demanded Grant.

McFall began to walk away from the cart, Grant walking with him. " 'What is to be done,' indeed. If you had just now for the first time come and given me a description of such symptoms I should have prescribed complete rest and a total absence of nervous excitement. I should also have felt obliged to prescribe a sleeping-draught, chloral being the most effective one I know. What is to be done *now* . . . either a private asylum, which is, if good, far from cheap, and, if cheap, far from good. . . . For, you see"—McFall stopped, faced Grant—"certainly he should have no more chloral. Certainly if it is cut off the results will be terrible. As for the public asylums . . . Perhaps he should have a keeper, one who is with him all the time. Several, in fact: round the clock. No money for that? No money, no money. Death or the straight-waistcoat; pleasant alternatives. Sometimes, you know, Mr. Grant, there are questions to which the only answer seems to be that there is no answer. A personality constitutionally strong . . . but when a personality is constitutionally weak—Ah well. If you believe that I have been remiss in my duties, you are at liberty to complain of me. Meanwhile, you may accompany me as I continue to attend to my patients. *If you wish.*" He walked off again.

Grant, after looking round the ward and at its many patients, and now for the first time listening to them as well, did not wish.

Along Upper Welchman Street there shambled—and finally stopped at the steps of the house and fumbled a ring of keys from his pocket, now and then mumbling a word or two to himself—a stooped old man with a white beard; his silk hat was older, taller, than those worn by the three men at the top of the steps, and he wore a long silk coat: each clean enough, hat and coat, though showing, each, the signs of long, hard wear. Suddenly he looked up and noticed the group in the doorway, and, clearly, noticed something more about them than their presences alone.

"What! What!" he exclaimed, a look of more immediate distress replacing the one of general sadness on his face, hollowed cheeks and pouchy eyes. "Gentlemen. . . . Gentlemen. . . . What is wrong? What is wrong?"

Tumbleton took this as a signal for a heavy sigh. "I am afraid that you have lost your tenant, Mr. Solomon," he said; "and we, our friend."

Mr. Solomon lifted a thin hand as one who wards off a blow. "Blessed be the True Judge," he murmured. "Oh. Oh. Oh. Oh. Oh—"

"Do you quite understand what Mr. Tumbleton has just told you, Solomon? Mr. Williams has *died*. Sometime last night."

The much-brushed, much-worn old hat bobbed. "I understand, I understand. I understood at once. Poor young man, eh? Poor Mr. Williams. And I thought he was getting better. Better, I thought he was getting. His illness returned after all, then?" This question was asked in a tone not confident. There was a silence.

"Well, you are entitled to know the truth. And would find out in any event. I feat that while the balance of his mind was disturbed, poor Williams took his own life. There is no doubt about it at all."

Harrison burst out, "Poor Eustace! It is ghastly!" His voice broke.

This time the old man lifted both hands. His face was horrified. "God help us! God have mercy on him. *Imbeshreer!*" He tottered a moment, took hold of the railing, steadied himself, moved hesitantly. "What should I do? Should I go inform the—Can I—" They beckoned him, and he went slowly up the steps. "Eh?"

Tumbleton: The fact is . . . The fact is. . . .

Solomon: Have you notified? He has family? What a shock for them. A, a priest? A minister? An undertaker, at least?

Grant (waves all this away): Harrison's *"fact"* is that Williams did it in his own bed and everything is drenched with blood. He should never have been allowed to shave himself.

The old man bared his teeth, drew in a hissing breath.

"There's not a clean sheet to be found," said Grant; "all the linens must have gone to the wash and not come back. The housekeeper has already gotten herself sodden with gin and is of no use at all. So we've covered him with a sort of tarpaulin we found out back, the coroner cannot come just yet, there's a policeman in there now—and the rest must wait. Family? An aunt in Wales, somewhere."

The old man said that a tarpaulin was not enough. "That's not a proper covering for anyone, a tarpaulin. Something better I must have upstairs in the storeroom. Must be. Let me think. Let me look."

Tumbleton said he was just about to suggest that. Grant growled, "You'll never be able to use it again, whatever it is; what? 'never mind that?' Then by all means go up and look." They turned and went into the hallway and toward the stairs to the upper floor. Harrison suddenly sat on the bench beneath the mirror, said he would wait.

Lighting the gas on each landing in the dark house, the old man laboriously climbed, talked on, talked on. "Poor Mr. Williams, these are terrible times we live in, gentlemen; murders, massacres, famines, plagues; poor man, I thought he was getting better: *why?* 'This new medicine helps me sleep,' he said, but that was last quarter day, more or less; terrible, terrible; the Shechinah is in exile and the Daughter of the Voice rings out, rings out, but we do not hear it, *'Repent! Repent!'* but we hear it not, we don't want to hear it, we don't want to repent; where is the key, the key, this one? no not this one. Mr. Williams! Aye!" At length the storeroom door was opened, it opened onto darkness and, another gas jet being lit (one without a mantle: high and red it flared, then was turned lower), onto clutter beyond cataloguing; the old man stood in a narrow way between items covered and uncovered, and he talked on. "—a terrible thing to be an artist today, gentlemen, and yet a fascination it has which cannot be denied; six or seven of the best, the leading artists of today—" He fumbled here and there, seemed sure of nothing. "—live in mansions and they lunch with lords, Sir Laurence, Sir John, the incomparable Landseer, Mr. Holman-Hunt who did *The Scapegoat,* he visited the Holy Land, what a blessed privilege, and how many others? a few others only"—he peered here and there around the crowded room— "and the rest? Poverty, decay, and worse. Making likenesses, perhaps it's not allowed, God says, what does God say? 'Thou shalt not make—' My cousin Simeon you may have heard of my cousin Simeon, let me remove a dust sheet here, sir—"

Grant said, impatiently, that a dust sheet would do. "But not a *dusty* dust sheet, Mr. Grant, sir; look: ah. . . ." Underneath the dusty one was a clean one, and underneath that something showed purple and gold. "My cousin Simeon was an artist, and a good one, too, and now look at him, or better yet don't; 'Here comes Moses,' he says when I visit him, which is perhaps not as often as—'Moses, with another half-crown and another half-drawsha, who needs your damned drawshas, Moses, a fig for your sermons and your *Shema Beni,* why don't you bring us a half-sovereign instead, Moses?'— because he would immediately convert it into drink, gentlemen, if not worse, gentlemen, a terrible disgrace for a family to have a drunkard . . . and worse: look." The dust sheets came off, one after the other; the old man carefully lifted up some heavy broad piece of stuff—"*This* would be nice for Mr. Williams, poor young man, poor young man. *Aye!*"

"Purple velvet!" exclaimed Tumbleton. "A gorgeous pall!"

Grant said he expected it was only velveteen.

"Beautiful gold bordering! Poor Williams would have admired—"

"Tosh, it can't be real gold, can't have real value, but it will do, hand it over, Solomon."

The old man said that everything which had to do with art had value, though seldom, he feared, to the benefit of the artist. "Sundry odds and ends I sold to Mr. Dante Gabriel when—"

"*Rossetti?*" exclaimed Tumbleton.

"Mr. Dante Gabriel Rossetti, a great artist, and sundry items here I bought back, after he died, a great poet he was, too; shame on them who said he wrote shameful poems, who—"

Grant swore, tugged the heavy purple cloth away. "Tumbleton, stay here listening to this babble if you like. I'm going down to lay this over Williams, damned pitiful poor fool; stopped *try*ing." They could hear his footsteps clump heavily and rapidly upon the stairs, slow down as he entered the bedroom below.

The old man lingeringly pulled the dust sheets back. "I came for this picture frame," he said, lifting it. "Only for this I came. And what did I find? May such a thing not happen to any of us, Mr. Williams, Mr. Williams! But let us not open Satan's mouth, lest he accuse us."

Tumbleton seemed by his glances here and there not eager to remain, but he seemed not eager to go below, either; certainly he did not wish to be alone. "So you knew Rossetti, eh?"

The old silk hat nodded, nodded. "Mr. William Rossetti, a kind gentleman. Miss Christina Rossetti, a very fine poet. Mr. Dante Gabriel Rossetti, I knew him best, a great artist, beautiful paintings he made, from my religion and from your religion; and poems as well. They say, some people say, he died of a sudden disease, other people say he died of a medicine of which he gradually took too great a quantity, so what was it? Opium? Not opium, what then, who remembers? Coral, why do I say 'coral,' coral is not a medicine, he could not sleep well, years and years he could not sleep, some wretched fellow broke his heart, said he wrote a shameful poem, poems, about love; they were beautiful poems, like *Shir Ha-Shirim,* Solomon's Song, is what they were like; look—"

He bent, he arose, he held something in his hand. "A skull!" cried Tumbleton, recoiled; said, "Not a skull," drew near again; the old man blew and blew, dust flew about, his thin beard fluttered, the gas flame trembled.

"A bust. I say, Mr. Solomon: a bust of *whom?*"

The old man nodded, nodded. "A plaster mold he was making; maybe, Mr. Dante Gabriel, almost the last thing he made, it may be. 'For this, Moses,' he said, 'I need no model, the man's malignant features haunt me forever.' His very words. See. What hate, eh? Jealous, jealous, hateful and malignant jealous, some penny journalist who made a great scandal out of envy of the great Mr. Dante Gabriel; with one hand who gave it such a blow, at last, the plaster was still wet: look—" He turned the object so the side misshapen might be seen.

Tumbleton seemed sickened, looked at the door, looked back. Asked, "But who? *Who?*"

A moment's thought. A long moment. "Who. His name. Let us not open Satan's mouth, lest. . . . Ah, yes. His name? Buchanan, his name. This is Buchanan's head. Look."

AFTERWORD TO "BUCHANAN'S HEAD"

In this tale of London sophisticates of the late nineteenth century, the hapless Williams falls victim to the malignant emanations of a certain hidden statue. English poet and painter Dante Gabriel Rossetti (1828–1882) was the founding force of the influential Pre-Raphaelite Brotherhood in 1848. His sister was the poet Christina Rossetti. His first wife died of an overdose of laudanum in 1862, apparently a suicide; Rossetti thereafter had a long affair with Jane Morris, wife of his friend William Morris. When she finally decided to return to her husband, Rossetti grew reclusive, and his addiction to chloral hydrate worsened, eventually killing him. In 1872, the artist was devastated when critic Robert Buchanan published his controversial attack on Rossetti and the Pre-Raphaelites, "The Fleshly School of Poetry and Other Phenomena of the Day." That Rossetti sculpted a portrait of his nemesis in his last years is not beyond conjecture.

—Henry Wessells

THE ODD OLD
BIRD

"But *why* a canal?"

"Cheaper, more, and better victuals."

"Oh."

Prince Roldran Vlox (to cut his titles quite short, and never mind about his being a Von Stuart y Fitz-Guelf) had "just dropped in" to talk to Doctor Engelbert Eszterhazy about the Proposed Canal connecting the Ister and the Danube . . . there were, in fact, several proposed canals and each one contained several sub-propositions: should it go right through the entirely Vlox-held Fens ("The Mud," it was fondly called . . . "Roldry Mud," the prince sometimes called himself)? should it go rather to the right or rather to the left? should it perhaps not go exactly "through" them at all, but use their sur-plusage of waters for feeder systems? and—or—on the one hand This, on the other hand That—

"What's that new picture over on the wall, Engly?" Guest asked suddenly. Host began to explain. "Ah," said Guest, "one of those funny French knick-knacks, eh? Always got some funny knick-knacks. . . . The British for sport, the French for fun. . . ." Still the guestly eyes considered the picture over on the wall. "That's a damned funny picture . . . it's all funny little speckles. . . ."

"Why, Roldry, you are right. What good eyes you have."

Promptly: "Don't soil them by a lot of reading, is why. Lots of chaps want to know about a book, 'Is it spicy?' Some want to know, 'Is it got lots of facts?' What *I* want to know is only, 'Has it got big print?' Shan't risk spoiling my eyes and having to wear a monocle. One has to be a hunter, first, you know." He made no further reference to the fact his host himself sometimes wore a monocle.

Eszterhazy returned to the matter of canals: "Here is a sketch of a proposed catchment basin—Yes, Lemkotch?"

"Lord Grumpkin!" said the Day Porter.

There followed a rather short man of full figure, with a ruddy, shiny, cheerful face. There followed also a brief clarification, by Lemkotch's employer, of the proper way to refer to Professor Johanno Blumpkinn, the Imperial Geologist; there followed, also, an expression on the Porter's face, indicative of his being at all times Doctor (of Medicine, Law, Music, Philosophy, Science, and Letters) Eszterhazy's loyal and obedient servant and all them words were not for a ignorant fellow like him (the day porter) to make heads or tails of; after which he bowed his usual brief, stiff bob and withdrew. He left behind him a slight savor of rough rum, rough tobacco, rough manhood, and rough soap . . . even if not quite enough rough soap to erase the savor of the others. The room also smelled of the unbleached beeswax with which they had been rubbing—polishing, if you like—the furniture's mahogany; of Prince Vlox, which some compared to that of a musty wolf (not perhaps to his face, though); of Eszterhazy himself (Pears soap and just a little bay rum) and of Professor Blumpkinn (Jenkinson's Gentleman's Cologne: more than just a little). Plus some Habana segars supplied by the old firm of Fribourg and Treyer in the Haymarket—London was a long way from Bella, capital of the Triple Monarchy of Scythia-Pannonia-Transbalkania (fourth largest empire in Europe) but so was Habana, for that matter. "Gentlemen, you have met, I believe," Eszterhazy said, anyway adding, "Prince Vlox, Professor Blumpkinn."

Further adding, "I am sorry that my servant did not get your name right, Han."

Blumpkinn waved his hand. "Calling me by the old-fashioned

word for the smallest coin in his native province really helps me to remember a proper value of my own worth.—Ah. *Canal* plans. I hope that when the excavations are in progress you will be sure to keep me in mind if any interesting fossils turn up." It was not sure that Prince Vlox would be able to identify an interesting fossil if one hit him in the hough or bit him on the buttock, but Eszterhazy gave a serious nod. *He* knew how such things were to be done. Offer a small gift for reporting the discovery of "any of them funny elf-stone things as the old witch-women used to use"—they used to use them for anything from dropped stomach to teaching a damned good lesson to husbands with wandering eyes: but now all that had gone out of fashion—should certainly result in the reporting of enough interesting fossils, uninteresting fossils, and, indeed, non-fossils, to provide coping-stones for the entire length of the Proposed Canal . . . if ever there was actually a canal. . . .

"And speaking of which," said Blumpkinn, and took two large sheets out between covers large enough to have contained the Elephant Folios; "I have brought you, Doctor 'Bert, as I had promised, the proof-sheets of the new photo-zinco impressions of the *Archaeopteryx,* showing far greater detail than was previously available . . . you see. . . ."

Doctor 'Bert did indeed now thrust in his monocle and scanned the sheets, said that he saw. Prince Vlox glanced, glanced away, rested a more interested glance at the funny French knick-knack picture . . . men, women, water, grass, children, women, women . . . all indeed composed of multitudes of tiny dots, speckles . . . points, if you liked . . . a matter easily noticeable if you were up close, or had a hunter's eye.

"Yes, here are the independent fingers and claws, the separate and unfused metacarpals, the un-birdlike caudal appendage, all the ribs non-unciate and thin, neither birdlike nor very reptilian, the thin coracoid, the centra free as far as the sacrum, and the very long tail. . . ." His voice quite died away to a murmur, Professor Blumpkinn, perhaps thinking that it was not polite to lose the attention of the other guest, said, "This, you see, Prince Vlox, is the famous

Archaeopteryx, hundreds of millions of years old, which the sensational press has rather inadequately described as the so-called 'no-
longer-missing-link' between reptiles and birds . . . observe the sharp
teeth and the feather . . . this other one unfortunately has no head . . .
and this one—"

Here Prince Vlox, perhaps not an omnivorous student of pale-
ontology, said, "Yes. Seen it."

"*Ah* . . . was that in London? or Berlin?"

"Never been in either place."

Blumpkinn gaped. Recovered himself. Looked, first amused, then
sarcastic, then polite. Eszterhazy slowly looked up. "What do you
mean, then, Roldry, 'seen it'? What—?"

Prince Vlox repeated, with a slight emphasis, that he had *seen* it.
And he bulged his eyes and stared, as though to emphasize the full
meaning of the verb, *to see.*

"What do you—Ah . . . 'Seen it,' seen it when, seen it where?"

"On our land. Forget just when. What do you mean, 'Am I
sure?' *I* don't need a monocle to look at things. Why shouldn't I be
sure? What about it?"

Blumpkinn and Eszterhazy for a moment spoke simultaneously.
What about it? There were only two known *Archaeopteryx* specimens
in the world! one in London, one in Berlin—think what a third
would mean! Not only for science, but for Scythia-Pannonia-
Transbalkania and its prestige.

Vlox, with something like a sigh, rose to his feet; clearly the
subject no longer much engaged him . . . possibly because his own
family and its prestige was incomparably older than the Triple Monarchy and *its* prestige. "Well, I'll have it looked for, then. Must be
off. Things to do. My wine-merchant. My gunsmith. My carriage-
maker. A turn of cards at The Hell-Hole. See if they've finished re-
upholstering my railroad car. Tobacconist . . . new powder scales. . . .
Can I execute any commissions for you, as they say? Haw haw! Tell
you what, Engly, damned if I know what you want with this odd
old bird, but tell you what: trade it for that funny French painting."
And he donned his tattered seal-skin cap (so that he should

not be struck by lightning) and his wisentskin cape (also fairly tattered, but wisents weren't easy to get anymore), picked up his oakstick, nodded his Roldry-nod, neither languid nor brisk, and went out into Little Turkling Street, where his carriage (as they say) awaited him. Some backwoods nobles kept a pied-à-terre in Bella in the form of a house or apartment, Prince Roldran preferred to keep a stable and to sleep in the loft. With taste and scent, no argument.

Silence for some seconds. Such was the prince's presence, that his immediate absence left a perceptible hole.

Blumpkinn: What do you say, Doctor 'Bert, is the prince *quite*, [a hesitation] . . . dependable?

Eszterhazy [removing his monocle]: In some things, instantly. He would think nothing of striking a rabid wolf with bare hands to save you. In others? well . . . let us say that fossils are not quite in his line. We shall see. Any kind of fossils from out that way should be interesting. If the old witch-women have left any.

The Imperial Geologist blinked. "Yes . . . if they've left any— Though I suppose . . . imagine, Doctor, they used to grind up dinosaur bones and feed them with bread and oil to pregnant women!!"

"That's what they did to my own dear Mother. Well, why not? Calcium, you know."

The Imperial Geologist (the King-Emperor, Ignats Louis, in authorizing the position, had hoped for gold and, no gold being found, had shrugged and gone out to inspect the new infantry boots)—the Imperial Geologist blinked some more. "Yes," he said. "Well, why not. Calcium . . . I know."

Some years before there had appeared the book *From Ram's Head to Sandy Cape on Camelback, by a New Chum* (Glasscocke and Gromthorpe, No. 3, the Minories, 12/–), and Eszterhazy had translated it into Modern Gothic, as he had its successors, *Up the Fly River by Sail and Paddle*, and *In Pursuit of Poundmaker, plus a General Survey of the Northwest Territories* (available at Szentbelessel's Book House near the New Model Road at two ducats *per* or all three for five ducats, each with eleven half-tone illustrations and a free patriotic bookmark; write for catalogue). From these translations a friendship had developed. Newton Charles Enderson was not really a "new chum," far from it: he was a "currency lad"; and now he was on holiday from the University of Eastern Australia and hoped to explore some more, in the lands of the Triple Monarchy.

There were a number of not-very-well explored (not very well explored by any scientific expeditions, that is; they had all been very well explored by the River Tartars, the Romanou, and by all the other non-record-keeping peoples who had gone that way since the days of [and before the days of: caches of amber had been found there, and Grecian pottery] the Getae, who may or may not have been close of kin to the ancient Scythian Goths) and rather languid waterways disemboguing into the Delta of the Ister. And New Chum Enderson had wanted Eszterhazy to go exploring with him, in a pirogue. And Eszterhazy had very much wanted to do so. There were several sorts of bee-eaters which had never been well engraved, let alone photographed; skins of course were in the museums, and several water-colors had been made by someone whose identity had been given simply as *An Englishwoman*, long ago; still semi-impenetrably wrapped in her modesty, she had withdrawn into her native northern mists, leaving only copies of the water-colors behind.

"But I am afraid that our schedules don't match. Really I do regret."

New Chum regretted, too. "But I must be back for the start of term."

"And I for the meeting of the Proposed Canal Committee. Well . . . I know that your movements are as precisely dated as those of Phileas Fogg, so just let me know when you'll be back, and I'll give you a good luncheon to make up for your privations. There's a person in the country who's promised me a fine fat pullet, and the truffles should be good, too, so—"

New Chum gave a bark, intended for a laugh, of a sort which had terrified Pommies and Abos alike. "I'm not one of your European gourmets," he said. "Grew up on damper and 'roo. Advanced to mutton, pumpkin, and suet pud. More than once ate cockatoo—

they'd told me it was chook—'chicken' to you—and I never knew the difference. Still, of course, I'll be glad to eat what you give me, with no complaint. . . . Ah, by the way. Don't depend on me much or at all to identify and bring back your bee-eaters. Know *nothing* of ornithology. Officially I'm Professor of Political Economy, but what I am, actually, is an explorer. Glad to give you a set of my notes, though." And on this they parted.

Two pieces of news. The country pullet would be on hand the next day. Also alas the sister-in-law's sister of Frow Widow Orgats, house-keeper and cook, had been Taken Bad with the Dropped Stomach— did she require medical advice?—an elf-stone?—no: she required the attentions of her sister's sister-in-law. The house, with the help of its lower staff, might keep itself for a little while. "And Malta, who I've hand-picked meself, will cook for you very well till I gets back, Sir Doctor." Malta, thought the Sir Doctor, had perhaps been hand-picked so as to prevent the Sir Doctor from thinking of her as a suitable full-time replacement—she was not perhaps very bright— but merely he said, "Tomorrow they are bringing up a special pullet for the luncheon with the foreign guest and it may not look just exactly as the sort they sell here at the Hen Mark in town; so mind you do it justice."

Malta dropped several courtseys, but not, thank God, her stomach; said, "Holy Angels, my Lard, whatsoe'er I'm given to cook, I shall cook it fine, for Missus she's wrote out the words for me real big on a nice piece of pasteboard." Malta could read and she had the recipe? Well, well. Hope for the best. New Chum would perhaps not mind or even notice if the luncheon fell short of standard, but Eszterhazy, after all, would have to eat it, too.

However.

The roof of the Great Chamber did not indeed fall in on the meeting of the Proposed Canal Committee, but many other things happened, which he would rather hope had not. The chairman had forgotten the minutes of the last meeting and would not hear of the reading being skipped, *pro hac vice,* so all had to wait until they had been fetched in a slow hack, if not indeed a tumbril or an ox-cart. Then the Conservative delegation had wished to be given assurances the most profound that any land taken for the Canal would be paid for at full current market value; next, well before the Conservoes were made satisfied with such assurances, the Workingchaps' delegation had taken it into its collective head that Asian coolie labor might be employed in Canal construction and demanded positive guarantees that it would not. Then the Commercial representation desired similar soothing in regard to brick and building-stone—not only that it would not be imported from Asia, but from anywhere else outside the Empire—"Even if it has to come from Pannonia!"—something which the Pannonian delegation somehow took much amiss. Cries of *Point of order!* and *Treason!* and *What has the Committee got to hide?* and *Move the Previous question!* were incessant. And Eszterhazy realized that he was absolutely certain to miss anyway most of his luncheon engagement with Enderson.

So he sent word that the meal was to proceed without him, and his apologies to his guest, and he (Eszterhazy) would join him as soon as possible.

"As soon as" was eventually reached, though he had feared it wouldn't be. As he was making his way out of the Great Chamber he encountered Professor Blumpkinn, almost in tears. "I have missed my luncheon!" said the Imperial Geologist (he did not look as though he had missed many) dolefully. "They have prepared none for me at home, and in a restaurant I cannot eat, because my stomach is delicate: if anything is in the least greasy or underdone or overdone, one feels rising, then, the bile: and one is dyspeptic for days!"

"Come home with me, then, Johanno," said Eszterhazy.

"Gladly!"

One might ask, How far can a pullet go? but the pullet was after all intended merely as garnish to only one course of several; also a cook in Bella would sooner have suffered herself to be trampled by elephant cows rather than fail to provide a few Back-up Entrances, as they were called, in case of emergencies. A singularly greedy guest might become an Untoward Incident in a foreign *pension:* but not in a well-ordered house in Bella: What a compliment! God—who gives appetite—bless the man! and the order would be passed on, via an agreed-upon signal, to bring out one of the back-ups.

Going past the porte-cochère of the Great Hall, which jammed with vehicles, Eszterhazy held up his hand and the red steam runabout darted forward from a nearby passage; almost before it had come to a stop, Schwebel, the engineer, had vaulted into the back to stoke the anthracite: Eszterhazy took the tiller. His guest, an appreciative sniff for the cedar wood-work (beeswax "compliments of Prince Vlox"), sat beside him.

"Who's *that?*" asked an Usher of a Doorkeeper, watching the deft work with the steering-gear.

"He'm Doctors Eszterhazy, th' Emperor's wizard," said Doorkeeper to Usher.

"So *that's* him!—odd old bird!" And then they both had to jump as the delegations poured out, demanding their coaches, carriages, curricles, hacks, and troikas. None, however, demanded steam runabouts.

"It will not offend you if we enter by way of the kitchen?" the doctor (although his doctorate was plural, he himself was singular . . . very singular) asked the professor.

Who answered that they might enter by way of the chimney. "Cannot you hear my stomach growling? Besides, it is always a pleasure to visit a well-ordered kitchen." Blumpkinn rang with pleasure the hand-bell given him to warn passers-by—the steamer was almost noiseless—and drivers of nervous horses.

"A moderate number of unannounced visits help keep a kitchen well-ordered." Besides, with a temporary cook and a guest with a very delicate stomach, an inspection, however brief, might be a good idea: and, in a few minutes, there they were!—but what was this in the alley? a heavy country wagon—and at the door, someone whose canvas coat was speckled with feathers—someone stamping his feet and looking baffled. "I tells you again that Poulterer Puckelhaube has told me to bring this country-fed bird, and to git a skilling and a half for it! 'Tain't my fault as I'm late: the roads about the Great Chamber was filled with kerritches."

But, like the King of Iceland's oldest son, Malta Cook was having none. "You's heard I'm only temporal here," she said, hands on hips, "and thinks to try your gammon on me!—but you'll get no skilling and a half at this door! The country chicking has already been delivered couple hours ago, with the other firm's compliments, and the foreign guest is eating of it now. Away with ye, and—" She caught sight of Eszterhazy, courtseyed, gestured towards the deliveryman, her mouth open for explanation and argument.

She was allowed no time. Eszterhazy said, "Take the bird and pay for it, we'll settle the matter later.—Give him a glass of ale," he called over his shoulder. Instantly the man's grievance vanished. The money would, after all, go to his employer. But the beer was his . . . at least for a while.

At the table, napkin tucked into his open collar, sunburned and evidently quite content, sat Newton Charles ("New Chum") Enderson, calmly chewing. Equally calmly, he returned the just-cleaned-off bone to its platter, on which (or, if you prefer, whereon) he had neatly laid out the skeleton. Perhaps he had always done the same, even with the cockatoo and the kangaroo. Eszterhazy stared in intense disbelief. Blumpkinn's mouth was opening and closing like that of a barbel, or a carp. "Welcome aboard," said New Chum, looking up. "Sorry you've missed it. The journey has given me quite an appetite." At the end of the platter was a single, and slightly odd, feather. Malta had perhaps heard, if not more, of how to serve a pheasant.

"My God!" cried Blumpkinn. "Look! There is the centra free as far as the sacrum, and the very long tail as well as the thin coracoid, all the ribs non-unciate and thin, neither birdlike nor very reptilian, the un-birdlike caudal appendage, the separate and unfused metacarpals, the independent fingers and claws."

"Not bad at all," said Enderson, touching the napkin to his lips. "As I've told you, I don't know one bird from another, but this is not bad. Rather like bamboo chicken—goanna, or iguana, you would call it. Though a bit far north for that . . . but of course it must be imported! My compliments to the chef! By the way. I understand that the man who brought it said that there weren't any more . . . whatever that means . . . You know how to treat a guest well, I must say!"

Contentedly, he broke off a bit of bread and sopped at the truffled gravy. Then he looked up again. "Oh, and speaking of compliments," he said, "who's Prince Vlox?"

"I see the French picture is missing," said Eszterhazy.

AFTERWORD TO "THE ODD OLD BIRD"

Of the Eszterhazy stories, Avram wrote: "The time was the late middle '70s; the place was the picturesque little city of Mill Valley, California (which *has* no other form of municipal incorporation— no towns, boroughs, villages, townships—they are all cities [except for the City-*and*-County of San Francisco, which is, of course, unique]).

"Gradually, it came to me that there had been an empire in Eastern Europe which had been so completely destroyed that we no longer even remembered it, rather like the Kingdom of the Serbs, Croats, and Slovenes, or the Dual Monarchy of Austria-Hungary; that being an empire, it had an emperor; that the emperor had a wizard; the wizard drove about the streets of Bella (*Bel*grade/Vienn*a*) in a steam runabout; . . . and that the wizard's name was . . . was . . . *Englebert Eszterhazy*. . . .

"I sat down at the typewriter, and in six weeks wrote all eight stories of the first series. No rewrites were ever even suggested. Everything came so clear to me . . . that now I recognize that I did not at all 'make them up,' that Scythia-Pannonia-Transbalkania *did* exist!, as surely as Courland, a Baltic duchy which once had colonies in America and Africa; and Lemkovarna, land of the Lemkos, those Slavs forgotten by everyone save themselves; . . .

"Among the admirers of Englebert Eszterhazy, Ph.D., D. Phil., Dr. of Science, Dr. of Music, Dr. of Literature, of Laws, of Engineering is George Scithers, who persuaded me to write a story of Eszterhazy as a young man. Which I did; . . . and from which came the other four stories of the second series. ('The Odd Old Bird' is the first of yet another series.')"

Alas, Avram did not live to complete any further Eszterhazy stories . . . although there are intriguing fragments. . . .

—George H. Scithers

THE DEED OF THE DEFT-FOOTED DRAGON

It was frightfully hot in the streets. Most of the shops were cooler, particularly since the day was fairly young, but some of the shops were even hotter, and behind the beaded curtain in one of them a man was taking advantage of the concealment thus offered to work stripped to the waist; and even so the sweat poured off his torso and on to his thin cotton trousers. He did not think of complaining about the weather, sent as it was by the inscrutable decree of Heaven. Still, it was necessary to admit that it did slow his work down. Not that he toiled one hour the less at the washtubs, not that he toiled one hour the less at the ironing-board. Man was born to toil, and—brutal though the savages were among whom he toiled—it was almost inevitable that eventually he would have saved one thousand dollars: then he might retire to his native country and live at ease. However, the heat. And the sweat. What slowed his work down was that from time to time he was obliged to wipe his hands dry and carefully fold the garments he had ironed; in order to avoid staining them with his perspiration he was obliged to stand far away as he folded: *this* slowed the work down. *Mei-yo fah-dze,* there was nothing to be done about it; he filled his mouth with water and carefully sprayed a small amount onto the garment on the ironing-board; then he picked up a hot iron from the stove and made it hiss upon the cloth.

"It is unfortunate about the girl-child's absence," one of his countrymen then present observed.

"So." The water had evaporated. Another mouthful. Another spray. Another hiss.

"She justified her rice by folding the garments while you ironed."

"So."

This countryman was called Wong Cigar Fellow. He rolled the cigars themselves, then he peddled them to others. Sometimes he carried other things for sale from his basket—these varied—but always the cigars; hence his name. "It is said that once you pursued a far more honored craft than this one, far away in the Golden Mountain City." The man said nothing. The pedlar said, "All men know this is so, despite your great modesty. Do you not regret the change?"

"Mei-yo fah-dze."

He puffed his cheeks with water, sprayed, ironed.

Wong Cigar Fellow made as though to rise, settled again. "It is too bad about Large Pale Savage Female."

The name on the shop was On Lung. Sometimes this caused the savage natives to laugh their terrible laugh. "Hey, One Lung," they would say, in their voices like the barking dogs. "Hey, One Lung, which Lung is it? Hey? No savvy? No tickee, no shirtee, hey?" And, baring huge yellow teeth, would laugh, making a sound like *hop, hop, hop.*

The wash-man dried his hands, dried his body, quickly packed up the shirt and, holding it at arms' length before he could begin to sweat heavily again, deftly folded it around a piece of cardboard.

"Ah, how swiftly the girl-child folded shirts."

"Mei-yo fah-dze." He took another shirt and spread it on the ironing board; then asked, indifferently, "What large pale savage female do you refer to?"

"Large Pale Savage Female, so we all call her. Eyes the ugly color of a sky on a bright day."

"Do not all the savages, male and female, have such ugly eyes?"

Wong Cigar Fellow was inclined to be argumentative. "No, not at all, all. Some have eyes the color of smoke. Some have eyes of mixed colors. And some even have eyes the colors of human beings' eyes. Ha! Now I know how you will remember! Did she not, as they say, 'teach a class'? On the morning of the first day of their week, in one of their temple-buildings which they erect with no thought to *feng-shui,* wind and water and other influences as revealed by geomancy—Yes. The one who taught fairy tales and savage songs to the children of our laundrymen, and did not the girl-child attend?— as why not? it may be that their strange god or gods have authority here in savage territory, so far from the Kingdom in the Middle of the World—besides: girls . . . one gives them away, merely; after eating one's rice for many years, they go off and live in another human's house . . ."

On Lung uttered an exclamation. Yes! *Now* he recognized Large Pale Savage Female. Not in the least pausing or even slowing his pace, he listened while Wong Cigar Fellow spoke on.

The father of Large Pale Savage Female had formerly been, it was said, a merchant. Next, by cleverly putting his money out at usury, he had gotten a great fortune and owned estates and houses and documents called stocks and bonds which also gained him money. His wife having died, he had taken a concubine. "They call her a wife, but she has had no children, how can she be a wife?" and between concubine and daughter there had grown enmity. . . .

"Even in our own country one hears similar stories," chattered Wong Cigar Fellow. "Still—why does the Old Father not adopt, say, a cousin's son? Marry off the daughter to—"

On Lung said, "Who would marry her? She has such big feet."

"True. That is true. And even while it is true that the savages never bind the feet of their girl-children and even prevent us from doing so, still, even for a savage, Large Pale Savage Female has big feet. Well!" This time he really got up and grasped the pole of his carrying-basket. "It is said that the second wife so-called is gradually obtaining all the old man's property and that, not content with this, has made plans to—as they say—make a will in her favor. He is old and when he dies, what will become of Large Pale Savage Female? She must either go and play for trade in a sing-song house, or stay at home at the second wife's (or concubine's) beck and call, toiling like a servant. It is to drink bitter tea. —Farewell, Deft-Footed Dragon. It may be cooler by evening."

On Lung worked on in his steamy back-room. "One Lung," indeed! The savages had no knowledge that *Lung,* besides being one of the Hundred Names, also meant *Dragon.* It was his success as a warrior which had gained him that full name. Ah, the war! Then came a day when the high military council had summoned him to their chamber. "A treaty of peace has been signed," said the spokes-man, "and one of the terms of the treaty—the others of course need not concern you—is that all such warriors are at once to leave the Golden Mountain City and depart for distant places. These august personages would not leave you without means of earning rice money in savage parts, of course. Here is your passage-ticket on the fire-wagon. It is to a town called Stream-by-a-Cataract, in a distant prov-ince whose name means nothing and the syllables of which no human mouth can pronounce. Here are fifty silver dollars. The sav-ages are so filthy that they are obliged to make constant changes of clothing, so you will never lack employment in the laundry which it has been arranged for you to assume. Therefore lay down your heart, Deft-Footed Dragon, and never worry about your rice-bowl."

The girl-child (her mother, being weak, had taken a fever and died quickly) was indeed of great use in folding shirts; the savages called her Lily Long. Indeed, after a while, he had found comfort in the child's company: perhaps it was not his destiny to have sons. Because she was needed to fold shirts, because she was rather shy, because there were anyway no children nearby to play with, "Lily" (it was, for a marvel, easy to say; often he said it) spent much of her time in the shop. Also she was useful in chattering with the savages, none of whom, of course, could speak, when they came with shirts and other garments. The farthest away she ever went, in fact, was to the so-called "school" held in the worship place in the morning of the first day of their week . . . as though it were in any way es-sential to divide the lunar months into smaller quantities. . . . Some-times she told him something of the strange tales and stranger songs learned there. Now and then he laughed. She was sometimes very droll. It was a pity she was so weak; her mother, of course, had also been so.

Almost as she entered he had recognized Large Pale Savage Female from the descriptions he had heard. "Lily was not at Sunday School today. Is she ill?" From the rear of the shop came the call of *Miss—Miss*—In the woman went. "Why, Lily, you are burning up. Let me put my lips to your brow . . . you have a terrible fever. Wait . . . wait . . ." Well did On Lung know a fever. Had the pills from the savages' apothecary helped? No they had not: therefore he was brewing an infusion of dried pomegranate rind, very good for restoring the proper balance of yin and yang, hot and cold. —In another moment, out rushed Large Pale Savage Female, swinging her mantle over her fleshy shoulders; it seemed but a second before she was back again, and this time she held the mantle in her arms as though she were swaddling a child; curious, he followed her behind the beaded curtain.

Curiosity gave way almost to alarm: Large Pale Savage Female at once set the mantle on a table and, picking up a cold iron, proceeded to strike it repeatedly upon the garment and its contents. Very nearly, it sounded as though bones were being cracked.

"Desist, 'Miss-Miss,'" he exclaimed. "That is clearly a costly garment as befits the daughter of a respected usurer and rack-rent landlord, and I fear it may be damaged, and the blame laid on me; desist!"

Smack! Smack! *Smack!*

In a moment the mantle was flung open, inside lay a mass of crushed ice, quicker than he could move to prevent it she had snatched from the pile first one clean wrinkled shirt and then another, tumbled the crushed ice into each and wrapped it up like a sausage; then she set one on each side of the small, feverish body.

"Doesn't that feel better now?"

The female child murmured something very low, but she smiled as she reached up and took the large pale paw in her tiny golden hand.

Large Pale Savage Female came often, came quite often, came several times a day; Large Pale Savage Female brought more ice and more ice; she bathed the wasted little frame in cooled water many times, she brought a savage witch-doctor with the devil-thing one end of which goes in the ears and the other end upon the breast; also he administered more pills. Large Pale Savage Female fed broth to the sick child—in short, she could not have done more if she were caring for a husband's grandfather.

Afterward, Wong Cigar Fellow commented, "Needless to say that I would have gone had it been a boy; although Buddhists have said that even the death of a son is no more than the passage of a bird across the empty sky, who can go quite that far? Forget the matter in much toil and eventually you will have accumulated the thousand dollars which will enable you to return to the Kingdom in the Middle of the World and live at ease forever."

Only On Lung himself had been present at the burial of the girl-child. He, that is, and Large Pale Savage Female whose much care had not prevailed, plus the priest-savage she had brought along. It was a wet, chill autumn day; the bitter wind had scattered rain and leaves . . . golden leaves . . . henceforth the tiny ghost would sip in solitude of the Yellow Springs beneath the earth. It was astonishing how very painful the absence of the small person was found. One would not indeed have thought it possible.

The heat had become intolerable; he thought of that sudden illness which was compared to the tightening of a red-hot band about the head: nonsense: he was still upright; merely the place seemed very odd, suddenly. Seemed without meaning, suddenly. Its shapes seemed to shift. It had no purpose. No wonder he was no longer there, was outside, was moving silently from one silent alley to another, on his shoulder the carrying pole of the two laundry-baskets, one at each end. No one was about, and, if anyone were, no one would have noted his presence: merely a Chinaman, which is to say a laundryman, picking up and leaving off shirts. No one. Everything was very sudden, now. He had hidden pole and baskets behind a bush. He had slipped through a space where a board was missing from a fence. He was in a place where wood was stored and split. He had a glimpse of someone who he knew. He must avoid such a one—indeed all others. Silently his slippered feet flew up the stairs. A voice droned in a room, Droned on and on. And on. ". . . come when I call you, hey, miss? Miss, Miss Elizabeth? Beneath you, is it? We'll see if you'll come when I call you pretty soon," the voice droned on. "I say. 'We'll see if you'll come when I call you pretty soon, miss.' Wun't call me, 'Mother,' hey, miss? Well, even if I be Mr. Borden's second wife, I be his lawful-wedded wife, him and me has got some business at the bank and the lawyer's pretty soon today, you may lay to that, yes, miss, you may lay to that; we'll see if you ain't a-going to come when I call you after that, and come at my very beck and call and do as I tell you must do, for if you don't you may go somewheres else and you may git your vittles somewheres else, too, though darned if I know where that may be, I have got your father wrapped around my little finger, miss, miss, yes, I say yes, I shall lower your proud head, miss," the hateful, nasal voice droned on.

So! This was she: the childless concubine of the father of Large Pale Savage Female! *She,* the one who planned to assume the rule of family property and cast out the daughter of the first wife? In this heat-stricken, insane, and savage world only the practice of fidelity and the preservation of virtue could keep a man's heart from being crushed by pain. He who had been known (and rightfully known) as The Deft-Footed Dragon, the once-renowned and most-renowned hatchet-man of the great Ten Tongs, hefted his weapon and slipped silently into the room . . .

AFTERWORD TO "THE DEED OF THE DEFT-FOOTED DRAGON"

Lizzie Borden took an axe and gave her parents forty whacks . . . But was it really Lizzie, or some mysterious other? We'll never know. We do know that Avram served in China with the US military at the end of World War II. His sojourn in China became an ongoing theme in many stories, in this collection and others, and in the fantasy novel *Marco Polo and the Sleeping Beauty* (reissued by Wildside Press), which I co-authored with Avram before he passed on. Avram knew something about China.

—Grania Davis

THE
MONTAVARDE
CAMERA

Mr. Azel's shop was set between a glazier's establishment and a woolen draper's; three short steps led down to it. The shopfront was narrow; a stranger hurrying by would not even notice it, for the grimy brick walling of the glazier's was part of a separate building, and extended farther out.

Three short steps down, and there was a little areaway before the door, and it was always clean, somehow. The slattern wind blew bits of straw and paper scraps in circles up and down the street, leaving its discarded playthings scattered all about, but not in the areaway in front of the shop door. Just above the height of a man's eye there was a rod fastened to the inside of the door, and from it descended, in neat folds, a red velveteen curtain. The shop's window, to the door's left, was veiled in the same way. In old-fashioned lettering the gold-leaf figures of the street number stood alone on the glass pane.

There was no slot for letters, no name or sign, nothing displayed on door or window. The shop was a blank, it made no impression on the eye, conveyed no message to brain. If a few of the many people scurrying by noticed it at all, it was only to assume it was empty.

No cats took advantage of this quiet backwater to doze in the sun, although at least two of them always reclined under the projecting window of the draper. On this particular day the pair were jolted out of their calm by the running feet of Mr. Lucius Collins, who was chasing his hat. It was a high-crowned bowler, a neat and altogether proper hat, and as he chased it indignantly Mr. Collins puffed and breathed through his mouth—a small, full, red-lipped mouth, grazed on either side by a pair of well-trimmed, sandy, mutton chop whiskers.

Outrageous! Mr. Collins thought, his stout little legs pumping furiously. *Humiliating!* And no one to be blamed for it, either, not even the Government, or the Boers, or Mrs. Collins, she of the sniffles and rabbity face. *Shameful!* The gold seals on his watchchain jingled and clashed together and beat against the stomach it confined, and the wind carried the hat at a rapid clip along the street.

Just as the wind had passed the draper's, it abruptly abandoned the object of its game, and the forsaken bowler fell with a thud in front of the next shop. It rolled down the first, the second, and the third step, and leaned wearily against the door.

Mr. Collins trotted awkwardly down the steps and knelt down to seize the hat. His head remained where it was, as did his hands and knees. About a foot of uncurtained glass extended from the lower border of the red velveteen to the wooden doorframe, and through this Mr. Lucius Collins looked. It almost seemed that he gaped.

Inside the shop, looking down at Mr. Collins's round and red face, was a small, slender gentleman, who leaned against a showcase as if he were (the thought flitted through Mr. Collins's mind) posing for his photograph. The mild amusement evident on his thin features brought to Mr. Collins anew the realization that his position was, at best, undignified. He took up his hat, arose, brushed the errant bowler with his sleeve, dusted his knees, and entered the shop. Somewhere in the back a bell tinkled as he did so.

A red rug covered the floor and muffled his footsteps. The place was small, but well furnished, in the solid style more fashionable in past days. Nothing was shabby or worn, yet nothing was new. A gas jet with mantle projected from a paneled wall whose dark wood had the gleam of much polishing, but the burner was not lit, although the shop was rather dark. Several chairs upholstered in leather were set at intervals around the shop. There were no counter, and no shelves, and only the one showcase. *It* was empty, and only a well-brushed Ascot top hat rested on it.

Mr. Collins did not wish the slender little gentleman to receive the impression that he, Lucius, made a practice of squatting down and peering beneath curtained shop windows.

"Are you the proprietor?" he asked. The gentleman, still smiling, said that he was. It was a dry smile, and its owner was a dry-looking person. His was a long nose set in a long face. His chin was cleft.

The gentleman's slender legs were clad in rather baggy trousers, but it was obvious that they were the aftermath of the period when baggy trousers were the fashion, and were not the result of any carelessness in attire. The cloth was of a design halfway between plaid and checkered, and a pair of sharply pointed and very glossy shoes were on his small feet. A gray waistcoat, crossed by a light gold watchchain, a rather short frock coat, and a wing collar with a black cravat completed his dress. No particular period was stamped on his clothes, but one felt that in his prime—whenever that had been— this slender little gentleman had been a dandy, in a dry, smiling sort of way.

From his nose to his chin two deep lines were etched, and there were laughter wrinkles about the corners of his eyes. His hair was brown and rather sparse, cut in the conventional fashion. Its only unusual feature was that the little gentleman had on his forehead, after the manner of the late Lord Beaconsfield, a ringlet of the type commonly known as a "spit curl." And his nicely appointed little shop contained, as far as Mr. Collins could see, absolutely no merchandise at all.

"The wind, you know it—ah, blew my hat off and carried it away. Dropped it at your door, so to speak."

Mr. Collins spoke awkwardly, aware that the man seemed still to be somewhat amused, and believed that this was due to his own precipitate entry. In order to cover his embarrassment and justify his continued presence inside, he asked in a rush, "What is it exactly that you sell here?" and waved his arm at the unstocked room.

"What is it you wish to buy?" the man asked.

Mr. Collins flushed again, and gaped again, and fumbled about for an answer.

"Why, what I meant was: in what line *are* you? You have nothing displayed whatsoever, you know. Not a thing. How is one to know what sort of stock you have, if you don't put it about where it can be seen?" As he spoke, Mr. Collins felt his self-possession returning, and went on with increased confidence to say: "Now, just for example, my own particular avocation is photography. But if you have nothing displayed to show you sell anything in that line, I daresay I would pass by here every day and never think to stop in."

The proprietor's smile increased slightly, and his eyebrows arched up to his curl.

"But it so happens that I, too, am interested in photography, and although I have no display or sign to beguile you, in you came. I do not care for advertising. It is, I think, vulgar. My equipment is not for your tuppeny-tintype customer, nor will I pander to his tastes."

"Your equipment?" Mr. Collins again surveyed the place. "Where is it?" A most unusual studio—if studio it was—or shop, he thought; but he was impressed by what he considered a commendable attitude on the part of the slender gentleman—a standard so elevated that he refused to lower it by the most universally accepted customs of commerce.

The proprietor pointed to the most shadowy corner of the shop. There, in the semidarkness between the showcase and the wall, a large camera of archaic design stood upon a tripod. Mr. Collins approached it with interest, and began to examine it in the failing light.

Made out of some unfamiliar type of hardwood, with its lens piece gleaming a richer gold than ordinary brass, the old camera was in every respect a museum piece; yet, despite its age, it seemed to be in good working order. Mr. Collins ran his hand over the smooth surface; as he did so, he felt a rough spot on the back. It was evidently someone's name, he discovered, burned or carved into the wood, but now impossible to read in the thickening dusk. He turned to the proprietor.

"It is rather dark back here."

"Of course. I beg your pardon; I was forgetting. It is something remarkable, isn't it? There is no such workmanship nowadays. Years of effort that took, you know." As he spoke, he lit the jet and turned up the gas. The soft, yellow light of the flame filled the shop, hissing quietly to itself. More and more shops now had electric lights; this one, certainly, never would.

Mr. Collins reverently bowed his head and peered at the writing. In a flourishing old-fashioned script, someone long ago had engraved the name of *Gaston Montavarde*. Mr. Collins looked up in amazement.

"Montavarde's camera? Here?"

"Here, before you. Montavarde worked five years on his experimental models before he made the one you see now. At that time he was still—so the books tell you—the pupil of Daguerre. But to those who knew him, the pupil far excelled the master; just as Daguerre himself had far excelled Niepce. If Montavarde had not died just as he was nearing mastery of the technique he sought, his work would be world famous. As it is, appreciation of Montavarde's style and importance is largely confined to the few—of whom I count myself one. You, sir, I am pleased to note, are one of the others. One of the few others." Here the slender gentleman gave a slight bow. Mr. Collins was extremely flattered, not so much by the bow—all shopkeepers bowed—but by the implied compliment to his knowledge.

In point of fact, he knew very little of Montavarde, his life, or his work. Who does? He was familiar, as are all students of early photography, with Montavarde's study of a street scene in Paris during the 1848 Revolution. *Barricades in the Morning*, which shows a ruined embattlement and the still bodies of its defenders, is perhaps the first war photograph ever taken; it is usually, and wrongly, called a Daguerreotype. Perhaps not more than six or eight, altogether, of Montavarde's pictures are known to the general public, and all are famous for that peculiar luminous quality that seems to come from some unknown source within the scene. Collins was also aware that several more Montavardes in the possession of collectors of the esoteric and erotic could not be published or displayed. One of the most famous of these is the so-called *La Messe Noire*.

The renegade priest of Lyons, Duval, who was in the habit of conducting the Black Mass of the Demonolaters, used for some years as his "altar" the naked body of the famous courtesan, La Manchette. It was this scene that Montavarde was reputed to have photographed. Like many popular women of her type, La Manchette might have eventually retired to grow roses and live to a great age, had she not been murdered by one of her numerous lovers. Montavarde's photographs of the guillotine (*The Widow*) before and after the execution, had been banned by the French censor under Louis Napoleon as a matter of public policy.

All this is a digression, of course. These asides are mentioned because they were known to Mr. Lucius Collins, and largely explained his awe and reverence on seeing the—presumably—same camera which had photographed these scenes.

"How did you get this?" he asked, not troubling to suppress or conceal his eagerness.

"For more than thirty years," explained the proprietor, "it was the property of a North American. He came to London, met with financial reverses and pawned his equipment. He did not know, one assumes, that it was the Montavarde camera. Nor did he redeem. I had little or no competition at the auction. Later I heard he had gone back to America, or done away with himself, some said; but no matter: the camera was a *bon marché*. I never expected to see it again. I sold it soon after, but the payments were not kept up, and so here it is."

On hearing that the camera could be purchased, Mr. Collins began to treat for its sale (though he knew he could really not afford to buy) and would not take no for an answer. In short, an agreement was drawn up, whereby he was to pay a certain sum down, and something each month for eight months.

"Shall I make out the check in pounds or in guineas?" he asked.

"Guineas, of course. I do not consider myself a tradesman." The slender gentleman smiled and fingered his watchchain as Mr. Collins drew out his check book.

"What name am I to write, sir? I do not—"

"My name, sir, is Azel. The initials, A. A. Ah, just so. Can you manage the camera by yourself? Then I bid you a good evening, Mr. Collins. You have made a rare acquisition, indeed. Allow me to open the door."

Mr. Collins brought his purchase home in a four-wheeler, and spent the rest of the evening dusting and polishing. Mrs. Collins, a wispy, weedy little figure, who wore her hair in what she imagined was the manner of the Princess of Wales—Mrs. Collins had a cold, as usual. She agreed that the camera *was* in excellent condition, but, with a snuffle, she pointed out that he had spent far too much money on it. In her younger days, as one of the Misses Wilkins, she had done quite a good bit of amateur photography herself, but she had given it up because it cost far too much money.

She repeated her remarks some evenings later when her brother, the Reverend Wycliffe Wilkins, made his weekly call.

"Mind you," said Mr. Collins to his brother-in-law, "I don't know just what process the inventor used in developing his plates, but I did the best I could, and I don't think it's half bad. See here. This is the only thing I've done so far. One of those old Tudor houses in Great Cumberland Street. They say it was one of the old plague houses. Pity it's got to be torn down to make way for that new road. I thought I'd beat the wreckers to it."

"Very neatly done, I'm sure," said his brother-in-law. "I don't know much about photography myself. But evidently you haven't heard about this particular house. No? Happened yesterday. My cook was out marketing, and just as she came up to the corner, the house collapsed in a pile of dust. Shoddy workmanship somewhere; I mean, the house couldn't have been more than three hundred years old. Of course, there was no one in it, but still it gave the cook quite a turn. I suppose there's no harm in your having this camera, but, as for me, considering its associations, I wouldn't have it in the house. Naked women, indeed!—saving your presence, Mary."

"Oh, come now," said Mr. Collins. "Montavarde was an artist."

"Many artists have been pious, decent people, Lucius. There can be no compromise between good and evil." Mrs. Collins snuffled her agreement. Mr. Collins pursed his little mouth and said no more until his good humor was restored by the maid's coming in with the tea tray.

"I suppose, then, Wycliffe, you wouldn't think of letting me take your picture."

"Well, I don't know why ever not," Mrs. Collins protested. "After the amount of money Lucius spent on the camera, we ought to make *some* use out of it, I think. Lucius will take your likeness whenever it's convenient. He has a great deal of free time. Raspberry jam or gooseberry, Wycliffe?"

Mr. Collins photographed his brother-in-law in the vicarage, garden—alone, and then with his curate, the Reverend Osias Gomm. Both clerical gentlemen were very active in the temperance movement, and this added a note of irony to the tragic events of the following day. It was the carriage of Stout, the brewer; there was no doubt about that. The horses had shied at a scrap of paper. The witnesses (six of them) had described seeing the two clergymen start across the street, deep in conversation. They described how the carriage came flying around the corner.

"They never knew wot 'it 'em," the witnesses agreed. Mrs. Collins said that was the only thing that comforted her. She said nothing, of course, about the estate (three thousand pounds in six percent bonds), but she did mention the picture.

"How bright it is, Lucius," she said. "Almost shining."

After the funeral she felt free to talk about the financial affairs of her late brother, and until the estate was close to being settled, Mr. Collins had no time for photography. He did keep up the monthly payments on the camera, however, although he found them rather a drain. After all, it had not been *his* income which had just been increased by 180 pounds per annum.

It was almost November before Mrs. Collins would consent to have a fire laid. The inheritance of her brother's share of their patrimony had not changed her habits for what her husband, if no one else, would have considered the better. Although he still transferred the same amount each quarter from his personal account to the household funds, there was less and less to show for it each week. Meat appeared on the table less often, and it was much more likely to be a piece of the neck than a cut off the joint. The tea grew dustier and the pieces of butter shrank in size, and more than once Mr. Collins had asked for another bit of cake at tea and been told (truthfully, as he learned by prowling around the kitchen later at night) that there wasn't another bit of cake in the house. (Perhaps it was his going to sleep on an empty—and hence, nervous, stomach—that caused the odd dreams which began about this time: confused scenes he could never remember, come daylight, and a voice—flat, resonant—repeating over and over, *"The life is in the light . . . the life is in the light."*)

He had, of course, protested, and it had, of course, done him no good at all. Mrs. Collins, with a snuffle, spoke of increased prices, the unsteady condition of World Affairs, and the necessity of Setting Something Aside For the Future, because, she said, who knows?

So, at any rate, here it was November, and a nice sea-coal fire in the grate, with Mr. Collins sitting by it in his favorite chair, reading the newspaper (there had formerly been two, but Mrs. Collins had stopped one of them in the interests of domestic economy). There were a number of interesting bits in the paper that evening, and occasionally Mr. Collins would read one of them aloud. Mrs. Collins was unraveling some wool with an eye toward reknitting it.

"Dear me!" said Mr. Collins.

"What is that, Lucius?"

" 'Unusual Pronouncement By the Bishop of Lyons' " He looked over at his wife. "Shall I read it to you?"

"Do."

His Grace the Bishop of Lyons had found it necessary to warn all the faithful against a most horrible series of crimes that had recently been perpetrated in the City and See of Lyons. It was a sign of the infamy and decadence of the age that not once but six times in the course of the past year, consecrated wafers had been stolen from churches and rectories in the City and See of Lyons. The purpose of these thefts could only indicate one thing, and it behooved all of the faithful, and so forth. There was little doubt (wrote the Paris correspondent of Mr. Collins's newspaper) that the bishop referred to the curious ceremony generally called the Black Mass, which, it would appear, was still being performed in parts of France; and not merely, as might be assumed, among the more uneducated elements of the population.

"Dear me!" said Mr. Collins.

"Ah, those French!" said Mrs. Collins. "Wasn't it Lyons—wasn't that the place that this unpleasant person came from? The camera man?"

"Montavarde?" Mr. Collins looked up in surprise. "Perhaps. I don't know. What makes you think so?"

"Didn't poor Wycliffe say so on that last night he was here?"

"Did he? I don't remember."

"He must have. Else how could I know?"

This was a question which required no answer; but it aroused other questions in Mr. Collins's mind. That night he had the dream again, and he recalled it very clearly on awakening. There was a woman, a foreign woman . . . though how he knew she was foreign, he could not say. It was not her voice, for she never spoke, only gestured: horrid, wanton gestures, too! Nor was it in her clothes, for she wore none. And she had something in her hand, about the size of a florin, curiously marked, and she offered it to him. When he went to take it, she snatched it back, laughing, and thrust it into her red, red mouth. And all the while the voice—inflectionless, echoing—repeated over and again, *The light is in the life . . . the light is in the life.* It seemed, somehow, a familiar voice.

The next day found him at his bookdealer's, the establishment of little Mr. Pettigew, the well-known antiquary, known among younger and envious members of the trade as "the well-known antiquity." There, under pretense of browsing, Mr. Collins read as much as he could on demonolatry in general, and the Black Mass in particular. It was most interesting, but, as the books all dated from the previous century, there was no mention of either Duval or Montavarde. Mr. Collins tipped his hat to the bookdealer (it was the same bowler) and left the shop.

He bought an *Illustrated London News* at the tobacconist's got a seat on top of the omnibus, and prepared to enjoy the ride home. It was a bright day despite the time of year, one of the brightest Guy Fawkes Days that Mr. Collins could remember.

The *Illustrated,* he noted, was showing more and more photographs as time went on, and fewer drawings. Progress, progress, thought Mr. Collins, looking with approval and affection at a picture of the Duke of York and his sons, the little princes, all in Highland costume. Then he turned the page, and saw something which almost caused him to drop the paper. It was a picture of a dreadnought, but it was the style and not the subject that fixed his attention to the page.

"The above photograph," read the caption, "of the ill-fated American battleship, the *U.S.S. Maine,* was taken shortly before it left on its last voyage for Havana. Those familiar with photography will be at once attracted by the peculiar luminosity of the photography, which is reminiscent of the work of the Frenchman, Montavarde. The *Maine* was built at—" Mr. Collins read no further. He began to think, began to follow a train of thought alien to his mind. Shying away from any wild and outrageous fantasies, Mr. Collins began to enumerate as best he could all the photographs known to him to have been taken by the Montavarde camera.

Barricades in the Morning proved nothing, and neither did *The Widow;* no living person appeared in either. On the other hand, consider the matter of La Manchette, the subject of Montavarde's picture *La Messe Noire;* consider the old house in Great Cumberland

Street, and the Reverends Wilkins and Gomm. Consider also the battleship *Maine.*

After considering all this, Mr. Collins found himself at his stop. He went directly home, took the camera in his arms, and descended with it to the basement.

Was there some quality in the camera which absorbed the life of its subjects? Some means whereby that life was transmuted into light, a light impressed upon the photograph, leaving the subjects to die?

Mr. Collins took an ax and began to destroy the camera. The wood was intensely hard, and he removed his coat before falling to work again. Try as he might, Mr. Collins could not dent the camera, box, brass or lens. He stopped at last, sweat pouring down his face, and heard his wife's voice calling to him. What*ever* was he doing?

"I'm breaking up a box for kindling wood," he shouted back. And then, even as she warned him not to use too much wood, that the wood had to last them another fortnight, that wood had gone up—even as she chattered away, Mr. Collins had another idea. He carried the camera up to the fire and thrust it in. He heaped on the coals, he threw in kerosene at the cost of his eyebrows, and he plied the bellows.

Half an hour's effort saw the camera not only unconsumed, but unscorched. He finally removed it from the fire in despair, and stood there, hot and disheveled, not knowing what to do. All doubts that he had felt earlier were now removed. Previously he had been uncertain as to the significance of Montavarde's presence with his dreadful camera at the Rites of Lucifer, at the foul ritual conducted by the renegade priest Duval. It was *not* merely as a spectator that the cameraman had attended these blasphemous parodies. The spitting on the crucifix, the receiving of the witch mark, the signing of the compact with his own blood, the ceremonial stabbing of the stolen Host while awaiting the awful moment when the priest or priestess of the unholy sect declared manifest in his or her own body the presence of the Evil One—surely Montavarde had *done* all these things, and not just seen them.

Mr. Collins felt that he needed some air. He put on his hat and coat and went down to the street. The breeze cooled his hot face and calmed his thoughts. Several children came down the street toward him, lighting firecrackers and tossing them into the air.

> *Remember, remember, the 5th of November*
> *Was gunpowder, treason, and plot*

the children began to chant as they came up to him. They were wheeling a tatterdemalion old bath chair, and in it was a scarecrow of a Guy Fawkes, clad in old clothes; just as Mr. Collins had done as a boy.

> *I see no reason why gunpowder treason*
> *Should ever be forgot*

ended the traditional phrases, and then the outstretched, expectant grimy paws, and a general cry of "Remember the Guy, sir! Remember the Guy!" Mr. Collins distributed some money to the eager group, even though he could see that his wife, who had come down and was now looking out of the first floor window, was shaking her head at him and pursing her lips, pantomiming that he wasn't to give them a farthing. He looked away and glanced at the Guy.

Its torn trousers were of a plaid design, its scuffed shoes were sharply pointed. A greasy gray waistcoat, a ragged sort of frock coat, a drooping and dirty wing collar, and a battered Ascot top hat completed its dress. The costume seemed unpleasantly familiar to Mr. Collins, but he could not quite place it. Just then a gust of wind blew off the old topper and revealed the Guy's head. It was made of one of those carven coconuts that visitors from southern countries sometimes bring back, and its carven features were a horrible parody of the face of the slender gentleman who had sold the camera.

The children went on their way while Mr. Collins remained standing, his mind a maze of strange thoughts, and Mrs. Collins frowned down at him from the window. She seemed to be busy with something; her hands moved. It seemed to him that an age passed as he stood there, hand in pocket, thinking of the long-dead Montavarde (How did he die? "Untimely" was the word invariably used), who had purchased, at a price unknown and scarcely to be guessed at, unsurpassable skill in building and using his camera. What should one do? One might place the camera in a large sack, or encase it in concrete, and throw it in the Thames.

Or one might keep it hidden in a safe place that one knew of.

He turned to his house and looked up at Mrs. Collins, there at the window. (What *had* she been busied with?) It seemed to him that she had never looked so much like a rabbit before, and it also occurred to him how much he disliked rabbits and always had, since he was a boy. That, after all, was not so very long ago. He was still a comparatively young man. Many attractive women might still find him attractive too.

Should he submit, like some vegetable, while his wife nibbled, nibbled away at him forever? No. The way had been shown him; he had fought, but that sort of victory was plainly not to be his. So be it; he would follow the way which had been open to him since the moment he took the camera. And he would use it again, this time with full knowledge.

He started up the steps, and had just reached the top one when a searing pain stabbed him in the chest, and the sun went out. His hat fell off as he dropped. It rolled down the first, the second, and the third step. Mrs. Collins began to scream. It occurred to him, even in that moment of dark agony, how singularly unconvincing those screams sounded.

For some reason the end did not come at once.

"I'm not completely satisfied with that likeness I took of you just before you were stricken," Mrs. Collins said. "Of course, it *was* the first time I had used a camera since we were married. And the picture, even while you look at it, seems to be growing brighter."

Logically, Mr. Collins thought; for at the same time he was growing weaker. Well, it did not matter.

"Your affairs *are* in order, aren't they, Lucius?" Her eyes, as she gazed at him, were bright, birdlike. A bird, of course, is not human.

He made no reply. "Yes, to be sure, they are. I made certain. Except for this unpleasant Mr. Azel asking me for money he claims is still owing on the camera. Well, I shan't pay it. I have all I can do to keep myself. But I mean to show him. He can have his old camera back, and much good may it do him. I took my mother's ring and I scratched the nasty lens up completely with the diamond."

Her voice was growing weaker now. "It's a tradition in our family, you know. It's an old diamond, an heirloom; it has been in our family ever so long, and they say that it was once set in a jeweled monstrance that stood upon the high altar at Canterbury before the days of good King Harry.

"*That* will teach that Mr. A. A. Azel a good lesson."

AFTERWORD TO "THE MONTAVARDE CAMERA"

Avram captured the essence of the nineteenth century like the Montavarde camera captured the essence of its subjects. He was fascinated by early photography. It turned up elsewhere in his fiction. In *The Boss in the Wall*, (Tachyon, 1999), a Civil War ambrotype, a cheaper successor to the daguerrotype, holds the key to the mystery. Say cheese.

—*Grania Davis*

WHAT STRANGE STARS AND SKIES

The terrible affair of Dame Phillipa Garreck, which struck horror in all who knew of her noble life and mysterious disappearance, arose in large measure from inordinate confidence in her fellow-creatures—particularly such of them as she might, from time to time, in those nocturnal wanderings which so alarmed her family and friends, encounter in circumstances more than commonly distressed. This great-hearted and misfortunate woman would be, we may be sure, the first to deplore any lessening of philanthropy, any diminution of charity or even of charitable feeling, resultant from her own dreadfully sudden and all but inexplicable fate; yet, one feels, such a result is inevitable. I am not aware that Dame Phillipa ever made use of any heraldic devices or mottoes, but, had she done so, "Do what is right, come what may," would have been eminently appropriate.

It is not any especial sense of competency on my part which has caused me to resolve that a record of the matter should and must be made. Miss Mothermer, Dame Phillipa's faithful secretary-companion, to say nothing of her cousin, Lord FitzMorris Banstock, would each—under ordinary circumstances—be far more capable than I of delineating the events in question. But the circumstances, of course, are as far from being "ordinary" as they can possibly be. Miss Mothermer has for the past six months next Monday fortnight been in seclusion at Doctor Hardesty's establishment near Sutton Ho; and, whilst I can state quite certainly the falsehood of the rumour that her affairs have been placed in charge of the Master in Lunacy, nevertheless, Doctor Hardesty is adamant that the few visitors she is permitted to receive must make no reference whatsoever to the affair of last Guy Fawkes Day, the man with the false nose, or the unspeakably evil Eurasian, Motilal Smith. As for Lord FitzMorris Banstock, though I am aware that he has the heart of a lion and nerves of steel, his extreme shyness (in no small measure the result of his unfortunate physical condition) must advertize to all who know him the unlikelihood of his undertaking the task.

It falls to me, therefore, and no one else, to proceed forthwith in setting down the chronicle of those untoward and unhappy events.

Visitors to Argyll Court, which abuts onto Primrose Alley (one of that maze of noisome passages off the Commercial Road which the zeal and conscience of the London County Council cannot much longer suffer to remain untouched), visitors to Argyll Court will have noticed the large signboard affixed to the left-hand door as one enters. Reading, "If The Lord Will, His Word Shall Be Preached Here Each Lord's Day At Seven O'Clock In The Evening. All Welcome," it gives notice of the Sabbath activities of Major Bohun, whose weekdays are devoted to his sacred labors with The Strict Antinomian Tram-Car and Omnibus Tract Society (the name of which appears on a small brass plate under the sign). Had the major been present that Fifth of November, a different story it would be which I have to tell; but he had gone to attend at an Anti-Papistical sermon and prayer-meeting holden to mark the day at the Putney Tabernacle.

The foetid reek of the Court, which has overwhelmed more than one less delicately bred than Dame Phillipa, bears—besides the effluvia of unwashed beds and bodies emanating from the so-called Seaman's Lodging-House of Evan-bach Llewellyn, the rotting refuse of the back part of a cookshop of the lowest sort, bad drains, and the putrid odors of Sampson Stone's wool-pullery—the tainted breath of the filthy Thames itself, whose clotted waters ebb and flow not far off.

On many an evening when the lowering sun burned dully in the dirty sky and the soiled swans squatted like pigs in the mud-banks of London River, the tall figure of Dame Phillipa would turn (for the time being) from the waterfront, and make her way towards the quickening traffic of the Commercial Road and Goodman Fields; proceeding through Salem Yard, Fenugreek Close, Primrose Alley, and Argyll Court. The fashionable and sweet-smelling ladies of the West End, as well as their wretched and garishly bedaubed fallen sisters, smelling of cheap "scent" and sweetened gin, just at this hour beginning those peregrinations of the East End's mean and squalid streets for which those less tender than Dame Phillipa might think them dead to all shame; were wearing, with fashion's licence, their skirts higher than they had ever been before: but Dame Phillipa (though she never criticized the choice of others) still wore hers long, and sometimes with one hand she would lift them an inch or two to avoid the foul pavements—though she never drew back from contact, neither an inch nor an instant, with any human being, however filthy or diseased.

Sometimes Miss Mothermer's bird-like little figure was with her friend and employer, perhaps assuming for the moment the burden of the famous Army kit-bag; sometimes—and such times Dame Phillipa walked more slowly—Lord FitzMorris Banstock accompanied her; but usually only quite late at night, and along the less-frequented thoroughfares, where such people whom they were likely to meet were too preoccupied with their own unhappy concerns, or too brutalized and too calloused, to stare at the muscular but mis-shapen peer for more than a second or two.

The kit-bag had been the gift of Piggott, batman to Dame Phillipa's brother, the late Lt.-Colonel Sir Chiddiock Garreck, when she had sent him out to the Transvaal in hopes that that Province's warmer and dryer air would be kindlier to his gas-ruined lungs than the filthy fogs and sweats of England. The kit-bag usually contained, to my own knowledge, on an average evening, the following:

Five to ten pounds in coins, as well as several ten-shilling notes folded quite small. Two sets of singlets and drawers, two shirts, and two pair of stockings: none of them new, but all clean and mended. A dozen slices of bread and butter, wrapped in packets of three. Ten or twenty copies of a pamphlet-sized edition of the Gospel of St. John in various languages. A brittania-metal pint flask of a good French brandy. A quantity of hard-cooked eggs and an equal supply of salt and pepper in small screws of paper. Four handkerchiefs. First-aid equipment. Two reels of cotton, with needles. A packet of mixed toffees. The Book of Common Prayer. Fifteen packets of five Wood-bine cigarettes, into each of which she had thrust six wooden matches. One pocket-mirror. A complete change of infant's clothing. Several small cakes of soap. Several pocket-combs. A pair of scissors.

And three picture-postcards of the Royal Family.

All this arranged with maximum efficiency in minimum space, but not packed so tightly that Dame Phillipa's fingers could not instantly produce the requisite article. It will be observed that she was prepared to deal with a wide variety of occasions.

Tragic, infinitely tragic though it is, not even a person of Dame Phillipa's great experience among what a late American author termed, not infelicitously, The People of the Abyss, could have been prepared either to expect or to deal on this occasion with such persons as the man wearing the false nose or the hideously—the unspeakably evil Eurasian, Motilal Smith.

The countenance of Motilal Smith, once observed, is not one likely ever to be forgotten, and proves a singular and disturbing exception to the rule that Eurasians are generally of a comely appearance; it being broad and frog-like in its flatness, protruberance of the eyes (which are green and wet-looking), reverse U-shaped mouth, and its multiplicity of warts or wart-like swellings. Most striking of all, however, is the air of slyness, malevolence, of hostility both overt and covert, towards everything which is kindly and decent and, in a word, human.

Motilal Smith has since his first appearance in the United Kingdom been the subject of unremitting police attention, and for some time now has gained the sinister distinction of being mentioned more often in the Annual Report of the League of Nations Commission on the Traffic in Women and Children than any other resident of London. He has often been arrested and detained on suspicion, but the impossibility of bringing witnesses to testify against him has invariably resulted in his release. Evidences of his nefarious commerce have come from places so far distant as the Province of Santa Cruz in the Republic of Bolivia and the Native Indian States of Patiala and Cooch Behar, as well as two of the Trucial Sheikhdoms, the Free City of Danzig, and Deaf Smith County in the Commonwealth of Texas; none of which, it must be regretted, is admissible in proceedings at the Old Bailey. As he is a British subject by birth, he can be neither deported nor denied admission on his return from frequent trips abroad. He is known to be always ready to purchase, he is entirely eclectic as to the nature of the merchandise, and he pays well and he pays in gold.

It is necessary only to add that, offered any obstacle, affront, or rebuff, he is unremitting in his hostility, which combines the industry of the West with the patience of the East. Smith occupies both sides of the semi-detached villa in Maida Vale of which he owns the freehold; its interior is crammed with opulent furnishings from all round the world, and stinks of stale beer, split gin, incense, curry, raw fish, the foul breaths and bodies of those he deals with, and of chips fried in ghee.

His long, lank, and clotted hair is covered in scented grease, and on his fingers are rings of rubies, diamonds, pearls and other precious stones worth with their settings a prince's ransom. Add only the famous Negrohead opal worn in his stained silk four-in-hand (and for which Second Officer Smollett of the *Cutty Sark* is said to have strangled Mrs. Pigler), and there you have the creature Motilal Smith in all his repulsive essence.

The night of that Fifth of November found the unfortunates among whom this great lady pursued her noble work no more inclined than in other years to celebrate the delivery from Gunpowder Plot of King James VI and I and his English Parliament. Here and there, to be sure, in the glare of the gin-palaces of the main thoroughfares, a group of grimy and tattered children had gotten up an even more unsavory Guy; for them Dame Phillipa had provided herself with a large supply of pennies. But that night as on most other nights there was little enough evidence of innocent gayety.

There are multitudes, literally multitudes, in this vast labyrinth of London for whom the normal institutions of a human society seem barely to exist. There are physicians in the East End, hospitals, and dispensaries; yet numbers past counting will suffer injury and disease and creep off to die like brutes in their dim corners, or, if they are fortunate, by brute strength survive. There are public baths in every borough, and facilities for washing clothes, yet many never touch water to their skins, and wear their rags unchanged till they rot. Babes are born without benefit of any human witness to the event save their own wretched mothers, though a word to the great hospital in Whitechapel Road will bring midwife and physician without charge. And while eating-places abound, from quite decent restaurants down to the dirty holes-in-the-walls offering tuppenny cups of tea and sixpenny papers of breaded smelts and greasy chips, and while private and public charity arrangements guarantee that no one need quite die of hunger who will ask to be fed, no day goes by without its toll from famine of those who—having their hoards of copper and silver—are disabled by their madness from spending either tuppence or shilling; or who find it much, much easier to die like dogs in their secluded kennels than come forward and declare their needs.

As the pigeons in Trafalgar Square have learned when and where the old man with the bag of breadcrumbs will appear, as the ownerless cats near Billingsgate can tell what time and in what place to scavenge for the scraps of fish the dustman misses, as the rats in the sewers beneath Smithfield Market know without error the manner in which "they seek their meat from G d"; just so, from this stinking alley and from that crumbling tenement, here from underneath a dripping archway and there from a disused warehouse, slinking and creeping and peering fearfully and furtively and sidling with their ragged backs pressed against ragged walls, there appeared by one and by one the cast-offs—one must call them "humans," for what other name is theirs?—the self-exiled, the utterly incapable, to take in their quick reptilian grasp the things Dame Phillipa had for them. She knew, knew by instinct and knew by practice, which ones would benefit by a shilling and which by half-a-crown; she knew those to whom money was of no more use than cowry-shells but who would relish the meat of a hard-cooked egg and the savor of the tiny scrap of seasoning which went with it; knew those who would be hopelessly baffled by the labor of cracking the shell but who could manage to rip the paper off a packet of bread and butter (huddled and crouched in the rank, familiar darkness of their burrows, tearing the soft food with their toothless gums); knew those who would fight, squealing or wordlessly, fight like cornered stoats rather than surrender a single one of the unspeakably filthy rags into which their unspeakably filthy bodies were sewn; and those who would strip by some forgotten water-tap and wash themselves and put on clean things—but only if provided them, having no longer in many cases the ability to procure either soap or singlets for themselves. She also knew who could be coaxed another foot or two up the path to self-respect by the tempting bait of mirror and comb, the subtle appeal such things made to the ravaged remnants of pride. And she knew when even a handful of toffee or a small picture of the charismatic King and Queen could brighten a dim corner or an eroded mind.

And often (though not always) with her on this humble and saintly mission went her faithful secretary-companion, Miss Mothermer, though by herself Miss Mothermer would have died a thousand dreadful deaths in such places; and sometimes Dame Phillipa was accompanied by her unhappy and unfortunate cousin, Lord FitzMorris Banstock, though usually he shunned the company of any but his few, familiar servants.

On this particular night, Mawhinney, his chauffeur-footman, had been obliged by a Guy Fawkes bonfire and its attendant crowd to drive the heavily curtained Rolls motor-car by a different and less familiar route; hence he arrived later at the usual place of rendezvous:

Miss Mothermer and Dame Phillipa, tall figure and tiny one, picture-hat and toque, had come by and, as was the unspoken understanding, had not tarried. So many considerations affected the presence or absence of Lord FitzMorris Banstock: was he engaged in a conversation particularly interesting by means of his amateur wireless radio equipment, was he in more pain than a certain degree, was he in less pain than a certain degree, was the moon too bright—for one or more of these reasons the star-curs't noble lord might not come despite his having said he might.

The obedient Mawhinney did not turn his head as his master slowly and awkwardly crept from the vehicle, inch by inch over the black silk upholstery. Nor, well-trained, did he suggest leaving the car in a garage and coming with his master. He waited a few moments after the door closed, then he drove straightaway back to Banstock House, where he stayed for precisely three hours, turning the Tarot cards over and over again with old Gules, the butler, and Mrs. Ox, the cook. On this Fifth of November night they observed that the Priestess, the Fool, and the Hanged Man turned up with more than their common frequency; and were much exercised to conjecture what, if anything, this might portend: and for whom.

And at the conclusion of three hours he put on his cap and coat and drove back to the place set.

Besides those nameless (and all but formless) figures from the silent world, of whom I had spoken above, there were others who awaited and welcomed Dame Phillipa's presence; and among them were women with names like Flossie and Jewel and Our Rose, Clarabel and Princess Mick and Jenny the Hen, Two-Bob Betty and Opaline and Queeny-Kate. She spoke to every one of them, gave them (if they required it, or thought they might: or if Dame Phillipa thought they might) the money needed to make up the sum demanded by their "friends" or "protectors"; money for rent or food or what it might be, if they had passed the stage where their earnings could possibly be enough to concern the swine who had earlier lived on them. She tended to their cuts and bruises the poor wretches received in the way of business, and which they were too ashamed to bring before the very proper nurses and the young, lightheartedly cruel, interns.

Sometimes she interceded for them with the police, and sometimes she summoned the police to their assistance; her manner of doing this was to direct Miss Mothermer to blow upon the police whistle she wore upon a lanyard, Dame Phillipa not liking the vibration this made upon her own lips.

Those to whom Dame Phillipa may have seemed but a tall, gaunt eccentric woman, given to wearing old-fashioned dresses, and hats which ill became her, would do well to recollect that she was among the very first to be honored with the title of *dame;* and that His Majesty's Government did not take this step exclusively in recognition of her career prior to her retirement as an educationist, or of her work, through entirely legal methods, on behalf of the Women's Suffrage Movement.

It was close to midnight when the two ladies arrived in Primrose Alley and Dame Phillipa rapped lightly with her walking-stick upon the window of a woman in whose maternity she had interested herself: actually persuading the young woman, who was not over-bright, to accept medical attention, eat something resembling proper food, and have the child christened in the nearby and unfortunately ill-attended Church of St. Gustave Widdershins. She rapped a second time—loud enough (she hoped) to wake the mother, but not loud enough to wake the child. As it happened it was the father she woke, a young man who circulated among three or four women in a sort of tandem polygamy; and who informed the lady that the baby had been sent to its mother's people in Westham, and who begged her, not altogether disdainfully, for sweet Christ's sake to bugger off and let him get back to sleep again.

Dame Phillipa left him to his feculent slumbers in absolute but resigned certainty that this time next year she would again be called upon to swaddle, victual, and renounce by proxy the World, the Flesh, and the Devil, on behalf of another squalling token of his vigour—unless the young woman should perhaps miscarry, as she had done twice before, or carry out her own suggestion of dropping the child in the river, by accident, like.

It was as she turned from the window, then, that Dame Phillipa first clearly observed the man wearing the false nose—as she thought, because of the Guy Fawkes festivities; though it appears Miss Mothermer instantly suspected that he did so by way of disguise—although she had been aware, without giving consideration to the matter, that there had been footsteps behind her. All inquiries as to this man's identity or motive have failed, but the singularity of his appearance is such that, unless he has been secretly conveyed out of the Kingdom, he cannot long continue to evade the vigilance of the police.

Thinking nothing further of the matter, as we may assume, Dame Phillipa and her companion continued their way into Argyll Court. The sound of voices, and the odor of hot gin and lemon, both proceeding from a bow window greatly resembling in carving and overhang the forecastle of an ancient sailing-ship, directed her attention to the gasjet which burned redly in the close air, illuminating the sign of the seaman's lodging-house. In times gone by, Evan-bach Llewellyn had been a notorious crimp. Board regulations, closely attended to, had almost put a stop to this, as far as vessels of British register were concerned. It was widely said, however, and widely believed, that the masters of foreign vessels putting into London with cargoes of coffee, copra, palm oil, fuel oil, hardwood and pulpwood; and finding members of their crew swallowed up by The Smoke, often appealed to the giant Silurian (he sang bass in the choir of Capel Cymrig) for replacements: and did not appeal in vain. Protests entered by surprised seamen, whose heads cleared of chloral in the Bay of Biscay, when they found themselves on board of strange vessels whose language they often did not recognize, let alone speak, would in the general course of things prove quite bootless.

As Dame Phillipa's attention was distracted to the window, two men, who must have been huddled silently at the other side of the court, came suddenly towards the two ladies, reeling and cursing, striking fiercely at one another, and giving off the fumes of that poisonous mixture of methylated spirits and cheap port wine commonly called *red biddy*. The ladies took a few steps in confusion, not knowing precisely what course to take, nor having much time to consider it: they could not go forward, because of the two men fighting, and it seemed that when they attempted to walk to the side, the bruisers were there, cutting off their way, too.

Dame Phillipa therefore turned quickly, leading Miss Mothermer in the same direction, but stopped short, as, out of Primrose Alley, whence they had just issued, darted the man who had been wearing the false nose. He made a curious sound as he did so; if he spoke words is not certain; what *is* certain is that he had plucked the false pasteboard from his face—it was hideously pockmarked—and that the flesh underneath was a mere convoluted hollow, like some gross navel, but nothing like a human nose.

Miss Mothermer gave a stifled cry, and drew back, but Dame Phillipa, though certainly no less startled, placed a reassuring hand on her companion's arm, and courteously awaited what this unfortunate might have to say or to ask. He beckoned, he gestured, he mewled and gibbered. Murmuring to Miss Mothermer that he evidently stood in need of some assistance, and that they were bound to endeavour to find what it was, Dame Phillipa stepped forward to follow him. For an instant only Miss Mothermer hesitated—but the two larrikins menaced from behind, and she was too fearful for herself and for Dame Phillipa to allow her to go on alone; perforce she followed. She followed into a door which stood open as if waiting.

If her testimony (and if one may give so succinct a name to confused and diffused ramblings noted down by Doctor Hardesty over a period of several months) may be relied on, the door lay but a few paces into Primrose Alley. The facts, however, are that no such door exists. The upper part of the Alley contains the tenements officially designated as Gubbinses' Buildings and called, commonly, "the Jakes": entrance is through a covered archway twenty feet long which divides into two shallow flights of steps from each of which a hallway leads to the individual apartments. It was in one of these, the window and not the door of which faced the Alley, that the young parents of Dame Phillipa Garreck's godchild were lodging. The lower part of the Alley on the same side is occupied by the blind bulk of the back of the old flour warehouse. The opposite side is lined with the infamous Archways, wherein there are no doors at all. There are, it is true, two doors of sorts in the warehouse itself, but one is bricked up and the other is both rusted shut and locked from the inside. A search of the premises *via* the main gate failed to show any signs that it had been opened in recent years—or, indeed, that it could have been.

It was at shortly after one o'clock on the morning of the sixth of November that Lord FitzMorris Banstock, toiling painfully through Thirza Street in the direction of Devenport Passage, received (or perhaps I should say, became aware of) an impression that he should retrace his steps and then head north. There is no need to suggest telepathy and certainly none to mention the supranormal in conjunction with this impression: Miss Mothermer was most probably blowing the police-whistle, blowing it with lips which trembled in terror, and so weak and feeble was the sound produced that no police constable had heard it. On the conscious level of his mind Lord FitzMorris did not hear it, either. But there are sensual perceptions of which the normal senses are not aware, and it was these, which there can be no doubt that he (perhaps in compensation, perhaps sharpened by suffering; perhaps both) possesses to an unusual degree, which heard the sound and translated it. He obeyed the impulse, walking as fast as he could, and as he walked he was aware of the usual noises and movements in the darkness—rustlings and shufflings and whispers, breathings and mutterings—which betokened the presence of various of Dame Phillipa Garreck's charges. It seemed to him that they were of a different frequency, as he put it to himself, accustomed to think in wireless radio terms, this night. That they were uncommonly uneasy. It seemed to him that he could sense their terror.

And as he turned the corner into Salem Yard he saw something glitter, he saw something flash, and he knew in that instant that it was the famous Negrohead opal, which he had seen that one time before when his lady cousin occasioned the assistance of the Metropolitan Police to rescue the girl Bessie Lovejoy, then in process of being purchased for the ill-famed Khowadja of Al-Khebur by the ineffably evil Motilal Smith.

It glittered and flashed in the cold and the darkness, and then it was gone.

Fenugreek Close is long and narrow and ill-lit, its western and longest extremity (where the Lascar, Bin-Ali, perished with the cold on the night of St. Sylvester) being a *cul-de-sac* inhabited—when it is inhabited at all—by Oriental seamen who club together and rent the premises whilst they await a ship. But there were none such that night. It was there, pressed against the blank and filthy wall, pressing feebly as if her wren-like little body might obtain entry and safety and sanctuary, sobbing in almost incoherent terror, that Lord FitzMorris Banstock found the crouching form of Miss Mothermer. The police-whistle was subsequently discovered by the infamous Archways, and Miss Mothermer has insisted that, although she would have sounded it, she did not, for (she says) she could not find it; although she remembers Dame Phillipa pressing it into her hand. On this point she is quite vehement, yet one is no more apt to credit it than her statement about the open door towards which they were led by the man without a nose: for if Miss Mothermer did not blow upon the whistle, who did?

The noble and misfortunate lord did not waste breath inquiring of his cousin's companion if she were all right, it being patent that she was not. He demanded, instead, what had become of Dame Phillipa; and upon hearing the name Miss Mothermer became first quite hysterical and then unconscious. Lord FitzMorris lifted her up and carried her to the place of rendezvous where, exactly on time, Mawhinney, his chauffeur-footman, had just arrived with the Rolls motor-car. They drove immediately to Banstock House where she was given brandy and put to bed by Mrs. Ox, the cook, whilst Lord FitzMorris summoned the police.

An alarum had already been given, or, at any rate, an alarum of sorts. One of the wretchedly miserable folk to whose succor Dame

Phillipa devoted so much of her time, having somehow learned that she was in danger, had informed Police-Sergeant L. Robinson to this effect. This man's name is not known. He is, or at any event was, called by the curious nickname of "Tea and Two Slices," these being the only words which he was usually heard to utter, and then only in a sort of whisper when ordering the only items he was known to buy. His age, background, residence, and present whereabouts are equally unknown. He had apparently an absolute horror of well-lighted and much-frequented places and an utter terror of policemen, one cannot tell why, and it may be hard to imagine what agonies and efforts it must have cost him to make his way to the police-station and inform Sergeant Robinson that he must go at once and "help the lady." Unfortunately and for unknown reasons, he chose to make his way to the police-station in Whitechapel instead of to the nearer one in Shadewell. His testimony would be of the utmost importance, but it cannot now be obtained, for, after giving the alarum, he scurried forth into the night again and has not been seen since.

The matter is otherwise with the testimony of the seaman, Greenbriar. It is available, it is copious, it fits in with that of Miss Mothermer, it is unfortunate that it is quite unbelievable. Unbelievable, that is, unless one is willing to cast aside every conceivable limit of credulity and to accept that on the night of Guy Fawkes Day in that year of our sovereign lord King George V the great and ancient city of London was the scene of a visitation more horrible than any in its previous history.

Albert Edward Greenbriar, Able-Bodied Seaman, is thirty-one years of age, and except for two occasions on which he was fined, respectively, £2 and £210s., for being drunk and disorderly, he has never been in any trouble with the authorities. On the first of November he landed at St. Katherine Docks aboard the merchant vessel *Salem Tower*, from the Straits Settlements with a cargo of rubber, copra, and tinned pine-apples. Neither the *Salem Tower* nor Greenbriar had been in the United Kingdom for the space of eleven months, and, consequently, when paid off, he was in possession of a considerable sum of money. In the course of one week he had, with the assistance of several women who are probably prostitutes, dissipated the entire sum. On discovering this the women, who share a communal flat in Poplar, asked him to leave.

It was Greenbriar's intention to obtain another ship, but in this endeavour he was unsuccessful. He managed to obtain a loan of half-a-crown from a casual acquaintance and spent the night at a bed-and-breakfast place in Ropemakers Fields, Limehouse. The following evening, footsore and hungry and, save for a single sixpence, penniless, he found himself in the Commercial Road, where he entered a cookshop whose signboard announced that good tea, bread, smelts and chips, were obtainable for that sum. Obtainable they were, good they were not, but he was in no position to object. Having finished, he inquired the way to the convenience, and there retired. On emerging he observed that he was next to the back door which opened onto Argyll Court, although he did not know that was its name, and on looking out he espied a sign.

The sign is still there; in white calligraphy of a fine Spencerian sort upon a black background it reads, *Seamen's Lodging House/Good Beds/E. Llewellyn, Prop.*

Albert Edward Greenbriar entered, rang the bell for the governor, and, upon the instant, saw a panel open in the wall, through which a face looked at him. It was the face of a gigantic cherub, white and dimpled and bland, surmounted by a pall of curly hair; in short, it was the face of Evan-bach Llewellyn. Greenbriar in a few words stated his situation and offered to give over his seaman's papers as a surety until such time as he might obtain a ship, in return for bed and board. The governor thrust forth a huge, pale hand, took the documents, slid shut the panel, and presently appeared to beckon Greenbriar down a corridor, at the end of which was a dimly lit dormitory. He gave him a thin blanket which was all in all not quite so filthy as it might have been, informed him that gaming and novel-reading were not permitted on the premises, invited him to take any bed he chose, and forthwith withdrew.

Greenbriar found an empty pallet, under the head of which he
placed his shoes, not so much as a pillow as a precaution, drew the
cover about him and fell instantly asleep. He was awakened several
times by the entry of other men, some of whom appeared to have
been flung rather than escorted into the room, and once he was
awakened by the sound of the proprietor playing upon a small patent
organ a hymn of his own composition on the subject of the Priest-
hood of Melchisedec. Greenbriar gazed at the tiny blue tip of the
night-light as it burned tremulously in the twisted jet and on the
odd and grotesque shadows cast upon the stained and damp-streaked
walls by the tossings and turnings of the lodgers, and listened to the
no less odd nor grotesque noises made by them. It was only by the
start he gave upon being awakened that he realized that he had gone
to sleep again.

Who awakened him he did not know, but, although the light
was no brighter, there was a stir in the dormitory and men were
getting to their feet and he heard the word "scoff" repeated several
times. He dashed water on his face and moved with the others into
what was evidently the main kitchen of the establishment. To his
surprise he observed that the clock there read eleven o'clock. It was
too dark to be morning. Evidently he had slept only a few hours or
he had slept round the clock and a bit more. It seemed an odd hour
for victuals but he was beginning to conceive the idea that this was
an odd place.

Broiled bloaters, fried sausage, potatoes, cabbage and sprouts
were being turned out of pots and pans and dumped higgledy-
piggledy onto cracked and not over-clean plates; and tea was steam-
ing in coarse crockery cups. No one ventured to eat or drink,
however, until Evan-bach Llewellyn had pronounced a grace in the
Cymric tongue and immediately after the Amen imparted a piece of
information, videlicet that he had a ship for them. It was a good
ship, too, he said; they would all be very pleased with it; it was not
one of their dirty old English tubs but a fine modern vessel: he urged
them all to eat hearty of the scoff, or victuals, so that no time need
be lost in getting aboard, and he then produced a large bottle of gin

and proceeded to pour a generous portion into each cup, with many assurances that it was free and would come out of his own commission.

No sooner had he given the signal, with a wave of his pale and dimpled paw, than the men fell to like so many ravening wolves, cramming the hot food into their mouths and gulping down the gin and lemon tea. Greenbriar concedes that the ailment was savory, and, finding himself hungrier than he had thought, took but a hasty swallow of the drink before addressing himself at length to the solids. A furtive movement at his elbow caused him to cease, abruptly. The man to his right, a hulking fellow with red hair and an exceedingly dirty face, was emptying a mug and looking at him out of the corner of his eye. It took but a second to ascertain that the wretched fellow had all but drained his own supply and then switched cups and was now doing away with Greenbriar's, who contented himself with stealing a link of the man's sausage whilst the latter was elaborately gazing elsewhere. Steeling himself to meet this man's resentment, he was dumbfounded to observe the fellow fall upon his face into the mashed potatoes and sprouts on his plate.

Within a matter of seconds, almost as if it were one of the contagious seizures which takes hold at times of the unfortunate patients of an institution for the epileptic—within a matter of seconds, then, all the others at the table sank down into unconsciousness, and Greenbriar, following suit, knew no more.

He awoke to a scene of more than Gothick horror.

He lay with his head against the silent form of another man, another one he could feel the weight of on his legs, and others lay like dead men all about. They were not dead, he knew, for he could hear them breathing. The room where they lay was walled and floored and roofed in stone and at regular intervals were carvings in *bas*-relief of a strange and totally unfamiliar sort. Paraffin lamps were set into niches here and there. There was a humming noise whose origin was not visible to him. Very slowly, so as not to attract attention (for he could hear voices), Greenbriar turned his head. As he did so he felt that there was a rope tied round his neck, and a sudden and quite involuntary convulsive movement which he gave upon this discovery disclosed to him that his hands were similarly bound. Thus urged on to even greater caution, the man took quite a long time in shifting his position so as to obtain some intelligence of his surroundings. If what he had seen before was strange and uneasy enough, what he saw now was sufficient to deprive him for the moment of the use of his limbs altogether.

Off to one side, bound and linked arms to arms and necks to necks like a prostrate caffle of slaves, and to all appearance also unconscious, were the bodies of a number of women; how many, he could not say, but evidently less than the number of the men. This, however, and however shocking even to the sensibilities of a seafarer, this was nothing—

Directly in front of his gaze, which was at an angle, and seated upon a sort of altar, was a figure as it were out of eastern clime: red-bronze in color, hideous of visage, and with six arms. Bowing low before it was a man, who addressed it in placatory tones and with many fawning gestures.

No other thought occurred to the British sailor at that moment but that he was in some sort of clandestine Hindoo temple and that he and all his other companions would presently be sacrificed before this idol; not being aware that such is not the nature of character of the Hindoo religion which contains, despite numerous errors and not a few gross importunities, many sublime and lofty thoughts. But be that as it may; the red-bronze-colored figure proceeded to move its limbs, the torso stirred, the entire body leaned forward. The figure spoke, and as it spoke, it seized the man with four of its limbs and struck him with the other two. Then it dropped him. As he scrambled to his feet his face was turned so that the sailor could see it, and he saw that it had no nose.

Greenbriar must once again have passed into unconsciousness. When again he awoke the altar was empty, and he could not see the "idol," but he could hear its voice. It was speaking in anger, and as one used to command. Another voice began when this one (deep, hollow, dreadful) had ceased; the new voice was a thin one, and it took a moment for him to realize that, despite its curious snuffling quality, it was speaking a sort of English. Two other voices replied to it, also in English; one was that of Evan-bach Llewellyn, the other one he did not know. By his description of both speech and speaker, for in a moment the latter moved into view, it is apparent that this was no other than the inhuman and unconscionable Eurasian, Motilal Smith.

Something, it seemed, was "not enough." There was an insufficiency of . . . something. This it was which occasioned the wrath of the person or creature with the six arms. And he was also in great concern because of a shortage of time. All four—the creature with six arms, the man without a nose, Smith and Llewellyn—kept moving about. Presently there was the scrape of wood and then a thud and then the wet and dirty odor of the River. The thought occurred to Greenbriar that they might be thrown into the Thames, which was then at high tide; he reflected that (in common with a great many seamen) he had never learned to swim; and then, for a third time, he fainted.

When he awoke he could hear someone singing the Doxology, and he thought—so he says—that he had died and was now in Heaven. One glance as he opened his eyes was enough to undeceive him. He lay where he had before and everything was as it was before, save that there were two people present who he is certain were not there before, and by his description of them they were clearly Dame Phillipa Garreck and her secretary-companion, Miss Mothermer.

Miss Mothermer was crouched down with her hands over her eyes, whether in prayer or terror or not inconceivably both, he could not say. Dame Phillipa, however, was otherwise engaged, for she moved from insensate figure to insensate figure and the light gleamed upon the scissors with which she was severing their bonds. She spoke to each, shook them, but was able to elicit no response. At this, Greenbriar regained his voice and entreated her help. She proceeded to cut the ropes which bound him, and left off her singing of the Doxology to enquire of him if he had any knowledge as to why they were all of them being detained, and what was intended to be done with them. He was assuring her that he did not know, when a door opened and Miss Mothermer began to scream.

That a fight ensued is certain. Greenbriar was badly cut about and Miss Mothermer received bruises which were a long time in vanishing, though in this I refer only to bruises of the flesh; those of the spirit are still, alas, with her. But he can provide us with few details of the conflict. Certain, it is, that he escaped; equally certain, so did Miss Mothermer. Dame Phillipa plainly did not. Greenbriar was discovered at about half-past one of the morning wandering in a daze in the vicinity of the Mile End Road by a very conscientious alien named Grebowski or Grebowsky, who summoned medical attention and the police. Little or no attention would or could have been paid to Greenbriar's account, had it not been for his description of the two ladies. His relation, dovetailing as it did with that of Miss Mothermer, left the police no choice but to cause a search to be made of the area of Argyll Court, in one corner of which a false nose was found.

Acting on the information received and under authority of a warrant, Superintendent Sneath, together with a police-sergeant and a number of constables, entered Llewellyn's premises, which they found completely deserted. Soundings of the walls and floors indicated the presence of passageways and rooms which could have had no place in a properly-conducted establishment licensed under the Common Lodging-houses Act, and these were broken into. A cap belonging to Greenbriar was found in one of these corridors, as was part of the lanyard of Dame Phillipa's police-whistle. There was a perfect maze or rabbit-warren of them, and, on the lowest level, there was discovered that chamber, the existence of which was previously publicly unknown, and which Professor Singleton of the University of London has pronounced to be a genuine Mithrarium of the reign of Marcus Aurelius, or perhaps, Nerva; and which was used by the unscrupulous Llewellyn for the illicit portion of his professional activity. It would have been here that the captives were assembled, if

Greenbriar's account is to be believed. What is, as a first premise, obvious, is that it cannot possibly be believed.

That Lord FitzMorris Banstock has chosen to believe it is, I am constrained to say, a greater testimony to the powers of his imagination than to any inherently credible elements in the story. The man Greenbriar now forms part of the staff of Banstock House; this is entirely the affair of Lord FitzMorris himself, and requires no comment on my own part, nor shall it obtain any. It may, however, be just as well to include some opinions and observations which are the fruits of Lord FitzMorris's very understandingly deep concern in this tragic and intensely puzzling affair.

He has collected a number of reports of some sort of aquatic disturbance moving downstream from London River early in the morning of the sixth November just about the time of the turning of the tide. To this he compares a report of the Astronomer Royal's concerning an arc of light which appeared off the Nore immediately subsequent. These have led him to the opinion that a craft of unknown origin and nature moved underwater from London to the sea and then rose not only above the surface of the water but into the air itself. This craft or vessel was captained by the creature with the six arms, and the man without a nose would have been an inferior officer aboard of her. Somehow this vessel became short of personnel and applied to Evan-bach Llewellyn to make up the shortage by crimping or shanghaiing the requisite Number. For reasons which cannot be known and concerning which I, for one, would rather not speculate, several women were also required (Lord FitzMorris is of the opinion that they were required only for such duties as members of their sex commonly fulfill in the mercantile navies of various foreign nations, such as service in the steward's branch). This being out of Llewellyn's line of business, an appeal was made by him to the notorious and wicked Eurasian, Motilal Smith, who is known to have left his headquarters in the semi-detached villa in Maida Vale on the Fifth of November, whither he never returned.

Lord FitzMorris suggests two possible provenances for this curious and hypothetical vessel. Suppose, he suggests, the being with the six arms to have been the original of the many East Indian and Buddhist myths depicting such creatures. It is likely, then, that the ship or submarine-aëroplane emanated from the vast and unexplored regions in the mountains which ring round the northern plateau of Thibet, the inhabitants of which have for centuries been rumoured to possess knowledge far surpassing ours, and which they jealously guard from the mundane world. The other possibility is even less likely, and is reminiscent, I fear, far more of the romances associated with the pen of Mr. Herbert G. Wells, a journalist of radical tendencies, than with proper scientific attitudes. Do not the discoveries of Professor Schiaparelli, establishing that there are canals upon the planet Mars, demonstrate that the inhabitants thereof must be given to agricultural pursuits? In which case, how unlikely that they should engage themselves in filibustering or black birding expeditions to, of all conceivable places, the civilized capital city of the British Empire!

Lord FitzMorris thinks that this theoretical craft of his must have carried off the unscrupulous Evan-bach Llewellyn in order to make up the tally of captives; how much more likely it is that this wicked man has merely fled to escape detection, prosecution, and punishment—perhaps to the mountains of wild Wales, where the King's writ runs scarcely more than it does in the mountains of Thibet.

Concerning the present whereabouts of Motilal Smith, we are on firmer ground. That he intended to devise harm to Dame Phillipa, who had on far more than one occasion interfered with him in his nefarious traffickings, we need not doubt. The close search of Superintendent Sneath of the premises on and about Argyll Court, Primrose Alley, Fenugreek Close and Salem Yard uncovered a sodden mass of human clay lying part in and part out of a pool of muck far under the notorious Archways. It was the drowned body of Motilal Smith himself; both from the evidence of his own powerful physique and the presence of many footprints thereabouts, it is clear that a number of persons were required, and were found, to force him into that fatal submersion. The friends—silent though they are to the world, dumb by virtue of their affliction and suffering—the friends of Dame Phillipa Garreck, the so-called and by no means ill-named People of the Abyss, whom she so constantly and so assiduously attended upon, had avenged their one friend and sole protector. It must now, one fears, go ill with them. The body of this unspeakably evil man, as well as his entire and vast estate (except the famous Negrohead opal, which was never found), was at once claimed by his half-brother, Mr. Krishna Bannerjee. The body was removed to Benares, and there subjected to that incomplete process of combustion at the burning ghauts peculiar to the Hindoo persuasion; and has long since become the prey of the wandering crocodiles which scavenge perpetually up and down the sacred waters of the River Gunga.

As I commence my last words for the present on the subject of this entire tragic affair I must confess myself baffled. Inacceptable as Lord FitzMorris's theories are, there are really no others that I can offer in their place. All is uncertainty. All that is, save my conviction that Dame Phillipa's noble and humanitarian labors still continue, no matter under what strange stars and skies.

AFTERWORD TO "WHAT STRANGE STARS AND SKIES"

The theme of "Lady Bountiful" appealed to Avram. Despite his own poverty, he was always sympathetic to the outstretched hand of a beggar on the street. Among his papers after he passed on, we found a manuscript titled "Everybody Has Somebody in Heaven," which appears in the collection of Avram's Jewish fantasies by the same title. It's the tale of Tanta Sora Rifka, a saintly Jewish woman who distributes bagels to the poor. Clearly Tanta Sora and Dame Phillipa are related, gracious sisters of generosity wherever they may appear.

—*Grania Davis*

THE LINEAMENTS OF GRATIFIED DESIRE

The mountain air was clear and sweet, scented with wild herbs, and although the young man had come quite a distance, he was not at all tired. The cottage—it was really little more than a hut—was just as it had been described to him; clearly, many people in the district had had occasion to visit it. At one side a tiny spring poured over a lip of rock and crossed the path beneath a rough culvert. At the other side was a row of bee-hives. A goat and her kid grazed nearby, and a small black sow ate from a heap of acorns with a meditative air.

A man with white hair got up from the bench and held out his hand. "A guest," he said. "A stranger. No matter, guest, all the same. Everyone who passes by is my guest, and the toll I charge is, I make them drink with me." He laughed, his laugh was infectious, and the young man laughed, too, though his sallow, sullen face was not that of one who laughed often.

The hand he shook was hard and calloused. "I am called Old Steven," the peasant said. "It used to be Black Steven, but that was a long time ago, even my moustache is white, now—" he stroked its length, affectionately—"except for here, in the middle. I am always smoking tobacco. Smoking and drinking, who can live without them?"

He excused himself, returned almost at once with bottle, glasses, and cigarettes.

"I do not usually—" the young visitor began, with a frown which seemed familiar to his face.

"If you do not smoke, you do not smoke. But I allow only Moslems to refuse a drink, and they do not often do so. One drink, a mere formality."

They had one drink for formality, a second drink for friendship, and a third drink to show that they did not deny the Trinity.

Steven wiped his moustache between index finger and thumb of each hand, thrust in a cigarette, lit it, and smiled contentedly.

"A good thing, matches," he said. "When I was a boy we had to use tinderboxes—how the world does change. . . . You came for a charm."

The young man seemed relieved, now that the preliminaries of the visit were over. "I did," he said.

"Your name?"

"Gabriel."

Old Steven repeated it, nodding, blowing out smoke. "I am, of course, well-known for my charms," he said, complacently. "I refer to those I make, not those with which Providence endowed me— although, there was a time . . . Well, well. My hair was black in those days. I can make quite a number of charms, although some of them are not in demand any longer. I don't remember the last time I supplied one to keep a woman safe from Turks. Before you were born, I'm sure. But, on the other hand, charms to help barren women conceive are as much called for as ever."

Gabriel said, scowling, that he was not married.

"My charges are really quite reasonable, too. I can guarantee you perfect protection against ghosts, vampires, werewolves, and the evil spirits of the hills and forests—their cloven hoofs and blood-red nails—"

"I am not afraid of those. I have my crucifix." His hand went to the neck of his open shirt.

"Very well," said Old Steven, equitably. "I've nothing to say against that.

"I also," he said, "prepare an excellent charm for success in the hunt . . ."

"*Ah . . .*"

"And an equally excellent one for success in love."

"*Yes . . .*"

Old Steven nodded, benignly. "That's it, then, is it? The love-charm?"

Gabriel hesitated, scowled again.

"Which one means most to you? Or, putting it another way, at which are you best? Take the charm for the other."

The young man threw out his hands. "I am good at neither! And it is important to me that I must excel in one of them."

Steven lit another cigarette. "Why only one? Take both. The price—"

But Gabriel shook his head. "It's not the price." He looked out on the wide-spread scene, the deep and dark-green valleys with their forest of oak and beech and pine, the mountains blue with distance, the silvery river. "It's not the price," he repeated.

"As far as you can see on all sides," the old man said, quietly; "in fact, farther, my reputation is known. People have come to me from across the frontier. If it is not the price, take both." He saw Gabriel shake his head, but continued to speak. "The hunt. A day like today. You take your gun and go off in the woods with a few friends. The road is dusty, but in the woods, in the shade, it is cool. Your friends want to go to the right, but you, you have the charm, you know that the way to turn is *left*. They may protest, but you are so certain that they follow. Presently you see something out of the corner of your eye. The others have not noticed it at all, or perhaps assume it is a branch of that dead tree. But you know better, your eye is clear, you turn swiftly, your arm and hand are quick as never before, the bird flushes, you fire! There it is, at your feet—a fine woodcock. Eh?"

Gabriel nodded, eyes gleaming.

"Or it might be a red doe, or a roe-buck. A fine stag! You can hardly count the points! Everyone admires you. . . . Perhaps in the winter the peasants come to you. 'Master, a wolf. No one is such a hunter as you are. Come, save our flocks.' They have not even seen the beast when your shot brings it down. You wait while they fetch it. They drag the creature along, shouting your praise: 'Only one shot, and at that distance, too!' they cry, and kiss your hand. 'Brave one, hero,' they call you."

A dreamy smile played on Gabriel's face, and he slowly, slowly nodded.

Old Steven waited a few moments; as his visitor said no word, he went on. "Then there is love. What can compare to that? A man who does not enjoy the love of woman is only half alive—if even so much. No doubt there is a young woman on whom you have looked, often, with longing, but who never returns that look. She has long, long black hair. How it glistens, how it gleams! Her lips are soft and red, and sometimes she wets them with her red little tongue. Inside her bodice the young breasts grow, ripe and sweet as fruit. . . ."

The young man's eyes seemed glazed. He did not stop the slow nodding of his head.

"You return, the love-charm is in your pocket, against your heart, *here.* There is a dance, you join in, so does she. Presently you come face to face. She looks at you as if she has never seen you before. How wide her eyes grow! Her mouth opens. Her teeth are small and white. You smile at her and instantly she smiles back, then looks away, shyly . . . but only for an instant . . . and you dance to-gether. . . .

"Soon the stars come out, and the moon rises. The old women are drowsing, the old men are drunk. You take her hand in yours and the two of you slip away. The moment you stop, she throws her arms around you and puts her mouth up to be kissed. The night is warm, the grass is soft. The night is dark and deep, and love is sweet."

Gabriel made a sound between a sigh and a groan. Slowly, he

reached into his pocket, took out his purse, and began to slide its contents into his hand. "You have made up your mind?" the old man asked. "Which is it to be, then?" There was no answer. Something caught the old man's eye. "This one is a foreign coin," he said, touching it with his finger. "But never mind, I will take it—it is gold."

Gabriel's eyes fell to his hand. He picked up the coin, and an odd look came at once over his face. The dreamy, undecided expression vanished immediately. His eyelids became slits, his lips turned down in an ugly fashion, something like a sneer.

After a moment the old man said, "You have made up your mind?"

"Yes," Gabriel said. "I have made up my mind."

There was only an old woman before him at the ticket-window. He had crossed the river just a few minutes before. The contents of his small suitcase had not engaged the attention of the customs officials for long; and from there it was only a short walk to the railroad station.

The old woman went away, and Gabriel stepped up to the window. On the wall of the tiny office, facing him, were two framed photographs, side by side. The likeness of the older man was the same one that had been on the coin which had caught Old Steven's attention; but Gabriel knew the younger man's face, too; knew it very well, indeed. Once again the odd, ugly, strangely determined expression crossed his face.

The station-agent looked up. "Yes, sir," he said, "where to?"

"One ticket, one way." Gabriel kept looking at the face in the photograph.

"Very well, sir, a one-way ticket—but, where to? Trieste, Vienna?" He was a self-important little man, his tone grew a trifle sarcastic. "Paris? Berlin? St. Petersburg?"

Slowly, Gabriel's eyes left the picture. He did not seem to have noticed the sarcasm.

"No," he said. "Just to Sarajevo."

AFTERWORD TO "THE LINEAMENTS OF GRATIFIED DESIRE"

With this story of a young man's visit to a hill-wizard, Davidson invokes the impending cataclysm of the First World War. The language of this story is plain, and the portrait of Gavrilo Princip is sympathetic and curiously innocent until the very end, when it becomes clear that one is in the presence of a fanatic.

In "The King's Shadow Has No Limits," the story opens with accounts of inter-ethnic squabbles in Scythia-Pannonia-Transbalkania, and follows Dr. Eszterhazy as he passes through the Empire's capital city and spies numerous emanations of the elderly King-Emperor. At the conclusion of this moving story, Davidson writes that Eszterhazy "heard, over and over again, in his mind, as though even now spoken next to his ear, the words which the aged Sovereign or else his very simulacrum or doppelganger had said. *'After me, this Empire will sink like Atlantis, and the children of these children will look for it upon the maps in vain . . .'* "

With the single word *Sarajevo* at the end of "The Lineaments of Gratified Desire," Davidson reminds us that it is not only a mythical empire that has vanished, but the entire old order of Europe, and that we too search for its traces in vain.

—Henry Wessells

THE ACCOUNT OF
MR. IRA
DAVIDSON

With some apologies to the readers, I must explain that this account, or Account, *is actually more the work of my younger brother, C. R. Davidson, who has insisted that my own name be attached hereto—"Because," he writes, with his usual modesty, "Because you have arranged it." This will be, then, the second time that experiences of the late Ira Davidson will have appeared in print, as some adventures of his when a boy formed the basis for another story, published in another magazine.*—A.D.*

Actual recollections of my Grandfather are, in my own mind, at least, few. My brother used to go to visit the grandparental home a few times a month, by trolley car; but I was deemed too young; and the visits were never returned: once my Grandfather had moved away from a neighborhood, he seldom cared to return. A typical memory might be of the time we met at the home of my Great-aunt Fannie (Mrs. Benjamin Webber). My Grandfather's greeting to me was, "Can you cipher to the Rule of Three?"

Grandmother: Now, Davidson, don't bother him with questions like that, he is only a little boy.

*"Grandpa and the Iroquois," *Colliers,* January 4, 1957.

Grandfather: What! I am not even supposed to speak to me own grandchild? (Strikes table with fist, stomps away, furious.)
Grandmother: Sshh, Davidson! Sshh!
Aunts: Now, Pa—
Uncles: Now, Pa—
Myself: (Exit, pursued by a bear.)

It was on another occasion that his temper, "uncertain at best," was displayed at its almost worst. Uncle Jacob—who was not really an uncle of ours at all, except as a courtesy title, being the brother of Great-uncle Benjamin—Uncle Jacob actually made a statement very sweeping in its inclusiveness, and one which (I now suspect) he had probably read in the New York *Sun,* to wit, that America was very fortunate because most of its great wealth was in the hands of men both moral and religious. My Grandfather at this seemed to go somewhat insane. His head snapped up, his mustache flew out, he pointed his finger at Uncle Jacob and in tones high and almost hysterical he cried out, each syllable separate, *"Ha! Ha! Ha!"* He was not laughing at all.

"Sshh, Davidson, *sshh!*"
"Now, Pa—"
"Now, *Pa*—"

My Grandfather was not a successful man; neither was he in the best sense of the word a philosophical one. His discovery of a means to keep scouring bars from crumbling came along just as America, almost overnight, converted to canned scouring powder. Many years he worked on developing auxiliary propellers for motor balloons; no sooner were they ready for testing than the motor balloon vanished from the heavens, and from history as well. I cannot tell you in details his system for bringing Grand Opera on a subscription basis into every American home via earphones hooked into the telephone; I *can* tell you that it was ready almost to the day that the radio vacuum tube came onto the market; and that after that, The Big Men, who until then had shown every interest, no longer answered my Grandfather's communications nor admitted him to their offices.

As for one or two, or three or four, other inventions and dis-coveries of his, he summed them up in the fell phrase (which I am sure spoke more of his natural disappointment than of the actual facts): "Stolen from me in the Patent Office!"

And, having said this, he would say one thing more, and he always said it, pointing to himself and crooking his head on one side. *"Condemned by the neck until dead . . ."*

The last time I heard and watched him say it was the last time I ever saw him, the one and only time I was ever in his own room. It was after my Grandmother's death. The room was small enough, but he had made space by taking out the bed and sleeping on the floor. Aunts and Uncles protested, but what could they do? Nothing. The quilt was neatly folded in a corner, books and magazines abounded, Grandfather sat in a straight-back chair at a roll-top desk, staring into an old notebook. A lodge fez, dusty, with missing span-gles, drooped out of a pigeon-hole. "They never forgave me," he said, gazing down.

("Mmm, Pa—")

But I was first: "Who didn't? Why didn't they?"

"Because of what I knew. Because of what I found out . . ." His head sank, his chin crept up towards his nose and his mustache flared out. His voice very low, he muttered, "But I would not do it. No, sir, never would I do it. That, I would, by God, never do . . ."

"Now, uh, *Pa*—"

Poor old head snapped back up, crooked itself to one side. *"Con-demned by the neck until dead."* Such as he was, he was his old self once again. To the end.

A few years ago I spent a couple of days with my Aunt Nettie. Halfway through the second day, and having realized that I was not really any more a little boy unable to cipher to the Rule of Three, Aunt Nettie began opening a few closed doors, metaphorically speak-ing. Now that my hair has begun to grey, I was told what Great-aunt Maude said to Uncle ——— in 1915, and Why (—— for instance ——). Also, how Cousin ——— chartered an airplane, or airplanes, and flew to Peru in 1930, and Why. The Real Reason why a certain Distant Relation obtained promotion in a certain Imperial Civil Service. And so then, for some reason, clued by something I cannot remember, I said, "Grandfather—"

And, as if reading what I myself could not read, namely my mind, Aunt Nettie said, "Yes, I was just about to," and got up and left the room. Returned with something I did not recognize until it was set on the table before me, and I opened it.

What it was, it was an antique loose-leaf notebook, bound in peeling but quite genuine leather. I opened it. Sure enough. The very same one which. "Wouldn't you like to have it?" she asked. "I'm sure that Pa would *like* you to have it." Aunt Nettie did sincerely mean to be kind, but I have seldom if ever heard any statement which I doubt as much as I do that one. Of course I did not say so, and I thanked her without falsehood, because, anyway, I myself liked to have it.

"Now," said Aunt Nettie, pleased. "Wasn't there something else? I think there is something else." She considered a moment. "There is a watch," she said. And added: "But I can't remember where it is."

Later, I called my brother.

"Hey, guess what *I've* got," I began the conversation—an admittedly childish locution. He answered:

"A certain muscle, formerly part of the Emperor Napoleon, for which £750 was asked at auction at Sotheby's, but failed of sale."

I laughed lightly, knowing his sense of humor. "No," I said. "I've got one of our Grandfather's old scientific experimental notebooks."

He said, "Goody"—rhyming it with "broody," as in, "A broody hen."

"At the top of the first page," I continued, "it says, PROPERTY OF MR. IRA DAVIDSON. CONFIDENTIAL AND SECRET. DO NOT STEAL.—"

"Death Shall Come On Swift Wings," my brother murmured.

Or perhaps "mutter" would be the correct word. Undaunted, I went on.

"Did you know that he was working on something called 'Crystal set photography,' " I asked.

"Jesus," he said. Adding, "No."

"I wonder whatever became of that?"

"Stolen in the Patent Office and then suppressed by *Them*. The family luck. How well do I know. Having inherited it. If nothing else. You must take after another side of the family." He paused a moment. "I forget which one," he said.

I chuckled. "Well, I'm going to see if I can figure it out."

"Listen, kid," my brother said, "let well enough alone. Confine your researches to interesting sidelights into the history of the provincial city of Garfield."

"Provincial it may very well be, but there are those of us who love it," I said, staunchly.

"Oh God."

Recognizing that he was under the spell of one of those moods of bitterness which sometimes mar an otherwise admirable character, I thought it best not to prolong the conversation. "Well, I just thought you'd like to know, and if I really find out any thing, I'll call you up—" I said.

"And therein fail not," were his parting words.

Probably the whole matter might be attributed to a desire on my Grandfather's part to entertain the tedium of his research by spinning a good yarn, so to speak. As for the pages and pages of diagrams, I once showed them to my close friend, Mr. Jeremy Knight, a computer expert.

"I couldn't make heads or tails of this," I said to him.

"Neither could anyone else," he commented, after scanning several of the pages—those with diagrams on them, I mean.

Besides these pages, which constitute by far the mass of notes, there were a number of others in my Grandfather's eager, rough calligraphy. Some of them are of a political nature, and have really no bearing on this account, or Account; but perhaps they may still be of some use in establishing even approximate dates for the Account, which is otherwise undated. For example, the lines,

"But Ira B.

Davidson, he

Says he *wun't*.

Vote fer Governor C.",

evidently refer to Calvin Coolidge, who had been the Governor of Massachusetts. A few other references to a "Governor S." almost certainly mean Alfred E. Smith, once Governor of New York. "Great Eng." must be Herbert Hoover, "the Great Engineer," (and a scholar of by no means slight attainments, as witness his translation from the late Latin of Georgius Agricola's *De Re Metallica*). And there can't be any doubt that "Pop. Ch. A." or "Sen. A." is Senator Magnus Abercrumbie, sometimes called "The old Champ" or "the People's Champion" or "The last of the Populists."

Purely for purposes of a smoother flow of narrative I am going to do what I never did or even thought of doing before in my life, and that is to call the protagonist of this Account by his first name. And I am not going to interrupt this same flow to distinguish what he saw, or what he *said* he saw, and put down in writing, from what he thought he saw and or pretended he had seen and illustrated with what are really very small and *very* rough little sketches—some in margins, some in between lines of text. I suppose that there must have been antecedent notes of the experiment. I do not suppose that Ira *began* his intense interest in and experiments with the notion of Crystal Set Photography already full-grown, but if there were other notes, they have not survived. I may wonder if even these ones would have done so, had they not been preserved in a binder of such obviously good quality.

So we don't know what Ira exactly had in mind when the Account begins. If we could make sense out of the diagrams—but we can't. What we know is that on a date, or day and *time* of day, not too helpfully set down as *Wed. afternoon*, a "wet plate" had cracked, and there were no replacements at hand. It was just then that, per-

haps glancing up and around in exasperation, he observed a conflu-
ence of moving blurs within his crystal. This struck him enough so
that he made almost the first of the sketches mentioned above. (The
very *first* actual sketch was of a cat, perhaps one belonging to the
family, and which anyway needn't concern us here.) Moving blurs
and moving *lines*. The general effect resembles some of the less picturesque of the cave paintings.

Intrigued at this unexpected and unexplained effect, Ira began to
reorganize, or, perhaps, organize, his equipment; and in this he was
somewhat successful, but whatever it was which he was seeing
seemed to be very far away. It occurred to him—and, I confess, it
would never have occurred to *me*—that if he could get hold of a
telescope or a set of binoculars—

He did. But evidently nothing more was to be seen. The notebooks continue with more diagrams, more diagrams, and more and
more diagrams. Then comes another dating. *Wednesday afternoon.*
He looked through his binoculars, and, for the first time, saw clearly.
A group of men were dressing, in a room somewhere; not, indeed,
from a state of complete nudity, but out of street clothes and into
more formal wear: frock coats or cutaways or something of the sort,
so much more common then than now. And, to his even greater
surprise, they began to put on something entirely unfamiliar, something which was attached with a sort of harness arrangement.

And then the scene vanished. That is, the entire scene vanished.

Fortunately, by this time Ira's children were all grown and married, although how he was able to support even himself and his wife,
whilst spending his days tinkering with such absurd conceptions as
"Crystal set photography," is itself a mystery. I suppose that he must
have had some savings and/or investments. That his mind was agitated by *some*thing, we may imagine from the brevity of the dia-
grammatic notes intervening between the above-noted, or second,
sighting, and the next reference: *Wednesday afternoon.*

This time, and after sundry adjustments and improvements to
his equipment, he saw, through what we as children still called "spy-
glasses," the group of men full-face-on. And he felt that they all

looked like high-school principals! I don't really know what sort of an image this may conjure up for others, but to me the picture is instant and vivid. The men are all spare; all wear thin-rimmed eyeglasses, have sandy to grey hair and mustaches; all of them have mustaches, the full yet neatly trimmed mustaches of a certain period in American history. Their hands are hard and bony, neither calloused nor soft, limp: hard! Their manner is crisp, curt. *"This won't do!"* they seem to say. Or, *"We can't do that!"* and, *"We can't allow that!"* *"You should have known that!"* *"We cannot make any exceptions!"* And, also, *"You have already been allowed extra time!"*

(In case it may seem that I am reading too much into a single phrase, I will have to admit, albeit a trifle sheepishly, that there is after all the evidence of the sketches—rough though they are.)

All this is familiar enough, I am sure. But what follows next certainly is not. The men now have on something vaguely resembling blacksmiths' leather aprons, reaching from just below the tiepin to just below the knee, and slashed in a very curious manner, and evidently decorated with very curious designs here and there.—This, you will recall, over their formal clothing!—And, what is more, and is more unusual: the men are evidently dancing!

Here we have eight or ten men, in early middle age and vigorous maturity, dressed (first) as though for an inauguration, let us say, and (secondly) as though for some sort of a fancy-dress ball—they are ranged in two ranks, and they are moving in their places, running in place, flinging their hands up in unison, flinging their legs up in unison—

Is this some sort of exercise? Something like the sitting-up exercises or the use of the "medicine ball," then so popular, both of them? If so, then why the curious combination of costume? In fact, why *either* element of the costume? Perhaps they were just having some fun? But the expression on their faces belies that, belies that entirely. Their faces are absolutely serious, their faces are in dead earnest. Not a ripple of either embarrassment or amusement stirs those stiff countenances by a hair. Slightly they lower their heads in unison, and each one lifts to each side of his head at the temples a hand with all fingers closed-in except the index finger, which points straight up; simultaneously they lift their feet so that the trousers move up and disclose the high-buttoned, highly polished shoes, lift their legs so that the knees are almost up to, *are* up to the line of the hips: they are prancing—there is no other word for it: they are prancing in place; then they toss their heads, keeping their hands in the same relative position and the same gesture—

Imagine, if you can, a chorus line. And now imagine that the same principle of movement in absolute unison applies, although of course an absolutely different sort of movement, and that instead of young women the line of dancers consists, as I have said, of mature men, the type which one would unhesitatingly describe as the leaders of their communities. They do not smile. They dance. They dance, they dance, they *dance*.

And, always as they dance, they gesture. They move their hands to a horizontal position and they pass their hands ever so swiftly across their throats. And now the pace of the dance becomes some-what swifter. The gestures become more and more bizarre . . . the gestures become almost shockingly so. . . .

Does the expression on the faces change? Not exactly. Yet there is a change—The angle of the faces changes slightly: *No!* It is the angle of their vision which changes. They are looking up, somewhat to the right (to their own left, that is) and above. They are looking up, yet, as it were, covertly. And now for the first time those secure and certain faces begin to show another emotion. Here and there sweat appears on the smooth-shaven line of a jaw. Here and there a mouth opens and does not close. The marks, one would say, of exertion? Of physical fatigue . . . nothing more? No. One would be wrong. One would be very wrong.

Now as they dance, their hands out, palms down, their heads bowed as in submission, still those eyes turn up, turn up as though seeking something which they fear to find. And here and there, watching closely, one observes a leg tremble, an arm jerk somewhat from its rigid position.

And Ira, watching, feels the glasses tremble in his own hands, and, although he cannot say why, he feels faint, he himself, not even present at this scene!—feels sickened.

He leaves. The glasses drop away, he lets them fall. He gets up and he stumbles away.

Well, what to *make* of it all? The likeliest explanation is that a too-close application to an impossible endeavor (I refer to the scientific experiment on which he had been working) resulted in loss of sleep, probably; in loss of appetite, probably; certainly to neglect of sound principles of health. With the result that he, Ira, probably—well, that is certainly too strong. One cannot say, *probably.* Let us say that it would not be at all surprising had he suffered from an acute form of eyestrain and that as the result of this he simply *saw things which were not there.* What is certain is that the experiment and the observations were not continued. They were certainly dropped for good. And yet, so strong was the impression left upon his mind that, as we have seen, almost at the last days of his life, he returned again to the perusal of the notes he had made of them.

One thing I suppose I should say in conclusion. My brother had made mention of my own personal hobby. (I can call it no more than that.) He refers to it, not very seriously, as my "researches into interesting sidelights on the history of the provincial city of Garfield." It is after all our native city, our own home town; if it is of no great interest to the professional historian, why need it escape the fond attentions of the amateur?

Ira had made one or two noted references (I mean only that he had noted them down) to "Sen. A.," and I have said I am certain that this refers to Senator Magnus Abercrumbie. I am afraid that Senator Abercrumbie has not yet found his true niche in our country's history. He died a disappointed man, certainly. He had perhaps lived into another era, one which was not suited to his hopes. His programs for what he called "The American People's Charter" were certainly not nationally popular in that period of firm faith in an expanding economy free of all governmental trammels. It is doubtful that, even had he lived, he would have succeeded in getting more than a fraction of his Charter into actual legislation. He had made many enemies. Still, who can really say? He was incorruptible. He was convinced. He was eloquent. We cannot forget the shock of his as-yet-unexplained death—in itself and by its manner so doubly shocking to the agricultural and working classes at the time. Nor should we forget the ripples of unease which spread throughout moral and religious circles later in that same year when it was learned that quite a number of our most prominent citizens, under the guise of acting on behalf of the Securities Registration Committee of the Fiduciary Trust Company, were actually meeting to worship the Devil, in a room hired for that purpose in the Garfield Building, between three and four in the afternoon on alternate Wednesdays (July and August excepted).

AFTERWORD TO "THE ACCOUNT OF MR. IRA DAVIDSON"

This tale is a curiosity . . . curiouser and curiouser. Where does the real-world autobiography end and the fantasy begin, or does it? Certainly the family names are real, at least some of them. The Davidson family temper, the family "luck," the family fascination with archaic oddities, all real. Computer expert Jeremy Knight is real; the Knights were dear family friends. But what is this mysterious dance, where does it come from?

—Grania Davis

TWENTY-THREE

Breakfast one day at the Sutters. Ellis looked up. "Say, do we have an Uncle Zachary?" he asked. Sound dies away, save for Samuel at an egg in its shell and Lewis clattering a coffee-spoon. Louise Sutter, their mother, slightly clears her throat. "Uncle Zachary had a weakness of the chest and his doctors thought he should go and live in the West where the air is dry. Samuel, don't fiddle. Lewis." If Ellis observes the difference between *Uncle Zachary has* and *Uncle Zachary had*. Ellis does not say so.

"Sidney Coolidge claims," is what Ellis next says.

"Sidney *Cool*idge!"—his sister Lucinda—"dirty-mouthed boy. Dirty-faced, too," she says.

Ellis emphatically agrees. "Dirty in lots of other places, too, say, you wouldn't believe—" His brother Lewis advises him to finish his fish-cake. His brother Samuel wants to know why they don't more often have bacon for breakfast, and Uncle Abel Sawyer, as though he had been waiting for the chance, says that bacon is *fourteen cents a pound!* Farmers never had it so good, Uncle Sawyer says. Aunt Effie (Sutter) Sawyer, pouring skim milk over something arid called Breakfast Food, declares, "The less pig, the more pie." Aunt Harriet Sutter looks at her nephews with perhaps something like foreboding. Perhaps not. What she says is not overheard. Aunt Sarah Sutter is

looking at her plate. And the discussion as to what Aunt Effie Sawyer's saying means causes Uncle Zachary and Sidney Coolidge to be
forgotten.

Agnes brings in the pie. The real and not the proverbial one.
There is always pie. And always Agnes. Not always the same ones,
of course.

Aunt Sarah eats well enough. And, as usual, she is silent.

Aunt Sarah is usually in the same chair in the library and doesn't
talk much, but saying this is not to describe a woman in rusty black
with massive hands on ivory-headed walking-stick: no. Sarah is really
quite slender, has been becomingly grey-haired since memory runs,
wears something quite too chic to be called a pants-suit: and besides,
pants-suits are yet to be invented. It is called *Aunt Sarah's house-
costume* and she does not wear it out of doors. Usually the costume
is grey, sometimes it has a small black checked pattern. Sarah reads
a lot. There is no television in the world, the radio yet has earphones, and would it still had. If one asks, and few do, "What are
you reading, Sarah?" one is quietly and quickly told the name of the
author. Never the title. Once in a long while someone ventures to
ask, "What's it about?" Really, what is Emerson, for example, *about?*
A brief and level stare, and her eyes return to her book. Sarah does
not suffer fools gladly.

Once, at least, Aunt Sarah tries to revive the pleasant old-
fashioned custom of reading aloud to the family circle. Her choice
is Longfellow's lovely poem *The Aftermath.*

> *When the summer fields are mown,*
> *When the birds are fledged and flown,*
>   *And the dry leaves strew the path;*
>
> *With the falling of the snow,*
> *With the cawing of the crow,*
> *Once again the fields we mow*
>   *And gather in the aftermath.*

Not the sweet, new grass with flowers
Is this harvesting of ours;
   Not the upland clover bloom;

But the rowan mixed with weeds,
Tangled tufts from marsh and meads,
Where the poppy drops its seeds,
   In the silence and the gloom.

The very brief silence at the poem's end is not broken by a murmur of pleasure; but by an alto, a tenor, and a baritone, guffaw. A voice says, "How well he knows—!" Says? Sneers?

Directly after this short poem comes by far a longer, beginning, *Should you ask me, whence these stories?* Nobody asks her, nobody at all. Aunt Sarah quietly closes the book. And—publicly, at least—never opens it again. The custom is not revived.

She reads, too, things unpublished. Family histories, letters, journals, diaries: these things she reads downstairs in the library.

Aunt Sarah knows all about, for instance, the question of the twenty-two and a half acres of good meadow-land on which the good fortunes of the Sutter family (*of the County of Berne in the Switzers Land*) are founded. Well, the good fortunes of one part of the Sutter family. Some say that land is rightfully the property of another part of that family. It is more than twenty-two and a half acres, some say. A bit more, some say, a good bit more. Ill feelings are often caused in families by the division of property. Or by its non-division.

Upstairs or down Aunt Sarah plays solitaire, or sets out what is understood to be the Tarot.

Mostly she is silent. One tends to leave her alone.

Sutter sisters and daughters are quiet and almost plain: very well, then: *plain.* Sutter brothers and sons are something else, and although there are older Sutter women at home, there are no older Sutter men. Wars consume them, they go to far-off places and do not return and neither do they write. There are in these days only three young Sutter brothers at home, and then there are none. Of the older set, Gerald is generally understood to be somewhere very far off where he wears a burnoose or a turban and perhaps it is not true that a foreign ruler places a price upon his head. Kingston's name is on a cross in France in a place of many crosses row on row. Woodruff's name is not, although he, too, goes to France and never returns. Unless his mother's belief, seldom expressed aloud, is true. And that it *is* Woodruff Sutter who is buried in the Tomb of the Unknown Soldier.

And if the older brothers do leave some memories of unfortunate *incidents* at home, surely their heroic deeds abroad, one year apart, redeem them. And more. And more. *Valiant and courageous* (official). *Reckless and suicidal in bravery* (unofficial). *Come on, you sons of bitches, do you want to live forever?* . . . echoes . . . echoes . . . dying, dying, dying. . . .

The younger set of this generation of young men Sutters at home consists of Lewis, Ellis, and Samuel, boys of great charm and rascal beauty and of, one hears, increasingly devilish behavior. So the Headmaster of Afton says (this last phrase). For a while they are away at school or college; one by one (again and again) are expelled . . . run off . . . invited not to return from vacation . . . suspended . . . dismissed. . . . Uncle Sawyer, the non-Sutter who actually runs the business, thinks it is time they settle down and learn something about running it themselves. So one hears. Uncle Sawyer is perhaps an optimist.

They all live together in a large, an immense, wooden house overlooking a river with an American Indian name, the river which (with all its rights) is sometimes described as "a wholly-owned subsidiary of the Sutter family." Its waters are imponded by a series of dams and by each dam is a dirty brick building wherein wool from far and wide is washed . . . spun . . . woven . . . made into rugs and blankets said to wear like iron: these both perhaps more sought after formerly than presently.

The water, thus collected, washes and scours the wool and carries

away the effluents of everything from sheep-dung to caustic soda and
solute suint or wool-sweat and overwashes of stinking dyestuffs: it is
long since the alewife or the shad were found in these streams. The
Sutter Corporation collects the waters in its pens and ponds, releases
them at times and between times to turn its wheels and fill its vats
and, of later days, kindle its electricity. And if the river, restive,
overflows its pent-up backwaters, converting tillable fields or sites for
houses into sog and bog, nourishing on others' lands instead of hay
or potatoes the coarse and uncommercial cat-tail, the rank and prof-
itless goldenrod and purple milkweed, and the frail, pale wild white
rose which cannot be cut and sold: why, what is this to the Corporation? nothing and less than nothing; let the former freeholders,
if they will, take the Pauper's Oath and receive fifty cents a day
viaticum and forfeit their suffrage: *root, hog, or die* is a saying worthy
of the saints, and *pecunia non olet*, of the sages.

Cousin Chester Boswell lives in a small house the other side of the
Village green. This, and shares in the Sutter Corporation, constitute
the larger part of his patrimony. Well . . . anyway, a *large* part. And
a large part consists of an intense interest in local and familial history,
and he shares this with Aunt Sarah. They also share a cousin Waldo
Sutter who lives in an even smaller house by a smaller river which
has yet to know its place, unlike Waldo Sutter, who does not choose
to get around much. Very rarely does Someone ask, "What does
Waldo Sutter do?" and the answer is that *He* minds his own business.
A . . . well . . . not exactly a message and not exactly a present but
Something of Interest has come from him. As it has about once a
year. Bridey has come in bearing a large brown paper bag, made in
the days before paper bags were made by machinery. It is thick and
heavy. And it is old. She says, "Waldo Sutter sends John Kelly with
this to drop off if he's coming this way." And adds, "Waldo wants
the bag back. And could you let him have a little kerosene in a
bottle." The words and deeds are invariable. So is Aunt Sarah's nod
as she empties the contents into a shallow wicker basket and hands
over the bag. Bridey takes it and goes out.

Invariably, too, the bag (and now the basket) contains some old papers and an old book, which they all know the cousin (not a first cousin and not even a second) has had delivered at the back door. There is no other reason in the world why he would have been coming "this way," but John Kelly is Waldo Sutter's (only) tenant and no longer employable at the mill. Not for money or any other consideration would their conjoint cousin dispose of any books or papers to a historical society or a college library, a dealer, or collector; but month by month as they work their way out of the disintegrating boxes in his closely packed little house (it smells strongly of many things and the rare callers are perhaps grateful for the kerosene) he drops them in the old brown paper bag, its smell now too faint than to more than guess if it had once contained say fresh whole nutmegs or macouboy snuff or pigtail twist chewing tobacco. Candied ginger. Something for old man Waldo Sutter to smell now and then besides his rancid socks. And once a year he sends these fragments to the large house which he himself never enters by the back door *or* the front.

Bridey or Agnes or Katie is even now handing over the kerosene in a gallon-jug as per instructions . . . a *full* gallon jug. And giving Old Man Kelly a doughnut. Or a piece of johnnycake.

"Well, what have we here?" asks Chester Boswell. Lame, pensioned. Part of the patrimony. A patriot, Chester, even if *he* is not left for dead two days at Chickamauga; but merely breaks his leg in camp at Tampa before he can get to Cuba; Chester Boswell never hears the bugle-call at Kettle Hill, the bone has not healed well and there is always talk that it will have to be re-broken and re-set. When Chester Boswell comes to visit the large house—which is fairly often—he stays put for the whole day. "What have we *here?*" He adds, "This time."

Here, and Chester handles it ver-ry carefully, is a sadly broken old book, pages worn and foxed and stained with candle-grease (to Old Sutter, kerosene is a modern invention). He points the title out to his cousin Sarah. *Wonders of the Invisible World / by the Rev[d]* M[r]

Cotton Mather, they exchange glances, she turns some soiled leaves, indicates with a finger the marginal notations; they nod. Out of the book slips a piece of flowered wallpaper, evidently trimmed with a knife. "Waste not, want not," Chester Boswell says. "Use it up. Wear it out. Make it do. Or do without." Part of the wisdom of their fathers. On the back of the wallpaper something is written with a lead-pencil made in the days when lead-pencils had lead in them and not graphite. He and she bend their heads to read. *Kin deamons marry?* "That's Crossley's writing.—Crossley's kind of question, too." The next question leaps across a vast sea of supposition. *Is the divorc leagle?* Crossley's spelling is not meticulous. But it is clear. *How are thes leagal and ill liegal children told apart?* How indeed; like someone better-known, Crossley Sutter does not stop for an answer: in smaller letters writes *prepar yͤ* The feast. Beneath that begins a list

frsh Porke

Samp

"When is the last time *I* ate samp?" asks Chester Boswell. "Boy," he answers. "Makes a rougher mush than regular hominy grits. *Well.* Taste and scent? No argument. Eh? Sal?" Aunt Sarah's part of the conversation is made chiefly by little motions of her mouth and brows. Though now and then she gestures. Slightly. *Feast?* Slattern hog and half-cracked corn? Crossley Sutter, their great-grandfather's half-brother, has not been known as a delicate eater. Has not been *deli*cate. Lines from his will are long repeated by generations of children when adults are not present. *To my Bastard son Nathaneal five pounds. To my basterd Son Slatheal Five pounds. To my imprudent dauhgther Prudence born in christain wedlock but most UnGreatful slutt Three cents and a buckit of ashes.*

Still . . .

And what have they *here?* Prudence's long-missing will they have *here* and she has made many dispositions and someone's heavy hand has printed DIED INTESTATE, for her Will is not signed, impetuous death does not wait for that. Prudence is Waldo Sutter's grandmother. She has never married. Its presence here signifies that he has at last given up all hope of getting any of those bolts of cloth, that cherrywood furniture (is it anything like this cherrywood furniture), those cases of pewter plates, sets of best blue chinaware. *A little kerosene in a bottle.* Last time he sends sixteen Old Farmers Almanacs, 1810–1826, and a straight razor in a flaking case; the boys, amused, use it in turn.

Old John Kelly is his only tenant, a gallon of lamp oil will last Waldo a long while, and the jugs are worth a penny apiece in trade. Pork. Samp. Chickamauga does not kill Waldo Sutter. Neither do the floods drown him. Certainly not the Spring freshets. Even if the Sutter Company will not adjust its river-level to his comfort.

What else is *here?* An old pamphlet on growing pot-herbs, an old booklet on raising silkworms (the smell is soon got used to), and exactly twenty small empty envelopes from a Department of Agriculture once generous with new types of seeds. All very old. But no doubt useful. And here is a note in age-browned ink on a part of a page torn from, it might be, one of those small bound "pocketbooks" in which thrifty goodwives record sales of Best Brown Eggs in terms of shillings, for complete changeover to dollars and cents has to await the later 1850s; on it a short note:

> *Salatheal Sutter*
> *old and mauger*
> *torn a part by wolves*

And a note upon the note, in somewhat darker ink, the iron nib biting deep into the page NOT WOLVES

No more.

And also just such a tiny volume and Aunt Sarah at once finds the half-torn page to match the torn-out note; in a tiny hand is neatly written, *John Q. Adams dead today.*

No more.

But enough of ancient history. Lewis, Ellis, and Samuel Sutter. "Charm and rascal beauty"? Yes. Increasingly "devilish behavior"? Yes. As children they are as sprightly and nimble as goat-kids. There is, later, something fawn-like (*faun*-like?) about the young Sutter boys, indeed devilishly bad as their behavior is sometimes said to be, eh? *their childish presences disarm*, eh? At twenty a growing heaviness becomes apparent, not fat, nothing like that, something immensely strong seems coming; the early wildness is replaced by a more deliberate quality, quite beyond description. And now they get into fights, fights—reports go about of a brutality which is not to be explained—though sometimes it has to be explained away.

Does Helen Sutter have a palsy? Dr. Brainert says no. Then what is the reason for the frequent trembling? Dr. Brainert prescribes this and suggests that. But Helen Sutter Woodruff Sutter continues so often to tremble. Aunt Harriet proposes a trip south. South Carolina. Northern Florida. "I will go with you," Aunt Harriet offers. "And Effie."

"There isn't enough money," Aunt Sawyer (Effie) says at once.

"There is enough money for that," her niece Lucinda insists. Cinda's sister Amy has married, and moved away to Portland, Oregon, which is about as far as she can move away and still keep her feet dry.

"Since Abel died," says her aunt, she means Uncle Sawyer, "there hasn't been enough money for anything." And, it is true that things seem shabbier in the very big house. Katie has died, and Mary, grown old, is retired. Neither has been replaced. Often there is talk of "having the carpenters in," but so far they are not being had. "I *wish* that the boys would set aside the nonsense. I *wish* that the boys would *take hold.*"

Aunt Harriet leaves for a moment the subject of Aiken or Vero Beach. "It is The Prohibition," she says. "The Volstead Act. It doesn't prevent. It *encourages.*"

Helen says that she hoped It would skip another generation. "I know that people blame Henry and me for marrying although we are cousins. But it had skipped two generations. And I had hoped

It would skip this one, too." Tremble. Tremble. "If Kingston or Woodruff had lived. If Gerald . . ." Aunt Sarah's mouth moves. But she remains silent.

"Does no one hear from Gerald?" asks Chester Boswell.

A universal silence. *No* one hears from Gerald.

Aunt Harriet looks all around. Almost furtively. As though she knows she should not ask, she asks. "How much money was settled on the De Sousa family?"

Aunt Effie Sawyer is a lady, and ladies do not glare. Almost, though, she glares. "You know very well how much. One. Hundred. Thousand. *Dollars.* Taken out of capital." She does gasp, however, and she rolls up her eyes: tightens, but does not clench, her fists. "Out of *cap*ital."

Lucinda reminds them (yet again) of the condition of Harry De Sousa's body. Witnesses report how the red touring-car (is there another custom-painted red touring-car in all the world?) backs up and runs over Harry De Sousa again and again. "There are five small children," Lucinda says. "If there is ever a prosecution . . ." Her mother trembles, trembles. Perhaps she remembers other . . . *incidents.* . . . Before. *And* since.

And other settlements.

It is long since that a settlement can be made (thus leaving Zachary free to absquatulate for Teckshus. *Free? Zachary? free?*) by giving someone a ninety-nine year lease on an ice-house for ninety-nine dollars a year. And, anyway, there is only one ice-house, for

scarcely flows
the frozen Tanais
through a waste of snows

Talk, before that, of giving Waldo Sutter the lease? Talk.

Lucinda does not now remind them that she herself witnesses the near-death on North Main Street of the Universalist minister. She screams and screams, warnings to the Rev. Mr. Showalter, appeals to her brothers. Mr. Showalter, after stoically refusing to acknowledge danger in the red touring-car's furious approach, finally with a squeak of fear barely flings himself to safety; a contemporary—Dr. Nickolson the homeopath—extends shaking hands to hold the trembling cleric up; cries, "Don't tell *me* those boys don't have the witch-bump!" The Nickolsons have lived here almost as long as the Sutters: no love lost.

The red touring-car continues to tear along the street like a whirlwind, madcap yells, howls, and cries coming from the front seat: Lewis at the Wheel. Mr. Showalter has suffered such a shock that he must retire; will place charges: *duty!*—doesn't care about himself but cares about the public safety. Uncle Sawyer speaks soothingly and speaks and speaks and gives directions for a new roof to be put on the Meetinghouse. Mr. Showalter shakes his head. And on the Manse. Mr. Showalter slackens, but feels that someone must be taught a lesson. Uncle Sawyer mentions faith and hope. Uncle Sawyer settles a ten-year endowment on the Universalist pulpit's everfaltering income. Mr. Showalter takes a vacation in the White Mountains, returns to preach with renewed vigor the doctrines of James Relly and Hosea Ballou (" 'No Hell! No Hell! No Hell! No Hell!' rings out the Universalist bell!'")—But even Uncle Sawyer cannot keep this up forever. And, it turns out, neither can Lewis.

If Aunt Harriet pretends to believe that her nephews' troubles stem from drink alone, *let* her. Does no one point out that Samuel, for example, does not drink. He is certainly never seen in any of the local saloons, but he is certainly talked about in them. "Sam Sutter? Know what they say about what his motto is? 'Women and children *first*,' that's what they say his motto is." People laugh at this. But their laughs are not nice ones.

Does Samuel suffer from amnesia? Sometimes people make references to the recent past, and his expression is a blank . . . that is if there can be a troubled blank. Can there be?

One afternoon in the early spring the ladies of the family are in the music room listening to the victrola. All, that is, save for Aunt Sarah, who is, as usual, in her place in the library wearing her neat house-costume; as usual, silent. Chester Boswell is, as usual, talking . . . perhaps in a lower tone of voice, even, than usual. "Gone upstairs to wash my hands," he says. "Samuel's door. Open." Everyone knows how such things are. One has *no* intention of *look*ing. At all. But there is a slight movement and it catches one's attention, Chester's head turns automatically. Samuel is sitting at his desk, holding his head in his hands, motionless save for a slight fidget of the fingers in the hair, slight but incessant. Aunt Sarah looks up and at her cousin Chester when he says this, and he imitates for her this slight (but steady) motion, somehow restless, somehow steady, of Samuel's fingers as he holds his head in his hands.

"I don't like to see this," Chester Boswell murmurs. "That's how it all started with Lew . . ." That's how it *start*ed with Lew? And how does it end with Lew? For it does end. At the age of only twenty-three, Lewis takes up a heavy old Colt Navy revolver, once the property of Selah Sutter, Waldo's elder brother, and shoots himself. Fatally.

No note. As Samuel murmurs to Ellis at the service, "Not even a forwarding address."

Mother Sutter (Helen) "takes it better than we would have thought." How, better? Does she not have practice? Never mind about Zachary, she is only a child when Zachary so hastily lights out for the Territories . . . and for oblivion. He is her uncle . . . *grea*-*t*uncle. Hardly counts . . . Uncle Zachary . . . though he lives on in local memory, in the minds and mouths of Sidney Coolidge and the like. Is Sid's an august name in these days? in this place? Less. Llewellyn in Wales. Cohen in Tel Aviv. *But.*

Kingston, Woodruff, Gerald. She doesn't see Kingston and Woodruff dead? She doesn't know for sure that Gerald—? She knows for sure. In her mind she sees them each dead a hundred thousand times. Perhaps there is even some comfort about Lewis. At least she touches the coffin. At least she stands by the grave. *She tries to live a little while without him, likes it not, and dies.* Waldo Sutter, he whom Chickamauga cannot kill, he whom none of them have seen in *years,* puts on his old Union uniform and attends the funeral.

Stands apart, speaks to no one, is covertly observed by those curious to see if they can observe traces of the alleged blood of the Narragansetts . . . or even of a darker and more vigorous tribe. He speaks to no one; on his way home, whom Chickamauga does not kill or the wolves tear apart, collapses by the side of the road. Old John Kelly, hopefully skulking (he who should have known better than hope) to see if Waldo perhaps goes to the postfuneral feast, returning with victuals in his pocket, finds him dead.

His will: *Them as gotten everthing else as ought to ben mine, let them git all I have to leave. . . .*

And, one year later, one year and some months, Samuel at twenty-three, after something not less horrible for being less describable, Samuel rushes, roaring, naked, through the woods and dives into the water and swims outward with powerful strokes until vanishing from sight. This is shortly after Chester Boswell sees Samuel in the room with his head in his hands, motionless save for that fidget of the fingers. The rains have been heavy, the river is high, surely Samuel *knows* this? Surely Samuel knows that he is swimming *toward* the dam? They find him dead at the foot of it, drowned, and with many bones broken.

Ellis's once-high spirits, slackened when Lewis dies, seem now suddenly and entirely checked. There are no more stories told about him. One sees him no more at meals even; Agnes brings him up a tray: reports that he sits with head in hands, fingers trembling. Chester Boswell, Cousin Chester? His bad leg? It *is* re-broken and it is re-set. A room on the first floor in the large house is cleared up for him: the office of *Henry,* lost and forgotten *Henry,* husband to Helen, father of Kingston, Woodruff, Gerald, Lucinda, Amy, Lewis, Samuel, Ellis. And there Chester sleeps—what formal sleep he gets— although he spends most of his time in the library with his leg in its cast up on an ottoman; Chester still suffers from the sinking of the *Maine,* on which he never sets eyes, sometimes murmuring to silent Aunt Sarah, sometimes dozing, to awaken abruptly with a little groan. There is perhaps a slightly warmer relation between Ellis and Chester than with the other boys, has he been more like an uncle than a cousin? Ellis never comes down to see him, sends him no general or especial messages. *His* door is open only to Agnes, and, twice a day, the tray.

Down below, they wait. And wait. As each day lengthens, so the tension. Yes, even so, a dreadful shock when, one morning, a great crash. And a quite frightful human sound, part scream, and—"What the devil—" cries Chester Boswell. And now another and rather lesser crash, and the scene is as one long prepared for some set piece, for a second all gape, then a wild rush up the stairs, somehow today the carpenters have been gotten in at last, large strong men—the thud of shoulders against a shuddering door. Voices cry out in horror, there are screams and shouts and—

Silent Aunt Sarah sits silently; unmoving, her neatly trousered legs in the grey with the small black check. Trembling Chester Boswell sits, too, a prisoner of his patriot leg in its heavy cast. Turmoil, terror, tragedy. Ellis has been shaving, pauses in mid-stroke and cries out and pushes over the heavy piece of cherrywood furniture with the mirror and the basin, slashes his throat. *Deeply.* Doctor Brainert is summoned, can do nothing.

Perhaps an hour or so later when there is something more like quiet once again, Chester Boswell, *"Why,"* he asks, in a trembling voice, *"Why* do all these devilish tragedies always seem to happen when they are twenty-three? Don't they always seem to happen when—"

Aunt Sarah breaks her silence. Her long, long silence. "Of course," she says. "That is when the horns begin to grow."

She leans forward and she begins to talk. And talk.

The "new" family burying-grounds make up part of the original property of twenty-two and a half acres. Some say, it is a bit more than that. A good bit more than that, some say.

AFTERWORD TO "TWENTY-THREE"

It is well known that Avram Davidson read and appreciated the work of H. P. Lovecraft; he made more than passing references to the gentleman from Providence in both his reviews and his fiction. I would like to assert that "Twenty-Three" can be viewed as a Davidson pastiche of Lovecraft—fully as bizarre and original as the pastiche of Sherlock Holmes, "The Singular Incident of the Dog on the Beach" (in which Davidson also did not imitate the style of the author).

Consider: the rich, eccentric New England family; the agrarian roots of an industrial fortune now in decline; allusions to the dae-monic connections of Crossley Sutter, possibly producing bastard children; Cotton Mather's supernatural writings; a reclusive elderly cousin "whom Chickamauga does not kill nor wolves tear apart;" the knowing helplessness of the Sutter women; the atmosphere of enforced New England rectitude and the abundance of antiquarian detail; and the explanation (almost too terrible to be spoken) in the final paragraphs of the story. Compare, for example, Lovecraft's sto-ries "The Dunwich Horror" or "The Shadow over Innsmouth."

—Henry Wessells

BUSINESS MUST BE PICKING UP

The scene was archetypal. The sweet gray-haired woman was trying to persuade the rugged gray-haired man to let her discard some of his old clothes. "No, I am *not* 'throwing them away,'" she said. "I am giving them to the town church for the annual sale."

"No, you are *not* 'giving them to the town church for the annual sale,'" he said. "I'll make a cash contribution instead, but I don't want a thing gotten rid of—not a thing!"

He was firm, but not angry. Neither was she. They knew each other well. "What, not even—not even," she groped, came up with several articles of old-fashioned look, "not even *these*, for goodness' sake? When was the last time you wore silk socks?—And besides, *what* cash?" She looked at him with affectionate impatience.

"Never you mind about that, it will be forthcoming when needed; no, not a *thing*. These old clothes, I can wear around the mill or the garden."

The room and the rest of its contents were neither new nor rich, but everything held and released the glow of things well made and well taken care of: paneled walls, furniture, bedspread and quilts. Stained-glass windows. Hand-crafted chandelier. Even the shade on the bedside lamp, and the bindings of the books.

"Ohhh, I suppose—" Her voice trailed off, then was renewed as she lifted her hands. "And the old stockings, will you wear them around the mill and the garden? One is red and—why, they don't even match! But, I suppose—"

They had had this scene before. She always lost. And she always tried again. "Look at them! I could almost swear that they've shrunk.— Anklets," she murmured, prepared to drop them, and the subject, too.

"Never mind," he said, also prepared to end it, but not for a few words more. "Never mind. I like things the way they are. No, don't throw away a thing. Do I tell you to throw away stuff in the kitchen?"

She shook her head. "No, you don't. And that's one reason we don't have to apply for food stamps. Yes, I know. I know all about it. Well. Be on about your business, you—you old master craftsman, you! Going to the kiln?" she asked, as he, with a final grunt, moved toward the door.

He tugged out his old watch, cupped and scanned it. "No, kiln won't be ready for over an hour." His rugged face split into a smile. "Man there waiting impatiently, even though I told him they'd have to *cool*, for gosh sake! 'I've come five hundred miles,' he says, 'and I'm not leaving without them soup bowls!' "

The gray-haired woman closed the closet door. "Well, I'm glad there are still some people who want them, big as they are. How long did it take the last batch to sell?" He did not answer, and she did not expect he would. So, "Find out how Sister Ferguson's arthritis is this morning" were her last words as he left.

A man of his own decade walked slowly along the graveled path, looked up now, and greeted him as "Brother Johnson."

"The gravel isn't here 'just for fancy,' as the Pennsylvania Dutch put it, no, Brother Washburne. Done with forethought. No mud in the springtime, no dust in the summertime. That is the way we work, here at the Dawnside Place. Forethought is an important Dawnside principle. Sister Johnson thinks the soup bowls may be too big for you," he said, with a slight quirk of his mouth.

Mr. Washburne's heavy face sagged. "Too big for *me*? Why, a soup bowl can't be too big, way *I* look at it!"

"Way *I* look at it, too—"

"When I want a bowl of soup, I want a *bowl* of it! Not a cup . . . Keep this place real neat, Brother, I see. Not a fallen leaf, so much as."

As they walked through the grounds, so carefully taken care of that a stranger might have thought that all the trees and shrubs had been hand-planted instead of—for a large part—being the carefully preserved original plant-cover of the landscape, Brother Johnson explained that not even a leaf was suffered to wither uselessly at the Dawnside Place, nor were they burned—so wasteful! Some went directly into the compost heap and some went there indirectly, after having been of service in the barn. That way Dawnside had to plant less grass for hay and could devote the land saved to other crops. No, of course the cows and goats did not eat leaves; the leaves were spread on the floors of their stalls. There was no "spoiled hay" at Dawnside.

"Nor much of anything else," he added.

Mr. Washburne was impressed. "Department of Agriculture comes up with some good ideas, sometimes," he said.

But that was the wrong thing to have said.

The Department of Agriculture had absolutely nothing to do with it, the Master Craftsman of Dawnside Place told him, using a good degree of emphasis. Employing fallen leaves for other purposes was just plain old-fashioned common sense and American know-how. "Department of Agriculture! Federal Government! People expect the government to do *everything* for them these days—the Federal Government, I mean. What's going to become of the good old American get-up-and-go, is what I'd like to know?"

Mr. Washburne said that he agreed with him a hundred percent.

"*We* don't expect some government bureau to do anything for us that we can do for ourselves," Brother Johnson swept on. "Oh, *this* is not one of your so-called art colonies, subsidized and federalized, no, not one of your factory-in-the-field kind of farms, either! Never let *anyone* do for you what you can do for yourself—oh, that's a very important Dawnside principle, Brother Washburne. Create your own beauty by your own honest toil is our motto. 'Whatsoever thy hands find to do, do it with thy might'—can't improve on *that*, can you now?"

Mr. Washburne said that he agreed with him a hundred percent.

"No!" cried the Master Craftsman of the Dawnside Place. "Elbert Hubbard showed us the way. The Shakers had already showed *him* the way. We raise our own food here—well, almost *all* our own food. We mostly make all our own clothes here. We make *all* our own furniture, we dip our own candles, we print our books on presses we have made ourselves, and we make our own pottery and glassware and paper. Some is wallpaper. I lost track of how many prizes our hand-printed wallpaper has won. And some is high-quality paper for our hand-printed books. We cast our own type and do our own engraving and coloring and binding and make our own cardboard and cartons for shipping and—"

Mr. Washburne, whose head had drooped slightly, now said that they were certainly beautiful books, for sure. "Wished I could afford to buy some. And some of your other beautiful stuff, too. Your stuff is kind of expensive, though—oh, mind you, not that I don't mean to imply, uh, why they are certainly worth every penny of it, and I don't begrudge the price of them soup plates which I've been saving up for, oh, two years now.—Say, how are you folks set up as a business here?" he asked, showing a slight embarrassment and a desire to change the subject.

They were set up as a corporation like any other corporation, the Dawnside leader explained. Receiving certainly no favors as such from the Federal Government. "We craftsmen and craftswomen hold all our stock ourselves, and I am merely the first among equals, as Chairman of the Board of Directors."

Mr. Washburne asked, "How's business?"

There was a brief silence. "Slow," said the Chairman of the Board. "Yes. Business is slow right now. Taxes are too high. People don't have the money to pay for quality right now." Nothing was said for a while. Presently they came to a low building of hand-pressed brick and unpainted timbers; it too had stained-glass windows of birds and flowers and plants.

"I'll just step into the office for a minute," said the Master Crafts-man.

Mr. Washburne said he'd wait outside and enjoy the air. A large automobile drove up to a halt and two grown-up people and two small children peered out of the windows. "Say, what is this place?" the man asked.

Mr. Washburne straightened up in his seat on the hand-fashioned bench. "Why, this is the famous Dawnside Place," he said.

The woman gave a sort of gasp of surprise. "Oh, is this the famous Dawnside Place?" she exclaimed. "Why, I heard about this place when I was just a little girl!"

"I want a hamburger," said a child.

"I want French fries," said the other child.

"Say, I thought they'd gone out of business," the man said. Mr. Washburne laughed at the very idea. "Yeah, sure, I heard they'd gone out of business. Or were *go*ing out of business. All that old-fashioned junk they make. Sure. I heard—"

"—hamburger—"

"—French fries—"

The woman asked if they served food here. Mr. Washburne nod-ded. At the Guest Table, he said. Three times a day. Not *now*, though. And he was in the midst of advising them that they wait around when the large automobile took off at high speed and was gone in a flurry of gravel and exhaust smoke.

The door opened and the Master Craftsman came out. His ruddy face looked much less than cheerful. "Didn't even say thank you," murmured Mr. Washburne.

Brother Johnson grunted. "What did *they* want—hamburgers? People *live* on that nowadays. Why, what is the matter with good old-fashioned meat-and-oatmeal-loaf? Good old-fashioned scrapple? With *hash?* Anything the matter with our old-fashioned-style hash and mashed turnips?"

"Not a thing," Mr. Washburne said staunchly. "Say, I guess I'm going to take a little rest-up before lunchtime. My soup bowls won't be ready for a while yet, I guess." He had a hopeful, questioning note in his voice.

"Be ready soon as they cool," the Master Craftsman said firmly. "Well, I got to go to town, do some bank business, so I'll give you a lift to the Guest House."

" '*Pre*ciate that."

In the car Mr. Washburne said nothing. Brother Johnson clutched the wheel, breathing heavily. "Sister Ferguson," he said. "Known that woman forty years. For-ty years. Taught her the ancient art of stained glass. The ancient arts of spinning and weaving. Taught her typing and double-entry bookkeeping. Taught her how to look on beauty, clear. Now she wants to sell out. To—sell—*out!* 'Either get one of those Federal grants like everybody else is doing,' is what she said. 'Never while I draw *breath.*' I told her, 'will I ask the Federal Government to do one thing for me which I can do for myself,' is what I said. Asked her, 'What? You going *soft* in your maturity?' "

Mr. Washburne's mild indeterminate sound might have been sympathy. Or sleepiness. The trees and shrubs and scattered buildings of the place looked rather bare under the gray sky. Brother Johnson made a surprised noise. "What? Gone past the Guest House?" he asked. He looked briefly aside at the other man. "Well, I'll back up, then. No problem. —Solve our *own* problems," he admonished.

He leaned over and opened the door. "Got a good three-quarter hour before the bell rings for lunch. Notice its mellow sound, by the way. Cast that bell my*self,*" he said proudly.

Alone in the car he continued his conversation. " 'Sister, you are not going to sell *out,* are you?' is what I asked her. For-ty *years,* oh, I saw it coming. I knew. I could tell. 'Either to Washington or to you or to Tom, Dick, or Harry,' she had the brass to say. Said, 'If no Federal grant, then buy my shares out,' says she. 'The grant will pay for an apprenticeship program, a lot of young people are interested in learning old arts nowadays, and we can install a new heating system; otherwise *I* am going to Florida and I am *not* going to spend one more winter shivering before my hand-crafted fireplace!'

"Apprenticeship program! *Young* people! *Hipp*ies! Sister *Fergu-son!*" he concluded.

"What's that, hey, Johnson?" asked the man at the gas station.

"Huh? *Oh.* Oh, just talking to myself. Fill 'er up. Regular."

The man at the gas station said, "Must have money in the bank, talking to yourself that way."

The Master Craftsman grunted and said, "I'm going to *put* some money in the bank, soon as you put some gas in my tank."

"Well, good. Guess I'll be able to deposit that post-dated check you gave me for last month's bill." He moved on back to take the cap off the tank. After a while he put it back on, made out the new bill with a small pencil stub, handed it in for the Master of Dawnside to sign. "My brother Bob," said the man at the gas station, "he draws disability, he draws Social Security, he draws Food Stamps, he don't have to worry about the oil company trying to force the independent distributors out of business, he don't have to get out of bed at half-past five in the morning."

The Master of Dawnside handed back pad and pencil. "The day *I* ask the Federal Government to do one single thing which I can do myself," he said grimly, "is the day I hope to die."

In town he parked carefully in front of where Snyder's Grocery used to be—Snyder's had often bought Dawnside products—and ignored the wide parking lot of the supermarket—which had never bought from Dawnside. He waited in the bank till Mr. Hopkins, the senior cashier, had finished with another customer, then stepped up to his window. Mr. Hopkins's small face smiled, cheeks as shiny as those on a crisp apple. Very softly he said, peering through his thick glasses, "Oh, good, you can catch up on your taxes, then." He picked up the deposit slip.

"Yes," said the Master Craftsman, "I can give the Federal Government some more of my money. So it can give it all away again to somebody else."

Mr. Hopkins sighed and nodded. "How true . . . One thousand, and one, two, three, four, five. Makes fifteen hundred. That's it?"

"That's it for *now.*"

"All in crisp new bills. Business must be picking up. Or"—and a roguish twinkle came into his faded blue eyes—"maybe you print them yourself, do you? Say, they look just about as good as what the government makes!"

"Just *about,*" said the Master Craftsman of Dawnside.

The two older gentlemen had a quiet little laugh together, at that one.

AFTERWORD TO "BUSINESS MUST BE PICKING UP"

Note the strict accuracy of the artisan's words: ". . . some more of my money." This story offers wry criticism of both modern commercialism, and the self-indulgent "self-reliance" of the American Arts and Crafts movement at the close of the nineteenth century.

Elbert Hubbard, a prosperous American soap salesman, founded the Roycrofters community in East Aurora, New York, after a visit to England. There, Hubbard had been impressed by the ideals of William Morris. Morris was indisputably a genius in addition to being a Pre-Raphaelite artist, wealthy socialist, pioneering designer, translator, poet, etc. Hubbard was at his best as a promoter—*selling* the ideals of the Arts and Crafts movement and the simple life to a vast, fee-paying bourgeois audience. At least one American genius did get his start in East Aurora: Dard Hunter, master papermaker and fine printer, whose influence remains strong today.

In the still unpublished *AdVentures in AutoBiography*, Davidson recalls the not-so-genteel poverty of the writing life of the 1950s; after the death of a fellow writer from those days, Davidson was told that his acquaintance had "had a damned fine plate" for printing twenties—*his own money*, in other words.

—*Henry Wessells*

DR. BHUMBO
SINGH

Trevelyan Street used to be four blocks long, but now it is only three, and its aft end is blocked by the abutment of an overpass. (Do you find the words *Dead End* to have an ominous ring?) The large building in the 300 block used to be consecrated to worship by the Mesopotamian Methodist Episcopal Church (South) but has since been deconsecrated and is presently a glue warehouse. The small building contains the only Bhuthanese grocery and deli outside of Asia; its trade is small. And the little (and wooden) building lodges an extremely dark and extremely dirty little studio which sells spells, smells, and shrunken heads. Its trades are even smaller.

The spells are expensive, the smells are exorbitant, and the prices of its shrunken heads—first chop though they be—are simply inordinate.

The studio, however, has a low rent (it has a low ceiling, too), pays no license fee—it is open (when it is open) only between the hours of seven P.M. and seven A.M., during which hours the municipal license department does not function—and lacks not for business enough to keep the proprietor, a native of the Andaman Islands, in the few, the very few things, without which he would find life insupportable: namely curried squid, which he eats—and eats and *eats*—baroque pink pearls, which he collects, and (alone, and during the left phase of the moon) wears; also live tree-shrews. Some say that they are distantly cognate to the primates and, hence, it is supposed, to Man. *Be that as it may.* In their tiny ears he whispers directions of the most unspeakable sort, and then turns them loose, with great grim confidence. And an evil laugh.

The facts whereof I speak, I speak with certainty, for they were related to me by my friend Mr. Underhand; and Mr. Underhand has never been known to lie.

At any rate, at least, not to *me.*

"A good moonless evening to you, Underhand Misterjee," says the proprietor, at the termination of one lowering, glowering afternoon in Midnovember, "and a bad evening indeed to those who have had the fortune to incur your exceedingly just displeasure." He scratches a filthy ear-lobe with a filthy finger.

—Midnovember, by the way, is the month which was banished from the Julian Calendar by Julian the Apostate; it has never appeared in the Gregorian Calendar: a good thing, too—

"And a good evening to *you,* Dr. Bhumbo Singh," says Mr. Underhand. "As for *them*—Ha Ha!" He folds his thin and lilac-gloved hands over the handle of his stalking-crutch. Even several so-called experts have declared the handle (observed by light far less dim than that in the shop of Bhumbo Singh) to be ivory: they are wrong: it is bone, purely bone. . . . Or perhaps one would better say, impurely bone. . . .

"Ha Ha!" echoes (Dr.) Bhumbo Singh. He has in fact no right at all to this distinguished family name, which he has assumed in dishonor of a certain benevolent Sikh horse-coper who in a rash and malignly constellated hour took the notion to adopt him.

Now to business; "A spell, Underhand Sahib?" he next asks, rubbing his chin. His chin bears a dull-blue tattoo which would strike terror to the hearts and loosen the strings of the bowels of the vilest ruffians in Rangoon, Lahore, Peshawar, Pernambuco, and Wei-hatta-hatta yet unhanged, save, of course, that it is almost always by virtue of dust, the inky goo of curried squid, and a hatred of water akin to hydrophobia, totally invisible. "A spell, a spell? A nice spell? A severed head?"

"Fie upon your trumpery spells," Mr. Eevelyn (two *es*) Underhand says easily. "They are fit only for witches, warlocks, and Boy Scouts or Girl. As for your severed heads, shrunken or otherwise: Ho Ho."

He puts the tip of his right index finger alongside of the right naris of his nose. He winks.

Dr. Bhumbo Singh attempts a leer, but his heart is not in it. "They cost uncommon high nowadays, even wholesale," he whines. And then he drops commercial mummery and simply waits.

"I have come for a smell, Doctor," Underhand says, flicking away with the tip of his stalking-crutch a cricket scaped from the supply kept to feed the tree-shrews. Dr. Bh. Singh's red little eyes gleam like those of a rogue ferret in the rutting season.

Underhand gives his head a brisk, crisp nod, and smacks his pursed lips. "A smell, subtle, slow, pervasive. A vile smell. A puzzling smell. A smell of seemingly ubiquitous provenaunce, and yet a smell which has no spoor. An evil smell. One which will, eventually, and to infinite relief, diminish . . . diminish . . . all but vanish . . . and then, rising like a phoenix from its bed of fragrant ashes, stalk abroad like a pest—worse, far worse than before . . .

"A smell disgusting beyond disgust . . ."

A slight shiver passes through Dr. (he has neither right nor title to this title, but who would dare deny it him? The AMA? The last platform which they could have occupied together even in combat was also occupied by Albertus Magnus.) passes through Dr. Bhumbo S.'s filthy, meagre frame. His tongue protrudes. (It *is* true that he can, when moved to do so, touch with it the tip of his rather *retroussé* nose; if it is also true that he can—and does—catch flies with it like a toad or chameleon, Mr. Underhand has not found the matter meet communicating to *me*.) His tongue withdraws. "In short, most valued customer, what is now requisite is a smell which will drive men mad."

" 'Men,' Dr. Bhumbo Singh? *'Men?'* I said nothing of men. The word never issued from my mouth. The concept, in fact, never formed in my mind." Bhumbo shakes with what may be a malarial spasm, but is probably silent laughter.

"I have just the thing," he says. "I have the very thing. The price is purely *pro forma,* the price is minimal, the price is 1500 golden gold pieces, of the coinage of Great Golconda. Per ounce."

Underhand's brows raise, descend, meet. " 'Of the imprint of Great Golconda'? Why, even the very schoolboys know that Golconda-gold was so exceedingly pure that it might be eaten like jam, which is why so few of its coins now remain. Damme, damme, Dr. Bhumbo Singh, if this is how you treat and charge your most valued customers, it is no wonder that you have so few." A mass of filth, matted together with cobwebs, slowly floats from the invisible ceiling to the unspeakable floor; is ignored.

The merchant shrugs. "Not even for my own brother, sir, am I willing to prepare the smell for less." Considering that Bhumbo's own (and only) brother, Bhimbo, has spent the last seven and one half years laden with chains in the sixth sub-basement of the gaol privily kept by that ugly, obese, and evil old woman, Fatima, Dowager Begum of Oont, without Bhumbo offering so much as two rupees two pice in ransom, this is quite probably the truth. "However, out of my great regard and respect for you personally and my desire to maintain the connexion, I shall not require you to purchase the full ounce. I shall sell it you by the drachm or scruple."

"Done, Bhumbojee, done!" cries Mr. Underhand. He thumps the stalking-crutch upon the filthy, filthy floor. The tree-shrew utter shrill little yipples of annoyance, and Bhumbo gives them crickets: they subside, aside from making nonverbal, crunching noises.

Nearby on the overpass a truck or lorry rumbles past; in its wake the frail building trembles, causing at least one of the shrunken heads to roll from side to side and grind its teeth. No one pays it mind. "Be pleased to return hither, then, Underhand Effendi, on (or, it may be, a trifle after) the Gules of December," Bhumbo Singh says. Then grows just a trifle uncertain. " 'December,' the giaours call the next half-past-a-month 'December,' do they not?"

Eevelyn Underhand (two *e*s) rises to go. "They do indeed. They have a high festival therein."

"They do, they do?" cries Bhumbo Singh. "I had not known. —What a thing it is to be wise!" He accompanies his customer to the dirty, dirty door with many bows, obeisances, and genuflections. Customer, having perfunctorily placed his foot once on Bhumbo's nasty neck, is long gone by the time the last of these is finished.

Gone, long gone, and the distant echo of the penny-whistle (on which he is wont to play the grace-notes to the *Lament For Nana Sahib* as he walks his spidery way through such dank ways and dark) long gone as well. . . .

In the next sundry weeks, either Bhumbo Singh or his very simulacrum is seen in a multitude of exceedingly diverse places. Abattoirs know him for brief moments; wool-pulleries and tanneries as well. He is seen to cast handsful of the Semi-silent Sands of the Hazramawut (or Courts of Death) at the window-panes of Abdulahi al-Ambergrisi (who sells asafoetida as well): and the Abdulahi (an Yezid of the Yezidi-folk) to open, blench, withdraw, thrust out by means of a very long-handled net an ampula of what-it-may-be. The Bhumbo—and if it be not he, who be it?—is observed out of the corners of eyes to scramble under the wharf at the Old Fish Market (condemned, since, by the Board of Health). He visits, also, the hovels of one or two and never more than three foreign folk who formerly fared at sea in tropic clime and who live now in tumbled sheds on the farther sides of disused dumps and show their ravaged faces only to the faces of the ravaged moons.

And on the nights when the moon is dark, he scrambles through ointment factories, in search of flies.

Now and then he whispers, and, did one dare come close and nigh, one would hear him calculate in somewise as this: "Such-and-such a number of golden gold-pieces! with some I shall buy me *more* baroque pink pearls and with some I shall buy me *more* curried squid and some I shall lay away to gloat upon and others—nay! one lone other!—shall I give to Iggulden the Goldbeater to beat me gold-leaf so soft and wide and thin: half of this I shall lay for a strangle-mask upon the face of a certain real-estate 'developer' and tother moiety shall She-Who-Makes-Sweetmeats roll round hot comfits and pasties and pastries for me and when this has melted like yellow butter I shall eat of them nor shall I invite even one other to join me and afterwards I shall lick my twelve fingers till they be somewhat clean. . . ."

Then he chuckles . . . a sound like the bubbling of thick hot grease in the foetid try-pots of a cannibal feast.

Meanwhile, and what of Mr. Underhand?

Mr. Underhand meanwhile makes visits, too: but of a more sociable nature: Mr. Underhand pays *calls*.

"Oh. Undy. It's *you,*" says a woman through the chink in the well-chained door. "Whadda *you* want?"

"Gertrude, I have brought you, this being the first of the month, the sum mulcted of me by the terms of our bill of divorcement," says he. As always.

He passes money through the crack or slit between doorjamb and door. Rapidly she riffles through it; asks, "Is this all I'm gonna get?" As always.

"No," sighs he, "I fear me not. It is, however, all that you are going to get in this or any other one month of the year; it being the extortionate amount wrested from me by compound, I do not say 'collusion,' between your attorneys and the judge upon the bench. Gertrude: good night."

He turns and departs. She makes a sound between her palate and her sinuses which experience has instructed she intends for scorn: then: cluntch-cluntch . . . thuckle-thuckle . . . the night-bolts. Cloonk. The door.

Mr. Underhand, an hour later, bathed and bay-rum'd and clothed in his best-of-best. Spats upon his glittering shoes. Hat and gloves and cane in one hand. Flowers in the other.

"Eevelyn," she says, hand to her gleaming, glittering throat. "What a lovely surprise. What quite lovely flowers. Oh, how nice."

"May I come in. My dear."

"Why of course. Need you ask. Now I shan't be lonely. For a while. Eevelyn." They kiss.

A wide glance he swiftly casts round. Then asks, "Do I interrupt your dinner?"

She looks about the apartment. Her expression is one of mild surprise. " 'Dinner'? Oh. That. Just a simple bowl of lobster salad on a heart of chilled iceberg lettuce. Chervil. Cress. A few spoons of caviare. Sweet butter, just a dab. A hard-cooked egg, cut fine. *Kümmelbrot.* And the smallest bottle of Brut. All far too much. But you know how Anna spoils one. You will join me."

He looks round, again. Crystal. Tapestry. Petit-point. Watteau. Chippendale. Asks: "You are not expecting—?"

"Oh, no. No. Not now. Shall we have some music. We shall have some music."

They do.

They dance.

They dine.

They drink.

They talk.

They—

They do not.

"Heavens, the time. You must go now Eevelyn."

"Then you are expecting—?"

How her fingers glitter as she raises them to indicate what words alone cannot. "Eevelyn. I do not. Know. I never. Know. —Go, my sweetest dearest one."

He picks up hat, gloves, cane. "How is it that I never—"

She places ring-crusted fingers across his livid lips. "Hush. Oh. Hush. The noblest kindest most generous man I know will never grumble. He will be understanding. Patient. A kiss before we part."

The Andaman Islander peers a moment through gummy eyeslits. Which now widen in recognition. "Underhand Sahib!"

"And whom else did you expect? Fat Fatima, perhaps?"

The islander shakes as with an ague. "Ah, Wisdom-wallah, do not mention her even obliquely! Has she not laid my miserable and I fear by now broken brother in a deep-dark dungeon, merely for having adventitiously broken wind in her outermost courtyard? Malignant she!"

Underhand shrugs. "Well, so be it. Or: so be it *not.* —*Well,* Bhumbo Singh, I have brought certain pieces of gold, contained, according to custom, in—hem, hem!" He coughs. "I need not name it." And looks up and around, expectantly.

At once the storekeeper begins to prowl and shuffle. " 'To afflict with impotence the Viceroy of Sindh.' No. 'To impose the plague of emmerods upon the anti-Pope of—' No. 'Lord Lovat's head, with tam o' shanter,' no. No. Ah. Ah." He lifts up a tiny container, begins simultaneously to read the label (scribbled in a most debased Pracrit) and to open—

"Hold! Hold! For pity's sake do not unstopple it!"

The dark man dumbly puts down the pottikin, no larger than a thumb or (say) the smallest sized can of Spanish truffles; turns to the next item on the cluttered, webby counter. " 'Will afflict with wens upon the forehead of the favorite of the Grand Bastard of Burgundy,' ah!"

Underhand is near-exasperated. "Bhumbo. Pause. Pause. Cease to dither. Lay down that spell. Down, I say, sir; down—Now. Pick up the previous item you had in hand. Yes. . . . And for the sake of Kali, *give* those shrews some crickets!"

The Andaman Islander still bumples around, so Underhand, with a click of impatience, follows both his own instructions. Also gives the fellow a keen glance of reproof, advises him henceforth to use either a better or a worse brand of opium; and places in his hands that which holds the golds. "You have weighed the preparation, I make no doubt; count therefore the coins, in order that—"

But his supplier declines the need. "It is enough, enough, Underhand Sahib. I feel the weight to be correct. Forgive my dithering: the *ah-peen,* as you say." The voice and manner are crisp enough now. "I would offer you cups of tea, but my own brutish brews are not fine enough for your exquisite palate, and the Lipton's I cannot find."

Underhand sweeps the filthy lair with a glance. (A broom would be better.) "And fresh out of viper's milk, too, I daresay. Pit-ty." He looks once, he looks twice around the darkly place, dirty almost beyond endurance, cluttered certainly beyond description. "Ah, the immemorial wisdom of the East. . . . Bhumbo: a good Gules to you."

The other bows. "Do I not live but to serve you with smells, Sahib?" he enquires. And begins the requisite series of prostrations. Presently he hears the sound of the penny-whistle.

Some time after that.

Anna's nose is very red; her voice is very thick. "Always mine lady liked nice things," she says. "Diamonts, chee liked. Poils, chee liked. 'Kebbiar, I could only itt a morsel, but it moss be the bast,' chee tal to me."

"Yes, yes, yes," Underhand agrees. "How true, how true. What a blow to you. To you *and* me." He wishes that Anna would twist her handkerchief less and apply it more.

"Always mine lady was very particular," Anna goes on. " 'Anna, how you minn, you couldn't smal it?' chee ask. 'Look maybe onder you choose.' I lat her see onder mine right chew: nothing. I lat her see onder mine laft chew: nothing. 'Nye, so, Mrs., how come soddenly mine kitchens not nice and clinn; come luke.' Chee come, chee luke, luke, luke. Nothing. Sneef, sneef, sneef. " 'Eeyoo, God-my, waht dradful smal,' chee say. And *say* and say—"

"My, my. Yes, yes. Don't distress yourself, they take very good care of her where she is now—"

Anna (fiercely): "What? Take care mine lady gooder than me? I visit, I bring mine spatial *grumpskentorten:* Chee scrim, only. 'Mrs., Mrs., you don't rackocknize Anna? *Anna?* Mrs. Goitrude, Mrs. Goitrude: is *Anna!*' But only chee scrim. And *scrim* and scrim." Anna begins to demonstrate, fists clenched, cords thrusting out from neck, voice a thin shrill grinding; Underhand begs her to desist.

Afterwards, Underhand, with some relief, returns to his own

home. Man is, certainly, a social being: but there are times when, the Author of Genesis (Underhand believes), notwithstanding, when it *is* good for man to be alone. Underhand has his roses; he prunes them. Underhand has his Newgate Calendars; he collates them. Underhand has his first editions (Mather, de Sade, von Sacher-Masoch); he reads them. Now and then he looks up. He finds, after a while, that he is looking up rather oftener than he is looking down. Then he looks further down than usual. First he lifts up his right foot and turns it sideways. He puts it down. Then he lifts up his left foot and turns it sideways. He puts it down. Then, room by room and closet by closet, he goes through the house, his nostrils dilating. "It is not what I think," he says, firmly. "It, is, *not* . . . what I *think.*"

Some time after *that.*

Underhand is in another place, and one which he doesn't much like. Endlessly he casts horoscopes, no pencils are allowed and so he uses crayons. The effects are certainly colorful but it is very hard to achieve fine detail. By one and by two, people pass by, and, pretending not to look, look. Underhand ignores them. Why he now, suddenly, does look up as someone stops—Look he does. This one, now, frankly gazes without pretense. Smiles.

Underhand stares. Starts. Speaks.

"Oh, my God. Oh. Oh. Bhumbo Singh. They told me he—told me *you* were dead. *Showed* me. Stuffed in between my inner and outer walls. *That* was what drove me mad. *That* was what I—*Not* what I had thought. *Not* what I had bought. Mistake. Must tell them: Bhumbo Singh: alive." He starts to rise, is stopped by a dark and gentle hand.

"Oh, no, Underhand Sahib and/or Effendi. Bhumbo *is* dead."

Underhand utters a small squeal, starts to sidle away.

"I am *Bhimbo,* own and only brother and twin to the faithless aforesaid. Who alas and regardless of the uterine ties between us let me languish in the lowermost dungeon of H. H. The Beebee Fatima, Dowager Begum of Oont, for seven years six months one week and several days, rather than pay ransom for my offense—*most* unintentional, I assure you: never eat legumes before transacting whatsoever even in the outermost courtyard of a descendant of Timur the Terrible. —The sixth sub-basement of her now-illegal gaol, whence I was released by the new and independent government, may Kali bestow blessings upon them with every pair of hands. Thence came I here. Wherefore I caused him, my natal brother Bhumbo, to be bitten to the heart by hungry tree-shrews imprisoned under an iron squid-pot which I held over his faithless heart; *how* he screamed."

He wags his head contentedly.

A moment Underhand ponders, ignoring whilst he does so the conduct of a neighbor who was now, as often, reciting what he claimed were the complete Songs of Ossian in the original Erse. From memory. Loudly. And at length. "Well, then, I understand why you put your brother to the death. *Nat*urally. But why, oh, why, Bhimbo, did you stuff him in between my innermost and outermost walls?—with such dreadful results to myself? And, oh! the black whirlwind!"

A shrug. A look of gentle surprise. "Why? Well, Sahib, one had to stuff him *some*where. —I had thought to return to my native Islands, there to start an independence movement which might result, who knows and why not? in my becoming President-for-Life. But in my brother Bhumbo's uncleanly shop I lingered too long, searching for his baroque pink pearls; whilst I was thus engaged, thither came the men called Inspectors of Buildings and of Healths. 'This one's *got*ta be nuts,' one said. '*Look*it this place!" He chuckles quietly.

Underhand gapes. Then thinks. Then says, " 'Escape,' yes. Bhimbo, we must put our wise heads together, cast cantrips, I cannot do it by myself alone; secure our release from—"

Bhimbo's rufous, jaundered eyes widen. "But, Sahib, I have already *been* released! To one, sir, who has spent seven and one half years, plus, in the lowermost dungeon of the fearful fat Fatima, female tyrant (since deposed), what is this place here but an hotel? Consider, Sahib: Clean clothes. Clean beds. Thrice a day, clean food—dispensed by servitors. Plus *snacks*. How fond of *snacks* I am,

Sahib! And also once a week one of the gurus called *Shrink* talks
with me in his sacred office; what honor. To be sure, there is no
palm-toddy to be had, but a certain servitor (in return for such
simple spells: Women. Gambling.) brings a savory wine called Ripple, concealed in bottles of the Dr. Pepper's medication. Betel-*pan*,
there is not, but there is *toombac*, Sahib; also the talking cinema in
the cabinet-boxes. *How* entertaining! *Much* murders! —And also,
shower-baths! sports! thrice a week, Therapeutic Handicrafts! *Such*
fun!"

He raises his voice, rather, so as to be heard not only over that
of the Ossianic bard, but over that of one who, crying the words
Hello Joe! in staccato bursts, would be good for at least a quarter of
an hour. "I know what your people call this place, Sahib. But, do
you know what *I* call it? Sahib, *I* call it Paradise."

Mr. Underhand feels again and sees again the approach of the
black whirlwind; smells again the ineffable evil smell . . . the one he
had bought? The one he had not? What matter. Grasping the table
for one moment's more contact with reality, he asks, "But does it
in no way bother you to be forever surrounded by madmen?"

Bhimbo looks at him. The reddish-yellowish glance is patient
and kind. "Ah, Sahib. Have you not learned the One Great Truth?
All men are mad." The immemorial wisdom of the East is in his
voice, and in his eyes.

Postscript to "Dr. Bhumbo Singh": A note by Avram Davidson (1983).

The name of *Bhumbo Singh* itself I encountered long ago in, I think,
the (very possibly spurious) account of (?) Zephaniah Howell concerning the Black Hole of Calcutta; it went something like this: *"We
tried to obtain boats from Bhumbo Singh, but could not do so."* That
was all. Why this name continued to ferment, or should I say, fester,
in my mind, I cannot say; but eventually, being (I suppose) somewhere without a tripewriter, I took up a ruled record book and began
to write this story. I set it aside unfinished, and indeed forgot about
it, until one day again finding myself without the use of the machine,

up again I picked the story and did not again set it aside until I had finished it. The scene of its completion was Peter Stein's boat, moored at Gate 6 in Sausalito, in that unique shanty-boat, home-made house-boat, and just plain *boat*, community; now alas in slow process of destruction. Peter, despite the fact that he is blind, builds good boats; and I dedicate this story to him.

AFTERWORD TO "DR. BHUMBO SINGH"

There is no doubt that this tale occurs in the days of urban renewal and highway expansion, and yet there is a curious paradox here, for Davidson's eccentric characters and the many allusions to the mysterious East evoke the late nineteenth century at the same time that they depict the perpetually renewed bubblings of the melting-pot that is America. The opening paragraphs describe a marginal neighborhood with considerable accuracy, and though the narrative ranges far afield, the arc of this crime story is rooted in that short stretch of Trevelyan Street. He had an eye for such neighborhoods: "And Don't Forget the One Red Rose" is a brilliantly crafted short tale set in a similar locale. Michael Dirda has written:

> [Davidson] made himself into a prose laureate of "the Old Country." He celebrated vanishing cultures and foods and customs and places, most of them now absorbed in the homogenized tele-glitz of modern American mall-life. There is no better sketch of the Slavic immigrant culture of my own youth—almost entirely gone now—than "The Slovo Stove."

—*Henry Wessells*

THE PENINSULA

"But Borski says that, selectively cut, there's enough good timber on the Peninsula to last for years," —she (Mary Blennerhassett).

"Borski's lying. Simple as that. Not with modern logging methods. Selective cutting, you'd be hard put to make logging-off the Peninsula stretch two years. Clear-cutting, the way he usually cuts, he'd have it flat in a year. *Less* than a year." —he (Victor Olauson).

Scene is in the reasonably modern office of "O & B." On the walls are large old photographs of Oscar Olauson and Robert Blennerhassett: all muscles; moustaches; watch-chains; whiskers; and wicked, wicked eyes. Mary and Victor are their grandchildren.

"And then what? After Borski logs off the Peninsula if he gets hold of it? Tree-farm?"

Victor doesn't think so. "Borski doesn't tree-farm. Never has. Why should he start now? What he'd have if he logged it clear would be one very valuable piece of real estate, you know the style: you cut down all the trees and then you plant saplings and you advertise **Lots in Woodland Acres**. Well. Not a bad stroke of business, ticky-tacky summer cottages cheek by jowl and the lake all full of motorboats. Very competent. Not a bad stroke of business for Borski. But I don't choose to allow it."

Old Oscar and Old Bob looked on with slight leers; *they* didn't choose to allow it, either. At least: they hadn't.

She asked if there hadn't been some suggestions, oh, a while back, that the whole Peninsula be turned into a memorial? Olauson, Blennerhassett State Park, maybe? or, "O & B" Forest Study Area? He said, yes there had been. But his father and her father hadn't chosen to allow it. Added, and neither did he.

And that, she understood, was that.

Mary recalled the first time she'd seen his wife, what was it *she* was called?, some improbably brief one-syllable Scandi name beginning and ending with a consonant. But you were also allowed to call her Emma. Victor was standing by himself with his hands hanging at his sides, no expression on his long flat face, surprisingly dark face with those very blue eyes. *One of my grandmothers was French Canadian,* perhaps a code phrase meaning *Indian blood.* In came Stig or Brum or Hoog or whatever, Emma came up to him and he didn't even look at her. And she brought her mouth to his ear and she spoke and she spoke and she spoke and he didn't even look at her, and then he turned his head and brought his mouth to her ear and *he* spoke. A very very few words. And his wife nodded. Turned. Left. And that was that.

Since then, of course, she—Mary—had met Emma. Had met Emma for a drink in the golf-club bar. One drink for Emma. Had met Emma at dinner in the enormous Olauson house, miraculously kept clean without a servant. Enormous dinner. Two children, *Christ* how clean and quiet. Lighter of hair and skin than Dad, but just as blue of eye. Emma looked a lot like the woman in *American Gothic,* but Victor didn't look a lot like the man. And Mary had met Emma for a lunch which she herself, Mary, had given them in the Vale Chalet, called the Valley Shalley for so long that this had become the place's *name*: given there because, where else? Not in Mary's tiny apartment over the dress shop. The Shalley had gourmet status, that is, no bouillon cubes were added to the French Dip's O Juice. And then, once more, one more time, she had met Emma at some semi-public function. She'd assumed that she and Emma were of a karma

to meet, say, every three weeks forever. To speak almost not at all:
to *meet*. But—

Mary Blennerhassett had spent Saturday night with Junius, the
fry-cook at the Busy Beaver; there really wasn't enough in her ice-
box to make a meal for two, and so off they went to have the
Loggers' Breakfast Special at the Mountain Brook Cafe, a good bit
more status than the Busy Beaver and an awful lot less than the
Shalley: *who* was there, non-messily also loading up on the Special
before (presumably) Church? the cleanly, neatly Victor-and-Emma-
Olauson Family. Was who. Victor nodded his invariable brief cool
Victor Nod. The kids showed no recognition. Maybe Junius was not
the most delicate sight. Emma was, on view of them together, first
terribly startled: then terribly shocked: then terribly, terribly tight-
faced. And after that, although now and then Mary passed within a
foot or two of Emma, she and Emma never again *met*. Tough titty,
Em. Let Victor call Mary "Miss Blennerhassett" till the moose came
home, sooner or later she would get her hands upon him, tawny
skin and all. He might be a man with whom you could only go so
far, but she would go as far as she could.

Although Mary B. and Victor O. perhaps should have been raised
together almost like brother and sister, or anyway cousins . . . but
they hadn't been raised together at all. All she had of her father was
the memory of a voice, before The Divorce, after which she neither
saw nor heard him at all: Mom had taken care of that. The late
Mom eventually went wherever the late Dad had gone. To their
daughter came lots of money from lots of stocks and bonds in a
Company and a Mill in a distant state. It had seemed like lots of
money, then it didn't seem like lots of money but just like money,
then it seemed like lots of money again. Because Mary didn't have
it anymore. For a while. She still had the stocks and bonds, yes, but
The Bank held them as security for The Loan. And The Bank took
dividends and interest to pay The Loan off. Whenever.

And rather than go around the familiar scene and ask for a job,
she being then *poor*, as all might know, why, she did what seemed

to her a sensible scene: she headed for the source of the money, in that distant state. The idea came in a flash as she read the news-item,

BORSKI PERSISTS IN O & B BID
Bill G. Borski, grandson of a Pomeranian pig-farmer, says he will continue his attempts to take over the Olauson–Blenner-hassett lumber interests in

Mary headed West. An old American tradition. Scarcely had she entered the state where the Mill was and had occasion to speak her family name—cashing a small traveller's check in a small roadside restaurant—when old plaid-shirt and bib over-hauls had spoken it himself. She hadn't even seen him there till then. "*Blenn*-der-hass-ett," he'd said, she not knowing if the mispronunciation were a trick of the old man's speech or a part of the local accent. "Say, you must be Old B. *B*'s daughter." God, he'd looked old, old as time. Probably *was*. There may have been, for all she knew, a thousand such old-timers. Okay, getting-used-to-it-time had just begun.

"Granddaughter," said she.

He looked at her through his cataract glasses. "*I* knowed dold B. *B.*," he said, in his oddly-parted speech.

If Mary knew nothing of her father, what did she know of her grandfather? "Oh, what kind of a man was he?" She wanted to know—

"*He* was, a nold, sund of a *bitch*." Well, now she knew. "An dold O. *O. He* was another." The veteran said these things without malice, or, for that matter, without affection.

As good an introduction as another.

As for . . .

Here is the picture. Mary got out of her car at Olauson, Blenner-hassett ("O & B"), and walked around here and there before asking directions to the main office, and by and by she found herself facing a pile of logs, rough and barky and even clotted with earth: there was a heavy-set man, no kid, taking his ease. Suddenly she was aware of another man, tall, business-suit. Not looking at her, looking at the workingman at ease. *What* it was, hard to define but making her happy the look was not being looked at *her*; exactly at this moment the burly man lounging became aware of the looker and the look. Perhaps he did not altogether go into a minor convulsion. Almost, though. Work resumed immediately for him. The man in the business suit turned. He saw Mary. He looked: and there was more in this look than the looks she was used to getting from men. Did he know who she was? Because at once she knew that she knew who *he* was. They had never met. But a hundred years of history connected them.

"Mr. Victor Blennerhassett Olauson?"

"I'm Vic Olauson, yes. Miss Blennerhassett?"

"Mary Blennerhassett."

They took, rather than shook, hands. She said, "Can you give me a job?"

"The union would say no. But as a partner, you—"

All around the life of the lumber mill went on, the saws screaming in one key and the little locomotive engines in another; and so it had gone on here for a century. "A partner? Oh, I thought I was a stockholder."

"In The Olauson and Blennerhassett Corporation, Miss Blennerhassett, you are a stockholder. But in Olauson, Blennerhassett, and Company, Miss Blennerhassett, you're a partner."

It wasn't that first day that she told him how she had "mortgaged" everything to get Flick out of his immense trouble. Or who Flick was . . . or had been . . . anyway . . . It wasn't that first day that she first heard aloud the name of Borski.

The old-timers are talking about the mill. That time of day, early afternoon, mostly it is just the old-timers at the bar, each one with his one shot, little water back.

"Startin t'cut *hem*-lock, I hear."

"*Uh*-oh."

"Whut *I* say." By their tones they might have been invited not alone to cut it, but to drink it.

Someone else, a not-so-old-timer: "What's the matter with that?"

"Whut's the *mat*ter with it?"

Old-timers turn, ready to turn belligerent. Not-so-old-timer not so ready to turn anything, not even away. Says, "Long's the mill keeps open . . . cut *some*thing . . . if Borski . . ." The bar no longer serves even sandwiches. Just whatever packaged snacks are in the racks and jars: jerky, Polish sausage, pigs' feet, cheese crackers. Chips, corn chips.

"They been bringin in cottonwood and turnin it in t'chips fr the Jap*nese* trade. The Jap*nese*, they bring the chips back in bulk nen they grine d'm *up*, make plywood 'r *pa*perboard," it is explained. Mouths are compressed, heads shaken.

An old-timer says that when O. *O.* was alive, mill wouldn't a bothered cuttin no hemlock, no fir, no cottonwood. "Cedarn pine, pinen cedar. Nuth nelse. Nuth nelse. Cream o' th' fawr'st. Nowdays . . . nowdays . . . all Jap*nese* trade . . . all Jap*nese* trade. . . . Jap*nese* buyin *horse*-chessnut?, mill'll cut *horse*-chessnut."

"Cut it metric, too," someone says, low-voiced. At this ultimate degradation, all sigh.

"Say, *I* did-dunt know the Jap*nese* were buyin *horse*-chessnut."

An old-timer has been watching this last old-timer for a while. Makes up his mind. "Say, 'n' I use ta see you sawin at Number 3 Mill, old O. *O.* still 'live?"

"Drine kill."

The first old-timer says he coulda swore he'd seen the second old-timer sawin at Number Three Mill, time old O. *O.* was alive. Second has had a chance to think it over, says, *Some*, he sawed at Number 3. But mostly he worked in the dryin kiln. He says, "I hear old B. *B.*'s daughter workin in thoffice now."

"No kiddin."

"What *I* hear."

"*Grand*daughter," says someone.

And someone, someone else, no old-timer at all but a younger man nursing a beer, says he hears that *she*. Is hot *stuff*. That she don't care what she does, or who she does it with. And an old-timer asks, Ain't they all that way anymore? Some of them declare loudly that they sure are. But some, those who've got their own grand-daughters, grunt. Look away. One says, again, Say, he didn't know the Jap*nese* were buying horse-chestnut. And it is explained to him that this was just made up as a for-instance. And then someone asks, "So you think the mill will maybe close?"

"*I* didn't say the mill will maybe close!"

"You think maybe Borski will take over?"

"*I* didn't say Borski will maybe take over!"

"He's trying to go where Vic is."

"Yeah, well you can only go so far with Vic, y' know."

"*I* know it. But does Borski?"

The younger man nursing the beer says that *he* doesn't give a shit, his brother's got a foreman's job in Oregon and can get *him* a job scaling anytime either of them want to. But he orders no second beer.

And a very old-timer, whose mind had drifted away, observes it come drifting back. Waits. The bartender meanwhile speaks up. "From what I hear," he says, "you don't want to count O. & B. out too fast. Whut I hear, they been down buhfore. But they never been out." And others say, *No no. Been down before but never been out, that's true*, they say. *That used to be true of even old O. O. even in the old country*, is what someone says. And someone else begins to chuckle. " 'Yust yerk it up and down,' " he says, in a sing-song. "What old O. O. used to say when the watchamacallit would stuck, by the donkey-engine; 'Yust yerk it up and down,' he'd say. Haw haw!"

And now the very old-timer says, "Plenny pinen cedar on th' P'*nin*-s'la."

Ah, they all say, *On the Peninsula....*

Ah....

As always in the office, Mary cannot keep her eyes off the co-founders. "Oh what a pair of robber-barons!" she says.

"Oh, no, Miss Blennerhassett. They were just competent businessmen. According to the standards of the day." Says Victor ("Vic") B. Olauson.

"Oh? And wouldn't you say the same is true of Borski?"

Well, no, he wouldn't. Not "just." It may have been competent of Borski to go secretly to Japan for business instead of waiting for the Japanese buyers to come over here. But it was in violation of the gentlemen's agreement between Borski and O–B not to cut each other's throat. Vic Olauson, you would at first be taking him for thirty. Then fifty. Or maybe vice versa. He was actually forty. Borski, he said, was willing to do anything, promise anything, so long as it would unbalance an adversary. Then he'd *push*— They had to watch out for Borski.

Borski (Mary was thinking as she got gasoline early one morning), Borski held proxies, was trying to hold more. Borski held O–B's paper. And was trying to hold more. Borski—

"Borski," said a voice. It was no thought-voice, it was a real, live, *voice*-voice. Someone had come up alongside her. The woman who owned the gas station. Her name? Forgotten.

"What about him," the name came suddenly, "Laurella?"

"None a my business," said Laurella, a weather-beaten person who had certainly slaughtered, gutted, scalded home-farm hogs before ever she had ten candles to her cake; well, if it's *none of your business* why mention it, shrilled Mary's voice. Though it was only a thought-voice. "But I hear Borski's goen to th' P'*nin*'s'la. And I seen fr myself that Prue Jensen rollin drunk over by the bar; early *start* what *I* mean. Tell Vic, 'f you like."

Mary, puzzled, thought best to say nought but, "Thanks, Laur'."

"You bet."

In the office. "Who's Prue Jensen?"

"Pruett Jensen?" Victor had his faults. But asking, *Why?* instead of first answering, this wasn't one of them. "He's the caretaker, the guard, at the Peninsula." Having said this, *then* he asked, "Why?" Was told Why.

Nothing flickered on that long flat face, dark secret-keeping face with its odd blue eyes. " 'Going to the Peninsula,' hey. Well, maybe a good place for him to go. Guess I'll go, too."

"And me." His eyes looked at her. "I'm a stockholder," she said. "And a partner. And, oh, damn it! I'm a grand*child*, even if not a grand*son*!"

And he said, "Yes."

But they said nothing to anyone as they got into his car and drove off. It was beautiful going there, and beautiful when gotten there. Now and then Vic pointed out where a narrow-gauge railroad line had been, and where oxen had once skidded vasty logs. The rocks and rills, the woods and templed hills, she could see for herself: they were beautiful.

"Jensen wasn't due to get drunk for another two weeks, at which time we would have relieved him. If he's drunk this early and if Borski's going to the Peninsula this early, then Jensen's drunk because Borski got him drunk. Him. Or his men. Or his women.— I'll have to get out and open the lock. Be a minute." The lock was on a chain and the chain was on the gate of a tall chain-mesh fence which came from the woods on one side of the road and entered the woods again on the other. There was a faint smell of balsam. She asked about the lock? About Borski's getting in?

Victor clicked his tongue. "Fence has mostly a moral effect. Pirate loggers know that Breaking and Entry's a more serious charge. Fence keeps out bikers and it keeps out poachers who want to jacklight deer and picnickers in cars who won't put out fires . . . like that. But this is a peninsula, you know, and it's surrounded on the other three sides by the lake and we never attempted to fence off the whole lakeshore or shoreline. Anybody can land in a boat and it's the caretaker's job to keep 'em off or send 'em back. Guess his job is now vacant." No curse. No anger. *Guess his job is now vacant.*

And, oh it was beautiful on the Peninsula! *Huge* pine. *Immense* cedar. The smell of balsam stronger. Place even had its own rivers! Time vanished. Suddenly— "Well, there's the caretaker's house. We have to get out of the car now. This is as far as the road goes. It's a good house, too, and rent and utilities free. Well. His choice."

The foot path wound on and on through the forest as though in a fairy tale; and Mary, reflecting, remembered that not everything which took place in those old Teutonic tales was merry and bright; and that an awful lot of Grimm was . . . well . . . *grim*. "What does Borski want here. Hm?"

Path skirted giant roots. "To spy out the land. Of course he's been over it by plane and helicopter and he's got mosaic photographs and he probably knows by expert analysis how many board feet of how many kinds of wood down to the last tooth-pick inch. But oh, there's nothing like seeing for yourself, *is* there, you forest-destroying, family-breaking, union-busting creep, Borski." Then they saw him.

At least she guessed it was. Who else?

The forest path went straight and it led straight up to a great rock and there was a man standing on top of the great rock. She said that it looked dangerous. Victor said that it *was* dangerous.

. . . and as they got quite close, he said in a low voice that they were not to make any noise. In her own mind Mary marveled at Vic's concern for the enemy's safety (the enemy had his back to them). But then—*no!* From somewhere Vic got a stick, a tree-branch it was, was it for a cudgel? Was he going to sneak up and bludgeon—? The man on the big rock never moved, as Vic began to walk around the rock to his right, dragging the branch after him. It was a long time, or so it seemed, before he returned. Still dragging it. He'd changed his mind, then. Well.

But how had Borski not noticed Vic circling the vast stone? Well, if Vic had stuck close to it, and it *was, vast.* . . .

Vic began to sing; *Vic* began to *sing!* What was it, the song? Not a single word could she make out, and it seemed awfully off-tune. He didn't even seem to want to face her and sort of bent down a bit with his damned stick and began to scratch the soil; was he printing something? Awfully odd letters; were the letters, was the song, even in English? Borski moved.

Borski of course turned around and looked down at them. Borski—there wasn't really another word for it—Borski snorted. He smiled, but only on one side of his face. *He* wasn't one of nature's noblemen. And then he moved to the far side of the rock and vanished from sight. Maybe he had a folding ladder. Maybe there were steps in the rock. What happened next? Next they heard his feet on gravel. He came into sight. Suddenly turned around and peered back behind him. As though he'd heard something. Not the singing. Something else.

It was inexplicable but yet it was funny: the way Borski suddenly began acting like a spooked old maid in an old movie: the way Borski put his hands straight up at right angles to his arms which he'd put straight out in front of him: the way Borski began to say, "Oooo oooo oooo." The way Borski's eyes began to bulge: all that was funny. It was funny for just a second or two, then Borski began to scream and that was not funny, and next Borski started to turn and run away on tottery rubbery legs: not funny. Then Borski, still screaming and moving in slow motion, was heard to lose control of his bowels. What came around the rock was about four or five times the size of a naked man; and the head and mouth were anyway disproportionately huge, and it came on in a sort of shambling lope, and it took hold of Borski and shoved Borski into its mouth head first and got him in up to the waist and began to bite and chew, and it kept on shambling and loping and biting and chewing, and it kept on shoving Borski into its mouth, and it vanished around the other side of the rock.

Olauson watched calmly. She fell against him and he got a hold of her and she said, "Save me. Save me." Again, just like in an old movie. "Don't let it get me; don't let it get me," she said.

"Oh it won't get *us.* Why I drew the circle and then those runes. My grandfather said—"

She sort of melted into him. "What was it? What is it?"

"Well, Miss Blennerhassett. The Indians call it the wendigo, but my grandfather said it was a troll. My grandfather was a very competent businessman and he had this *meth*od, you know, from the old country, and—"

She had control of herself. "Can we just get out of here, real quick, right now, right now?" She was pressing, pressing against him.

He nodded. "Yes. But it's gone, you know. That's all it ever wants, and it gets it and it goes. So just let me rub out the circle and the runes."

They walked away, and it was she who set the pace—pretty fast—did the Peninsula woods seem less safe now? Safer? Was this the real reason why their grandfathers hadn't wanted them cut and why their fathers hadn't even wanted them to pass out of family hands? The breeze was clean and the odor of the balsam was very strong. But she began to tremble; she hadn't trembled, really, before; but she was trembling now. "There's the house," Vic Olauson said. "And the car." What was he made of? Was he made of *ice?* There was the car, there was the house, there—

"I want you, I want you," she said.

He had bent over to open the car door. He turned. "What?"

"You and I. There—there—in the house. Together. In bed—"

He straightened, pulled the car door open. Gestured to her. "No, no, Miss Blennerhassett," he said. "I am a married man."

AFTERWORD TO "THE PENINSULA"

During his last years, Avram lived in the Pacific Northwest, much of the time in and around Bremerton, Washington. This tale grew out of his stay in those heavily wooded hills and waterways, and out of his always perceptive ear for regional dialects. It was my very great pleasure to use this story in *Amazing Stories* during my editorship of that venerable magazine.

—George H. Scithers

SUMMON THE WATCH!

If you want to see New York as New York used to look, there is no point in looking around Manhattan, the only place which practices autocannibalism as a matter of policy. The few—the very few—blocks of old buildings which survive on Minuit's island have, for the most part, become slums. Old New York, however, does survive, but in the sister borough.

Upshurr Street in Brooklyn is not very long, and the legend that it is easy to get lost in Brooklyn is, unfortunately, all too true. Perhaps that is why so much that is old and good still survives in Brooklyn—perhaps the wreckers have merely been unable to find their way, and, finally baffled, have given up and retreated to destroy yet more areas across the East River.

The two men who arrived at the house at the corner of Upshurr and Huyk Streets one winter afternoon surveyed it with interest, despite the cold. It was a well-kept building in the Georgian style, three stories high, and surrounded by garden. The smaller trees and bushes were carefully muffled in burlap. The two men mounted the steps.

"Where's the bell?" one of them asked, after fumbling with his gloved hand.

The other man shifted a camera he was carrying, bent over, and looked. He straightened up and shrugged. "Ain't none. Try that doojigger there," he said.

The knocker—in the form of a lion's head with a long tongue—was banged a few times. The two men waited, stamped their feet, blew out vapor, rubbed their noses. Then the door was opened by a short heavy old woman with long gray ringlets clustering around her broad pink face. "Come in," she urged. "Come in."

"Miss Vanderhooft?" the first man asked. The old woman nodded vigorously, setting the ringlets to bouncing like springs. "My name is—"

"Your name will still be the same if you come inside," she said crisply. They entered, she shut the door. The house was warm, and well furnished in the style of the early nineteenth century.

"My name—" the man began again.

"*My* name is Sapphira Vanderhooft," the old woman said. "My sister, being elder, ought properly to be addressed only as 'Miss Vanderhooft,' but since this fact seems to have passed out of all common knowledge, you may address her as Miss Isabella—come along, come along," she urged, gesturing them to precede her; "and me, as Miss Sapphira."

They found themselves in the living room, or parlor. A coal fire burned in the high basket grate. A few candles shed a soft light which melted into the ruddy glow from the fireplace. Seated in an upright chair was a second old woman, tall and spare, with her white hair parted in the center and drawn back.

"You will excuse me if I do not rise," she said, nodding to them and making a slight gesture with an ivory-headed cane. Embroidery work, hooped and needled, lay in her lap.

"This is my sister," said Miss Sapphira. "Isabella, these gentlemen are from the newspaper. That is, I *hope* that they are gentlemen," she added.

"And I hope that they are from the press," Miss Isabella said. "Have you seen identification, sister? If you are on another errand—soliciting contributions, for example—you won't get any," she went on, as the younger of the two men fumbled in his pocket. "Mr.

Caldwell, at the Trust Company, takes care of all that for us. Hmm. What is this?" She examined the card offered her. "It has last year's date on it; how is that?"

The man said that the card's validity ran from April to April, and—as Miss Isabella nodded, and handed it back to him—he at last managed to get out the information that his name was Dandridge and that his photographer-companion was called Goltz.

"Let me have your greatcoats," Miss Sapphira said. "There's no need for you to stand, we aren't royalty. Have whatever chairs you like, but the settle is mine."

Mr. Dandridge, who was thirtyish and thin, and Mr. Goltz, who was fortyish and squat, looked around the cozy, quaintly furnished room.

Miss Isabella broke the momentary silence. "If you've come to do a sensational article for the penny press, young man, the point cannot be too strongly emphasized that we are *not* recluses," she said.

"Certainly not," agreed Miss Sapphira. "The fact that we receive *you* is—or should be—proof of *that.*"

Dandridge said, "Well—"

"After that unfortunate affair of the Collier brothers," Miss Isabella swept on, "there was a reporter here from the Brooklyn *Eagle*, and he at once conceded that there was no similarity at all."

"None whatsoever," said Miss Sapphira. "We knew Homer and Langley when they were very young. The trouble with them was simply that they were spoiled. Aren't you going to say anything for yourself?" she demanded of Mr. Dandridge.

He smiled. Goltz looked bored. "I might begin by saying that my paper isn't a sensational one—and that it's been many years since any newspaper sold for a penny."

The older Miss Vanderhooft sniffed. "Well, it has been many years since we have cared to purchase one," she said. "So your information is of no particular use."

"Also," Goltz growled, "the *Eagle* is outa business."

For a moment the sisters were startled. Then they regained their aplomb. "Ah, well," said Miss Isabella, "it doesn't signify."

Dandridge looked down from a portrait labeled "General J. Abram Garfield." "Our editor thought it would be of interest to the readers to see how the calm and gracious life of another day is still being kept up amid the hustle and—and—" he stumbled, hesitated.

The sisters smiled. "We are, I suppose, old-fashioned, to be sure," said Miss Isabella, "but we will not be shocked if you say the word 'bustle.' Silly fashion, we always thought. And our dear papa used always to say that the garments Mrs. Amelia Bloomer was condemned for wearing were not so very much sillier than the ones she was condemned for *not* wearing."

Miss Sapphira said that she had put the kettle on. "It will sing, presently, and then we shall have tea. Would you like tea? Capital."

Her sister picked up the hoop and took the needle in her fingers. She looked at the reporter, nodded to him encouragingly. Miss Sapphira, on the settle, slid her hand into her pocket, slipped out a tiny silver box, and—when she thought no one was looking—hurriedly took a pinch of snuff.

"Well, now that we are agreed that you are not recluses," Dandridge said, "may I ask if it is true that you have no radio, telephone, or television?"

The younger sister said that it was true. Such devices, she explained, as she might to a child, exuded a malign magnetical influence. Indeed, if it were not for their dear brother's insistence, they would never have allowed the electrical incandescent lamps to be installed. He was dead, poor Cornelius, and they now lived quite alone.

No servants? Ah, that *was* a problem, wasn't it? Well, Emma came in thrice a week to clean—not today, being Monday, but on Tuesdays, Thursdays, and Saturdays. She did the shopping. The sisters would endorse the bills and send them to Mr. Caldwell at the Trust Company, who mailed checks to the merchants. In clement weather the two sisters often walked to the end of the block and back; no farther.

To church? No, no longer, but of course they always had evening prayers, and on Sundays they took turns reading sermons—one of Dr. Talmage's or, sometimes, one of the Reverend Henry Ward Beecher's. They did not, they assured Dandridge, believe a *word* of that dreadful scandal.

"Was there a scandal about him?" asked Mr. Dandridge. "I didn't know that."

The sisters exchanged gratified glances. "You see, Sapphira," Miss Isabella said. "I *told* you it would die down in time!"

"And have you no fears about living alone like this?"

Certainly not. Why should they have? It was a respectable neighborhood. The police always tried the doors at night—not that it was really necessary.

Dandridge cleared his throat. "Now—I don't mean to ask personal questions—but there seems to be a sort of, ah, legend, to the effect that a large treasure is hidden on the premises. . . ." He tapered off with a chuckle.

"Treasure?" asked Miss Isabella, looking at Miss Sapphira.

"Treasure?" asked Miss Sapphira, looking at Miss Isabella.

"No," they said simultaneously. Then, "Do you suppose, sister, that the young man could be referring to the gold"—the photographer, for the first time, looked interested—"which dear papa brought here following the panic of 'seventy-three?" suggested Miss Isabella.

"Are you?" asked Miss Sapphira. The reporter nodded.

Miss Sapphira said, "Well, well. It isn't here any longer. No. We have *long* since turned it over to the government. Now, when was it? Nineteen twenty-three? Nineteen thirty-three?"

"Usurpation!" cried Miss Isabella, thumping her stick on the floor. A faint pink suffused the pallor of her cheeks. "Usurpation and confiscation—though I suppose we could expect little better, with the Republicans in office."

Miss Sapphira, for her part, brushed aside Dandridge's comment that the Democrats were in office at the time privately owned gold was called in. Dear Grandpapa Vanderhooft, she told him, had said often enough that the nation's fiscal policy had never been sound since the Whigs went out of power. And the two old women nodded soberly at this sage, though melancholy advice.

Miss Isabella poured the tea, Miss Sapphira passed around the cake. Mr. Dandridge brushed his lips with a heavy monogrammed linen napkin. "Why do you call it 'usurpation and confiscation,' ma'am—the government's calling in your gold, I mean? After all, you received—they didn't just take it—you got money for it, didn't you?"

Miss Isabella waved her cane. "Only bank notes!" she said angrily. "Shinplasters! And to think they took our good northern gold to Kentucky—a nest of rebels!"

But Mr. Dandridge was no longer concerned with the gold. "And what did you do with all those shinplasters?" he asked. Miss Isabella was drinking tea, so her younger sister replied.

"It is somewhere around, I suppose," she said. "It doesn't really signify."

Mr. Dandridge got up. "It signifies to *us,*" he said. He pointed to Mr. Goltz, who had put his camera to one side and had something else in his hand. "Now, ladies, you are going to show us to your money and we are going to take it. Everything will be done quickly and quietly, and no one will be hurt. Up, please."

The two old women looked from him to the revolver in Mr. Goltz's fist.

"And you a photographer!" said Miss Sapphira, her pink cheeks very pink indeed. "Why, poor Mr. Brady would turn in his *grave* if he knew."

"Led'm," said Goltz, briefly. "C'mon, where's the money, ladies? Where ya goddit stashed away?"

Miss Isabella sighed and started to rise upon her cane. Dandridge reached to assist her, but she drew back with such an expression of disdain that he let his hand fall. "I suppose the quicker you have it, the quicker you'll leave. And 'tis only greenbacks, after all—no better than the credit of the government, and if the government allows banditti such as you to roam the peaceful streets of Brooklyn it has very little credit indeed. . . . I think they may be in the cedar chest."

The cedar chest proved, after prolonged searching, to contain four bolts of linen and approximately one hundred copies of *Godey's Lady's Book,* all in perfect condition. While Goltz glowered, Miss Sapphira picked up a magazine and let out a little cry of pleasure. "Look, Sister! A story by dear grandpapa's friend whom he so often told us about, poor Mr. Poe. I'm *so* glad I've found it. I shall read it tonight."

For the first time Dandridge's control slipped its mooring. "Quit this fooling around!" he shouted. "I want that money located in ten minutes—or—"

Miss Sapphira said that she wondered if he fully realized what effect this episode would have on the *young* people of the country if it became known. A most deleterious one, she was afraid.

Her sister stood in a pose of deep thought. "It's been so many years—" she said. "Now, could it be in the mahogany press? That is in the next room. I have the keys on my chain, here, but one of you will have to bring the candles."

The afternoon had grown late and dark and the candles, held by Dandridge, shed a scanty light in the cold room while Miss Isabella fumbled for her keys. Goltz said, "I had enough of this. Them candles are too spooky, and I like ta see what I'm doing." He reached up and tugged the cord of the dusty electrolier overhead. The cord snapped off in his hand, but the lights went on. Miss Isabella and her sister clicked their tongues. Dandridge blew out the candles.

"Open it up," he ordered. Miss Isabella complied. Two large cloth bags tumbled out, and—as the two men exclaimed—quantities of paper money poured from them. Dandridge fell on his knees, grinning. Then, as he examined the money, his grin faded. He waved one of the bills toward the Misses Vanderhooft. "Is *this* what the government gave you for your gold?" he demanded incredulously. "The Planters and Merchants Bank of Boggs County, Missouri?"

The sisters sighed, shook their heads.

"So that is where it was? Dear me."

"An unfortunate speculation in wildcat currency on the part of Great-uncle Isaac—dear grandpapa's brother. We never knew him.

He fell at the Battle of Pittsburgh Landing in the year—"

A heavy hand beat loudly on the front-door knocker. A heavy voice called, "Is anything wrong, ladies? Hello, hello! Is anything—"

Miss Isabella, looking Goltz straight in the eye and without changing by a hair's breadth the expression of calm disdain on her face, opened her mouth and called. "Help!" in a clear, level voice. Goltz went livid, raised the revolver, shook his head threateningly. "Help! Footpads!" Miss Isabella called out.

Miss Sapphira took the candelabra and, with an underhand pitch, threw it through the windowpane.

"Stop, thief!" she sang out. "Summon the watch!"

"I hope you don't mind eating from the same cake as those two scant-soaps fed upon," Miss Isabella said. This time *she* cut and passed, while Miss Sapphira poured the tea. Patrolmen Freitag and Johansson shook their heads, swallowed, accepted more. "This recipe comes down to us from the days of Abraham Vanderhooft's second wife. They say that she was an indentured servant before he married her, but it doesn't really signify, does it? And we ourselves descend from the first wife. . . . Dear me, what an afternoon!"

Patrolman Freitag washed down his second slice of cake with half of his second cup of tea. "This guy Dandridge—the real one, I mean, the reporter—he better be careful what he does with his old press cards from now on, instead of throwing them away. I hope," he said, rather anxiously, "that you ladies won't mind too much having to go to court and all that? Because—I guess—well, we could maybe say you were sick and have them come here to take your testimony—maybe."

Miss Sapphira shook her head, setting the long gray ringlets in motion around her pink face. "It is very kind of you young men to be so considerate—but I trust that my sister and I are sensible of our duty as citizens."

Her sister nodded, then asked, as if the thought had just struck her, how it was that the attention of the two policemen had been drawn to the house so much earlier than usual. Johansson smiled. Freitag smiled. The former answered.

"It was the electric light," he said. "We were just cruising down Huyk Street and we saw the electric light—I mean, the shade and the curtains were drawn, but we could see it was electric. So I says to Freitag, I says, 'Oh-oh. I been living in this neighborhood for thirty years and I never saw no electric lights burning in the Vanderhooft house, not since Mr. Cornelius passed away.' And he says, 'Neither did I, Nels. Never anything but candles.' So we figured we'd better investigate. I gotta give you both credit—what you did, it took courage."

Miss Isabella said, "Poo." Her sister said, "Pshaw. Hog-snatchers is all they were, trying to get above themselves."

"It was not our idea at all, to install the incandescent lamps," Miss Isabella explained. "It was our brother's. But we have never used them since he died. Such devices exude a malign magnetical influence."

"Isabella," asked Miss Sapphira, "now that so much attention has been drawn to the matter I confess that I am mildly curious myself as to where those bank notes are."

The older sister's ivory forehead creased in thought. Then she said, "Do you know, Sister—I wonder if we did not ask Mr. Caldwell to take them down to the Trust Company and purchase bonds or something with them during the war."

Miss Sapphira considered. "Did we? Perhaps you are right. Perhaps we did."

"Ah, well," said Miss Isabella. "It doesn't signify. More tea for the watch?" she asked.

AFTERWORD TO "SUMMON THE WATCH!"

"Summon the Watch!" is one of a number of Davidson's stories set in New York City. Even more than he did in "Lord of Central Park," Davidson has woven into the tale allusions to bygone events and

customs that evoke a particular mood. Any one of these references—
the Collier brothers, the "malign magnetical influence," Mathew
Brady, wildcat currency, or a story by Poe in *Godey's Lady's Book*
("The Cask of Amontillado," most probably)—would require more
than this brief paragraph by way of explication. You may be certain
that Davidson could have supplied the details in a narrative meander
(and in other instances he did so). In "Summon the Watch!" these
little sparks of information are gold strands in a complex fabric:
tantalizing evidence of the writer's learning, inseparable from his
narrative skill.

—Henry Wessells

DRAGON SKIN
DRUM

When Corporal Bill Howard, USMCR, of Headquarters Company, 2nd Battalion, Fifth Marines (currently quartered in the old Austrian Legation), arranged with his friend, Gunnery Sergeant Jackson, to go on liberty together and have some roast duck, he had the exact restaurant in mind. The background was as follows: not long after the Regiment had arrived in Peiping from Okinawa he went sight-seeing one afternoon in the Forbidden City. Howard did not spend his money on fast living as so many of the Marines unfortunately did, so he was able to hire an interpreter-guide and this man (considering the fact that his black robe was going green with age he was unreasonable in the fee he demanded, but Howard was able to beat him down without difficulty), in pointing out places of interest, had mentioned—several times—a certain class of Imperial officials. This aroused Howard's interest. It was not a morbid or indecent interest, of course, it was just that, after all, this same class was mentioned in the Bible. So Howard had asked if it might be possible to meet one of these people, and the interpreter-guide had put on quite an act. He said it was impossible just to walk in on this particular one outright because he was very famous, and so forth and so on. Finally Howard agreed to give a dinner for him, and when he arrived at the restaurant he found he was entertaining, not just the interpreter and the ex-official (a Mr. Chen), but a supernumerary interpreter as well, also a man who had acted as go-between, and his small son. Although expensive ($6.00, gold—that was what they called U.S. money, "gold"), it was not without interest, and the interpreter told him he had gained much face by giving the dinner. That was why he picked the same restaurant to eat at with the Gunny.

"How's about we bring some women?" the Gunny said, ribbing Howard as usual. "Nice Chinee girl, huh? One for you and one for me?"

"Chacun à son goût," was Howard's answer. And he told Gunny Jack he was thinking of asking a former official of the Imperial Court to join them over the *kow yahdza*, or roast duck; promising him that this man was worth meeting. "Okay by me," said the Gunny. And he curled his long and black handle bar mustache. This gunnery sergeant was tall and dark and fierce-looking and had a dent in his nose. Like so many others in the Corps then stationed in China, he led a rather dissolute life. Indeed, he once persuaded Bill Howard to accompany him to a place called The Palace of All Seasons.

"Let your hair down, damn it," he said. The place was full of smoke and noise and everyone was drinking freely. A Chinese woman came and sat down, uninvited, next to Howard, and tried to show off that she knew a little English. She called in a coarse voice to another woman, "Sister! Come over here, Sister! I want you to meet this nice American." And the other woman, also garishly painted, came and sat down on Howard's other side. From the ribald comments of the other Marines he gathered that these women were not "hostesses" as they claimed to be, but just common prostitutes, so he made only perfunctory replies to their questions and they finally let him alone. The older one, Blossom, was a disgusting sight, with cigarette smoke dribbling out her flat nose; but the younger one, May (or "Sister"), was rather pretty underneath the paint. It was too bad she lived a sinful life.

On this particular afternoon Corporal Howard and Gunnery Sergeant Jackson got into two rickshaws and went off through the maze of crooked streets and dirty alleys until they reached the place where

Old Mr. Chen lived, somewhere in the quarter known as the Imperial City. The elderly gentleman was obviously very pleased to see them, and when Bill Howard said to him (in Chinese, for, instead of wasting time talking pidjin-English to prostitutes, he took Chinese lessons at the Y), *"Chir fahn, low yay"*—"low" rhyming with "cow"—which is to say, "Sir, I invite you to dinner," he agreed at once. The old man put on a robe of black silk or satin, with a flowery design, over his knitted upper and lower garments, and they hired a third rickshaw and off they went. Jackson was moody and silent, which pleased Howard just as well because, once or twice before, Gunny Jack under the slight influence of liquor had called out something in a loud voice which amused the rickshaw-coolies and other lower-class Chinese very much, until Howard asked him not to. The Gunny protested it was the only Chinese he knew. Indeed, this friendship, with two people so different in their habits and whole outlooks, was rather puzzling to some people. Only the wonderful *esprit-de-corps* of the Marines could explain it.

As the three rickshaws rolled down the street and the shouts of the coolies mingled with the cries of the street vendors and the sound of the phonographs playing Chinese music in the shops crammed with strange merchandise, Bill Howard felt as if he were witnessing something unreal from a novel by Mrs. Pearl S. Buck or other commentators on the Oriental scene—picturesque and exciting, but impossible to understand despite the many attempts he made to do so because of the importance of China in the world scene. They crossed Morrison Street and rolled to a stop inside the East Bazaar. This was a large building containing stalls and shops where absolutely every kind of ware was sold, and upstairs was the Mohammedan restaurant where they were going to eat. Two of the coolies accepted their money at once, but the third one demanded more. At this Old Mr. Chen made a noise of shock and outrage and he took the Americans by their hands and stalked them away like an indignant old grandmother. While they were walking past the curio section he stopped and began to talk to a man who had a briefcase under his arm. This man wore a very tired-looking felt hat and on the whole looked the picture of failure, but he turned out to speak perfect English. It seemed that Old Mr. Chen asked him to join the party to interpret, and although for a moment Bill was annoyed—because each time he came here to eat he seemed fated to feed half the population of Peiping—it was just as well, because his own knowledge of Chinese, while equal to the stresses and strains of shopping, was certainly inadequate for conversational purposes, and there was absolutely no point in just *feeding* Mr. Chen.

He wanted him to talk about the old days before the monarchial system was overthrown, and he wanted to see if he could get some interesting stories out of him. Something that, in the future, in later years, when he was a father and had all his children gathered around him, he could say, such as, "Listen closely, now, and I'll tell you a story that an old Chinese nobleman told me once." And they would shush one another and snuggle up close.

So the four of them went upstairs, and by some miracle they were still only four when they reached their private dining room (actually a small cubicle with a curtain across the door). A fat man with a wispy mustache had set up a cry as soon as he saw them come in. Little Mr. Wong (this was the interpreter's name) fiddled with his dirty fedora and started to speak to him, but the fat man interrupted after a few words. Mr. Wong laughed. The Chinese laugh when they are embarrassed or when they hear bad news or even when they tell it. One of them had said to Bill Howard once, "My concubine dies last week, hah-hah-hah!" and Howard did not know whether to be more shocked at this easy confession of loose living or at the callous way the man laughed, but after a while he came to understand the Chinese character better. And it must be admitted you cannot judge them altogether by American standards: first, because they are not a Christian nation, and second, because they have been so long engaged in unremitting struggles for their liberties against external and internal enemies.

The time before, when Howard was here in this restaurant, and roast duck was ordered, a delicacy for which Peiping is famous, there took place an amusing incident. The waiter had led him downstairs and out through the kitchen, which was full of steam and sizzling and half-naked men shouting and little boys running about, down to the backyard where there was a pen full of white ducks quacking around, and the waiter asked him to pick out the ducks he wanted! This time he told them to fix a duck they had on hand ready to go, but they still insisted on bringing in several plucked ducks, with the heads still on them, for him to pick. Meanwhile Sergeant Jackson was getting restless.

"How's about some beer?" he demanded. *"And* some whiskey?" And he said loudly, "Hey, boy, got-chee bee'jo? Gotchee whiskey-jo?"

"Oh, never mind that pidjin-English," Howard protested. "That's what Mr. Wong is here for, to interpret. Not that we aren't glad to have you with us anyway, I mean, Mr. Wong." Mr. Wong sat up straighter and opened his mouth. He looked kind of sad and soiled and crumpled.

"Bring three piecee bee-jo, chop-chop," the Gunny said.

The waiter, who was just a boy in a dirty apron, yelled something. Outside, someone yelled back.

"They have no whiskey," Mr. Wong explained. "They have wine. I shall order wine?"

"You're doggone-ay right, order wine," said the Gunny, only he used another word instead of doggone. Mr. Wong spoke to the boy, and looked more cheerful. Mr. Chen just sat back and smiled blandly and benevolently. The table was spread as follows: a clay pot (with a wire tripod around which was coiled a long piece of glowing punk to light cigarettes on) to hold the ashes, three tall brown bottles of lager beer, glasses, five pairs of chopsticks (one to serve with), some squares of soft paper (to wipe the chopsticks on), two teapots, cups, and four small dishes of chopped raw vegetables. These last Howard would not have sampled at any price because what the Chinese use to fertilize their vegetables with is too disgusting to mention. Jackson and Wong began drinking the beer and the wine and Howard and Old Mr. Chen had tea. Then the old man had some beer and wine, so that left only Howard sticking to tea.

"Very good wine," Mr. Wong said. His cheeks were flushed. The wine was in one of the teapots, as is seen in moving pictures about Prohibition days. It wasn't really wine, but was distilled from grain of some sort and was a very pale yellow. "You are a Moslem?" Mr. Wong asked.

"No, I just don't drink," Howard said.

"Have you been long acquainted with famous Mr. Chen?" On hearing his own name, the old man beamed and nodded.

"What makes him famous?" asked the Gunny, wiping beer off his long mustachioes and pouring his cup full of "wine."

"Oh, he is a very famous eunuch." (Gunnery Sergeant Jackson said, "Well, J————C————!") "Oh, yes. You see his eyes? They are eunuch's eyes. His face is the face of a eunuch. All have the same eyes, face. The lids—see how they droop? The face has no hair, only a soft down, it is like a face made of very pure but un-bleached beeswax, in which grooves have been scored with a hot knife—no wrinkles. And his voice is the voice of a eunuch."

Mr. Wong, his tongue perhaps loosened by his potations, went on to explain that the Imperial Government used the eunuchs as a kind of civil service. There were two grades. One was recruited from the lower classes to be servants of the Imperial Family—barbers, valets, and so on. The other was recruited from the upper classes, and these became government officials.

"They don't do that any more, do they?" the Gunny asked.

"No, not since the tyrannous Imperial power was overthrown. It was a very wicked government."

Corporal Howard quoted the text from Mark which says, "Some are eunuchs from their mothers' wombs, some are made eunuchs by men, and some become eunuchs for the sake of the Kingdom of Heaven. He that can receive it, let him receive it."

"Well, don't look at me," the Gunny said. Mr. Wong drank some more wine. "The Chinese Revolution was nurtured in the United States," he said. Then he belched. The Chinese consider this the height of politeness. "It is one reason why I love the United States," he said. Then he made quite a speech about Sun Yat-Sen and the wonderful work Chiang Kai-Shek (which he pronounced Jong Gay-Shur) had done, and the traditional friendship between the United States and China.

"I'm getting hungry," the Gunny interrupted. He, too, had been drinking, not wisely, but too well. "How about a oyster, Samivel," he said. "Or a srimp?"

The Corporal asked, "What?" Just then they brought in a great big fish with the head still on it. In fact, the Gunny mumbled something to the effect that in China they leave the heads on everything but the people. Old Mr. Chen took the extra pair of chopsticks and was about to start serving the fish, but Mr. Wong took them away and poured hot tea over them and wiped them clean and gave them back. After Mr. Chen had very deftly taken off the skin and then all the fish on the top side, he turned it over and as he was carving it out he said something. Mr. Wong translated.

"Ah, yes, you see, this is very interesting: at the table of the Empress Dowager, whose aide he was, they only served the fish on top. As it was beneath their dignity to turn the fish over, the rest was sent to the servants. See, how proud and haughty the Manchus were. Now everything is democratic."

"Does Jong Gay Shoo give his servants half his fish?" the Gunny asked.

"Mohammedan cooking is very good," Mr. Wong said, ignoring this foolish question.

The Gunny wiped his mouth. "By Allah, yes," he said. "I desire more."

But the fish was already gone. They brought in a big plate of shrimp cooked in some kind of yellow batter, and after that there was paper-thin mutton and vermicelli, cooked together over charcoal, with cabbage, and about ten different sauces. Old Mr. Chen asked if they had vermicelli in America.

"Yes," Howard told him. "Marco Polo brought it from China to Italy, and the Italians brought it to America."

"The trouble is, the old man really does not understand anything foreign," Mr. Wong said. "Certainly nothing modern. If you ask him about Russia, for example, he will tell you about the presents of Catherine the Great to Ch'ien Lung."

"If you ask *me* about Russia, for example," said Gunny Jack, "I will tell you the following story: when I was a young and ardent sixteen, and had not yet developed these bar-muscles amidships, my father was convinced there would be war with Russia at any time, and he sent me to military school. One morning while we were very spartanly getting in some mileage in the streets near the school, clad only in sneakers and shorts, I chanced to see a very pretty woman giving me the eye as I jogged by her house. So I let everyone else get ahead of me, then I jogged back, straight to her welcoming arms, and there I stayed for two days and two nights, practically a prisoner, as she refused to get me any clothes. Finally, unable to continue my feats of war on a diet of soda-crackers and peanut butter, which was all she had in the house, I departed. When I got back to school I told them I'd had amnesia and remembered nothing. This important part of my education I owe entirely to the Russians, and I have endeavored to show my gratitude to the women of that nation here in Peiping."

Howard didn't know exactly what to say, so he asked Mr. Wong his profession.

"I am a school teacher. Soon I shall tell my classes of this meeting of ours, how two young Americans in military service spent time in inquiring of the Old China and the New . . ."

Corporal Howard was very glad he had gotten the floor away from Gunny Jack. As soon as the latter had a few drinks his whole manner changed, including his manner of speech. This had proven embarrassing before. And then the Gunny broke in.

"If I might ask the New China a question?"

"Why, certainly," Mr. Wong said, very politely.

"You're a sympathizer of the Kuomintang?"

"Oh, yes. For over thirty years—"

"And the school teachers are on strike?"

Mr. Wong laughed in embarrassment.

"Because they can't get their salary, right?" Mr. Wong looked at his plate. "And the government said it will give them free cornmeal, didn't it? And the teachers won't go back to work until they get the cornmeal, right?" Mr. Wong's cheeks were very red. He nodded. "Well, doesn't the New China notice that plenty of people are making plenty of money? Why doesn't it raise hell? Less corn and more hell; I mean, more hell to get more corn."

Mr. Wong said, "It is the Communists. The war is costing our government too much money, that is why."

Old Mr. Chen drank some tea. The boy felt the teapot and yelled and another boy, even smaller, came and brought a fresh pot and took away the old one. There was no more food on the table. Then they brought in the duck, a beautiful golden brown color, and a platter of wheat cakes like flapjacks, and green onions or scallions, and a soya sauce. They carved pieces of duck meat and sliced the green onions and put them on wheat cakes with sauce and rolled them up. All four began to eat. Mr. Chen made loud noises, to show how good it was. He shoveled rice into his mouth, holding the bowl right under his lips.

"Oh, boy, how the people here cheered when the Marines came to town!" said Gunny Jack. "You cheer, too, Mr. Wong?"

"I wept with joy," Mr. Wong said.

"Will you cheer when the Communists march in?"

"They will never come. The Chinese and American people will never permit it."

"Roger and wilco," the Corporal said.

"Oh, don't be so damned gung-ho," the Gunny said. "What do you know about real fighting? Okie was practically secured by the time you got there. Don't you *know* by this time that nothing short of full-scale intervention can stop the Reds? And don't you *know* that there isn't going to be any?"

"Then the Chinese will fight alone!" cried Mr. Wong.

"When? They're not doing it so far. A wonderful series of strategic retreats. Nope. Uh-uh. The Reds will march in, all right. And when they do, you will cheer, all right. And you'll tell your classes to cheer. Know why?"

Mr. Wong appeared very angry. "Why?" he asked. He was trembling.

"Because otherwise you won't get any cornmeal, that's why. And I am greatly afraid you won't get any more roast duck, no matter *how* loud you cheer. So eat up now, my brave Pekinese."

Once again Corporal Bill Howard felt constrained to change the subject. Besides, the purpose of this gathering was not being achieved. So he asked Mr. Chen questions about his career. The old man began to tell scandalous stories of the Empress Dowager, of whom, for some reason, he seemed quite proud, despite everything. She became empress simply because she bore a child to the then emperor, and this was typical of her life, because she was never really married to him. Then there was the Boxer Rebellion, and she pushed her nephew's concubine down the well—actually, she had some eunuch do it, Mr. Chen very calmly said—and kept him, her nephew, the emperor, locked up because he disobeyed her and she was very strong on filial piety. But this wasn't what Bill wanted, either. He asked Mr. Wong to ask Mr. Chen to tell them a story. Mr. Chen thought very deeply in silence. Then he began to speak.

"In the palace there was a drum made from the skin of a dragon. When there was a bad drought, the emperor—but only he—would beat upon this drum, and it would rain and the crops grow again."

And after finishing this statement the old man smiled.

"Is that the whole story?" asked Gunny Jack.

"Of course not, let him finish."

"But he is finished. As I told you, he understands nothing of foreign things." Mr. Wong's face was shiny from the grease of the duck. He licked a grain of rice from his lip-corner.

"Ask him, has he got any children?" said Gunny Jack.

"How can he have any children? He's a eunuch, didn't you hear?"

"Well, he coulda had them before he took the veil."

"Sometimes it was so," said Mr. Wong, "but not with him. He lives with his nephews. He became a eunuch when he was eighteen, and now he is over eighty." Gunny Jack swore loudly. Mr. Wong

explained that Mr. Chen had handled much money and was considered to be beyond temptation by women.

"The subject is too sad," Jackson observed. "Listen. I desire to
hear his views on the current situation. Ask him who, in his opinion,
is to blame for it. Tell him he may speak without fear."

Mr. Wong cleared his throat and spat in the corner. The two
Chinese spoke together. *"Yuan Shih-Kai,"* said the old man. He
spoke in a tone of cold contempt. As if you ask a rich old lady, who
made those marks on your lovely wallpaper? And she tells you the
name of a dirty little boy from the next block.

"Yuan Shih-Kai," said Mr. Wong. "The first president of China.
Because he broke the link."

Both Americans asked together, "What link?"

"The link between China and its past. Under the empire, he
says, we were the Children of Heaven. The emperor was our earthly
father. Once a year he, as Son of Heaven, would go to the Altar of
Heaven at the Temple of Heaven, and worship Heaven. And so,
whatever was wrong, it was still one family. But then Yuan Shih-
Kai, under pretense of establishing reforms, overthrew the Imperial
House. He made himself president, then he proclaimed himself emperor and ascended the Dragon Throne, but the link was broken
and the armies rebelled, so he swallowed his ring and died. Then
there was Sun Yat-Sen and the war lords and the Kuomintang and
the Japanese and the Communists. All—he says—because Heaven
is not worshipped and there is no harmony either above or below,
no filial piety, no national unity; and it is all the fault of Yuan Shih-
Kai, who broke the link." Mr. Wong drank.

The Gunnery Sergeant put his head on one side and nodded it.
"Well, it's a point of view," he said. "Not without merit."

"He is a very stubborn old man," Mr. Wong said. "He never
recognized the Republican Government, even though they gave him
a free pass to the Forbidden City, where he lived and worked in
imperial times."

"When did the last emperor die?" Howard asked.

"Ho, he is not dead. He is a prisoner of the Russians."

Jackson said, *"What?"*

"Oh, yes," said Mr. Wong. "The last emperor was only a boy of four when he ascended the Dragon Throne."

Two waiters came in with hot towels rolled up, very gray-looking, and probably crawling with diseases, which Howard waved aside; but the two Chinese swabbed their faces in them with loud grunts of pleasure, and even the Gunny used one.

"The Japanese made him emperor of Manchuria, the land of his ancestors, and he was captured there by the Russians when they went to war against Japan . . . his first wife is dead. A Manchu princess, I remember the wedding. 1922? or 1924?"

The Gunny, tugging each end of his mustache in turn, said, "Am I to understand—that the Emperor of China—of *China?*—is not only *alive,* but is a prisoner in the hands of the Russians?"

"That is quite correct. A foolish boy."

"Fabulous!" the Gunny exclaimed. "And nobody knows, and nobody even cares." He shook his head.

"All that belongs to the *Old* China," said Mr. Wong. They began to clear off the table. "The *New* China, with the friendly assistance of the United States—who, by returning the Boxer Indemnities for scholarships, enabled so many Chinese to secure a Western education—the New China will arise, like the phoenix from its ashes, and drive the rebels back beyond the Kalgan, beyond the Great Wall."

He tilted the teapot, or, rather, the winepot, but it was empty, so he finished the old man's beer instead. He tried to fix his eyeglasses, but they kept slipping off on one side.

"Why won't they fight, these phoenixes?" asked the Gunny. "I desire to know why the armies of the New, or should I not say, the middle-aged, China—the Kuomintang forces—will not fight? Hey? Why no fight Reds? Retreat, only."

Mr. Wong waved his hand. "They fight." He fell off balance, but quickly righted himself. "They fight"—he waved his hand and moved his mouth—"fiercely," finally finding the word.

"They run like hell, is what you mean."

Howard, to divert the subject, said, "This is very good tea."

"It is very *bad* tea!" Mr. Wong exclaimed. "They cheat you here. Swindle."

The Gunnery Sergeant said, "Well, that's the New China for you. We give them artillery, and they leave it behind. We give them cartridges, and they retreat without shooting them. We give them gasoline, and then it turns up on the black market."

"Lies," muttered Mr. Wong. "All lies."

Suddenly Old Mr. Chen gave a tremendous yawn. They all looked at him. He smiled and murmured something.

"We must take him home now," Mr. Wong said. "He is old and sleepy tired."

Howard realized that he wasn't going to get any more stories, or, rather, that he wasn't going to get *any*. But there was nothing to be done about it. He paid the bill and left cumshaw money, and they were bowed out of the restaurant.

It was dark out, but the streets were as full as ever. The trolley-cars, coupled together tandem-fashion, rattled by, the people hanging on the outside, and the rickshaws and bikeshaws swirled around. Private cars blew their horns furiously. The street lights went on and off, as they always did, but all the sidewalk vendors and shopkeepers had little gasoline or oil lamps. There was a yelling and clamoring and the sound of gongs and cymbals. Pretty soon they arrived at Mr. Chen's stop and they got out and Howard paid off two of the rickshaws. While he was doing so a Marine from their company came along and greeted them.

"What's the news from Kalgan?" the Gunny asked.

"Please tell Mr. Chen how much I enjoyed being with him," Howard said. Mr. Wong was taking a package from the hollow place under the rickshaw seat, and grunted.

"The way them Reds are acting, there ain't going to *be* no more Kalgan before very much longer. *We* sure aren't going to stick it out, and *you* know Chiang's boys, Gunny," the Marine said.

"You are speaking of the New China," said Gunny.

Mr. Wong and Mr. Chen conferred.

"Now, when I was in the *Old* Corps, in the *Old* China, we had a way of dealing with such a situation. We beat the drum. The dragon skin drum. We beat the cotton-picking hell out of it. That saved the day."

"Mr. Chen says, he thanks you. He asks you to give him a dollar, gold."

"What," asked Howard, startled.

"One dollar—not Mex, U.S.—for a souvenir."

"Gunny," said the Marine from Kalgan, "what in the *hell* are you talking about?"

Corporal Howard took out a dollar bill and gave it to Mr. Chen. The old man took it, but his face fell, and he pouted and muttered. Bill asked what was the matter. Mr. Wong laughed. This time he didn't sound embarrassed. He adjusted the bundle under his arm. It was beginning to show stains on the newspaper wrappings, and from it came the smells of the fish and the shrimps and the duck and the mutton, and Bill realized what had happened to the food that wasn't on the table after the first helping. Mr. Wong had claimed it from the restaurant as his cumshaw for interpreting the orders.

"Mr. Chen is angry. He says that you have made him lose much face by giving him the money in public as if he were a beggar. But he says you have lost face yourself by doing so."

"Why didn't you *tell* me how to do it?" Bill cried.

He felt terrible. The old man cast him a reproachful look as he left, but Mr. Wong laughed and walked off with a swagger.

AFTERWORD TO "DRAGON SKIN DRUM"

In his autobiographical sketch "The Great Coast of China" Davidson laments that he wrote so little of his stay in China at the close of the Second World War. The two Chinese fictions he crafted ("Dagon" and "Dragon Skin Drum") are brilliant—rich in observed detail and arcane knowledge, and alert to the contrasts that postwar

China presented to an American. "Dragon Skin Drum" is a deftly rendered clash of cultures from which there emerge images and incidents of heart-stopping intensity—punctuated by the caustic remarks of Gunny Jack. "Dragon Skin Drum" is one of the few pieces by Davidson published in a "mainstream" literary journal, the *Kenyon Review*. In a 1991 letter to R. W. Odlin, Davidson wrote that *Kenyon Review* editor Robie Macauley "advanced to be fiction ed at *Playboy* and thence onto Houghton, Mifflin . . . and he never ceased to say of whatsoever story, 'Not as good as the Dragon Skin Drum, of course.' "

—Henry Wessells

EL VILVOY DE
LAS ISLAS

Ah, las islas encantadas! Ah, in fact, the visions which the name itself enconjures! How many other archipelagoes, some of them quite non-existent, have borne that enchanted name, before it was finally settled on the group of islands in the South Atlantic . . . settled at least by some, that is. Perhaps these wild, wild islands had indeed not ever been visited by Da Gama, Vespucci, the brothers Pinzón, Sebastian Cabot, Ponce de Leon, Cartier, Drake, Sir Jno. Hawkins, and many another. And then, after all, perhaps they had. As Lope de Vega (¿Cervantes? ¿Calderón?) puts it in his dry, spare style, ¿Quien Sabe?
   Not I.

My friend Diego had driven up with the Land Rover of his choice—
a Safari Wagon, with space for twelve passengers and the driver (much good it would be without one), or, say, two people and lots and lots of baggage: a point which he made almost at once.
   "Oh, I don't doubt it," I said, admiring the spare tire, and fan-cying myself . . . almost . . . in Kenya, with Papa.
   "How would you like to drive down to the Straits of Magellan?"
   "Sorry. I just washed my beard, and I can't do a thing with it."
   "No, I am not joking; how would you like—"
   "Diego. Please."

And that was how I came to be driving down to the Straits of Magellan. Can one drive *up* to it? (them?) Certainly . . . if you start in Tierra del Fuego. Nothing to it, I suppose. Diego told me many stories of his boyhood, his family, his young manhood, his family, his country. And his family. After we crossed the Equator (I had crossed it twice, by sea, and was able to contain my enthusiasm this third time) the stories grew fewer, and his sighs more frequent. I do not wish to, indeed I can't, dismiss the entire South American continent cavalierly (or, for that matter, in any other way)—but this is not that story. As we went further and further South, of course, it grew colder and colder. As for the land along the Straits of Magellan, I realized that they had never been fully developed as Summer resorts; they were, I understood, cold. Very cold. And very, very wet.

After rising from sleep and sleeping bag one morning almost in slow motion, I faced not only the foothills of the Andes (I was looking westward), but the fact that I was not only no longer young, I was not even middle-aged any more. "Diego," I said, "my osteopath told me there would be days like this: plain old degenerative osteoarthritis done got me. Leave me here to sink my bones into some hot bath, and catch me when you come back." Although Diego gave me much sympathy, I felt that he was in some way rather relieved. Often and vividly as he had described to me his family, it was by now certain that he faced returning to them with something less than the wilder zeals. Folklore has prepared us for the Latin Americans with very many stereotypes, so that when they pick up their guitars and burst into "*¡Alla en rancho grande!*"—and sometimes they really do—we feel that this is all as it should be, and we are prepared for that. But folklore has not prepared us, in North America, with any stereotypes at all, really, for Latin Americans of the deep south of South American latitudes. Reunited with his family after many years in the United States, how would Diego react? How would his family react? And how would *I* react? Perhaps these considerations also engaged Diego's mind, for, although he assured me that hot baths were available in his family home, his tone lacked something of its once-enthusiasm.

"At any rate," he said at last, "I cannot simply leave you," his arms swept the chill, sparse landscape, *"here."*

"Well, in the next town or city, then."

"No, no: *mucha bronca gente.* Ah!" his face lit up, "I shall leave you with people I know, in Ereguay! It is not far, no, no, not even so far as the distance between New York and Milwaukee. I know some people there very well, no, nonsense, they are very nice people, they will be very glad to have you." All this (I thought to myself) was as it may be; but it was no time nor place for an argument; once there in that other country, about which I knew next to nothing, surely I could find what we used to call "reasonable accommodations"; Diego might assure me till his breath stopped smoking, but, face to face with the realities of the situation, he would accept my decision.

Gad! he'd better!

The rest of the trip, that is, of my trip to Ereguay, was rather painful, bodily; but the spirit or the journey seemed to have lightened with our common realization that, after all, Diego would not have to explain his family to me, and me to his family. That all the reproachful scenes beginning, "Far be it from me to reproach you, but," could now do without the intrusive presence of an outsider and a foreigner, *de populo barbaro,* as it were. Pop*u*lo? Pop*o*lo? Oh, well.

Descriptions of the fertile vineyards, the empires of wheat, the plantations of yerba mat(t)e, herds of kine and swine: these I must leave to others: lo! are they not already waiting in the wings?

The weather grew warmer, though never hot. The suburb where my friend's friends lived was old, and, I have imagined, Roman-suburb-like, with many a well-tended vegetation, lots of well-kept walls, and even (the plant which I chiefly recognized) roses, roses; the señores Murphy were at home—what? yes, Murphy. It would be indeed charming to write they still, after three, or who knows maybe more, generations, still spoke English with a lovely brogue; not so. No brogue at all? No brogue at all, he had brought me to Murphys with no brogue at all. Of course, yes, they did speak En-

glish, only English did they speak as soon as it was realized that this
was my language; it was a rather flattened-out English, you would
never in a million years have guessed, had you met them in, say,
Switzerland, what part of the world they were from. And they expressed no surprise at all on learning that Diego proposed to deposit
me with them; evidently this was, really was, the way things were
done down there. Diego lingered three days, so it was scarcely that
he was dropping me abruptly. And, as we waved him off, laden with
gifts for his parents, I seemed to be part of the family which belonged
in that villa, in that never-before-heard-of-by-me suburb of Ciudad
Ereguay—of which, in fact, I had hardly heard of, itself, until then.
A papal person had not long before said, publicly, that he was there
to represent church interests in Paraguay, Uruguay, Ereguay, "and
every other kind of-guay" (i.e. "woe"); it was curious how very suddenly the Vatican had need of him at home, after all. I make no
claim that I saw "the real Ereguay," indeed, even the unreal Ereguay
I scarcely saw outside the very far-stretching walls of the villa where,
twice a day, a hot bath was drawn for me, and where I received
every conceivable creature comfort and every conceivable courtesy.
In very little time the youngest children climbed into my lap, and
even the next to youngest also came over and gave me a good morning and a goodnight kiss. Beside my ample bed, a *"matrimonial"* in
the grand old style, upon the nightstand were laid such items as an
English-language newspaper (rather thin, as though the fat had been
stripped off it), an elderly novel by Michael Arlen, but one which I
had never read, and a fairly recent copy of the *Illustrated London
News.*

But if I were to go into detail we should never get anywhere, so
let us gel to a sort of small garden party, no, not a party, an informal
gathering, well, it was in the garden; it was only a few days that I
had been a guest, I was sure that I had yet to meet every single
member of the extended Murphy family, let alone very many members of the English-speaking population of Ciudad Ereguay. There
was a señora Angela de Something, whose husband was Someone in
the civil service, *un burócrata,* as it was, I thought, succinctly put; a

doctora Maria del Pilar Guzman, I am not certain of the area of her doctorate—gastroenterology perhaps, early colonial rent-rolls perhaps, you can't tell any more, men or women; however—I am aware of opening myself to all sorts of attacks, but nevertheless I shall make this statement: I seldom saw a woman of the upper middle or upper classes there who did not have lines of discontent around the mouth, and I seldom saw a woman of the working class there who was not happy and smiling and laughing. Spit on me, stone me, that's the way I saw it. There was an older man all in black and white, who at first glimpse I thought was a priest, but upon further attention was revealed to be an attorney; and there was a younger man, light-haired, in open shirt and khakis, whom I did not assess: he turned out to be a priest. Presently there entered a young man who was not introduced, he had rather longish and very brown hair, a farmer or perhaps a hunter by the look of him, and I don't recall that he said three words all the time he was there. And also someone was there, a doña Alberta, certain to be recognized everywhere as a Universal Grandmother; she was a moderately well-known British novelist on a visit from her home in the Isle of Wight. There were one or two others. I do not remember.

Someone had politely asked doña Alberta something, and she said, "I am always interested in hearing of the legends and folklore wherever I am. *Vin du pays,* one might say. Won't someone please tell me something of that?" She was a courageous woman; very often one is told fairly crisply that there are no legends, no folklore, all such things have passed quite away. But now, almost at once, licenciado Huebner said, "Ah, of course! We have the tragical tale of *la llorona,*" and he proceeded to tell us, in great detail and with much local color, the story of The Weeping Woman, which is found wherever Spanish is spoken and mis-spoken throughout the world; right at this moment in your city someone is telling it *now,* and naming the very neighborhood, through which you have unwittingly passed, where the unfortunate events occurred. I purposely do not tell it here; let it come, perhaps, as a surprise.

Someone said, *"Muy tragico."* Heads were nodded. And then

someone else said, "Well, we have also the legend of *el vilvoy de las islas.*"

The novelist asked, "Did you say 'veal boy'? Or 'beel voy'?"

Our host spelled it for her (and for me, too), "V–i–l–v–o–y," and added, "We pronounce it—"

But I did not then hear how they pronounced it, because before the attorney had more than begun, the young priest—not meaning, I am sure, to be impolite, merely he was a bit emphatic—said, " 'El Vilvoy,' but that is surely a collection of nonsense!"

The attorney said, very calmly, and as one certain of his facts, "Sometimes we provincials, with all our naif enthusiasm, nevertheless arrive at a conclusion more veridical than the sophisticates of the metropolis."

"Oh, but surely I did not say 'provincials'; and if, by 'the metropolis,' you mean Spain, or Madrid in particular, certainly I am a Madrileno, but—"

A servant approached with a tray. " 'El *vil*voy,' " repeated Mrs. Phlux (her real name), the novelist. "But what does that *mean?*" More than one person began, perhaps, to reply.

Our host, taking advantage of the abrupt silence which fell after several people had realized that they were all speaking at once, said, in a rather musing voice, "It is certainly rather curious, indeed coincidental, but . . . just this morning I was in the library, looking through some old volumes, especially a set of Dickens which I suppose my grandfather had had bound as it had his rubrico embossed on the covers, when I found a sort of scrapbook which had been maintained on this subject. Here is Ruy with the chocolate for which his wife is famous, and I shall ask him to bring the scrapbook while we are sipping some of it."

The chocolate well deserved that she should be famous, it was excellent (Lina had made it. Her name was Lina), it was miraculous. And while Alberta Morris (her maiden- and pen-name) was drinking it, her eyes seemed to grow larger and larger. She gave a perceptible smack as she took the cup away from her mouth, and then she said, " 'El *vil*voy'! But what does that *mean?*"

From *La Voz de la Nación, With Seccion in ingles:*

What a storm of outrage swept through the streets and houses of our Ciudad Ereguay when one heard yesterday night that affront had been offered to our well-known and well-beloved mis Brethe ohara by a bruto whose name will shortly be discovered by our conscientious polis who all night sourced the meaner streets and alliedways which do no honour to us. The dear mis Vertha the grand daughter of capitan Monserrat our great Patriotic Hero had been delayed on some errand of merci to an umble casa near the port section of «town» when coming out en route to the awaiting carriage of her Papa the inglis coronel OHara (the idiom ingles does not contain of the letter R, hence coronel=colonel and Londres=London, how curious) when from the penumbrous area of some copse of trees there emerged that criminal Typico with pistole in hand who seized this innocent Mis roughly by one arm and exclaimed,—I will have at least jour money and ¡perhaps more!

In the opinion of some people (in fact, of lots), a little of such style goes a long way. A very long way. And yet . . . someone many years ago told me, as regards "more accurate" translations of the Bible, that he would rather read *Arise, O Lord* than *Get up, God.* And although we are dealing here with an entirely secular text, yet there is a something in the flavor of the Basic Form of it which appeals to me more than a smoother version might. Readers who disagree will still, I hope, excuse me if some more of the original from time to time seeps through.

Avanti.

Leaving to one side his discursions about the importance to the national economy of the Col. O'Hara's factory where Ereguayan cattle were processed into an essence of beef much advertised in the United Kingdom, and reminders of the late and great Cap. Monserrat's famous charge up the slope of Castel Ereguay to bring the Royal Spanish flag tumbling down; our reporter (Señor Cruz) at length describes the young girl's piteous cries for help, the shameful cowardice of some unnamed "citymen" who were nearby but evidently afraid of the "pistole"—and finally plunges into the matter of our story, videlicet that there then stepped forward with impetuous gait a most remarkable young man in almost ragged garments in antique cut of "raw hyde" and upon his feet curious footwear devised also from the uncured skin of an animal, such as one has not observed in years but only in illustrations of some old leyendas. Upon his head also a hat of shaggy leather.

This young man of such startling appearance, when he heard the cry of fear and pain from the defenseless girl, Mssi Evereth, uttered a savage shout and leaped forward swinging his bushknife, or machete. Quickly he slashed in such a way as to draw the scoundrel's blood, who [the scoundrel] was immediately lost to sight as he fled, the coward, into the enveloping darkness.

It appears that he made his way, the monster, to the night clinic of the Medical Hospital where he attempted to have reattached the severed ear, which he had brought with him "untidily wrapt" in a rag. But the "advanced medical student" on duty insisted that "a chirurgeon" would have to be summoned. Whereat "the retch fled yet again into the night. And one hears that he is attempting to depart our Countery by the back trials. But the frontera guards have been alerted by telegraph and he must soon be catched, the fiend. Unless of course he may find refuge amongst the teeming criminals which always protect the profugitives in the adjacent republic (so-called) of Bobadilla y Las Bonitas (el B & B, as we crisply put it). Falseley does that other country claim the Las Islas Encantadas, for which we are ready to shed our blood."

Further, *La Voz de la Nación* had gathered the following information: The young man whose manners and appearance reminds one of the works of Juan Jacques Ruso or the novel Paul y Virginia, not to mention the arcetypo classico Robisson Cruso, is Antonio the son of the pioneer settlers Kielor, Swiss or perhaps Baltico in origin. The patriarco Kielor's son resides with his parents and "some infant bothers" in the island Encantada Grande, whence he has come with his father to the mainland of our Republic to purchase what few supplies their humble and hard-working efforts have enabled them to afford. The europeans Sr. and Sra. Kielor have for several years inhabited all by themselves and young children this rugged Island part of that archipelago. ¡See, how they naturally regard their capital city as Ciudad Ereguay and not of some other nacion as it speciously proclaims! And there they have lived alone for most of one year to another, it being unusual to have even a visit from a fisherman's bote because of distance and the savage seas.

Having been thus raised practically alone in a wildness, he has grown up, as one says, «a wild boy», wearing no clothes not a produduccion of that wildness and "never was sick a day in his life," as he declares in his simple wholesome and naif way. Although void of any artifice and entirely sans sophistication exactly as one has read about in books by european savants. But consider the bravery of this doubtless Wilde Boy who has never been one day in school, how he rushed forward, careless of his own life, a true cavalier of the wilderness, he well deserves to be considered a noble son and citizen of this Republic, the justly named wildboy without a thought of fear, so similar to the bravo capitan Monserrat, our National Hero, whose garnddaughter [here the clipping ends]

Thus the report as written by Gustavo Gomez Cruz, who for many years wrote the English-language column Amigos Friends, for the daily *La Voz de la Nación* of which allegedly his brother-in-law was sole proprietor; but what difference does it make? As for this first mention of "Antonio" Kielor, it seems certain that mostly it was true. Thus the legend of the Wild Boy of the Islands sprang almost full grown in an instant, or anyway in a night. A few comments now to those sceptical persons who are everywhere. It is said that the boy certainly did not wear a goatskin hat in the manner of Crusoe, but that the hatband may have been goatskin. It is said that his clothes were certainly not all made of rawhide, though parts of them may have been—and certainly his shoes or sandals or boots, whatever one may call them (moccasins?) had been made by the elder Kielor himself; and why not? Furthermore, in regard to the incident at the Night Door of the hospital, there has been some sceptical insistence that the man who had appeared there for medical or surgical attention to his ear had certainly not carried it with him in a rag, despite the firmness of the legend on this detail; but that it had been severely bitten in a cantina brawl and bore no mark of a slash with a sharp weapon such as a machete. (As for the Legend, it adjusted itself on this point: the Wild Boy had both slashed the thug with his machete and *then* bitten off his ear . . . which the thug then wrapped in a rag and carried with him to the Infirmary: a newspaper drawing not long after showed a figure looming out of darkness and carrying in one hand a pistol and in the other an Object out of which blood dripped along the ground. It was very vivid; indeed the stuff of legend.) As for the subsequent history of this man—or, if there were indeed two—either man: there is no subsequent history; fables of an earless man howling for revenge in the moonlight are, simply, fables. The darkness had swallowed him or them and the darkness continued to, as it were, keep him/them swallowed. Which, since we are in the presence of Legend, is perhaps as it should be.

And in regard to the young man's given name, really it was not Antonio, an understandable mistake; evidently his full name was William Washington Kielor; this not having been fixed into law by the Medes and the Persians, he was sometimes called "Bill," sometimes "Billy," and sometimes (often) "Tony." And the elder Kielors were, very simply, from the Isle of Man . . . perhaps this is not as simple as it sounds . . . it may be that Sr. Gomez Cruz really did think that Man was a canton in Switzerland or an island in the Baltic Sea (there, after all, *are* islands in the Baltic Sea . . . *are*n't there?), or, it might be, that the word *Manxman* was a bit beyond him. At any rate, the elder Kielors had had some earlier experiences with island life. Why didn't they, if tired of, say, life in London, simply go back to the Isle of Man? Perhaps because it was full of English tourists, all hoping to hear one of the eleven or fifteen people who could still speak Manx. And as for that simply despicable person sitting over there in the corner and muttering that the old Manx form of the name was Illiam (cognate Gaelic *Liam*), without an initial "W"—why, let him go back where he came from.

Señor Murphy having paused at this point to wet his whistle, like, with a sip of chocolate, Señora Murphy turned to the? hunter? farmer? fellow; "Your family, they are all well, I trust?" The young man answered, simply, "Yes." After a moment she said, "My aunt will appear presently."

I had, somehow, a faint impression that she had forgotten or simply did not know his name, but she had evidently touched the right note, because he then said, "Ah." Not one of your very talkative types, evidently. Afraid he might scare away the game, or make the off-ox turn left instead of right. Ivan Sanderson once said that people speak of "the silence of the jungle," when, really, they are very noisy places . . . or did Ivan Sanderson say just the opposite? I met him once or twice, a very nice man: but he is gone now.

But, as to the matter of "William" or of "Bill," that is nothing compared to the word(s) . . . phrase, perhaps . . . title, perhaps . . . set down crisply enough by Gomez Cruz at least twice (if not consistently) as "Wild Boy." Although one stands, shall we say, surprised at his statement that "English contains no 'R,' " it certainly seems that Spanish does not make abundant use of "W." Let us, however, not forget that "W"=Double "U," that "U" and "V" are variant forms of the same letter, and that there are a number of languages (including Spanish) in which "V" and "B" are not what one would call clearly distinct: consider Servia and Serbia, Habana and Havana, Sevastopol and Sebastopol—and, for that matter, Avram and Abram. The second given name of old Kielor's oldest son was to cause the journalists and typesetters of Ciudad Ereguay enormous difficulties: sometimes it appeared as Vashington, sometimes as Boshindon or even Uachignton, or . . . sometimes . . . Washington. (Old Kielor was much impressed by Immense Liberator Figures.) But mostly young Kielor was referred to in the press as The Wild Boy, two

English words also not without their transliterational difficulties and which went through sundry forms as El Vild Boy, Wild Voy, Vildouy, or—finally and eternally—Vilvoy: a headline from some time later: BIENVENIDA VILVOY. Further transmutations and confusions, such as Bill Boy, Billy Boy, and Bell Boy, we will leave as well enough alone. *Vilvoy.* There! The Ereguayans knew a good loanable word when they saw one; it just took them a while to pin it down and stabilize it. And have we of the inglish idiom done a sight better with Montecuzuma or whatever, and—for that matter—*batata?*

No *indeed.*

Well, that more or less completes our survey of what we might call El Vilvoy, Part One.

Onward.

It was the practice for many years of Col. O'Hara, in his capacity as Honorary British Vice-Consul, to call formally once a year at the Presidential Palace and deliver a Note reminding the Republic of the British Claim to Las Islas Encantadas (H.M. Government, what with the Maori and the Mahdi and other such vexatious people, having other matters than that small southern Atlantic archipelago on the front of their desks. What? "its"? "desks"? Nonsense. "Her Majesty's Government *are*," no more to be said)—Claim to Las Islas Encantadas (or, as My Lords preferred to call them, Lord Iggen's Islands); after the delivery of which The President would give him a glass of sherry and a segar . . . both, we understand, very good . . . and then they would enjoy a half-hour's pleasant conversation on the subject of, as it might be, horseflesh . . . that is to say, not hippophagy, but breeding. French reminders of the French Claim were more sporadic (echo in *Cada Dia,* of Ciudad Bobadilla: NAPOLEON III HAS ESCAPED FROM ENGLAND AND IS DESTINED TO ARRIVE IN THE ISLAS ENCANTADAS. Nap Three never made the scene, alas). But the Claims of the adjacent Republic (adjacent to Ereguay, that is; not to France) of Bobadilla y Las Bonitas were something else. True that both Republics were agreed that Spanish sovereignty of the Islands, after the overthrow of Spanish colonial rule, had

passed to . . . had passed to . . . passed, aye, there's the rub! Passed
to *whom?* Or, to *which?* Opinions differed. They very much differed.
And continued to differ.

Nine Days Wonders we always have with us, and perhaps interesting news was a bit scarce at that time, at any rate, the newspapers
in Ciudad Ereguay certainly made very much of the Vilvoy. And so
did opinion in the not-inconsiderable portion of the public which
did not read newspapers. Tributes to his modesty and, if not to his
piety (old Kielor, on the single occasion when he was solicited about
theology, declared himself to be a believer in An Universal Force or
Influence, y nada mas), then anyway to his filial piety: headline in
La Prensa Nacional: VILVOY THINKS ONLY OF HIS PAPA. We
who described yesterday the collection of a purse to reward the Wil
Voy for his courage are now proud to disclose that, when asked what
gift he desired, the vil voy replied, "Only a pouch of good English
tobacco for his papa!" It seems that the father Kielor grows naturally
his own tobacco in those Islands which pertain to our Country, but
this year the crop was not all what was hoped for. Colonel Ohara,
father of the augustly descended sweet and becomingly timid girl
whose life the Vil Dvoy saved, immediately ordered purchased and
placed on board the fishingvessel by which father and son will return
to their chosen island of settlement an entire case of the best Inglish
pipe tobacco available from the enterprising merchants here. El Vilvoy professed himself delighted. The Prensa has learned that the
coronel has offered either or both of the Kielors good employment
at the factory which produces the beef essence that the English use
as tea, but that they both declared that nothing will make them
surrender their residencia and small farm which with such hard la-
bour they have acked, or hewn as one might say, from the wilness.
We are also precisely informed by the Ministry of National Lands
that a writ of title to the aforesaid terrain will be most immediately
issued to the señor Kielor.

Señora K. had remained in the Islands with her younger children;
when asked if he were not afraid of her safety the father Kielo declared that no one who lives under the flag of the Republic of

Ereguay need fear any man. Also he reminds us that in a true state of the Natura one lives in harmony with nature's laws, and then remains always without the well-founded fears to which the urban dweller is a prey. Both he and his brave son el vilvoy wear their hair much long except that the latter of course has almost no veard upon his manly young face. Observe please readers the likeness of his fearless and untainted countenance in this Press via means of the latest photographic process . . .

Thus it is possible precisely to date the first-known photograph of el Vilvoy; and in fact this photograph was reproduced and sold widely for quite a while through the ciudad and in one or two provincial towns, both in black-and-white and in sepia.

Father and son (and a cargo of more supplies than either had hoped for; old Kielor would not accept money, which he in fact called by many harsh names; but he agreed to accept agricultural tools, seeds, and nursery stock, fishing lines and hooks, gunpowder, lead, cartridges, and a nice new shotgun) returned presently to their far-distant Island Home. Quite a throng saw them off at the mole. And the Ministry of Correction and Justice quietly put away its plans to locate a penal colony somewhere in the Islands.

When the newspapers said (as say they did) that the President of Ereguay, Eduardo Gaspar de la Vara, D.D.S., had promised that he would visit the pioneering family when he could manage to find the time to escape from the cares of state, they said but the truth. Dr. de la Vara was then in his forty-second year, he had attained to office entirely by constitutional means and he was determined to leave office in the same manner. His physician, Dr. Cipriano Madariaga, said to him one day after the routine examination, "Previous holders of your august office have been either soldiers or attorneys; you are unique in having a scientific degree, therefore may I speak with you, not as citizen to president, but as one scientist to another?"

"Securely you may," said el doctor don Eduardo. "Proceed."

"If I were to work too hard," said Madariago, "my assistant could always assume my duties—for a limited period of time, of course. ("Of course.") Only . . . the lay person scarcely appreciates that the corpus and the spiritus are entirely intertwined; do you agree?"

"Agreement the most absolute."

"We say of a garment made of good sound cloth, that 'it wears like iron,' do we not? and yet even iron may eventually wear out, so—"

Here the president interrupted. He was a small man. But he was courageous. "Are you about to tell me, Sir Medicin Doctore, that I am about to wear out?"

The physician crossed himself three times. "I beg of you, my friend, do not jump to conclusions. Any man who works hard may require a rest in order to recuperate his powers. But if, unlike, say, *me*, you should require a rest, is there someone who could assume your duties until—"

Perhaps Gaspar de la Vara rapidly considered the political state of affairs in Ereguay. "Sir Medical Doctor, you have reason!" he exclaimed. "No, there is not . . . save, perhaps for the very shortest period of time."

Dr. Madariaga nodded. "How short a period of time? Could you not take a rest for . . . say . . . two weeks? Only two weeks? As your friend, I implore you. As your physician, I order you!"

Gaspar de la Vara came to a, perhaps, rapid decision. "And what sort of a rest?" he enquired. "For two weeks, not more."

"Alas," said the physician, "we have here not healing springs, spas, they are called in Europe. How they invigorate! How they juvenescate! But . . . facts are facts . . . and in the absence of any such in our own country, and as it is impossible to go to Europe right now, I have no hesitation to recommend . . ." He hesitated. ". . . a short sea-voyage," he concluded. And watched the other's face.

Immediately the President exclaimed, "I shall make a cruise of our overseas territories!"

"You will sail around the Enchanted Islands in the national yacht?"

"No, I shall go via the steam vessel—and I shall keep well in mind the maritime wisdom of the Liberator!" His friend the medical doctor slapped him on the back, and they embraced.

From a contemporary statement in *La Voz:* "The President will make a voyage of inspection beyond the seas in keeping with the famous maritime maxim of the Liberator. Did not the Liberator himself declare that, 'Whoso controls the sea, controls the coast; and whoso controls the coast controls the interior. Therefore, whoso controls the sea, paradoxical as it may seem, he controls the interior'? Indeed. It is not necessary to explicate the reference to the Liberator Ignacio Gomez de la Cedilla, often called the San Martin (or the Bolivar) of Central Coastal South America, East; of whom the whole world has heard. Almost."

In fact, the Republic of Ereguay was the current owner of the locomotive vessel *La Victoria* (formerly Her Britannic Majesty's Steam Ram *Sink*); and this at a time when the adjacent Republic of Bobadilla y Las Bonitas had only recently recognized that the gallery was obsolete, and the adjacent Republic of Nueva Andorra had acquired the former Confederate privateer *Arkansas* (it had been engaged, in the interim, in the corned-mutton trade out of Port Bangalong, Eastern Australia). This exemplum of "the fleet in being" had struck terror into the hearts of all would-be invaders of the Ereguayan littoral (not even do we exempt Brazil). Commanding the *Victoria* was the capitan da Costa, and also present was the learned and unpredictable Dr. Hector Macvitty.

Capitan da Costa made up for his Brazilian birth by voicing objections whenever the Emperor's name was mentioned; "a tawdry fellow," he called him, "a freemason, a yanqui-lover, a friend of the Negroes, and an imperialista." The capitan da Costa had visited the not-often-visited Islands, and so knew anyway something about them, besides the fact that they were there. (That was something. It was often reported and often denied that Nueva Andorra had once sent *La Desiderata* [formerly the *Arkansas*], under a politically-appointed and inexperienced commander, on a voyage to Brazil; asked, upon his return, how were things in Brazil, he had replied, with a shrug, "Brazil isn't there.") Dr. Macvitty did not engage in much conversation, but all the while he made sketches, of the sort for which he was almost famous. And it is indeed from these sketches, and from letters to his brother Sawney (the Rev. Alexander Macvitty), that a number of the details of this voyage have been supplied. (The letters and sketches mostly repose in the Lord Marechal's Library and Museum in Edinburgh, to the learned Curators of which we express our thanks; their charges have been, considering inflation and rates of exchange, almost modest.)

Nevertheless, we will not bore readers—at any rate, I hope I am not boring mine—with many details. Though the South Atlantic seas can be very rough indeed, one reason no doubt why the Islas had been so seldom visited the voyage of *La Victoria* was fairly untroubled. She anchored in the windward of Encantada Grana and several times a day people put ashore in her small boat, or "launch"; and of course the shore visits of the passengers were more frequent than those of most of the crew, who, truth to tell, were not much inclined to land on these Isles containing none of the amenities which sailors prefer to encounter whilst ashore. And a very wild and rocky shore it was, too, though little did this seem to disarrange the famous Great Tortoises.

"See these great tortoises, Your Excellency!"

"Never mind such titles, Capitan; call me simply 'Doctor'; but where are they all going? So very, very slowly?"

"Either to crunch the flesh of the prickly-pear cactus between their horny jaws, or in search of those hidden springs which they alone, mostly, know about."

Consider, then, at this time, the President of the Republic—no silk hat, no frock coat, no sash of office, no: clad in simple costume borrowed from the third mate, and with the same well-worn *sombrero de jipijapa* which he wore (almost one wishes to say, *wears*, so strong is habit!) at home, how eagerly he traverses the rocky landscape of the largest of the Islands which never before had been trodded by presidential foot; observe the slight flush of pleasure and the quick degree of impatience, he brushes aside all offers of "helping hands," and soon, with only a single guard to accompany him, he vanishes into the brush, or bush, or however one wishes to describe it; those trees of which the sound of an axe has seldom menaced, the dense thicketry, the—

"Come, follow me!" exclaims the capitan da Costa in a tone of command which never he would have used to the President himself; "I know of a short-cut, we will soon encounter them!" Everybody obeys; sure enough, a trail is found, all follow it, birds call out, the small animalitos or insectivos also appear, what glorious and one may accurately say, gorgeous, butterflies: but what care, momentarily, the visitors, save for the taciturn Dr. Macvitty, who, almost as he moves, he sketches, sketches—behold! the party has reached at last the small plantation which the pioneer settler family, those profugitives from the scurrying and unhealthy throngs of European city-dwellers, has cleared, with great labor, from the bosque: there is the Family Kielor, almost as though they had gathered for the Purpose of welcoming the President. The father Kielor greets his civic leader with a warm handshake and an embrace, the mother Kielor leaves for a moment the home-made frame on which she embroiders, so to speak, textiles made from the wild flax with threads spun from a local fibre and dyed with local dies-stuff, representations of the autochthonous flora and fauna, and waves her hand at the great chief magistrate; several small boys of various sizes at first stand off shyly, then slowly creep forward and are greeted with paternal pats upon their heads. A delicious odor fills the air—to be specific, a "lunch" was cooking, of goatsflesh and several sorts of ñames and patatas, as well as the famous wild spinaches so good against the dreaded scurvy. After some few minutes the President says, "But I do not see here your oldest son, whom always we fondly remember by the name of *el vilvoy,* forever will we remember with what bravery he bit off the ear of that savage fellow, a foreigner I need not say, whilst defending the sweet mis Ohara, la bertita chica; where is he?"

Scarcely has [The above account, transposed from the holographic, seems rather confused: on the one hand the President has vanished into the woods with one single naval guardsman, and yet here he is described as being already present at the Kielor house and farm, with no explanation or transition. Well, we must take history as we find it, and, as the almost fabulous capitan ser Júan Smiht so aptly puts it, History without Geography is a wandering carcase, or perhaps it is the other way around; the capitan ser Juhan Esmiss, rescuer of las pocahontas, was not a literary man] scarcely has the initial burst of enthusiasm subsided sufficiently for the babble of voices to terminate for a moment, when distinctly are heard some distant shots, securely of firearms. Exclaims the elder Kielor, "That is not my son, he took with him this morning only a machete when he left to examine some traps and snares; let us go at once in that direction!" And, directly he trots off in another direction. Navy officers cry commands to their few men and they begin to run in a more direct direction; but the doctor Macvitty calls out to warn them of the dangers of the hedge of prickly-pears which they are about to charge through: of their large thorns which draw blood—and, much more dangerous, their tiny and usually at first glance unseen spines, those which break off in the flesh, and fester, causing more infection and sores of great pain, often indeed leaving scars. In a moment prevail the heads more cooler, it is realized the patriarco Kielor doubtless knows best the paths of his "own" island; if he runs off in a certain direction, doubtless it is to find a passable lane through the wilderness which will presently change its direction according to the contures of nature. (It is not to be thought that these considerations are the results of subsequent meditations.) And the reader already knows that the shots had been fired by certain troops of the Counter-Claimant Nation for the sovereignty of las Islas: in other words, not to cavil at the truth, the Republic of Bobadilla and Las Bonitas, as it is commonly and simply called. El B & B only in the vulgate.

When the Intelligent Semaphore on the well-sited Goat's Head Hill, overlooking la Ciudad de Ereguay and the circumjacent waters had signaled with both its arms out straight that (in other words) a side-wheel steamer was approaching—the black ball hoisted at the same moment indicating that it was one of our Naval vessels, and next

T H E   O T H E R   N I N E T E E N T H   C E N T U R Y

went up the Presidential flag; at once a crowd began to gather at the mole, for it was realized that this meant the return of the steam Ram *La Victoria,* with the President on board. Meanwhile, of course, as the semaphore continued working while the ship drew nearer, and both were sending and transcribing messages to each other; but little heeded this the throng, most of whom naturally could not read the Semaphore letters, nor had they telescopes to see what the Ship was saying. But those who had the knowledge and the means, including of course several people in the Department of Naval Affairs; as well, naturally, one need hardly say, the journalists: they were transfixed, electrified, by what these messages implied. And as word of this spread so rapidly through the City, of course the crowd grew vast.

The Questions at the "Interview"

Q. Mr. Dr. President, is it indeed true that you had been as it were lost in the jungle on Encantada Grande and that the Vilvoy himself then rescued you?

A. With the frankness which characterizes my nature, I answer, simply, Almost I might have become alarmed, but the Vilvoy heard my calls, and fairly at once he rescued me.

Q. Ah, thank God! You seem to be in entire good health, in fact one might say, in better, is it not true?

A. Yes.

Q. And is it also true that this is because the Vilvoy led you to some medicinal springs of the sort called *spa?*

A. Perceiving that I was very hot and somewhat fatigued, he did indeed lead me to some springs in an obscure place, in which certainly I bathed. As to its medical qualities, Dr. Macvitty regrets that I did not carry away with me a sample of the spring water, but I had no thought of that. As for my health, it may be that the exercise and the sea breezes had something to do with it. But there are more important matters, and if you will excuse me, I observe that my carriage is over there, and—

Q. Ah, but sir doctor president, what of these important matters? It is true, then, that some troops of the Counter-Claimant Country,

I refer to el B & B, had landed and were attempting an invasion? the shameless ones.

A. Yes.

At this, roars of indignation swept the crowd, and, almost immediately, the City. The survivors of the Invasion had been observed making an escape in a small bote, from which, it is adjudicated, they transferred into a larger one. Nothing more than that the coal-supplies of our Steam Vessel were limited for a return to port only, prevented the capitan da Costa from at once pursuing this estimated other vessel. But our Nation was well-satisfied that the villians had suffered a sufficient punishment in that fearlessly El Vilvoy had attacked with his machete, and, it cannot be doubted, cut off six of their heads! Effectively, how they could have resisted with their *"superior fire-power,"* as it is called, save only his already-perceived famous wild bravery struck terror to their hearts, the cowards. And they fled. As to the flag which they had previously succeeded to plant on the volcanic soil of las Islas, one may behold it any day at the Museum of the National Patrimony, hours from three to four in the afternoon, a very small surcharge is necessarily made for the benefits of Widows and Orphans. But the public may donate the dueños such gratuities they wish. What greater evidences of breach of faith is needed to condemn a neighboring nation with whom we were legally at peace for invading our quasi-paternal soils? Well could we of the Republic of Ereguay have stricken back and given then, as one says, "titt for tatd," save that the generous heart of our then Presidente doctor Gaspar de la Vara was moved to avoid any breach between two adjacent nations of this Continent; and so, after a period marked by recriminations on their part and of cold silence on our own (imagine, they accused us of Fabrication of the acCount of the Heads!), the matter has passed off and no longer espoils the cordial relations which now obtain between our two countries, brothers as we are in blood and language anyway.

But think! of this mere youth, how he fearlessly struck of the heads of sixteen necessarily much larger grown men! What an ensample for our jung people to admire! Ah how very well-founded is this leyyend of El Vilvoy de las Islas.

At this point (or perhaps at some other nearly-contemporary point) the Counter-Claimant Nation simply turned its back on the whole thing: headline in the *Cada Dia* newspaper, widely recognized as government organ: DECLARES THE KING OF SWEDEN AND NORWAY / *The Nations of Europe Are Very Contented to Recognize That the Confederational Union of Bobadilla AND LAS BONITAS IS INDISSOLUABLE.* The King of Sweden and Norway, that civilized and civil man, was always willing to issue such declarations whenever his ministers asked him . . . and much it helped the union of Sweden and Norway; its effects on South American sales of canned sardines and wooden matches cannot be precisely calculated.

So far as is known, only once did El Vilvoy travel into the Interior of Ereguay . . . at least only once which is known . . . it is realized that the generosity of the vaqueros was almost an embarrassment, they incessantly surrounding and offering him many copas of Rum Dinga, their famous naive but strong drink; also constantly they surrounded his horse and soon all its tails hairs had been plucked out for souvenirs and alleged cures for the infirmities of the male person; in these matters of *"Ffolk-wisdon,"* who indeed can say? And as it was seemingly impossible, if not indeed difficult, to avoid almost similar seens in the Ciudad, if thereafter for sundry times of sundry years he came to the capital and port, it would have been as incognito, slipping in and out and then away again: his arrival, departure, presence, alleged comments and appearances, almost in the popular mine and pewrhasp higher, in some essential details resembles the doctrine of Sebastianism, as within the memories of some old and still-living people one found it yet in Brazil, let alone the Question of in Portugal. But of course the mysticism or not, in essential detail this difference: El Vilvoy was not dead!*

---

*And one remembers with some small dismay the so-called Riots of Rosarosa, in that remote rural region, which began when someone in a cantina allegedly denied that El Vilvoy had cut

But—

Ah, the sceptics! The sceptics, O! Of much would the sceptics have liked to dismiss entirely the matter of the Twenty-six Severed Heads as lies, old crones' tails, and propaganda . . . but little have they been able. There is, for one thing, the testimony of President Doctor Eduardo Gaspar de la Vara, and if revisionist historians would dismiss that: there was, for another thing, the testimony of the Doctor Macvitty: was not the Dr. Macvitty the Author of a learned monograph on Certain Disorders of the Metatarsals, printed in the Journal of the National Scottish Medical Association? Little recked the ravings of the *Cada Dia* newspaper of the Ciudad de Bobadilla against the inflexible probity of the Journal of the National Scottish Medical Association (alleged activities of the dr. Alejandro Nkox and the uneducated Herr Burc are entirely beside the point). It is of course unfortunate that doctor Macvitty's renewed testimony was not available at a later date, but he had returned to his native Land, there to engage upon his life-long crusade to test and maintained the wholesome nature of Scotch whisky as compared to brandy; and died in Peebles under muffled circumstances. And there is furthermore the errefutable testimony of the Sketches: the Sketches, four in number, clearly show each one clearly six of the Severed Heads reposing on their ledge or ledges in the Secret Cave, and how respectful were all the parties involved to refuse to disturb their repose or even to disclose their location, merely to satisfy a rude curiosity. Or for any other reason. As for the claim that the four Sketches show the same six heads from slightly different angles, or that four times six equals twenty-four and not twenty-six—this is a mere quibble. And also remains unidentified the alleged medical spring.

It is secure that, so far as goes impartial evidence and testimony, El Vilvoy never acknowledged his heroism in this matter, merely giving

off seventeen of the heads of the misfortunate invaders. Small wonders that he therafter preferred, so it seems, the shadows of bein unrecognized, to the full noontine glare of the Publicity.

a slight jesture and a «grunt» and a movement slightly of the mouth whenever asked of it. How this proves his essential Modesty, that of the Gentleman of Nature, too educated even to deny what his interlocutter has enquired.

"Well indeed," commented the Spanish Priest (in a former time not yet so very far back at all, priests did not go about in casual dress ever, and with what dignity, too!) "But it now seems quite evident that those heads had probably nothing to do with the so-called Invasion, the Las Bonitas Incursion. Scientists tell us that probably they were the heads (if they existed at all) of pre-Columbian Indians, there on the Islands for mysterious and uncertain reasons." And it is true that the Heads appear to be entire heads, unlike those prepared by the Jivaro Indians rather on the principle of a stuffed olive: this the priest conceded. Then he said, "But modern science has determined that organic matter stored, so to speak, well within a cave at the well-known and naturally-maintained 'Cave Temperature,' cool but not freezing-cold, well may last forever in its original form. Witness," he said, "the hide of the megatherium in Patagonia, and the deposits of sloth-dung in the cave in North America.

"—The Vilvoy led the president and Dr. Macvitty to the cave where the heads were? Well, perhaps he did, but that in no way proves that he had put the heads there, let alone removed them from the shoulders of the soldiers of Las Bonitas." The others there in the garden of la Villa de Murphy, moved just a bit restively at this statement, but perhaps all were too polite to dispute, or even to deny. The rural-looking young man said nothing; he seemed, if anything, politely a bit bored. Whiffs of memory, like faint scents of some aromatic plant growing not within sight, began to be perceived by me. Had he been, perhaps, the man with the gun and the game-bag, who had nodded to us from the berm of the road near the forest as we slowed down to avoid a mud rut? I could not be sure. Or was he one of a couple of people considering a bogged-down piece of equipment in a field just before we stopped for water?

"Perhaps, sir, you will give us your opinion," suggested licenciado Huebner, politely.

The young man seemed to consider the question for a second, then he said, very calmly and equitably, "No."

And as though the attorney had asked *her:* "To me," said la doctora, after a moment, "the evidence upon the shell of the great tortuga is a most remarkable thing." There was a murmur of agreement; and, seeing that I knew nothing of these things, two or three people recapitulated for me a conversation back there on Great Enchanted Island. Imagine! they directed me; imagine that black soil composed of volcanic origins ground so very fine, and the black rocks scattered around, almost a terrain of the inferno; here and there, going infinitesimally slowly, the giant tortoises, moving their flipper-like legs and making so little distance with each step that one might walk alongside them as they did so. And in fact, walking exactly so, is President E. Gaspar de la Vara, and so is capitan da Costa. One points out to the other curious and atypical markings on the giant carapace of one huge crawler. "¡Mira. *MAP* and *VYP!* Are these not the initials of the explorer-brothers Martin Alonso and Vicente Yáñez Pinzón?"

"Indeed, indeed! What else? And examine this set carved on the other side!"

"JPdL. Juan Ponce de Leon! Ah, that great pilot; señores, we are in the presence of history!"

And of those there in the garden of the villa in that suburb of that southern South American city, several look directly at the young priest to see if he is not impressed. "Why," he asks, "should I doubt that they saw such initials? And why should I not doubt that they saw what had been put there by hoaxers, or shall we say, 'jokers'? Giant tortoises may live long, but—*that* long? On Santa Elena there is a great tortoise, said to have been there in the time of Bonaparte. *Said.* And on Tonga, in the Pacific, there is another one, said to have been brought there by capitan Cooke. *Said.* Humanity continues to divert itself with fables, and meanwhile it continues, largely, to refuse to accept the truth. Therefore we all suffer." He said this with a certain intensity, low-keyed but emphatic. Said the attorney, dressed in that meticulous black and white, "But . . . Father Juan . . . it does not follow does it, that because we believe that certain tortoises may live to be old, very very old, surely it does not follow that we deny the One Holy, Catholic and Apostolic Church?" And the young priest answered, slowly, almost I would say, reluctantly, that, No, it did not follow.

But although El Vilvoy made no further, as it were, public appearances in the Capital and Port, he continued to be seen from time to time by visitors from there to his almost-native Island (after all, he had been very young and small when his parents made their landing). From time to time parties of such visitors, it depended always upon the weather, at least, and sometimes also upon other conditions—in time of prosperity perhaps a bit more often, in times of civil unrest certainly somewhat less often; parties of visitors would make what one might call a cruise, one might call it an excursion. Few indeed made the trip, which had to be made by foot, all the way from the shore to the farm. For one thing it was not easy, for another it was known that the senior Kielors did not favor such visitations, interruptive of their private schedules and their private peace; also they said that visitors brought colds. It became the custom for one of the landing parties to fire three shots when they had landed. And, eventually, usually while they were eating their picnic lunches, silently out of the wilderness there would appear upon the upper edges of the shore, *El Vilvoy*. What exclamations! What risings to the feet. What, one might say, clamors. Cheers! And always, always . . . or anyway, usually, or at any rate: often . . . someone would level a camera.

"Ah, Toño," the skipper would say, casually (imagine speaking *casually* to someone so remarkable.); "Toño, here are the things ordered by your Papa. [aside] Here, you, fellow, pile them well back from the tideline."

And so on.

Sometimes, as the visitors were returning to whichever small ship by row-boat or by motor-launch, sometimes they looked back, El Vilvoy raised a hand in farewell, abruptly let it fall. What a waving of handkerchiefs! What cries of *Luego, Vilvoy!* et cetera.

But when they looked back again, always he was gone.

Full-page spread in La Voz. Headline: El Vilvoy, Does His Natural Life Keep Him Youthful? Is it his total revulsion of the semi-artificial foods of the civilized living which maintains the Vilvoy in his youthfulness? Is it the conditions so devoid of stress or pressure, in complete harmony with the rhythms of the tides and the cycles of the Nature, which is preventing him from showing the signs of inevitable decay? Has his metabolism thus been slowed? Is he indeed, so to speak, *un pieter-pan?* Let us regard these incontestable photographical evidences . . . And there they were, each captioned with the names of the photographer and the date of the photograph, an entire series of pictures of el vilvoy, over a period of I forget how many years, numbers do not settle well in my mind. Sometimes his hair was a little shorter and sometimes a little longer, sometimes he was wearing such and such a garment, sometimes another: but always, always, not "usually" but always, really, the same face. And it did not really seem that he was any older in the last one than in the first one.

"I believe that it is the fruitarian diet," said la doctora, emphasizing that this was her opinion, with slow, deep nods of her handsome head. "I have known really remarkable results to occur with the fruitarian diet. I would observe it myself, but my family will not allow."

But the other señora, señora Alvarado? was of a different opinion. "It is because he knows of a certain yerba which grows in a hidden vale there on that island, or, some say, on another of those Islands. Twice a year he goes there, secretly, and he eats that secret yerba. And it purifies his blood. Once in January and once in June he purifies his blood with the substance of this secret yerba. And it is that which prevents him from the aging."

Mrs. Phlux said, "How very selfish of him. I am sure that we would all *love* to know the name of this herb! Why don't we?"

Said the señora, "Because it is a secret one." She said this very mildly, conscious of no artifice herself, and she nodded two or three times, not very deeply but somewhat less than rapidly. Clearly, to her, that was all the explanation needed.

Said the Spanish priest, "Old Padre Lizarraga, of the Botanical Gardens," everyone nodded at this reference; afterwards I learned that it was not that they all knew Padre Lizarraga, but that they all knew the Botanical Gardens. Or knew *of* the Botanical Gardens. "Told me that he had spent forty years investigating the native herbal medicaments, so often said to be so good for this ailment and for that; and the result of his studies was that he found that ninety-five percent of them were purgatives."

I felt that he expected that this statement would make some certain effect, but none was visible. Only the usual polite nods. After a moment, he went on. "Surely we have all heard of the Deception Theory?" And the attorney said, "The malice of the press of Las Bonitas is almost beyond belief. Conceive with what effort this theory must have been compounded."

So now I heard, if only in faintly greater detail, for the first time more about Old Kielor's other sons than the sole fact of their existing. Old Kielor's sons had been named, one after the other: Washington, Bonaparte, Jefferson, Lincoln, and Masaryk . . . called informally, Tony, Bony, Sony, Cony, and Max. Either History had ceased to supply Old Kielor with Immense Liberator Figures, or Time had changed the angle of the telescope. Or else Old Kielor had been simply consistent, and it was we who had underestimated Masaryk. And the Deception Theory was, simply, that the entire Kielor family (prompted, so it was implied, by the government of Ereguay) had conspired to deceive the visitors to las encantadas by replacing each brother, as he grew older, with the next youngest brother. That is, the tourists or trippers, the visitors, had only seen the real Tony for an unnamed period of time; after that, the one who came down to the shoreline and was photographed would have been Bony. And, when his own inevitable maturity would have become obvious, the one who was introduced as El Vilvoy was actually Sony. And so on, down through Cony and Max.

And here one heard certain other variations in the conventional legend. Bony would make a patriotic speech. Cony performed a certain dance, presumably of his own invention. Sony would hang from a branch of a tree by the shoreline and swing back and forth. Max brandished a machete and demanded assurance that the party was really from Ereguay, and not las Bonitas.

Mostly I had just looked and listened. Now I asked a question. Had anyone here ever been to Grand Encantada?

"But one does not go there anymore," said the señora whose husband was *un burócrata.* "Because it is uncomfortable the voyage, and on the Island there is no retrete, and nowadays one has the cinema."

The youthful stranger had rolled himself dexterously a cigarette in what looked like a leaf of pale tobacco, and now he lit it and sat forward in his chair, watching the smoke. It was not rank, merely somewhat strange. I thought that perhaps it reminded me of the small puro being smoked by the man, his face I did not see, who had brought the side of venison to the ristorante where Diego and I had eaten the morning before our arrival in the Ciudad. Only, perhaps I did see his face.

—But when had these visitations left off? Opinion was divided. And how many years had separated the brothers Kielor one from the other? No one had any idea. There were, however, any number of ideas involving such reference-points as the Revolution of the Year of Drought, and the Interim Presidency of the Very Sad Leap Year, and the Battle of Apostolo Santiago: events clearly as significant to those others present as The Bonus March or Pearl Harbor was to me; but of which we, all of us in the Northern Continent, were but utterly ignorant. Every Latin American republic has its own Alamo, its own Gettysburg, and we have never heard of any one of them. Nearer to us than to Ereguay is a country once convulsed by a great civil war during a period which we remember chiefly for the wearing of sleeve-garters, and funny female hats.

It was, however, where I now tarried, absolutely a matter of national belief that on the Islas Encantadas lived *El Vilvoy*, who had (a) come to the rescue of an innocent young girl, daughter of a national hero, who was once menaced by a thug; he immediately bit off the thug's ear, thus causing him to flee into the night with his bleeding ear in one hand; (b) this same wild but inestimably praiseworthy young vilvoy had upon a subsequent occasion rescued none other but the President of the Republic from a gang of invaders intent upon depriving Ereguay of the sovereignty of the Islands, and (c) had cut off the heads of twenty-seven of them and hidden the heads in a cave; and (d) he—

Mrs. Phlux said, "In a way it rather reminds me of Arthur and the Island of Avalon, or of Barbarossa in his cavern asleep with his beard still growing . . . and, of course, of poor young King Sebastian, who didn't really die in battle five hundred years ago was it? and will of course some day return. My. I do rather like it."

The priest, Padre Juan, had taken up his cup of chocolate, and now he put it down again. "We have all heard," he said, "of something which was done in another country, which should not have been done," and again he took his cup, and again he put it down. And it seemed that there was now a bit more interest displayed; could it be that people had been just a bit restive at hearing their own legend put down, and were now pleased to be hearing of some other nation being blamed for . . . for what? "I refer," said the priest, "to the Julio Castillano forgeries." People were being, definitely, more interested. *I* was certainly even more interested, for I had never heard of the matter.

"What was that?" I asked. Julio Castillano, it was explained to me, had been a well-known journalist in Nueva Andorra; perhaps he was at least as well-known for his candid camera as for his candid commentaries. And in a celebrated series of news articles he had supplied, I did not learn exactly how many photographs, of a Leading Political Figure in the company of a Leading Theatrical Artiste who was not his lawful (or even unlawful) wife. To make the matter very short, if not indeed curt: the photographs were revealed, exposed as we might say, as forgeries, hoaxes . . . of a sort . . . that is, they had all been taken of the two people involved in entirely different pictures, and the clever scoundrel had somehow joined the two together. Indeed, there was no real evidence that they had ever *been* together at any time in any place. Sought by the law and by the outraged husband of the Leading Theatrical Artiste, Julio Castillano had fled the country for another: and there he had shot himself.

"What do you suggest, then, Father?" the attorney asked. "That the photographs showing the vilvoy were all hoaxes? In what way?"

Padre Juan hesitated for a moment. "What proof do we have," he asked, "that all or most of those pictures had not been taken in the course of, say, one or two years? with fictitious date subsequently ascribed to them? Or what proof do we have that the dates may have not been let us say confused?"

Asked la doctora, "But what proof do we have that they were?"

It was, he said, a deduction, a theory, not an accusation. The press was almost everywhere of a sensationalist tendency, ready to manufacture exciting news when that happened to be in short supply. It would not have been difficult to assemble a collection of photographs and to misascribe, or even to confuse, their dates. "Thus gratifying," he said, "he jaded tastes of a public unnaturally eager for, always, more novelty more and more novelty. Even when it involves an interference in the natural law, whereby all men are mortal, and whereby all who live an age must become aged."

The attorney made a gesture which foretold a comment, then for a moment he withheld his comment. Then he said, "I believe, reverend sir, that you wish to remind us that the Church cautions us against accepting a miraculous explanation for anything as long as a mundane explanation is acceptable." He did not put it in the form of a question.

And the priest slowly nodded his agreement that this was, indeed, just what he meant. A murmur was heard, as that of several people all saying *Mmmm* at once.

While the latter part of the conversation had been going on I was aware of a figure walking very slowly around the other end of the gardens (it was a large garden and might very well have rightfully deserved the plural form), but this had not been in the forefront of my mind. Presently the figure came gradually nearer, and I saw that it was an old woman. Whoever said that in passing through life (or however does it go?), be sure to pause and smell the roses, would have been pleased with this elderly person. Stopping, stooping, bending her face to the blossoms, almost she seemed to be stroking the plants; and perhaps she was. "What a shame you had not been here even a few years ago," the attorney said to me. "You would have been able to meet the former President Gaspar de la Vara, who was tragically killed whilst driving his motor car, when he was ninety-six." And the señora said, "Ninety-seven."

Slowly the woman drew nearer, then slowly she wandered on away. Eventually I formed the thought, and leaned over and asked my host, "Who is that?" and I gestured. It was a small gesture.

He gave her only the slightest of glances, smiled (so it seemed, fondly), and then he said to me, "That is my great-aunt Bertha. She never goes out, and socially she sees almost no one." Scarcely had I engaged this answer to my question than another question formed, for the young—as I had thought, hunter or farmer, perhaps—who had, save for occasionally touching his very slight moustache, and smoking his cigarette, hardly moved; he had gotten up and, walking through the lower part of the garden, had come face to face with the old woman. She looked up as he stood before her, and then in a rush she held out her hands, and he took them. "Oh, Tony!" she cried, "Oh, Tony! You never grow old!"

AFTERWORD TO "EL VILVOY DE LAS ISLAS"

This poignant tale of the miseries of old age was written when Davidson was in his mid-sixties and confined to a wheelchair. His linguistic and narrative acrobatics give form and history to a character unique in fantasy literature. The vilvoy's antecedents are complex: one can discern traces of Rousseau's Noble Savage, Melville's "The Encantadas" (sketches of life in the Galápagos), a clear nod to the Tarzan novels of Edgar Rice Burroughs, a satire of the *Swiss Family Robinson,* etc. "What if Henry James wrote Tarzan with a wacky foreshadowing of magic realism?" is how Don Webb described the story. Howard Waldrop has observed that "El Vilvoy de las Islas" is like a Tarzan "archetype written by a Spanish-surnamed magic realist . . . Davidson's stories were usually lots wider and deeper than they were long."

—Henry Wessells

MICKELREDE; OR, THE SLAYER AND THE STAFF: A GHOST-NOVEL BY AVRAM DAVIDSON

edited, with interpolations,
by Michael Swanwick

OUTLINE IN WHITE GIRDERS

Introduction: Here and there and everywhere: AD set out to write a novel and failed to complete it. No surprise in *that*. How many books are begun and not finished? How many stars are in the sky? How many broken hearts on Broadway? Fragments, notes, and a cursory outline, however, he left behind. Enough to provide a taste, a holographic glimpse of what might have been.

I lifted these pages from a box full of such: bits and shards, stories begun and galleons launched for faraway cities of gold; but never, alas, arrived at; nor readily made publishable, alack, any of them. Save this. With a little shuffling and a few speculative additions, I've arranged a construct something like Philadelphia's famous Ghost

House, which is a three-dimensional outline in white girders of the long-gone house wherein Benjamin Franklin dwelt, not a reconstruction but a map of our knowledge, and of our ignorance as well.

Here: See, taste, enjoy. In the theater of your mind, reconstruct the whole. AD's ghost-novel is laid before you like a brass horn upon the table; put your ear to its mouth. Let it speak.

NONMYSTICAL MOTIONS OF TEMPERATURE AND PRESSURE

California: The campus had begun to be shrouded with fog which, seemingly, had ridden on high, mad winds, all the way from the Pacific, past the crag and sea-flung Farallones, over the tide-rushed Golden Gate, across the darkened Bay; before swooping down and settling on the trees and lawns and buildings gathered there on the hills rimming round them. But it was all illusion, Casey Swift knew. The fogs had not ridden in from anywhere—not from the ocean, not from their legendary breeding ground in a particular potato patch in Marin County there north across the straits from Frisco—they were forming right here now in front of his eyes, changing out of one state of vapor invisible into another state of vapor coalescent in response to certain nonmystical motions of temperature and pressure. My doctrine shall drop as the rain, my speech shall distill as the dew.

ALONG CURVED TIMELIKE ARCS

Explication: They are born of course, are the fogs, when worlds collide. Which happens more often than you might think. Every day, on every continent, new timelines are constantly being split off underfoot. The universe reaches an instant in which two outcomes of a choice are equally likely and, in the spirit of a greedy three-year-old confronted with a choice of two equally large slices of cake, reaches for both. But *unlike* the three-year-old, the universe is by this very act ripped in two. The two scion timelines race away from each other along curved timelike arcs of virtual existence that may last anywhere from 2.225 nanoseconds to (in rare cases, admittedly) three weeks before their divergent paths again converge and, like quarreling lovers, they fall into each other's arms, kiss, and are reconciled.

These secret divergences sometimes leave their mark in divergent memories. "You remember the time . . ." you begin, and "It wasn't like that at all!" your Significant Sweetie says. He said, she said. Maybe you're both right.

Maybe not.

BUDDHIST BEGGARS WITH BOWLS OUTSTRETCHED

California: "We're not where we were the last time you were here," he said to the other man in the car. "They finally broke down and gave us the new facilities we asked for."

"The Regents?" asked Dr. Galloway. His ego did not much at all miss the *sir* but his ears noticed its absence immediately; at the British "redbrick" university where he had spent the recent year it had so invariably been forthcoming that now a sort of visible or auditory lacuna seemed to take shape. He was faintly bothered that he should in any way be bothered by it, so asked the question in whose answer he had no great interest. Facilities were either existent or nonexistent; where they were not, there was not Herbert Galloway. Mildly he pitied the scholars of the permanent faculties, obliged to come like Buddhist beggars with bowls outstretched.

LIKE A LEOPARD-FISH OR A MORAY EEL (I)

Elsewhere: He saw something moving through the star-lit sky, moving oddly, oddly, very oddly, its outlines and its markings as faint as the faintest star. A plane? No plane moved in that curious, sinuous, curving fashion. Nor were birds shaped like that, nor did birds have markings like a leopard-fish or a moray eel.

He stood amazed.

This strange place was an In-Between. It lay in-between times, spaces, dimensions, worlds: by itself and of its own. But it wasn't hermetically sealed. There was a certain . . . seepage . . . not much; enough to have seeded the place with the elements of its present population. A band of women and children who, following too slowly after their men-folk who were hunting down a woolly rhino, took a wrong turn and left the Aurignacian forever. A group of veterans of the Varingarian Guard, returning from long service in Byzantium, never reaching their old homes in Norseland. The last of the Martians. Other. Others. And, at length, Casey Swift.

"Do you often . . . just have people *stolen* . . . like this? Simply for your own use or pleasure or convenience?" Casey asked.

"Of course. Oh, quite often, said the Green King. "With my arcane powers, it's easy." He chuckled fatly.

"Oh. Then . . . uh . . . how come you don't just, well, take over? The Earth, I mean."

The Green King shrugged. "A headache," he said. "Who needs it?"

THE PERPETUAL ODDITIES OF MANY GREAT MEN

California: Casey guided the little MG along roads already glistening wet and black, still rather amused that he had only had to go as far as the railroad station and not all the way to the airport to pick

Galloway up. Not for the first time he considered the perpetual oddities of many great men: Galloway, for instance, whose professional climate was one in which the jet plane was already as good as obsolete, crossing the continent by train. Casey hadn't even known that the trains, whose rattle and honk he was sometimes aware of as background sounds on quiet nights, still stopped here for passengers at all.

"The Regents, yes," he said; "plus about two and a half rich old alumni who'd been considering the matter for a couple of years. Fortunately the money came through before the enthusiasts started getting enthusiastic and the demonstrators started to demonstrate, or we'd never have seen a penny of it ... Do you know what I'm talking about? I suppose it must have made the papers over there— people who want the University run by a Committee of Workers, Peasants, and Students."

Galloway watched the fog swallow up a grove of eucalyptus trees. "Your characterization seems a bit severe," he suggested. "Of the Free Speech Movement, I mean."

THE RITUALIZED POLITICS OF THEIR WORLD

Elsewhere: He took the stuff for kicks, despite the yatatata about "expanding his horizons and perceptions" with which he justified it. Stepping through the jeweled mists he came upon a place frozen still ... then moving slowly ... then in full motion. He was In-Between, though he didn't know it yet. Nor did he know that he'd been procured by the Green King to be a gamesman for him: a "slayer." He learned that quite quickly, though.

The Kings did not spend all their time watching games. Politics, the ritualized politics of their world, was their main occupation. They had no actual countries, they had their seats, and outside of them—in province and in city—they worked endlessly, sometimes in alliance, sometimes in enmity, for control. In Iddinan, where the Green King had a palace, he currently held six places on the council against the nine of the Yellow King and the six divided between three other kings. It was impossible for him to move openly, nakedly, for greater strength. He had to juggle the status quo in a dozen cities and a score of provinces against such factors as his own liberality in holding games and the niggardliness of his current ally, the Yellow. And, always, the great imponderable of the runesmen or redesmen, the Servants of Mickelrede.

THE PEDIATRIC BURN WARD

Interpolation: Why would the Green King select an academic to be a slayer? On this AD was silent. Surely, though, R. Caswell Swift was chosen for his mathematical skills, which will prove decisive to his meteoric rise through training to stardom as a gamesman. Never particularly physical, much less the object of popular adulation, Casey will experience the heady intoxication of the intellectual who finds himself magically transformed into a jock.

But every self-absorbed hero needs a wake-up call. I'll let Casey's be a post-coital conversation with a woman of affordable virtue (provided him by a grateful home-team booster), who lets drop the info that *this* particular gig is, among whores, just about as popular as assignment to the Pediatric Burn Ward is among nurses. Soon as you get attached to one, she says, he dies.

For the first time, Casey applies his mathematical insights to the game *as a whole,* and sees what should have been blindingly obvious all along: it's a zero-sum game, a rigged wheel. For every winner, there's a loser. For every game, so many deaths. As an individual gamesman, he's doing fine; as a statistical gamesman he's already half-dead.

A TIGER BY THE TAIL

California: The younger man laughed—not scornfully—said, "Oh, I suppose they would run the store about as well as the Regents and the two and a half rich old alumni who run it now. Differently, of course, but no worse. I frankly don't care. I'm like the Vicar of Bray . . . We park here." He showed something in his wallet to the attendant, slid the car smoothly into the space between the white lines, briefly displayed the items in the wallet to Galloway. "My neck-verses," he commented, grinning. And got out and walked away.

Such frankness might well be disarming had I arrived armed, Galloway thought. Young Swift's British equivalent would surely have gone around and opened the door for the newly-arrived savant. But then *he* wouldn't have *had* a car of his own to drive. Anyway, it was an attempt to compare incomparable categories. Mr. Caswell Swift had no foreign equivalents. It didn't matter. The junior must be competent enough, or Brannard wouldn't have him. And it was only competence that counted. Galloway got out of the little car and followed. He wanted to meet Brannard again after all this time, but even more than that he wanted to see for himself something of what Brannard had been doing here. He wanted this so much he could almost taste it. Time enough after for trifles like his baggage, where he was going to stay, or washing after his journey.

I've got a tiger by the tail, Brannard had written; *and I don't know whether it's going to turn out to be a camera or a cannon. Maybe you'll know. Somebody had damned well better.*

THINGS AFAR OFF . . .

Elsewhere: Casey, doing his own juggling, heard of the redesmen. Heard, too, of Mickelrede, the great, holy, and numinous rune-stave, the source of all knowledge. Including technical knowledge. For this world did have its technology. There were firearms, forges, mills, engines . . . There was a science, a science sealed. Not for a while did Casey realize that he had to break the seal. Much more to the immediate moment was learning to handle the lance and the sword and the other implements of the games; that the users of local technology did not stand as employers vis-a-vis the technicians, that the technicians were redesmen, consulted like oracles—he pieced this together later.

The world of the gamesmen was abrupt, a mixture of brutality, cunning, vainglory—and occasional sparks of love and mercy. True, one of his fellow-gladiators, surprising Casey in the chance act of scribbling in the sand, then and forever after insisted that Casey was—must be—an outcast redesman. Other than such odd bits, the Servants of Great Mickelrede remained as vague in Swift's mind as the Jacks o' the North: rulebreakers, these: rebels, raveners, rabble, rioters, owing fay to no king, no color. Things afar off . . .

AS THOUGH SHE HAD INVENTED THEM

California: Coming out of the mist and fog as though she had invented them Casey Swift saw the girl the same second she saw him; he looked at her straight on, but she only peeped at him out of the corners of her eyes as she went on along, perhaps not quite so serenely self-pleased now. Llewellyn Thompson, or so she incredibly called herself—perhaps she was really so, officially and actually, a product of the creeping custom of giving male names to female children, although with the increasing emancipation of the masculine sex little boys might soon enough find themselves being christened Margaret or Mary. Likelier, though, Miss Thompson had merely co-opted to become Llewellyn as part of her own personal make-yourself-more-interesting program. Casey Swift, in a burst of anger which had surprised him as much as it could have her, had once told her that "Sadie" would go much better with her last name than any other. It had flown straight home, too, and she showed it whenever she met him; but of course that didn't do Joe Foyle any good. Not a bit of good.

Because Joe Foyle had gone right to pot when Llewellyn T. began putting him through the wringer. Joe Foyle had flunked out, been fired, rusticated, sent down. And had in consequence lost his neck-verses and was semi-immediately conscripted and sent to East Iridium or some such hellhole rich in bullets and beriberi and where the West Iridiumese were now trying to blow his ass off, which had been made for better things.

Casey was damned sorry for Joe, but he was (he felt) *manageably* sorry, which meant being damned sure not to make the same mistake. No medieval student was ever more careful of the scrap of parchment bearing a Latin verse or two of the Psalms, ability to read which would obtain him benefit of clerical privilege if accused of any of the many capital offenses and thus save his neck from the gallows or the block (hence "neck-verses"), than Casey Swift was of the card which declared him a graduate student in physics or the card which stated his consequentially deferred draft status. He fooled around with girls, true; he drank on occasion into merriment; true; he fenced and skied and swam in due season, true. But he never allowed any of these things, or any other things, to bring down his marks by a hair or a minus-sign. He avoided political activity not only of the far right or of the far left but of the bland and ever-shifting center as well. You never knew. There were only a few years to carry him beyond draft age and into some well-furnished and well-paying corporation lab of the sort which was always so roomy along its constantly expanding sides as to make the presence or absence of room at the top a matter of indifferent definition only.

THE ANNUAL FREE AND FOLLY

Elsewhere: The tricorn crouched in the shadow almost beneath the Royal Seat and it glared and it growled. The slayer held out his lance, shaft under armpit, and hissed invitingly. His free hand swung loose in an almost effeminate gesture. But it never swung very far from the short sword in the short scabbard. And then the tricorn charged.

Oh, it was an episode . . . only an episode. Of more import were those previously-mentioned Things afar off . . . Which abruptly came close without pausing to be merely closer. For it was Jack-wards that Casey and his small group of fellows headed after their escape from the barracks-lodge during the annual Free and Folly.

For the Jacks were on the move again. And so, Casey learned, was Mickelrede. Moved to avoid capture, it was nevertheless captured. Freed. Re-captured. Experience, though brief, with the Jacks o' the North had convinced Casey Swift of two things: One, that they were no mere rabble. Two, that they were not for him, whatever they were. Things might be no better with the redsmen, but he had to try them and see.

BANDY-LEGGED AND HEAVY OF BROW

Interpolation: The Jacks o' the North are only vaguely described in the sixty grams of typescript (fourteen pages, xerographed, cover page and two copies of page 1 inclusive) that AD left behind. Presumably he was saving the fun of creating them for that happy day when he held a living contract in his hand.

So I shall insert six tyrants seated upon seven thrones (one empty), who command the absolute allegiance of all Jacks. They are large and brooding creatures, bandy-legged and heavy of brow, capacious of skull and yet lacking the high foreheads we ourselves rejoice in: Neanderthalers. They are also, through a process that will be explained later, immortal.

Bestial, apish, and cunning, the Six (once they were Seven; one died, and is still mourned) have gathered together the runaways and renegades of In-Between and imposed upon them discipline and some mocking semblance of social order. Their ultimate objective is to avenge themselves upon the species that killed off all their kind but they Six—the human race.

To exterminate the brutes.

EXPERIMENTAL DRUGS OF AN ILLICIT NATURE

California: Needless to say that Mr. Casey Swift never but never indulged in exotic herbs or experimental drugs of an illicit nature. He was heart and soul of the opinion of that noted jazz musician whose comment on the alleged innocuousness of such substances was, "What do you mean, 'What can it do to you?' It can put you in jail, that's what it can do to you!"

QUAINT AND CURIOUS IN ITS FASHIONING

Elsewhere: The Great Rune-Stave had been carried off again from captivity, and had passed across The Gap, where no Jacks dared follow the bridge. Small wonder! Who, unprotected by runish magic, would venture to set foot upon a causeway that the winds palpably blew through, the stones of which were so unsolid as to be transparent? But Casey disbelieved in magic. *All chance is but direction which thou canst not see.* He believed that.

The bridge materialized beneath his feet, revealing the simple fact that his bodily presence polarized its molecules into solidity. The runesmen had vanished into the darks and snows by the time he crossed the gap, but he kept on. He wanted them now more than ever. For, if they could do *this,* then—surely—they could get him out of In-Between. And home again.

The awe of Mickelrede was great upon the land. But the plain people did not understand why it didn't simply destroy the Jacks. And the Jacks, having found—when they'd had it—that they could not use it: had come over to a half-don't-believe-in-it state . . . there was a serious chance they might destroy it.

They caught up with it again about the time Casey did. The fight was hot and close—so close that Casey, fighting hard and side by side with the runesmen, caught a glimpse of the thing when its covering robes were momentarily torn away. And in that second he knew what it was. Mickelrede. "Great Counsel." The Great Rune-Stave, the foundation of wisdom and power and technology. It was a slide-rule! The size of a man, quaint and curious in its fashioning—but a slide-rule!

CREATOR OF THE STACKED EQUATIONS

Interpolation: If it were written, 'twere well it were written quickly. Nothing ages so fast as science fiction, and, having hesitated, there surely came a moment when AD realized that his fractional novel, partially prosed and roughly outlined, was never going to be written. That damned slide-rule! "Mickelrede" was written some thirty-five years ago on a manual typewriter, in those long ago halcyon days before personal computers crept into our homes to gladden our lives. At some point the very notion of an all-powerful slide-rule became ridiculous. Cumbersome. An embarrassment. Yet it was central to the plot. Excise it and all that depended upon it, and what remained? Damned little, sir. Very little more than what fuels your standard fantasy-unit (*Book One,* let us say, of the *First Nounword Trilogy* of *Ye Encyklopedia of Magycke*) today.

And yet. And yet . . .

Suppose it were not *precisely* a slide-rule, but rather something akin to Babbage's stillborn yet demonstrably workable difference engine? (Which same gizmo was employed in Gibson and Sterling's *The Difference Engine.* But they were not the first to bring it to public attention. Nor will they be the last.) Imagine a device of gleaming, intermeshing brass gears—a primitive cruncher of numbers, a hand-cranked equation mill.

Such a device would need an operator, a programmer. And—since the invention and loss of such a technological chimera *twice* in human history is a monstrosity of unlikelihood so great as to derail even the most gullible reader—let that programmer be somebody connected to Babbage's folly: Ada Byron, the daughter of the more famous George Gordon, Lord Byron, and creator of the stacked equations upon which the difference engine would have run, had its inventor only the sense to refrain from making improvements before the bloody thing was finished.

Ada makes a particularly attractive heroine: a genius, a programmer, and beautiful to boot. And—since her personal history is quite adequately documented and it is known (or can easily be ascertained) that she did *not* fade softly and silently away from the world as we know it—let her be a mirror-Ada. A duplicate and splitting-away of the original such as can only occur under special conditions, when the deviating timelike arcs of quantum reality *never* reunite to cancel out their differences.

I'll also postulate—why not?—that by the nature of the event, Ada was made immortal, just as the Six (once Seven) were, before her. That the redesmen have elevated her in rank to a kind of priestess. And that Casey Swift falls in love with her.

THE CRASH OF MATTER AND THE WRACK OF WORLDS

California: So there he was, Richard Caswell Swift, white, American, male, early middle twenties in age, calm in spirit and sound in health, well-adjusted and well-contented; dusty-brown-blond of hair and modestly brown of eye, muscled without being muscle-bound, too fond of himself to spare much of him for others but canny enough not to spare none. It was, he thought, another stroke of luck that he was able to feel an interest in his work as a research assistant to Professor Brannard quite in addition to its utility for him in his own plans for himself. Not that he would have devoted less care and effort to it had it not been so. His work and studies dealt with "the crash of matter and the wrack of worlds" but he would have pursued them just as diligently had they been concerned with the statistics of industrial lard rendering.

TIME AND ANTI-TIME

California: Sometimes, more often than he was perhaps aware of, Dr. Galloway, that peripatetic natural philosopher, considered that he did not like fluorescent lighting. It was, he considered, as noisy as gaslight though less warm. Now, however, as he half-sat and half-crouched, talking to his old friend and current colleague, Jack Brannard, it would have made no difference if the lab had been illuminated by slut-lamps or neon signs.

Two-dimensional mirrors, i.e. our mirrors, leave out a dimension: depth. Is there a mirror which shows three dimensions? Yes—a moving picture film projected will show length, breadth, and time. But this is still losing one dimension: again, depth. A mirror which does display three dimensions is still leaving out one dimension, i.e. time.

Dr. Brannard had built a sort of shadow-box or cloud-chamber which shows length, width, and depth—but not time: Action is in it suspended. It had some semblance or relation to a hologram, in which one can "look around the tree and see the man behind it." Still, it was not the same thing: no.

But then Casey poked or was pushed or fell into the box/chamber (an accident, seemingly, though not in reality), turned silvery/opalescent around the edges, appeared flat and one-dimensional: vanished. The scene vanished. Casey Swift's clothes were left behind. Witnesses assumed he was in all probability annihilated by the intraposition of time and anti-time.

THE STATUS OF MECHANICS

Elsewhere: He found the redesmen, battle over, and his knowledge confided to them, not about to pop with joy over him. It was certainly no matter of, "You who know the Secret are therefore of us." Contrariwise. They were sour, suspicious. Unauthorized knowledge.

Bad show. What does the County Medical Association do about an outsider who can perform appendectomies? Warn him he'd damn-well better not.

In a way, he had finally broken the seal. He found the scientists reduced to the status of mechanics—in one way. Enhanced to the status of priests—in another. Obliged to treat with barbarians and tyrants to uphold the status quo . . . or, actually, to drag it back-wards. Were they actually withdrawing devices, one by one? Why? Or were the devices merely falling from their failing grasp? Civili-zation sliding slowly backwards while the Servants of Mickelrede encouraged the petty kings to occupy themselves with games and petty wars? The Chief of the Servants should have been able to tell Casey. But it wasn't protocol even to put the question. Would (for example) the Pope see some tatterdemalion jackleg infidel who claimed to know all about transubstantiation? Not likely. But sup-pose that same also claimed to know where the bones of St. Peter lay . . .

Casey saw him, he saw Casey, and he saw through Casey. Who, he flatly said, was a menace. With Swift's dangerous knowledge, all Hell could break loose. Only when things in In-Between reached a low enough level, technologically, and there remained indefinitely, would there be hope of beginning to achieve moral improvements to provide a truly safe base for future physical advances. Against that day the Servants of Mickelrede would preserve their knowledge . . . the basis of which was the use of that instrument without which pre-computer technology is impossible. And thereunto they, in times before, captured Mickelrede in order to keep their world from the plunder and ravishment of industrialism, doling out its knowledge carefully, grudgingly. To all of this, Casey represented a threat.

WITH CHINTZ CURTAINS AND A PIANOFORTE

Interpolation: The miracle-bait AD had in mind for Casey to employ was Mickelrede's location. But I'm going to do a little bait-and-switch here, and posit that Casey knows where Ada Byron, long believed slain, is being held prisoner.

My own impulse would be to place her in a stone tower amid the cold vapors of some Ultimate dim Thule. Someplace archetypal. AD, I suspect, would more likely ensconce her in a comfortable suite of rooms, with chintz curtains and a pianoforte, warded by a gaoler who, while unbribable, can yet discuss Aeschylus and Calculus in the original Greek equations.

So: Let it be both: In a stone tower in the cold North in a well-appointed room does Ada languish, whose single door is barred by a warden of perfect culture and bestial appearance: one of the Six.

Casey tells of seeing Ada in the heated hand-to-hand fight for Mickelrede. He does not mention (so conflicted are his feelings: of loathing, of love) that her face is familiar to him from of old, for he has seen her before. Many times. In California. As Llewellyn—sometimes "Sadie"—Thompson. A girl who has been known to come out of the mist and fog as though she had invented them.

ALL WAS STILL AND MOTIONLESS

Neither Here nor There: He felt himself as though prisoned within a dream, and, as within a dream or nightmare (though otherwise there was nothing of the nightmare about it) when one knows or partly knows that the paralysis is of the same stuff as the dream and thus one by main effort forces motion upon the body, slowly, slowly, weighted down by some devilish and stifling gravity—so, that way, equally slowly, by heavy effort and with heavy weight opposing him, he forced himself to move. And as though the scene itself responded to his effort and was somehow acted upon and released by it, so, slowly, slowly, the scene melted into action.

He felt a puff of slow, sluggish air upon his skin. He saw . . .

Great glittering gouts of moisture hung from the strange mosses pendant from the stranger trees and refracted, diamond-like or crystalline, glittering and glowing. And yet no sun was visible as the source of this bejeweled light, but all was obscured by wraiths and shreds of mist. The great peacock-like birds stood on one leg each, the other leg drawn up body-close with foot dangling foppishly, tails partly unfanned in a display of brilliant color and fantastic design totally unearthly. The flock of white birds with crimson bills and scarlet feet and carmine pinion-plumes remained fixed and hovering in middle air and middle distance. The stand of flowers bowed their golden heads. The man in the strange green habit still inclined his head and still beckoned with his hand and finger. And all was still and motionless.

A MULTITUDE OF KING STORKS

Elsewhere: But the Jacks o' the North represented a greater menace: a multitude of King Storks against the status quo of the petty few King Logs: Casey might (if allowed) tip the molten mixture out of the caldron before the mold was fixed. But the Jacks would destroy caldron and mixture and furnace and all. No safe, controlled descent towards watchful waiting. All-destroying savagery, instead. And Casey offered a package deal. Cancel his status as the chattel of the Green King, agree to return him whence he came, back him up all along the line—and he would rid them of the Jacks o' the North.

BUT THIS WAS LONG AGO AND FAR AWAY

Neither Here nor There: Once, the only single once (but that was in another country), as one of a tiny company among whom the sacred cigarette with the greenish herb which was not tobacco circulated from hand to hand and mouth to mouth like a sacrament around the candlepoint of light in the darkness, and then, later, floating upon the sweet sea of euphoria (but this was long ago and far away and besides, the lad was young), something else began to happen to him. Time ceased to exist. That which he had just said, he had never said; that which he had just said, he had always been saying; that which he had just said, he was yet to say. He saw his words as though embossed on sand, he saw them vanish away as though absorbed in sand. Nothing happened, everything was about to happen, action was distilled into inaction, inaction was pregnant with action.

Something not at all the same as that but yet inescapably reminiscent of that was in this strange compelling silently unmoving scene which drew and had drawn him in. Amazement still held him in thrall but now present was the sudden element of terror. Was he to remain here fixed and unmoving forever, another motionless figure in this scene neither living nor dead?

DID HE INHALE?

Exegesis: Did Casey smoke dope? And if he did, was it only once and long ago? Or was it often and recently? Did he inhale? Was it dope that brought him to the In-Between? Or was it the good Doctor Brannard's ghost box? The Green King summoned him—would it have profited him one whit, had he steered a wide course of drugs and hard physics?

The simplest demonstrable mindfuck in physics is the experiment in which a beam of light is revealed to be either wavelike or particulate in nature—whichever one the experimenter chooses. After which, and called upon to explain themselves, scientists split the difference and call it a "wavicle."

AD didn't bother being consistent with the mechanism that swept Casey out of reality as we know it altogether, because it was a negligible matter, what Alexander Pope called the *Machinery:* that Part which the Deities, Angels or Daemons (or Scientists) were to play in the matter. Calling upon Deities, Angels, Daemons, or Scientists to do your enabling for you, is to admit that it cannot be done by sensible means.

Besides, I like the thought that the story itself partakes of quantum uncertainty. Two plots diverge and race away from each other on timelike arcs, only to meet again somewhere In-Between. Let's not reconcile them.

THUMBS WERE PRICKED AND SQUEEZED

Elsewhere: The Battle of the Plains of Quore had been of the illustrious and classical kind. Arquebusiers in black-and-gold, arquebusiers in red-and-gold, had filed and defiled to the music of drums and trumpets and oboes until they were within fire-shot of each other. Then the heralds had stepped forward, and the augurs. Thumbs were pricked and squeezed, blood was ceremoniously declared to have been shed, both sides were asked to accept this as sufficient. Both sides ceremoniously refused. The black and white bones were cast, the omens taken, the choice of first fire given and accepted. Heralds and augurs retired, walking backwards. Fifteen volleys were exchanged, the side with the fewest men then standing was adjudged to have lost and was permitted to retire with its wounded and its banners. Commissioners presently followed to accept its change of rule. Thus, the battle; thus the war.

But this newest and latest battle by the Jacks o' the North against the Seat of the King of the Yellow was something else again. The attack had actually occurred in the night! without heralds! without augurs! *without warning—!* The comment most frequently quoted was the Yellow King's, "This isn't war, this is chaos." However, as he had said it in exile and defeat, it was doubtful if his was the ultimate and definitive comment after all.

The chessboard "armies" of the Kings of the Colors were worthless in this new kind of warfare. But there was another body of disciplined fighters: the gamesmen. The slayers.

SHE WHO PROGRAMS

Interpolation: The narrative seems to have lost sight of Ada: our heroine: She Who Programs. She is nobody to lose sight of. Too, there are no surprises in the late synopsis, and AD was a writer of ample and commodious surprises, the ground shifting underfoot, revelation abruptly veering into the Unknown. AD was saving his inventions for the actual writing. I, perforce, cannot wait that long.

What is she doing in her well-appointed room in that stone tower in the Nordmost north of the frozen North? Her guardian watches over her, enamored and ignorant of his own infatuation (for it has been so long since the last female of his kind died that he has forgotten what that state *feels like*), and even he, shrewdest of anthropoids, does not know. To what purpose do her nimble fingers trip so lightly over the brass mill of fate, the cog-wheeled decoder of runes, which y-clept Mickelrede?

Weaving.

The brass gears and teeth of the mighty difference engine spin under her hands, and she looks upon their permutations with cool and knowing eyes. Which device she had tricked and politicked the Six into capturing for her. To what purposes does this warrior-faced woman, this chill and cerebral immortal, this long-experienced and deep-thinking minder of her own counsels weave?

Why, to her own, of course.

THE HAND THAT BINDS

Elsewhere: A faction within the runesmen warned Casey Swift that the Chief could not be depended on—that, in fact, the greater Swift's success, the less likely the Chief was to be dependable.

But Casey was not actually aiming all this at the Chief. He was aiming it at the Green King. *The hand that binds is the hand that loosens.* Cunning king, would he want the balance of power entirely thrown up for grabs by the total destruction of the Jacks? Not bloody likely. And it was he, after all, who had had Casey brought to the world of In-Between in the first place.

Time passed. Events occurred.

The slayers and their new commander had driven the Jacks back into the very frosts and snows of the wild North. And then it was, as he knew it must be, that Casey saw the ignorant armies slow to a crawl . . . then go stiff and rigid . . . and all motion cease . . .

And back he went through the jeweled mists and into the cortex of his own old body once again. Forever. Forever? Perhaps not forever . . .

> *For hers is the hand that loosens*
> *And hers is the hand that binds*
> *Hers is the hand that releases*
> *And hers is the hand that winds*

LIKE A LEOPARD-FISH OR A MORAY EEL (II)

Envoi: "the idea for this came to me one night in 1963 in Berkeley Cal. when in the near night sky I saw an unexplained aerial phenomenon like a moray eel or a leopard shark. Not sure why I never finished this, it looked real good at the time. It was to have involved gladiators, probability theory, and the slide rule. Chee."

—AD, 02 October 1976

AFTERWORD TO "MICKELREDE"

What could represent the vanishing past more clearly than the slide-rule? Would today's high-tech students even recognize a slide-rule, let alone worship one?

Michael Swanwick, an extraordinary, award-winning author of speculative fiction, has taken the posthumous fragments and shards of an incomplete manuscript, and fashioned them into a narrative that is unique in form and style, and a unique blend of two great writers' minds.

—*Grania Davis*

AFTERWORD
BY GRANIA DAVIS

"He is not antagonistic toward all mechanical devices; he is quite fond of the water wheel and maintains a strict neutrality toward the spinning jenny." Thus spoke author Michael Kurland, describing Avram in the recent mystery story collection, *The Investigations of Avram Davidson.*

Science fiction is a form of virtual time-travel. Most writers and readers of SF like to travel into the distant future. But Avram Davidson (1923–1993) was often a time traveler into the past, both in his writing and in his own life. The old, the archaic, the antique fascinated him. Snuff was his preferred recreational drug. He loved to delve into the mysteries of the past in his stories, and in his *Unhistory* essays. Futuristic technology did not attract him. Avram never nuked his food (horrors!) in a microwave, but was famous for his slowly simmered kettles of soup. This was a man who never drove a car, whose transportation system was his feet.

Avram was also famous for his stories, which brought him many prestigious awards, if little material wealth. "The Necessity of his Condition" won the (Ellery) Queen's Award for best mystery story in 1957. In 1958 his classic exploration of the breeding habits of safety pins and bicycles, "Or All the Seas with Oysters," won the Hugo Award for best science fiction short story. In 1962 his homage to Rudyard Kipling, "The Affair at Lahore Cantonment," won the Edgar Award for best short mystery story. 1965 saw two nebula Award nominations—"The House the Blakeneys Built," for best short fiction, and *Rogue Dragon* for best novella. 1966 saw two more: for *The Clash of Star-Kings* (a.k.a. *Tlaloc*) in the best novel category, and *The Kar-Chee Reign* for best novella.

In 1975 his Doctor Eszterhazy tales, set in a fantastical Eastern

European monarchy before the Great War, first saw print. One of them, "Polly Charms, the Sleeping Woman," was a finalist for the Nebula Award for best novella. They were collected as *The Enquiries of Doctor Eszterhazy,* and won that year's World Fantasy Award for best collection. (A later Eszterhazy story, "The Odd Old Bird," is reprinted in this collection.)

Avram picked up an Edgar nomination for best short story in 1977 for "Crazy Old Lady," then hit a streak of World Fantasy Awards. He was nominated for best short fiction in 1978, for "Manatee Gal Won't You Come Out Tonight." In 1979 he was nominated for "A Good Night's Sleep" for best short fiction, and for *The Redward Edward Papers* for best collection. That same year he won (finally!) the World Fantasy Award for best short fiction, for his story "Naples."

In 1980 "There Beneath the Silky-Tree and Whelmed in Deeper Gulphs Than Me," was nominated for the Nebula Award for best novella. In 1983 another Eszterhazy tale, "Eszterhazy and the Autogondola-Invention," was nominated for the Nebula Award for best novella and in 1984 yet another Eszterhazy story, "Young Doctor Eszterhazy," was nominated for the Nebula Award for best novella.

In 1986 "The Slovo Stove" was nominated for the World Fantasy Award for best short fiction. And finally, in 1986, he received the World Fantasy Award for Lifetime Achievement. Add to this one more Nebula nomination for post-lifetime achievement, for his 1999 novella *The Boss in the Wall* (posthumously completed by Grania Davis).

Most of these stories can be found in the recent Locus-Award-Winning, World-Fantasy-Award-nominated collection, *The Avram Davidson Treasury* (Tor, 1999).

This latest collection, *The Other Nineteenth Century,* contains Avram's stories set in the not-so-distant past. These are his tales of the Nineteenth Century and related eras, a time of gaslights and steam runabouts and snuff. In this book you will find alternate histories, unusual events, and strange and steamy gadgets. Turn up the gaslight and enjoy the shadows on the wall.

I want to thank my esteemed co-editor Henry Wessells, who came up with the idea for this book; George Scithers (who contributed story Afterwords) and Darrell Schweitzer of Owlswick Literary Agency; and Teresa Nielsen Hayden of Tor Books, who brought the idea to life. I also want to thank Jack Dann, my co-editor on the recent Avram Davidson Jewish fantasy collection, *Everybody Has Somebody in Heaven* (Devora Press), who taught me new editorial tricks. I especially want to thank Ms. Sarah Fishman, who has prepared a preliminary catalogue of the Avram Davidson Archive. And thanks, of course, to our beloved readers, families, and friends.

GRANIA DAVIS
San Rafael, California
North Shore Oahu, Hawaii

ABOUT THE AUTHOR

AVRAM DAVIDSON was born in 1923. He won the Hugo Award, the Edgar Award, the Ellery Queen Award, and three World Fantasy Awards. He died in 1993.

ABOUT THE EDITORS

GRANIA DAVIS is the author of the novels *The Rainbow Annals* and *Moonbird*, and was married to Avram Davdison for many years. She and Davidson collaborated on several works, including *The Boss in the Wall*. She lives in California.

HENRY WESSELLS is an antiquarian bookseller in New York and the author of *Book Becoming Power*. His fiction and essays have appeared in *Nature*, *Interzone*, *The Washington Post Book World*, and *The New York Review of Science Fiction*. He is publisher of *The Nutmeg Point District Mail* and maintains the Avram Davidson Web site at http://ad.kosmic.org.